OXFORD WORLD'S CLASSICS

THE TRIAL

MIKE MITCHELL taught at the universities of Reading and Stirling before becoming a full-time literary translator. He is the co-author of *Harrap's German Grammar* and the translator of numerous works of German fiction, for which he has been eight times shortlisted for prizes; his translation of Herbert Rosendorfer's *Letters Back to Ancient China* won the Schlegel–Tieck Prize in 1998. His translation of Georges Rodenbach's *The Bells of Bruges* was published in 2007.

RITCHIE ROBERTSON is Fellow and Tutor in German at St John's College, Oxford. He is the author of *Kafka: A Very Short Introduction* (2004) and editor of *The Cambridge Companion to Thomas Mann* (2002). For Oxford World's Classics he has translated Hoffmann's *The Golden Pot and Other Stories* and introduced editions of Freud and Schnitzler.

OXFORD WORLD'S CLASSICS

*For over 100 years Oxford World's Classics have brought
readers closer to the world's great literature. Now with over 700
titles—from the 4,000-year-old myths of Mesopotamia to the
twentieth century's greatest novels—the series makes available
lesser-known as well as celebrated writing.*

*The pocket-sized hardbacks of the early years contained
introductions by Virginia Woolf, T. S. Eliot, Graham Greene,
and other literary figures which enriched the experience of reading.
Today the series is recognized for its fine scholarship and
reliability in texts that span world literature, drama and poetry,
religion, philosophy, and politics. Each edition includes perceptive
commentary and essential background information to meet the
changing needs of readers.*

OXFORD WORLD'S CLASSICS

━━

FRANZ KAFKA

The Trial

━━

Translated by
MIKE MITCHELL

With an Introduction and Notes by
RITCHIE ROBERTSON

OXFORD
UNIVERSITY PRESS

OXFORD
UNIVERSITY PRESS

Great Clarendon Street, Oxford OX2 6DP

Oxford University Press is a department of the University of Oxford.
It furthers the University's objective of excellence in research, scholarship,
and education by publishing worldwide in

Oxford New York

Auckland Cape Town Dar es Salaam Hong Kong Karachi
Kuala Lumpur Madrid Melbourne Mexico City Nairobi
New Delhi Shanghai Taipei Toronto

With offices in

Argentina Austria Brazil Chile Czech Republic France Greece
Guatemala Hungary Italy Japan Poland Portugal Singapore
South Korea Switzerland Thailand Turkey Ukraine Vietnam

Oxford is a registered trade mark of Oxford University Press
in the UK and in certain other countries

Published in the United States
by Oxford University Press Inc., New York

Translation © Mike Mitchell 2009
Editorial matter © Ritchie Robertson 2009

The moral rights of the authors have been asserted
Database right Oxford University Press (maker)

First published as an Oxford World's Classics paperback 2009

British Library Cataloguing in Publication Data

Data available

Library of Congress Cataloging-in-Publication Data

Kafka, Franz, 1883–1924.
[Prozess. English]
The Trial / Franz Kafka ; translated by Mike Mitchell;
with an introduction and notes by Ritchie Robertson.
p. cm. — (Oxford world's classics)
Includes bibliographical references.
ISBN 978-0-19-923829-3 (pbk. : acid-free paper)
I. Mitchell, Michael, 1941- II. Title.
PT2621.A26P713 2009
833'.912—dc22
2009005382

Typeset by Cepha Imaging Private Ltd., Bangalore, India
Printed in Great Britain
on acid-free paper by
Clays Ltd., St Ives plc

ISBN 978–0–19–923829–3

5

CONTENTS

BIOGRAPHICAL PREFACE

FRANZ KAFKA is one of the iconic figures of modern world literature. His biography is still obscured by myth and misinformation, yet the plain facts of his life are very ordinary. He was born on 3 July 1883 in Prague, where his parents, Hermann and Julie Kafka, kept a small shop selling fancy goods, umbrellas, and the like. He was the eldest of six children, including two brothers who died in infancy and three sisters who all outlived him. He studied law at university, and after a year of practice started work, first for his local branch of an insurance firm based in Trieste, then after a year for the state-run Workers' Accident Insurance Institute, where his job was not only to handle claims for injury at work but to forestall such accidents by visiting factories and examining their equipment and their safety precautions. In his spare time he was writing prose sketches and stories, which were published in magazines and as small books, beginning with *Meditation* in 1912.

In August 1912 Kafka met Felice Bauer, four years his junior, who was visiting from Berlin, where she worked in a firm making office equipment. Their relationship, including two engagements, was carried on largely by letter (they met only on seventeen occasions, far the longest being a ten-day stay in a hotel in July 1916), and finally ended when in August 1917 Kafka had a haemorrhage which proved tubercular; he had to convalesce in the country, uncertain how much longer he could expect to live. Thereafter brief returns to work alternated with stays in sanatoria until he took early retirement in 1922. In 1919 he was briefly engaged to Julie Wohryzek, a twenty-eight-year-old clerk, but that relationship dissolved after Kafka met the married Milena Polak (née Jesenská), a spirited journalist, unhappy with her neglectful husband. Milena translated some of Kafka's work into Czech. As she lived in Vienna, their meetings were few, and the relationship ended early in 1921. Two years later Kafka at last left Prague and settled in Berlin with Dora Diamant, a young woman who had broken away from her ultra-orthodox Jewish family in Poland (and who later became a noted actress and communist activist). However, the winter of 1923–4, when hyperinflation was at its height, was a bad time to be in Berlin. Kafka's health declined so sharply that, after moving through several clinics and sanatoria around Vienna, he died on 3 June 1924.

The emotional hinterland of these events finds expression in Kafka's letters and diaries, and also—though less directly than is sometimes thought—in his literary work. His difficult relationship with his domineering father has a bearing especially on his early fiction, as well as on the *Letter to his Father*, which should be seen as a literary document rather than a factual record. He suffered also from his mother's emotional remoteness and from the excessive hopes which his parents invested in their only surviving son. His innumerable letters to the highly intelligent, well-read, and capable Felice Bauer bespeak emotional neediness, and a wish to prove himself by marrying, rather than any strong attraction to her as an individual, and he was acutely aware of the conflict between the demands of marriage and the solitude which he required for writing. He records also much self-doubt, feelings of guilt, morbid fantasies of punishment, and concern about his own health. But it is clear from his friends' testimony that he was a charming and witty companion, a sportsman keen on hiking and rowing, and a thoroughly competent and valued colleague at work. He also had a keen social conscience and advanced social views: during the First World War he worked to help refugees and shell-shocked soldiers, and he advocated progressive educational methods which would save children from the stifling influence of their parents.

Kafka's family were Jews with little more than a conventional attachment to Jewish belief and practice. A turning-point in Kafka's life was his encounter with Yiddish-speaking actors from Galicia, from whom he learned about the traditional Jewish culture of Eastern Europe. Gradually he drew closer to the Zionist movement: not to its politics, however, but to its vision of a new social and cultural life for Jews in Palestine. He learnt Hebrew and acquired practical skills such as gardening and carpentry which might be useful if, as they planned, he and Dora Diamant should emigrate to Palestine.

A concern with religious questions runs through Kafka's life and work, but his thought does not correspond closely to any established faith. He had an extensive knowledge of both Judaism and Christianity, and knew also the philosophies of Nietzsche and Schopenhauer. Late in life, especially after the diagnosis of his illness, he read eclectically and often critically in religious classics: the Old and New Testaments, Kierkegaard, St Augustine, Pascal, the late diaries of the convert Tolstoy, works by Martin Buber, and also extracts from the Talmud. His religious thought, which finds expression in concise and profound aphorisms, is highly individual, and the religious allusions which haunt his fiction tend to make it more rather than less enigmatic.

During his lifetime Kafka published seven small books, but he left three unfinished novels and a huge mass of notebooks and diaries, which we only possess because his friend Max Brod ignored Kafka's instructions to burn them. They are all written in German, his native language; his Czech was fluent but not flawless. It used to be claimed that Kafka wrote in a version of German called 'Prague German', but in fact, although he uses some expressions characteristic of the South German language area, his style is modelled on that of such classic German writers as Goethe, Kleist, and Stifter.

Though limpid, Kafka's style is also puzzling. He was sharply conscious of the problems of perception, and of the new forms of attention made possible by media such as the photograph and cinema. When he engages in fantasy, his descriptions are often designed to perplex the reader: thus it is difficult to make out what the insect in *The Metamorphosis* actually looks like. He was also fascinated by ambiguity, and often includes in his fiction long arguments in which various interpretations of some puzzling phenomenon are canvassed, or in which the speaker, by faulty logic, contrives to stand an argument on its head. In such passages he favours elaborate sentences, often in indirect speech. Yet Kafka's German, though often complex, is never clumsy. In his fiction, his letters, and his diaries he writes with unfailing grace and economy.

In his lifetime Kafka was not yet a famous author, but neither was he obscure. His books received many complimentary reviews. Prominent writers, such as Robert Musil and Rainer Maria Rilke, admired his work and sought him out. He was also part of a group of Prague writers, including Max Brod, an extremely prolific novelist and essayist, and Franz Werfel, who first attained fame as avant-garde poet and later became an international celebrity through his best-selling novels. During the Third Reich his work was known mainly in the English-speaking world through translations, and, as little was then known about his life or social context, he was seen as the author of universal parables.

Kafka's novels about individuals confronting a powerful but opaque organization—the court or the castle—seemed in the West to be fables of existential uncertainty. In the Eastern bloc, when they became accessible, they seemed to be prescient explorations of the fate of the individual within a bureaucratic tyranny. Neither approach can be set aside. Both were responding to elements in Kafka's fiction. Kafka worries at universal moral problems of guilt, responsibility, and freedom; and he also examines the mechanisms of power by which authorities can subtly coerce and subjugate the individual, as well as the individual's scope for resisting authority.

Placing Kafka in his historical context brings limited returns. The appeal of his work rests on its universal, parable-like character, and also on its presentation of puzzles without solutions. A narrative presence is generally kept to a minimum. We largely experience what Kafka's protagonist does, without a narrator to guide us. When there is a distinct narrative voice, as sometimes in the later stories, the narrator is himself puzzled by the phenomena he recounts. Kafka's fiction is thus characteristic of modernism in demanding an active reading. The reader is not invited to consume the text passively, but to join actively in the task of puzzling it out, in resisting simple interpretations, and in working, not towards a solution, but towards a fuller experience of the text on each reading.

INTRODUCTION

EVER since Aeschylus' *Oresteia*, the motif of the trial has been fundamental to literature. Ideally, the trial serves to bring the truth to light and to assign people their just deserts. In practice, literature questions and complicates this simple conception of a trial. It shows that the meaning and purpose of a trial depend on the legal system, the society, and the people among whom it is conducted. An unjust judge may himself be put on trial, as in Shakespeare's *Measure for Measure*. The legal system may be so heavily satirized, as in Dickens's *Bleak House*, as to make it doubtful whether a trial can resolve anything of importance. Or it may be suggested, as in Dostoevsky's *The Brothers Karamazov*, that a judicial investigation opens up a series of moral and ultimately religious problems which no legal system can handle.

In Kafka's *The Trial*, there is no courtroom scene in which the issues are debated by lawyers before a judge. In keeping with the continental system in which Kafka, a law graduate, was trained, the procedure is not adversarial but inquisitorial. Once Josef K. is arrested, an examining magistrate inquires into the case against him. Hearings are held. K. engages a lawyer to advise and defend him. He hears of a vast, impenetrable legal organization, where the highest judges are wholly inaccessible, and where the trial merges imperceptibly into the verdict. No charge against Josef K. is ever formulated. The real trial is elsewhere. It may be, as Heinz Politzer argued, that we should read the novel as a 'trial against the court', in which the court is gradually exposed as relentless and malicious.[1] Or perhaps we should see the trial of Josef K. as moral rather than legal: the question is not whether he is guilty of a misdemeanour, but how he responds to the increasing pressure under which the court places him. On this reading, it is Josef K.'s whole character, the extent of his human and spiritual resources, that is put on trial.

Given the vast implications of the trial metaphor, we need not expect Kafka's own biography to yield more than trivial clues to the meaning of the novel. Nevertheless, it is striking that the main

[1] Heinz Politzer, *Franz Kafka: Parable and Paradox* (Ithaca, NY: Cornell University Press, 1962), 163–217—still one of the most stimulating critical studies of Kafka.

female character, Fräulein Bürstner, is usually referred to in Kafka's manuscript by the abbreviation 'F.B.', which also forms the initials of his fiancée Felice Bauer. Soon after their first meeting, in August 1912, Kafka began to correspond with her—she lived in Berlin, he in Prague—and on 1 June 1914 they celebrated their official engagement. Kafka, however, had profound misgivings about marriage. It would provide an escape from solitude, but then solitude was what he needed in order to write. In his diary he wrote that at the engagement party he was 'chained like a criminal' (6 June 1914). Very unwisely, Kafka confided his doubts in letters to Felice's friend Grete Bloch, who passed the bulk of the letters on to Felice. Learning about the misgivings which he had concealed from her, Felice was understandably furious. She summoned Kafka to what he described as a 'court' in a Berlin hotel, where she was supported by her sister Erna and by Grete Bloch (diary, 23 July 1914). It was in the aftermath of this experience that Kafka began writing *The Trial*.

After writing the first long section, beginning with Josef K.'s arrest and leading up to his sexual assault on Fräulein Bürstner, Kafka immediately turned to the last chapter, in which K. is executed exactly a year after his arrest. This was in part a precautionary measure. From the difficulties he had already had in writing *The Man Who Disappeared*, Kafka knew that his stories tended to run away with him, especially as he did not make plans, drafts, or sketches, but relied on the inspiration of the moment. But it also shows that the fictional K. had to be punished, and that his punishment would in some undefined way be connected with his treatment of F.B. In the final chapter, as K. is being led to his execution, he tries to resist his executioners. Just then, however, somebody who is either Fräulein Bürstner, or strongly resembles her, appears in front of them, and K. instantly feels that his resistance is pointless. In Kafka's original conception, therefore, K.'s relations with Fräulein Bürstner were to give the novel its overarching coherence.

As Kafka worked further on the novel, its shape became less clear. Each chapter he wrote was placed in a separate folder with a brief indication of its contents (corresponding to the chapter headings in the published text). Not all of the chapters were finished. Even the long and important chapter in which K. dismisses his lawyer breaks off in the middle of the action. Others tell us more about figures who are only mentioned briefly in the completed chapters, such as K.'s mother, his girlfriend Elsa, and the state prosecutor Hasterer.

K.

Despite the origins of the story in Kafka's painful relationship with Felice Bauer, Josef K. is not a portrait of Kafka. He is, rather, a type—the modern professional man who suppresses his private life in his devotion to his work. At the age of 30, he has already attained a prominent position in a bank; the manager thinks highly of him, and much of his time is spent in playing office politics against his rival, the deputy manager. Instead of owning a house commensurate with his professional status, however, he rents a room in a flat which is occupied by numerous tenants. He has a complex relation with his landlady, compounded of suspicion, resentment, emotional need, and willingness to exploit her servile devotion to him.

K. has little contact with his family. We learn from the unfinished chapter 'Going To See his Mother' that K., three years earlier, promised his mother to visit her annually on his birthdays, and has failed to do so for the last two birthdays. K. shows no concern over her failing eyesight. He reflects only that 'various afflictions of old age had got better instead of worse, at least she complained about them less'. His only affective reaction is his revulsion at his mother's increasing piety. Are we to see K.'s failure to visit his mother as the specific crime for which he is arrested? That explanation, proposed by Eric Marson, is certainly neat. It is supported by K.'s awareness of the old woman who lives opposite gazing at him from her window, 'with, for her, quite unusual curiosity'. And it may be more satisfactory to find a concrete reason for K.'s arrest than to impute it to vague existential guilt.[2] That would imply, however, that K.'s neglect of his mother was part of Kafka's original conception of the novel. Yet Kafka mentions in his diary for 8 December 1914 that he wrote 'the first page of the Mother chapter' on the previous day—in other words, at a very late stage in the composition of the novel. That would suggest that the relationship between K. and his mother was an afterthought. It is consistent with what we have already seen of K.'s character. Although his seventeen-year-old niece is attending a boarding-school in the city, K. has no contact with her; to disguise his negligence, she tells her father the white lie that he sent her a box of chocolates on her name-day, and K. resolves at least to send her theatre tickets in future, but not to see her personally.

[2] Eric Marson, *Kafka's Trial: The Case Against Josef K.* (St Lucia: University of Queensland Press, 1975), 44.

K.'s work dominates his life. He is obsessed by order and hierarchy. His arrest leaves him with the vague feeling that disorder has been created and that he must restore order, after which every trace of his arrest will be erased (p. 17). Confronted with something unfamiliar, he tries desperately to maintain his familiar reality. He explains to Frau Grubach that he was caught off guard, whereas in the bank he would have been protected in advance against anything unexpected: 'In the bank, for example, I am prepared, it's impossible for something like that to happen to me there, I have a man of my own there, the outside telephone and the office telephone are on the desk in front of me, people are always coming in, clients and clerks; moreover, and above all, I'm constantly involved in my work, therefore always on the alert, it would be a real pleasure to be faced with such a situation there' (p. 19). Later he tries to reassure himself that his trial is 'nothing more than a piece of business, such as he had often transacted with profit for the bank' (p. 90). That the court might represent an alien reality, not dreamt of in his professional philosophy, is an idea which he tries to fight off, even in conversation with the prison chaplain. K.'s claim to understand the court better than the chaplain does provoke the latter to give a horrified cry of warning: 'Can't you see even two steps in front of you?' (p. 152).

Although we cannot know what the court intends, we can see its effects on K. It gradually breaks down the defensive façade which he constantly tries to maintain. When arrested, he suddenly finds himself contemplating suicide, even though he promptly dismisses the idea as absurd. His conversation with his landlady, in which he tries to make her agree that his arrest is meaningless, ends with his sudden and unexplained outburst: 'Purity! . . . if you want to keep the guest-house pure, you'll have to give me notice first of all' (p. 21). Although he uses his first and only hearing to deliver a defiant speech, his second visit to the court premises leaves him unable to endure the bad air, dizzy and seasick, hatless and dishevelled, until he regains the fresh air and normal life. He becomes unable to concentrate on his work, ignores his clients, and allows the deputy manager to take over more and more of his business. In his conversation with the prison chaplain we see a different K. He still considers himself unjustly victimized, and believes he understands the court, but his manner is quiet, free from his usual arrogance, and he shows a touching need for friendship which he believes he has found in the chaplain.

However, the court's intervention in his life also opens up other sides of K.'s character, especially his sexual appetite. Previously, like Meursault in Camus's *The Stranger*, he satisfied his sexual urges with a weekly visit to a prostitute. Now he suddenly develops an interest in Fräulein Bürstner which finds expression in a sexual assault: he is 'like a thirsty animal furiously thrusting its tongue over the water of the spring it has found at last', a complex comparison suggesting brute appetite alongside an elemental need. In the court premises he is enticed by the usher's wife, who is apparently also the sexual victim of the examining magistrate, and in the lawyer's office he is easily led into an affair with the housekeeper Leni. There is undoubtedly some misogyny in the portrayal of these women. The endearments of the usher's wife ('you can do whatever you want with me', p. 45), and the promiscuity ascribed to Leni, recall the pseudo-scientific theory of Otto Weininger, vastly popular in turn-of-the-century Central Europe, that all women could be classified as either mothers or whores.[3] Leni's webbed hand, which K. calls 'a pretty claw', suggests an evolutionary throwback to a more primitive phase of humanity.

K.'s interest in these women is exploitative as well as physical. 'I'm enlisting women helpers,' he thinks as Leni sits in his lap, 'first of all Fräulein Bürstner, then the usher's wife and now this little nurse' (p. 77). The chaplain warns him against seeking such help. And Leni at least has her own agenda. She urges K. to surrender to the court, to give up his intransigence and to confess. She is thus trying to bring him under the power of the court. This illustrates the role of temptress that Kafka sometimes ascribed to women. Although he was far from inexperienced sexually, with many brothel visits and some short-lived holiday romances, Kafka often felt a disgust with sexuality and an ascetic desire to escape from it. In such moods he felt that women—whom he blamed, following a common misogynist tactic, as the projection of his own sexual desire—were dragging him down into repulsive material existence.[4]

---

[3] Otto Weininger, *Sex and Character: An Investigation of Fundamental Principles*, tr. Ladislaus Löb, ed. Daniel Steuer and Laura Marcus (Bloomington and Indianapolis: Indiana University Press, 2005). See Chandak Sengoopta, *Otto Weininger: Sex, Science, and Self in Imperial Vienna* (Chicago: University of Chicago Press, 2000), esp. 137–56 on responses to Weininger; Kafka's response is discussed briefly (p. 143), and more fully by Politzer (pp. 197–200).

[4] See Ritchie Robertson, *Kafka: A Very Short Introduction* (Oxford: Oxford University Press, 2004), 62–3.

In 1918 he wrote in his notebook: 'Sensual love deceives one into ignoring heavenly love.'[5]

The Court

At the same time as the court breaks down K.'s professional façade, it appears like a parody, a projection, or a counterpart of his professional life. Its hierarchy of judges corresponds to the bank hierarchy of which K. is sharply conscious: we see from his treatment of Rabensteiner, Kullich, and Kaminer how condescending he is towards junior employees. The court too is full of surreptitious sexuality. The examining magistrate is reported to be an inveterate womanizer (p. 49); what K. takes for law-books turn out to be cheap pornography (p. 42). The painter Titorelli is plagued by young girls with unsavoury erotic overtones.

It is even uncertain how far the court exists independently of K. Often it seems to read his mind. Not having been told when to attend his hearing, K. resolves to turn up at 9 a.m., arrives at 10.05, and is told: 'You should have been here an hour and five minutes ago.' His enquiry for a carpenter called Lanz is answered in the affirmative when a young woman shows him into the courtroom. After K. has slammed the lumber-room door on the thrasher and the two guards, they are still there twenty-four hours later; no time seems to have passed. K. goes to the cathedral to meet an Italian business colleague, who does not turn up; soon after he enters, the priest calls to him by name, and says he has had him summoned.

There are even suggestions that K. brings the court into being. The guard enters K.'s bedroom only after he has rung a bell for his breakfast. Later we are told the view of one judge that the ringing of a bell marks the real beginning of the trial (p. 141). Perhaps K. has thus unwittingly initiated his own trial? In the same way, it is he who acknowledges 'the stranger's right to keep him under surveillance' (p. 5), and who defines the strangers as guards—'they had to be guards' (p. 7). K. too declares in his speech at his first hearing that there is 'a large organization at work', with ushers, clerks, police officers, and executioners (p. 37); the organization only appears after K., without any knowledge, has asserted its existence.

[5] Kafka, *Nachgelassene Schriften und Fragmente II*, ed. Jost Schillemeit (Frankfurt a.M.: Fischer, 1992), 68. My translation.

Mostly, however, the court seems to exist in parallel to the familiar world. Its premises are in attics and garrets all over the town. To visit them, K. has to penetrate unfamiliar slum quarters. Their construction is ramshackle and absurdly inconvenient. Even in the cathedral, the prison chaplain addresses K. from a small pulpit that stands beside the main pulpit, and seems so badly designed that a preacher cannot stand upright in it. The lumber-room scene especially implies that the court exists in spaces that people have locked up and forgotten about, and invites a psychoanalytic interpretation in which the court occupies the space of the unconscious.

Such an interpretation, however, would be difficult to pursue consistently, for in other respects the court seems formidably real. Its behaviour towards K. can be construed as a sadistic cat-and-mouse game. At first the court seems cooperative, even obliging, yet everything it does is in some way disagreeable to K. It sends three junior colleagues from the bank to make his late arrival less obvious; K., however, is reluctant to recognize them as colleagues and resents their presence. In order not to disrupt K.'s work at the bank, the court schedules hearings for Sundays. Yet by doing so it already interferes with his professional life by obliging him to refuse the flattering and politically important invitation to a trip on the deputy manager's yacht (p. 27). By deciding to compose a submission, K. imperils his own professional career and his competition with the deputy manager. K. finds himself unable to discuss business with the factory-owner; the deputy manager has to take over and deal with the matter. He leaves the bank, even though three clients want urgently to speak to him, in order to visit the painter Titorelli, and the deputy manager deals with the clients instead.

One could to some extent interpret the court's behaviour as pressing K. to become an autonomous human being. Instead of fencing himself off from the rest of the world through an apparatus of telephones, servants, and documents, he may be required to confront himself and acknowledge the possibility of his own guilt. The supervisor admonishes him: 'Think less about us and about what is going to happen to you, think more about yourself instead' (p. 13). K., uneasily conscious of hierarchy, rejects this advice because it comes from somebody who may be younger, and, as so often, seeks to shelter behind somebody else—in this case, by the brief impulse to contact his friend the state prosecutor Hasterer. Later the lawyer admits:

'They wanted to eliminate the defence counsel as far as possible, everything should depend on the accused alone' (p. 82). The chaplain rebukes K. for seeking help from women, yet without explaining to him what real help would be.

If so, however, the court has set K. a task too hard for him to accomplish. Instead of relying on himself, he enlists women and lawyers in his service. His inevitable failure is announced in the scene with the information clerk. This court employee is supposedly able to answer any question that a client wants to put. When he meets this official, however, K. is already almost overcome by the bad air in the court premises, and the ground seems to be rocking under his feet like the deck of a ship. All he wants is to be guided out of the court premises and back into ordinary life. The ironic smile of the information clerk seems to acknowledge that K. will not be able, or will not want, to ask him any question that might lead to a true understanding of his case.

The power of the court, like all political power, rests ultimately on violence. This is drastically brought home to us in the lumber-room scene, where the two guards are thrashed—an inordinate as well as brutal punishment for their misdemeanours. The thrasher has no misgivings about what he is doing, but does his job as unfeelingly as a concentration-camp guard: 'I'm employed as a thrasher, so I'll thrash them' (p. 60). K.'s execution in a lonely quarry, where two executioners plunge a knife into his heart, is even more barbaric.

Dr Huld, the lawyer whom K. engages at his uncle's behest, is not part of the court. He describes at interminable length his cultivation of contacts with court officials, while admitting that these contacts have not yet produced any result. He conveys an impression of a huge hierarchy of officialdom, stretching upwards and out of sight. He acknowledges that in essence he can do nothing for K., since the court discourages defence lawyers. A lawyer can only wait outside the door during hearings and, when the defendant emerges, try to gather from his confused and fragmentary reports something that might be of use in pursuing the case. Yet the lawyer refuses to admit that this makes the defence unnecessary. Nor is there any prospect of improving the workings of the court: 'The only correct approach was to accept things as they were' (p. 85). He urges K. to accept passively the methods of the court and to place himself blindly in his lawyer's power, and to accept servitude: 'it is often better to be in chains than free' (p. 136).

The exercise of power, in fact, is the lawyer's real reward. K. realizes at an early stage that the lawyer is humiliating him. He only realizes how much power the lawyer acquires over his clients when he sees him humiliating the corn-merchant Block. Block turns out to be a defendant who has devoted himself entirely to his case, allowing his flourishing business to decline, and employing five lawyers besides Huld. He spends almost every day in the corridor waiting to see a lawyer. We see Huld exercising his power on Block, telling him that whenever he comes, he comes at the wrong time, and obliging him to spend the day in a tiny room reading legal documents. Servitude is expressed through bodily prostration: Block, angrily resisting K.'s attempts to prevent him, kneels before the lawyer and kisses his hand.

A different kind of help is offered by the court painter Titorelli, who explains the three possible outcomes of a trial. Real acquittals occur only in legends, which the hard-headed K. instantly dismisses. That leaves only apparent acquittal, when the defendant is released but may be rearrested at any time, and protraction of the proceedings, which prevents them ever coming to a final trial but also requires a vast expenditure of energy by the defendant. The latter two prevent a condemnation, but they also prevent a genuine acquittal (p. 114). The three identical pictures perhaps suggest the equivalence in K.'s mind of all three solutions (p. 117). The episode is an ironic reflection on the role of art. Art can tell us about matters that have no direct connection to mundane reality, like the real acquittals recorded in legends. Whatever value legends—and by extension, imaginative fiction in general—might have, K. dismisses them. To people like K., uninterested in lateral thinking or imaginative leaps, Titorelli has no solution to offer. In the mundane world, art is not a means of discovering truth but an instrument of power. The pictures of judges that Titorelli paints do not correspond to reality but follow a set of prescribed conventions. Thus, the judge in the picture in the lawyer's room, who looks large and menacing, is in fact, according to Leni, a tiny man who sits not on a throne, but on a kitchen chair covered by an old horse-blanket. Titorelli's landscape paintings, 'Sunset on the Heath', are all alike, presenting a bleak landscape with a suggestion of decline in the setting sun, but no prospect of transcendence. Kafka was himself sceptical about the relation between art and truth, comparing art to a moth that flies round a candle: 'Art flies round the

truth, but is determined not to get burnt. Its ability consists in
finding a previously unsuspected place in the dark void where the ray
of light can be unexpectedly and powerfully caught.'[6]

Although K. does muster enough independence to dismiss his
lawyer, he is thrown back on his own resources and in practice adopts
the method of protraction or dragging his case out. As his obsession
grows, he plans to compose a submission reviewing his entire life,
explaining his reasons for action in every event of any importance.
Such a submission will of course be an enormous, time-consuming
undertaking which can only by chance contain anything relevant to
his trial. It is not an attempt to deal with his case, but rather a massive and laborious diversion from trying to pinpoint the real reason
for his arrest.

Law, Metaphysics, Religion

What does the court have to do with the real legal system? Kafka, a
law graduate, was familiar both with the legal system of the Habsburg
Empire and with its history. Theodore J. Ziolkowski has related *The
Trial* to two conceptions of law that were in conflict among jurists in
Kafka's day. One was the strictly Kantian philosophy of law enshrined
in the legal code of the German Empire (1871), which regarded the
criminal as an autonomous person with full moral responsibility for
his or her actions. Hence the German legal code attended only to the
act committed, and prescribed punishment in accordance with the
nature of the crime (though with allowance for mitigating circumstances). The Austrian legal code (going back to the *Josephina* of
1787) defined crime not only as an act but also with reference to the
'evil intent' of the accused: hence it attended not only to the act itself
but also to the motivation of the accused. Accordingly, it became an
axiom of Austrian law that there could be guilt without illegality:
somebody might plan a crime but be prevented from carrying it out
by an external accident. Hence: 'In line with his training in Austrian
law, Kafka has constructed an absurd paradigm of the legal system
that believes in a theoretical "guilt without illegality" and that concen-
trates on the criminal rather than on the criminal act.'[7] The authorities

---

[6] Ibid. 75–6. My translation.

[7] Theodore J. Ziolkowski, *The Mirror of Justice: Literary Reflections of Legal Crises*
(Princeton: Princeton University Press, 1997), 128.

are interested not in the act Josef K. may have committed—which is never specified—but in his guilt (*Schuld*), and the word slides from meaning 'responsibility for an act' to 'subjective feelings of guilt'. Being accused seems to mean being a special type of person.

This conception of the criminal as a special type of person is also founded in Kafka's legal training, and, more widely, in late nineteenth-century anthropology. The Italian criminologist Cesare Lombroso famously argued, in *L'uomo delinquente* (*Criminal Man*, 1875), that a 'criminal type' existed, distinguished by a number of physical features which in turn revealed his aberrant personality. Thus, a low forehead, a twisted nose, a wild look or unsteady gaze, might reveal an innately criminal character, even if the person concerned had not (yet) committed a crime.[8] These doctrines derived from the eighteenth-century 'science' of physiognomy, and found further support in Darwin's *The Expression of the Emotions in Men and Animals* (1872). They were developed by the Austrian criminologist Hanns Gross, whose lectures Kafka attended at the University of Prague. In his handbook, *Criminalpsychologie*, Gross lists and classifies the features that disclose criminality. In order to interpret them, one must study a person as a whole, assigning meaning to his most involuntary actions and gestures. It is not the crime, but the criminal inclination, that is the object of inquiry. The basic principle of modern criminal investigation, according to Gross, is: 'Not the crime, but the criminal, is the object of punishment; it is not the concept but the person that is punished.'[9]

The contrasting legal philosophies reconstructed by Ziolkowski are both present in the novel. At times, as we have seen, the court seems to be inviting K. to assume a Kantian autonomy, to confront his possible guilt directly without intermediaries. But at other times it seems to be identifying him as an individual who is guilty by nature, whether or not he has committed any actual crime.

Here the novel slides from legal to moral and metaphysical discourses. The very opening sentence elides the boundaries among them, for 'anything wrong' is in the original 'etwas Böses', and the semantic range of 'böse' stretches from 'nasty' to 'evil'. Often the court sounds

[8] See Mark Anderson, *Kafka's Clothes: Ornament and Aestheticism in the Habsburg Fin de Siècle* (Oxford: Clarendon Press, 1992), 146–7.

[9] Hanns Gross, *Criminalpsychologie* (Graz: Leuschner & Lubensky's Universitäts-Buchhandlung, 1898), 89.

like an impersonal mechanism concerned with guilt. It does not go looking for guilt, but is ineluctably drawn to guilt, which implies that nobody can ever be wrongfully arrested. The thrasher asserts that the guards' punishment is 'as just as it is inevitable' (p. 59), implying again that whatever the court ordains must be accepted. The prison chaplain underlines that the court bears K. no personal ill-will: 'The court does not want anything from you. It receives you when you come and dismisses you when you go' (p. 160). Yet at the same time this impersonal authority clearly humiliates and ultimately destroys its victims. The defendants whom K. sees in the corridor are hunched like street beggars. The significance of the court is most strongly suggested by the allegorical figure on the back of the chair in which Titorelli has painted a judge. It represents the goddess of justice and of victory in a single figure. She has wings on her heels and is running, though justice should be stable. As K. looks more closely, she seems to be the goddess of the hunt. This anticipates an aphorism that Kafka wrote a few years later: 'The hunting dogs are still playing in the courtyard, but their prey will not escape them, no matter how fast it is already rushing through the woods.'[10]

If we take the court to be a religious or metaphysical authority, we may want to pay particular attention to an exchange between K. and the chaplain, where K. objects: 'How can a person be guilty anyway? We're all human, every single one of us.' 'That is correct,' said the priest, 'but that's the way guilty people talk' (p. 152). K. is saying in effect that 'guilt' is an inappropriate concept for ordinary weak human beings. The chaplain's rejoinder suggests that such a remark is a mere attempt at self-exoneration by people who know they are guilty. That implies further that ordinary human weakness *is* guilt, and might also make us invoke such a concept as original sin. Such a move would reinforce doubts about whether the court embodies any kind of justice or simply the relentless exercise of power. The thought ascribed to K. just before his death, when he cannot bring himself to commit suicide—'the responsibility for this last failing lay with the one who had refused him the necessary strength to do that' (p. 164)— might be read as an indictment of an all-powerful being. And it would link up with an intriguing conversation that Kafka had in February 1914, a few months before he started *The Trial*, with the religious

---

[10] Kafka, *Nachgelassene Schriften und Fragmente II*, 55. My translation.

philosopher Martin Buber in Berlin. As Buber later recollected, Kafka asked him about a puzzling passage in the Bible. Psalm 82 begins:

God standeth in the congregation of God; he judgeth among the gods.
How long will ye judge unjustly, and respect the persons of the wicked?
Judge the poor and fatherless; do justice to the afflicted and destitute.
Rescue the poor and needy: deliver them out of the hand of the wicked.

Buber explains this psalm as referring to a number of subordinate deities to whom God gave a position of power which they abused. He traces it back to a Gnostic myth that says the world is under the dominion of evil spirits, from whom man can free himself by turning to the hidden light that comes from the supreme God.[11] Should we understand the unseen supreme judges as evil divinities? And if so, is the hidden light to be identified with the radiance streaming from the Law that the man in the chaplain's legend sees just before his death?

These questions, however intriguing, are ultimately unanswerable. The novel does not disclose a metaphysical system, a message, or a doctrine. It hints, suggests, and implies. Its characteristic mode is ambiguity. Hence the long, sometimes over-long, discussions about how to interpret the behaviour of the court, or the relations of the doorkeeper and the countryman in the chaplain's legend. Ambiguity was important to Kafka, an essential part of his experience of the world, and no less essential to his fiction.

Images and Perspectives

Turning from the *what* to the *how*, Kafka renders his novel hard to interpret by confining us almost entirely to the perspective of the central character and denying us any narratorial comments that would help us to orient ourselves. This narrative method, first identified by Friedrich Beissner over half a century ago, and often called 'mono-perspectival narration', accounts also for the sense of confinement and entrapment that the reader can easily share with Josef K.[12] However, Beissner's path-breaking account has since been qualified. There are a few moments (see the notes) when the narrator shows us things which K. is not in a position to see. More importantly, we can often

[11] Martin Buber, 'Schuld und Schuldgefühle', in *Werke*, 3 vols. (Munich: Kösel, 1962–4), i. 499. See further Julian Morgenstern, 'The Mythological Background of Psalm 82', *Hebrew Union College Annual*, 14 (1939), 29–126.

[12] Friedrich Beissner, *Der Erzähler Franz Kafka* (Stuttgart: Kohlhammer, 1952).

surmise a discrepancy between an event and K.'s reaction to it. When the supervisor offers him some advice in the first chapter, it hardly seems appropriate for K. to respond with indignation at being lectured like a schoolboy. Gradually we can collect many examples of K.'s ill-judged reactions, self-deceptions, and faulty reasonings, and argue that he consistently misreads the—teasingly ambiguous—clues to his situation that the court offers him.

Kafka also helps us to make sense of his story through his imagery. In his stripped-down fictional world, ordinary mundane objects, such as windows, accrete significance. Eric Marson, who has given the most detailed and at the same time the most illuminating inter-pretation of *The Trial*, observes: 'The person who gazes out of a window in Kafka's fiction has often fallen into a state of abstraction whilst pondering or reflecting narrowly upon a matter of concern to himself. What he sees beyond the window is often a significant com-ment on the content or implications of his thoughts—a neat shortcut for authorial information in a limited-perspective story.'[13] Thus, in *The Metamorphosis* Gregor Samsa, on waking up, looks out of the window and sees the rain—an image for his dismal life; and later, as his eyesight fades, he spends a long time leaning on the windowsill of the room to which he is now confined, yet cannot see even to the other side of the street. And on the winter morning at the beginning of the chapter headed 'The Lawyer. The Factory Owner. The Painter', we see K., unable to concentrate on his work, gazing out of the window, where 'snow was falling in the murky light'.

Light and darkness, in particular, have symbolic overtones through-out the novel. K.'s day-to-day environment—his lodgings and his office—has modern electric lighting, but the entrance to the lawyer's house is lit by an old-fashioned 'open gas flame', which burns with 'a loud hissing noise' but gives off little light, and the lawyer's bedroom is illuminated only by a candle. Similarly, the lumber-room where K. finds the guards being punished is lit by a candle, in contrast to the electric lamp outside. The cathedral where K. is summoned is lit by candles, which are gradually extinguished, leaving K. and the chap-lain in virtual darkness; K. has come equipped with a modern imple-ment, the electric pocket torch, which, however, prevents him from seeing the paintings except by illuminating a few inches at a time.

---

[13] Marson, *Kafka's Trial*, 26–7.

All of these images suggest that the court represents an archaic world, in contrast to the brightly lit settings of modernity.

However closely we read the text, many details must remain opaque. Why is the audience at K.'s first hearing divided into two parties? Why are his executioners dumb, eunuch-like, and compared to actors? Such details are really less important than the imaginative power which made Kafka's novel into a basic text for the twentieth century, and perhaps beyond. Whatever Kafka's intentions, his insight into the workings of power, the ability of a bureaucratic system to grind down its victims, and the mechanisms by which they acquiesce in the process, have made many people, especially in the former Soviet Union and its satellites, feel that Kafka was writing for them.[14]

The Trial is not hopeful about the possibilities for human freedom. It seems to present K. with two undesirable alternatives—an impossibly demanding ideal of autonomy, and a slavish submission to the system in which he is enmeshed. The consequences of obeying authority are shown in the legend about the man from the country, who spends his entire life waiting for permission to enter the Law by a door intended specifically for him, and dies with only a glimpse of the object of his desire. But the reader is never told what the man should have done instead, any more than we are told how K. should have managed his case.

On the other hand, by thus withholding easy answers Kafka affirms the freedom of the reader, and thus shows himself to be in the forefront of modernism. Modernist writers offer difficult, challenging texts in order to stimulate the reader's creative involvement. Another modernist, Bertolt Brecht, insisted that his epic theatre was not meant to be passively consumed, but to provoke his audience to indignation and outrage. The spectator was to say: 'I'd never have thought it— That's not the way—That's extraordinary, hardly believable—It's got to stop—The sufferings of this man appal me, because they are unnecessary.'[15] Similarly, we are invited to read Kafka's novel not with acquiescence but actively, against the grain, looking for the possibilities which K. himself rejects or is denied. The freedom which the fictional protagonist cannot use is still available to the reader.

[14] On such readings, and the features of Kafka's writing to which they are a valid response, see my *Kafka: A Very Short Introduction*, ch. 4.

[15] 'Theatre for Pleasure or Theatre for Instruction', in *Brecht on Theatre*, ed. and tr. John Willett (London: Eyre Methuen, 1964), 69–77 (p. 71).

NOTE ON THE TEXT

KAFKA never produced a final version of *The Trial*. After working on it intensively in the second half of 1914, he abandoned it in January 1915, leaving many textual problems. He had begun by writing the first chapter and the last, so that the narrative should not run away with him. With the intervening chapters, Kafka gave no clear indication of the order in which they should appear. Chapters tend to open with a vague indication of time—'during the next week' (p. 40), 'one evening soon afterwards' (p. 58)—which does not commit Kafka to any strict sequence. The broad development of the novel is admittedly clear. After K.'s arrest, there is a movement in which the court has repeated contact with him, summoning him to a hearing, allowing him to meet court officials a week later, and staging the punishment of the offending guards in a lumber-room in the bank where K. works. In a second movement, the court withdraws and K. seeks help, first from the lawyer to whom his uncle introduces him, then from the painter Titorelli, and, when these advisers prove disappointing, by composing his own submission to the court. The sombre episode in the cathedral clearly occurs a short time before the end. This pattern is reinforced by reference to the seasons and their atmosphere. The novel begins in spring; the court offices are rendered stifling by the hot sun, suggesting summer; a later chapter begins on a snowy winter morning, and a visitor complains of a 'horrible autumn' (p. 95), while the darkness of the 'Cathedral' chapter implies that winter is persisting.

Within this scheme, the main uncertainty concerns the placing of the 'Thrasher' chapter. In response to the complaints about his guards' misbehaviour that K. uttered at his first hearing, the court has them brutally punished in a lumber-room in K.'s bank. Eric Marson, in a searching study of the novel that deserves to be far better known, argues that this chapter ought to follow immediately on 'The First Hearing'.[1] That location would show even more unnervingly how promptly the court reacts. By providing more variety, it would also be more artistic than the present arrangement, in which

---

[1] Eric Marson, *Kafka's Trial: The Case Against Josef K.* (St Lucia: University of Queensland Press, 1975), 134–5.

complaint and punishment are separated by the long chapter 'In the Empty Conference Hall'.

The Trial was prepared for publication after Kafka's death by his friend Max Brod, and appeared in 1925. Brod had to decide for himself on the best sequence of chapters. He inserted the short, unfinished chapter 'B.'s Friend' into the main text, and did not include the other fragments. These were included in subsequent editions. They are, however, omitted from most English translations. In an afterword to the third edition of *The Trial*, Brod considered the possibility that the 'Thrasher' chapter might have been intended to come earlier, perhaps after 'The First Hearing', but he did not change the sequence.

In the 1970s work began on a proper critical edition of Kafka's work, supported and published by the S. Fischer Verlag in Frankfurt am Main. It was undertaken by an academic team, mostly based in Germany but including the Oxford scholar Malcolm Pasley, who in 1961 had, with the permission of Kafka's heirs, transported his manuscripts for safe keeping to the Bodleian Library. *The Trial* was not at first available for editing, since Max Brod had retained the manuscript and bequeathed it to a close friend, but eventually it was bought by the Deutsches Literaturarchiv (German Literary Archive) at Marbach am Neckar, the great centre for research in modern German literature. The text, critically edited by Malcolm Pasley, appeared in 1990.[2] The present translation follows it. In the Critical Edition, 'B.'s Friend' is consigned to the fragments, and the 'Thrasher' chapter retains the place that Brod gave it, after 'In the Empty Conference Hall'.

The peculiar character of the novel, however, means that an edition which arranges the text in a fixed linear sequence must inevitably be somewhat misleading. The sequence of chapters cannot be definitively settled, and the status of the fragments remains unclear. Since Kafka never finally discarded them—in contrast to some short passages which he stroked out in his manuscript—they form a kind of penumbra, offering further information which we as readers can use as we please. It has been argued that the only way to present the text

[2] Franz Kafka, *Der Proceß*, ed. Malcolm Pasley, 2 vols. (Frankfurt a.M.: Fischer, 1990). The first volume consists of the text; the second contains a description of the manuscript, an account of its composition, a list of editorial interventions (such as writing out abbreviations like 'F.B.' in full as 'Fräulein Bürstner'), and the alterations made by Kafka in the course of writing.

without misrepresenting its character is as a facsimile of Kafka's manuscript, and the Roter Stern Verlag in Germany has published, as part of its series of Kafka facsimiles, such an edition, in which the chapters are in separate folders and can be moved about as the reader prefers.[3] However, the advantages of a do-it-yourself text do seem to be outweighed by those of a reading edition in which readers are appropriately informed about the kind of novel they have before them.

[3] This is the first volume of the Historische-kritische Ausgabe sämtlichen Handschriften, Drucke und Typoskripte, ed. Roland Reuss and Peter Staengle (Basel: Stroemfeld/ Roter Stern Verlag, 1995–).

SELECT BIBLIOGRAPHY

(CONFINED TO WORKS IN ENGLISH)

Translations of Non-Fictional Works by Kafka

The Collected Aphorisms, tr. Malcolm Pasley (London: Penguin, 1994).

The Diaries, tr. Joseph Kresh and Martin Greenberg (Harmondsworth: Penguin, 1972).

Letters to Friends, Family and Editors, tr. Richard and Clara Winston (New York: Schocken, 1988).

Letters to Felice, tr. James Stern and Elizabeth Duckworth (London: Vintage, 1992).

Letters to Milena, expanded edn, tr. Philip Boehm (New York: Schocken, 1990).

Letters to Ottla and the Family, tr. Richard and Clara Winston (New York: Schocken, 1988).

Biographies

Adler, Jeremy, *Franz Kafka* (London: Penguin, 2001).

Brod, Max, *Franz Kafka: A Biography*, tr. G. Humphreys Roberts and Richard Winston (New York: Schocken, 1960).

Diamant, Kathi, *Kafka's Last Love: The Mystery of Dora Diamant* (London: Secker & Warburg, 2003).

Hayman, Ronald, *K: A Biography of Kafka* (London: Weidenfeld & Nicolson, 1981).

Hockaday, Mary, *Kafka, Love and Courage: The Life of Milena Jesenská* (London: Deutsch, 1995).

Murray, Nicholas, *Kafka* (London: Little, Brown, 2004).

Northey, Anthony, *Kafka's Relatives: Their Lives and His Writing* (New Haven and London: Yale University Press, 1991).

Storr, Anthony, 'Kafka's Sense of Identity', in *Churchill's Black Dog and Other Phenomena of the Human Mind* (London: Collins, 1989), 52–82.

Unseld, Joachim, *Franz Kafka: A Writer's Life*, tr. Paul F. Dvorak (Riverside, Calif.: Ariadne Press, 1997).

Introductions

Preece, Julian (ed.), *The Cambridge Companion to Kafka* (Cambridge: Cambridge University Press, 2002).

Robertson, Ritchie, *Kafka: A Very Short Introduction* (Oxford: Oxford University Press, 2004).

Rolleston, James (ed.), *A Companion to the Works of Franz Kafka* (Rochester, NY: Camden House, 2002).

Speirs, Ronald and Beatrice Sandberg, *Franz Kafka*, Macmillan Modern Novelists (London: Macmillan, 1997).

Critical Studies

Alter, Robert, *Necessary Angels: Tradition and Modernity in Kafka, Benjamin and Scholem* (Cambridge, Mass.: Harvard University Press, 1991).

Anderson, Mark, *Kafka's Clothes: Ornament and Aestheticism in the Habsburg Fin de Siècle* (Oxford: Clarendon Press, 1992).

—— 'Kafka, Homosexuality and the Aesthetics of "Male Culture"', *Austrian Studies*, 7 (1996), 79–99.

Boa, Elizabeth, *Kafka: Gender, Class and Race in the Letters and Fictions* (Oxford: Clarendon Press, 1996).

Corngold, Stanley, *Lambent Traces: Franz Kafka* (Princeton: Princeton University Press, 2004).

Dodd, W. J., *Kafka and Dostoyevsky: The Shaping of Influence* (London: Macmillan, 1992).

—— (ed.), *Kafka: The Metamorphosis, The Trial and The Castle*, Modern Literatures in Perspective (London and New York: Longman, 1995).

Duttlinger, Carolin, *Kafka and Photography* (Oxford: Oxford University Press, 2007).

Flores, Angel (ed.), *The Kafka Debate* (New York: Gordian Press, 1977).

Gilman, Sander L., *Franz Kafka, the Jewish Patient* (London and New York: Routledge, 1995).

Goebel, Rolf J., *Constructing China: Kafka's Orientalist Discourse* (Columbia, SC: Camden House, 1997).

Heidsieck, Arnold, *The Intellectual Contexts of Kafka's Fiction: Philosophy, Law, Religion* (Columbia, SC: Camden House, 1994).

Koelb, Clayton, *Kafka's Rhetoric: The Passion of Reading* (Ithaca and London: Cornell University Press, 1989).

Politzer, Heinz, *Franz Kafka: Parable and Paradox* (Ithaca, NY: Cornell University Press, 1962).

Robertson, Ritchie, *Kafka: Judaism, Politics, and Literature* (Oxford: Clarendon Press, 1985).

Sokel, Walter H., *The Myth of Power and the Self: Essays on Franz Kafka* (Detroit: Wayne State University Press, 2002).

Zilcosky, John, *Kafka's Travels: Exoticism, Colonialism, and the Traffic of Writing* (Basingstoke and New York: Palgrave Macmillan, 2003).

Zischler, Hanns, *Kafka Goes to the Movies*, tr. Susan H. Gillespie (Chicago and London: University of Chicago Press, 2003).

Historical Context

Anderson, Mark (ed.), *Reading Kafka: Prague, Politics, and the Fin de Siècle* (New York: Schocken, 1989).

Beck, Evelyn Torton, *Kafka and the Yiddish Theater* (Madison, Wisc.: University of Wisconsin Press, 1971).

Bruce, Iris, *Kafka and Cultural Zionism: Dates in Palestine* (Madison, Wisc.: University of Wisconsin Press, 2007).

Gelber, Mark H. (ed.), *Kafka, Zionism, and Beyond* (Tübingen: Niemeyer, 2004).

Kieval, Hillel J., *The Making of Czech Jewry: National Conflict and Jewish Society in Bohemia, 1870–1918* (New York: Oxford University Press, 1988).

Robertson, Ritchie, *The 'Jewish Question' in German Literature, 1749–1939* (Oxford: Oxford University Press, 1999).

Spector, Scott, *Prague Territories: National Conflict and Cultural Innovation in Franz Kafka's Fin de Siècle* (Berkeley, Los Angeles, and London: University of California Press, 2000).

The Trial

Dodd, William J., *Kafka: Der Prozeß* (Glasgow: University of Glasgow French and German Publications, 1991).

Dowden, Stephen D., *Sympathy for the Abyss: A Study in the Novel of German Modernism* (Tübingen: Niemeyer, 1986), 94–134.

Goebel, Rolf, 'The Exploration of the Modern City in *The Trial*', in *The Cambridge Companion to Kafka*, ed. Julian Preece (Cambridge: Cambridge University Press, 2002), 42–60.

Grundlehner, Philip, 'Manual Gestures in Kafka's *Prozeß*', *German Quarterly*, 55 (1982), 186–99.

Leopold, Keith, 'Breaks in Perspective in Franz Kafka's *Der Prozeß*', *German Quarterly*, 36 (1963), 31–8.

Marson, Eric L., *Kafka's Trial: The Case Against Josef K.* (St Lucia, Queensland: University of Queensland Press, 1975).

Pasley, Malcolm, 'Two Literary Sources of Kafka's *Der Prozeß*', *Forum for Modern Language Studies*, 3 (1967), 142–7.

—— 'Kafka's *Der Process*: What the Manuscript Can Tell Us', *Oxford German Studies*, 18/19 (1989–90), 109–18.

Robertson, Ritchie, 'Reading the Clues: Kafka, *Der Proceß*', in David Midgley (ed.), *The German Novel in the Twentieth Century: Beyond Realism* (Edinburgh: Edinburgh University Press, 1993), 59–79.

Sheppard, Richard, '*The Trial/The Castle*: Towards an Analytical Comparison', in Angel Flores (ed.), *The Kafka Debate* (New York: Gordian Press, 1977), 396–417.

Sokel, Walter H., 'The Programme of Kafka's Court: Oedipal and Existential Meanings of *The Trial*', in Franz Kuna (ed.), *Franz Kafka: Semi-Centenary Perspectives* (London: Elek, 1976), 1–21.

Stern, J. P., 'The Law of *The Trial*', in Franz Kuna (ed.), *Franz Kafka: Semi-Centenary Perspectives* (London: Elek, 1976), 22–41.

Further Reading in Oxford World's Classics

Kafka, Franz, *The Castle*, tr. Anthea Bell, ed. Ritchie Robertson.
—— *A Hunger Artist and Other Stories*, tr. Joyce Crick, ed. Ritchie Robertson.
—— *The Man who Disappeared*, tr. and ed. Ritchie Robertson.
—— *The Metamorphosis and Other Stories*, tr. Joyce Crick, ed. Ritchie Robertson.

A CHRONOLOGY OF FRANZ KAFKA

1883 3 July: Franz Kafka born in Prague, son of Hermann Kafka (1852–1931) and his wife Julie, née Löwy (1856–1934).

1885 Birth of FK's brother Georg, who died at the age of fifteen months.

1887 Birth of FK's brother Heinrich, who died at the age of six months.

1889 Birth of FK's sister Gabriele ('Elli') (d. 1941).

1890 Birth of FK's sister Valerie ('Valli') (d. 1942).

1892 Birth of FK's sister Ottilie ('Ottla') (d. 1943).

1901 FK begins studying law in the German-language section of the Charles University, Prague.

1906 Gains his doctorate in law and begins a year of professional experience in the Prague courts.

1907 Begins working for the Prague branch of the insurance company Assicurazioni Generali, based in Trieste.

1908 Moves to the state-run Workers' Accident Insurance Company for the Kingdom of Bohemia. First publication: eight prose pieces (later included in the volume *Meditation*) appear in the Munich journal *Hyperion*.

1909 Holiday with Max and Otto Brod at Riva on Lake Garda; they attend a display of aircraft, about which FK writes 'The Aeroplanes at Brescia'.

1910 Holiday with Max and Otto Brod in Paris.

1911 Holiday with Max Brod in Northern Italy, Switzerland, and Paris. Attends many performances by Yiddish actors visiting Prague, and becomes friendly with the actor Isaak Löwy (Jitskhok Levi).

1912 Holiday with Max Brod in Weimar, after which FK spends three weeks in the nudist sanatorium 'Jungborn' in the Harz Mountains. Works on *The Man who Disappeared*. 13 August: first meeting with Felice Bauer (1887–1960) from Berlin. 22–3 September: writes *The Judgement* in a single night. November–December: works on *The Metamorphosis*. December: *Meditation*, a collection of short prose pieces, published by Kurt Wolff in Leipzig.

1913 Visits Felice Bauer three times in Berlin. September: attends a conference on accident prevention in Vienna, where he also looks in on the Eleventh Zionist Congress. Stays in a sanatorium in Riva. Publishes *The Stoker* (= the first chapter of *The Man who Disappeared*) in Wolff's series of avant-garde prose texts 'The Last Judgement'.

1914   1 June: officially engaged to Felice Bauer in Berlin. 12 July: engage-
       ment dissolved. Holiday with the Prague novelist Ernst Weiss in the
       Danish resort of Marielyst. August–December: writes most of *The
       Trial*; October: *In the Penal Colony*.

1915   The dramatist Carl Sternheim, awarded the Fontane Prize for
       literature, transfers the prize money to Kafka. *The Metamorphosis*
       published by Wolff.

1916   Reconciliation with Felice Bauer; they spend ten days together in the
       Bohemian resort of Marienbad (Mariánské Lázně). *The Judgement*
       published by Wolff. FK works on the stories later collected in
       A Country Doctor.

1917   July: FK and Felice visit the latter's sister in Budapest, and become
       engaged again. 9–10 August: FK suffers a haemorrhage which is
       diagnosed as tubercular. To convalesce, he stays with his sister
       Ottla on a farm at Zürau (Siřem) in the Bohemian countryside.
       December: visit from Felice Bauer; engagement dissolved.

1918   March: FK resumes work. November: given health leave, stays till
       March 1919 in a hotel in Schelesen (Železná).

1919   Back in Prague, briefly engaged to Julie Wohryzek (1891–1944).
       In the Penal Colony published by Wolff.

1920   Intense relationship with his Czech translator Milena Polak, née
       Jesenská (1896–1944). July: ends relationship with Julie Wohryzek.
       Publication of *A Country Doctor: Little Stories*. December: again
       granted health leave, FK stays in a sanatorium in Matliary, in the
       Tatra Mountains, till August 1921.

1921   September: returns to work, but his worsening health requires him
       to take three months' further leave from October.

1922   January: has his leave extended till April; stays in mountain hotel in
       Spindlermühle (Špindlerův Mlýn). January–August: writes most of
       The Castle. 1 July: retires from the Insurance Company on a pension.

1923   July: visits Müritz on the Baltic and meets Dora Diamant (1898–1952).
       September: moves to Berlin and lives with Dora.

1924   March: his declining health obliges FK to return to Prague and in
       April to enter a sanatorium outside Vienna. Writes and publishes
       'Josefine, the Singer or The Mouse-People'. 3 June: dies. August:
       A Hunger Artist: Four Stories published by Die Schmiede.

1925   *The Trial*, edited by Max Brod, published by Die Schmiede.

1926   *The Castle*, edited by Max Brod, published by Wolff.

1927   *Amerika* (now known by Kafka's title, *The Man who Disappeared*),
       edited by Max Brod, published by Wolff.

1930 *The Castle*, translated by Willa and Edwin Muir, published by Martin Secker (London), the first English translation of Kafka.

1939 Max Brod leaves Prague just before the German invasion, taking Kafka's manuscripts in a suitcase, and reaches Palestine.

1956 Brod transfers the manuscripts (except that of *The Trial*) to Switzerland for safe keeping.

1961 The Oxford scholar Malcolm Pasley, with the permission of Kafka's heirs, transports the manuscripts to the Bodleian Library.

THE TRIAL

CONTENTS

The Arrest

SOMEONE must have been telling tales about Josef K., for one morning, without having done anything wrong, he was arrested.* Frau Grubach's cook, who brought him his breakfast at around eight every day, did not appear. That had never happened before. For a while K. waited—from his pillow he saw the old woman who lived opposite watching with, for her, quite unusual curiosity—but then, both perplexed and hungry, he rang. Immediately there was a knock at the door and a man he had never seen in the apartment came in. He was slimly yet solidly built and was wearing a close-fitting black suit which, like an outfit for travelling,* was equipped with a variety of pleats, pockets, buckles, buttons, and a belt that made it appear especially practical, without its precise purpose being clear. 'Who are you?' K. asked, immediately half-sitting up in bed. But the man ignored the question, as if his presence there had simply to be accepted, and merely said, 'You rang?' 'Anna's to bring me my breakfast,' said K., then tried to work out who the man actually was by observing him in silence and racking his brains. However he didn't expose himself to K.'s scrutiny for very long, but turned to the door and opened it slightly to say to someone who was obviously standing just behind it, 'He wants Anna to bring him his breakfast.' Brief laughter in the neighbouring room ensued; from the sound it was unclear whether there were several people joining in or not. Although he could not have learnt anything he didn't know already, the stranger now said to K., as if reporting someone else's words, 'It's not possible.' 'It's the first time that's happened,' said K., jumping out of bed and quickly putting his trousers on. 'I want to see who these people in the next room are and what explanation Frau Grubach has for this disturbance.' It did immediately occur to him that he should not have said that out loud, that in a way it was recognizing the stranger's right to keep him under surveillance, but that didn't seem important to him at that moment. That was certainly the way the stranger interpreted it, for he said, 'Wouldn't you prefer to stay here?' 'I have no desire to remain here, nor to be spoken to by you, as long as you have not introduced yourself.' 'It was well meant,' the stranger said, opening the door without being asked.

At first glance the neighbouring room, which K. entered more slowly than he intended, looked almost exactly the same as it had been the previous evening. It was Frau Grubach's living-room, crammed full with furniture, rugs, china, and photographs; perhaps there was a little more space there than usual, it was impossible to tell at a glance, especially since the main change consisted of the presence of a man who was sitting by the open window with a book, from which he looked up. 'You should have stayed in your room. Did Franz not tell you?' 'What is it you want?' K. said, looking from his new acquaintance to the one referred to as Franz, who had stayed in the doorway, and then back again. Through the open window the old woman could once more be seen. With truly geriatric curiosity she had gone round to the window opposite this room, so that she could continue to watch everything. 'But I just want to tell Frau Grubach—' K. said, making a movement as if to tear himself free from the two men, who, however, were a good distance away from him, and setting off towards the door. 'No,' the man by the window said, tossing the book on a little table and standing up. 'You are not allowed to leave, you are our prisoner.' 'That's what it looks like,' said K. 'May I ask why?' 'It is not our place to tell you that. Go to your room and wait. The proceedings have been set in motion and you will be told everything at the appropriate time. I am exceeding my instructions in talking to you in this friendly manner, but I hope there is no one to hear it apart from Franz, who himself has behaved towards you in a friendly manner, contrary to all regulations. If you continue to enjoy such luck as you have in the allocation of your guards, you can face the future with confidence.' K. wanted to sit down, but then he saw that there were no seats in the room, apart from the chair by the window. 'You will come to realize how true all that is,' said Franz, at the same time moving towards him together with the other man. The latter in particular was significantly taller than K. and patted him on the shoulder several times. Both felt K.'s nightshirt and said that from now on he would have to wear a much poorer-quality one, but that they would look after his nightshirt together with the rest of his shirts and underwear and, if his case should turn out favourably, would give them back to him. 'It's better if you hand over your things to us now, rather than in the depot,' they said, 'things are often misappropriated in the depot and, anyway, they sell everything off after a certain time, whether the case in question has been concluded or not. And the time these trials take, especially recently! It's true that you would eventually receive the proceeds of the sale from the depot, but in the first place the proceeds are small, for what decides the sale is not the amount of the offer, but the amount of the bribe, and in the second place it's well known that such proceeds get smaller as they pass from hand to hand and from year to year.'

K. hardly paid any attention to what they were saying. He perhaps still had the right to dispose of his things, but that seemed much less important to him than clarifying his situation. In the presence of these people, however, he couldn't even think. The belly of the second guard—they had to be guards—kept prodding him in a way that was positively friendly, but if he looked up he saw a dry, bony face that did not go with the fat body and which, with its large, sideways slanting nose, was passing messages to the other guard over his head. What kind of people were they? What were they talking about? Which department did they belong to?* After all, K. had rights, the country was at peace, the laws had not been suspended—who, then, had the audacity to descend on him in the privacy of his own home? He had always tended to avoid taking things too seriously, not to assume the worst until the worst actually happened, not to make provision for the future, even when everything looked black. In this case, however, that did not seem to be the right approach. He could, of course, regard the whole thing as a joke, a crude joke his colleagues at the bank were playing on him for some unknown reason, perhaps because it was his thirtieth birthday. That was always possible, perhaps he just had to laugh the guards in the face somehow and they would join in, perhaps they were porters from the street corner, they looked not unlike them. Be that as it may, ever since he first saw the guard called Franz he had been positively determined not to relinquish the least advantage he might perhaps hold over these people. The danger that it might later be said he could not take a joke K. regarded as minimal, though he did remember—not that it was usually his habit to learn from experience—a few occasions, unimportant in themselves, where, in contrast to his friends, he had deliberately, without the slightest thought for the possible consequences, acted carelessly and been punished by the outcome. It was not going to happen again, at least not this time. If it was a hoax, he was going to play along with it.

For the moment he was still free. 'Excuse me,' he said, going quickly between the guards into his room. 'He seems to be being sensible,' he heard one of them say behind him. In his room he immediately pulled out the drawers of his desk, everything in them was neat and tidy, but in his agitation he could not find his proof of identity, the very thing he was looking for. Eventually he found his cycling licence and was going to take it to the guards, but then he felt the document was too trivial and continued looking until he found his birth certificate. Just as he was going back into the next room, the door opposite opened and Frau Grubach was about to come in. She was only visible for a moment, for hardly had she seen K. than, clearly embarrassed, she apologized and disappeared, closing the door with the greatest care. 'Do come in,' K. had just had time to say. It left him standing with his papers in the middle of the room still looking at the door, which did not open again, and he was only roused by a call from the guards, who were sitting at the open window and, as K. now saw, eating his breakfast. 'Why didn't she come in?' he asked. 'She's not allowed,' said the tall guard, 'you've been arrested.' 'How can I have been arrested? Especially in this manner?' 'There you go again,' the guard said, dipping a slice of bread and butter in the honey pot. 'We don't answer questions like that.' 'You will have to answer them. Here is my identification, now show me yours and, above all, your warrant.' 'Good Lord!' said the guard, 'why can't you just accept the situation instead of pointlessly insisting on trying to annoy us; at this moment we're probably closer to you than anyone else in the world.' 'That's true, you'd better believe it,' said Franz, not raising the cup of coffee he had in his hand to his lips, but giving K. a long, probably significant but incomprehensible look. Without wanting to, K. became involved in a dialogue of looks with Franz, but then he did tap his papers, saying, 'This is my proof of identity.' 'What's that to us?' the tall guard cried. 'You're worse than a child. What do you want? Do you think you can bring your damned trial to a rapid conclusion by arguing with us guards about identity and warrants? We're minor officials who hardly know what proof of identity looks like, and have nothing to do with your case apart from standing guard ten hours a day in your apartment and getting paid for it. That's all we are but we're still able to understand that, before they order such an arrest, the authorities in whose employment we are will go into the reasons for the arrest and the particulars of the person to be arrested. There is no mistake. Our department, as far as I'm acquainted with it—and I'm only acquainted with the lowest grades—does not seek out guilt in the population but, as it says in the law, is attracted by guilt and has to send us guards out. That is the law. Where could there be an error?' 'That is not a law I am acquainted with,' said K. 'All the worse for you,' said the guard. 'I suspect it only exists inside your heads,' said K. He was trying to worm his way somehow or other into the guards' thoughts, to divert them into channels favourable to him or to make himself at home there. But the guard simply said coldly, 'You'll feel the full weight of it soon enough.' Franz joined in and said, 'Look, Willem, he admits he doesn't know the law and at the same time claims he's innocent.' 'You're quite right, but you can't get him to see anything,' the other replied. K. said nothing more. Do I have to let myself get even more confused, he thought, by the non-sense from these lowest of officials—as they themselves admit they are? They're certainly speaking of things they don't understand. It's only their stupidity that gives them such assurance. A few words with someone of my own kind will make everything clearer by far than any amount of conversation with these two. He walked up and down a few times in the space left free in the room. Across the street he could see the old woman, who had dragged an even older man to the window, where she held him clasped in her arms. K. had to put an end to this spectacle. 'Take me to your superior,' he said. 'When he wants us to, no sooner,' said the guard who had been addressed as Willem. 'And now I advise you to go to your room,' he added, 'to remain calm and wait and see what decisions are taken in your case. We advise you not to waste your energy on pointless thoughts but to compose yourself, great demands are going to be made on you. You have not treated us as our obliging attitude deserved, you have forgotten that, unlike you, we, whatever we may be, are at least free men, and that is no small advantage. Despite that, we are prepared, if you have some money, to fetch you a small breakfast from the café across the street.'

K. did not respond to this offer, but stood still for a while. Perhaps if he opened the door to the adjoining room, or even the door going into the hall, the two of them would not dare to stop him, perhaps the simplest solution to the whole business would be for him to fling caution to the winds. But perhaps they would grab him, and once he'd been thrown to the floor all his superiority over them, which to a certain extent he still maintained, would be lost. He therefore opted for the security of the solution that was bound to emerge in the natural

course of events, and went back into his room without a further word
being uttered, either by him or by the guards.

He dropped onto his bed and took a juicy apple* off the bedside
table; he had put it there the previous evening, ready for his breakfast. Now it would be all he would have for breakfast, but at least it
was much better, he assured himself as he took his first big bite, than
a breakfast from the grubby all-night café that he could have had as
a favour from the guards. He felt at ease and full of confidence. It was
true that he would be absent from the bank that morning, but that
would be no problem, given his relatively senior position there. Should
he state the real reason as his excuse? He intended to do so. If they
didn't believe him, which would be understandable in this case, he
could cite Frau Grubach as a witness, or the two old people across
the street, who were presumably now making their way to the window
facing his room. K. was surprised, at least it surprised him from the
point of view of the guards, that they had driven him into the room
and left him there alone, where he could kill himself ten times over.
At the same time, however, he wondered, from his own point of view
this time, what reason he might have to do so. Because the two of
them were sitting in the next room and had intercepted his breakfast?
It would have been so pointless to kill himself that, even had he
intended to do so, the pointlessness of the act would have made it
impossible for him to carry it out. If the guards' limited intellect had
not been so obvious, he could have assumed that the same logic had
led them to see no danger in leaving him by himself. As far as he was
concerned, they were welcome to watch him go over to a little wall
cabinet, where he kept a bottle of good schnapps, knock back a first
glass to make up for his missed breakfast and a second to give him
courage, the latter merely as a precaution for the unlikely case that it
should prove necessary.

Suddenly he was so startled by a call from the next room that his
teeth knocked against the glass. 'The supervisor's calling for you,' he
was told. It was just the tone of the shout that had startled him, a
curt, clipped, military shout he would not have believed Franz capable
of. The command itself was very welcome. 'At last,' he called back,
locked the wall-cabinet and immediately hurried into the adjoining
room. The two guards were standing there and, as if it were the most
natural thing in the world, hustled him back into his room. 'What are
you thinking of?' they cried. 'Going to see the supervisor in your

nightshirt? He'd have you given a good thrashing, and us too!'
'Leave me alone, dammit,' K. cried, having been forced back against
the wardrobe. 'If you descend upon me while I'm still in bed you
can't expect me to be in my Sunday best.' 'There's no need for that,'
the guards said. Whenever K. started shouting they became calm,
almost sad, confusing him or, in a way, bringing him back to his senses.
'Ridiculous formalities,' he muttered, but already he was taking a
jacket from the chair and holding it in both hands for a while, as if he
were submitting it to the guards for approval. They shook their heads.
'It has to be a black jacket,' they said, at which K. threw the jacket on
the floor and said—he had no idea himself what he meant by it—
'But it isn't the main hearing yet.' The guards smiled, but stuck to
their 'It has to be a black jacket.' 'That's fine by me if it'll hurry
things up,' said K., opening the wardrobe himself. He spent a long
time looking through all the clothes in there before choosing his best
black suit, that had almost caused a stir amongst his acquaintances
because of the jacket's fitted waist. He also changed into a shirt and
began to dress himself carefully. Secretly he believed he had gained
time by the guards forgetting to force him to go and wash. He observed
them to see if they would remember, but of course it never occurred
to them; on the other hand, Willem did not forget to send Franz off
to report to the supervisor that K. was getting dressed.

When he was fully dressed he had to walk across the adjoining
room, just in front of Willem, into the next room, the double doors of
which were already open. As K. very well knew, this room had recently
been taken by a Fräulein Bürstner,* a typist, who went off to work very
early and came back late; K. had done little more than exchange greetings with her. Now the bedside table had been moved from her bed
into the middle of the room and the supervisor was sitting on the other
side of it. He had his legs crossed and one arm draped over the back of
the chair. In one corner of the room were three young men who were
looking at Fräulein Bürstner's photographs, which were attached to a
mat hung on the wall. The window was open and a blouse was hanging
from the handle. The two old people were leaning out of the window
opposite again, but their number had increased, for behind and tower-
ing above them stood a man with an open-necked shirt* who was
squeezing and twisting his ginger goatee with his fingers.

'Josef K.?' the supervisor asked, perhaps just to get K., who was
glancing round the room, to look at him. 'I presume you are very

surprised at this morning's events?' the supervisor asked, using both
hands to adjust the position of the few objects on the bedside table,
the candle and matches, a book and a pincushion, as if they were
objects he needed for the interrogation. 'Certainly,' K. said, filled
with a sense of gratification at finally finding himself in the presence
of a rational person and able to discuss his case with him, 'certainly
I am surprised, but I wouldn't go so far as to say I'm very surprised.'
'Not very surprised?' the supervisor asked, placing the candle in the
middle of the table and arranging the other things round it. 'You
misunderstand me, perhaps,' K. hastened to add. 'I mean—' At this
point K. broke off and looked round for a chair. 'I can sit down, can't
I?' he asked. 'That is not usual,' the supervisor replied. 'I mean,' K.
went on without further ado, 'I am, it is true, very surprised, but
when you've reached the age of thirty and had to make your own way
in the world, as I've had to, you get inured to surprises and don't take
them to heart. Especially today's.' 'Why especially today's?' 'I'm not
saying I regard the whole thing as a joke, the arrangements that have
been made seem much too elaborate for that. All the tenants in the
boarding house would have to be involved and all of you as well, that
would be beyond the bounds of a joke. So I'm not saying it's a joke.'
'Quite right,' said the supervisor, counting how many matches there
were in the matchbox. 'On the other hand, however,' K. went on,
addressing all of them; he would even have liked to include the three
looking at the photographs, 'on the other hand, however, the matter
cannot be that important. I deduce that from the fact that I have been
accused but cannot find the least thing I am guilty of with which
I could be charged. But that, too, is a matter of secondary importance, the main question is, by whom have I been accused? Which of
the authorities is conducting the proceedings? Are you a state official?
None of you is in uniform, unless your suit'—here he turned to
Franz—'could be called a uniform, but it's more of a travel outfit.
I demand that these questions be cleared up and I am convinced that
once they are cleared up we can part amicably.' The supervisor tapped
the table with the matchbox. 'You are very much mistaken,' he said.
'These gentlemen here and myself are of minor importance as far as
your case is concerned, indeed, we know almost nothing about it. We
could be wearing the most proper of uniforms and your situation
would be no worse. I cannot inform you that you have been charged
with anything or, rather, I do not know whether you have been or not.

You have been arrested, that is a fact, and that is all I know. Perhaps the guards have told you something different, but if so, then it's just idle talk. But even if I cannot answer your question, I can advise you. Think less about us and what is going to happen to you, think more about yourself instead. And don't go on about your feeling of innocence so much, it spoils the not exactly unfavourable impression you otherwise make. In general you should exercise more restraint in speaking. Even if you had only said a few words, almost everything you have just said could have been deduced from your behaviour and did not particularly redound to your credit anyway.'

K. stared at the supervisor. He was being talked to like a schoolboy by a man who was perhaps younger than he was. His reward for his openness was a rebuke. And he was told nothing about the reason for his arrest, nor about whoever had given them their orders. He became somewhat agitated and walked up and down. No one stopped him. He tucked his cuffs in, felt his chest, smoothed his hair down, walked past the three men, and said, 'It's pointless,' at which they turned round and regarded him with sympathetic but serious expressions. Finally he stopped at the supervisor's table again. 'Hasterer,* from the state prosecution service, is a friend of mine,' he said, 'may I phone him?' 'Certainly,' the supervisor said, 'but I don't know what would be the point, unless you have some private matter to discuss with him.' 'What would be the point?' K. cried, dismayed rather than annoyed. 'Who are you anyway? You expect there to be some point and yet isn't what you're doing the most pointless thing imaginable? It's enough to make you weep. First of all these men descend upon me and now they're sitting or standing around here making me jump through all kinds of hoops for you. What would be the point of telephoning a public prosecutor when I've supposedly been arrested? All right, I won't telephone.' 'Please do,' said the supervisor, stretching out his hand and pointing to the hall, where the telephone was, 'please do telephone.' 'No, I don't want to any more,' said K., going over to the window. The group across the street were still gathered at the window, only their quiet enjoyment of the scene seemed somewhat disturbed by K.'s appearance at his window. The older pair tried to get up, but the man standing behind them calmed them down. 'We've got an audience, you see,' K. shouted quite loudly at the supervisor, pointing outside. 'Get away from the window,' he shouted across the street. The three immediately took a few steps back, the old couple even retreating behind the man, who concealed them with his body and, from the movement of his lips, seemed to be saying something which was not comprehensible at that distance. They did not disappear completely, however, but seemed to be waiting for the moment when they could return to the window unnoticed.

'Prying, inconsiderate people!' K. said, turning back to the room again. The supervisor possibly agreed with him, as K. thought he saw from a sideways glance. But it was just as possible that he had not been listening at all, for he had pressed one hand flat on the table and seemed to be comparing the length of his fingers. The two guards were sitting on a trunk covered with a patterned blanket, rubbing their knees. The three young men were standing, arms akimbo, looking round aimlessly. It was quiet, as if in some abandoned office. 'Well, gentlemen,' K. cried—it felt for a moment as if he were carrying them all on his shoulders—'from the way you look, my case could well be over. In my view it would be best not to waste any more time wondering whether your action was justified or not, and to settle the matter amicably with a shake of the hands.* If you agree with my view, then—' saying which, he went up to the supervisor's table and held out his hand. The supervisor raised his eyes, chewed his lip, and looked at K's outstretched hand; K. still believed the supervisor would take it. He, however, stood up, picked up a hard, round hat lying on Fräulein Bürstner's bed, and put it on carefully, using both hands, as one does when trying on a new hat. 'How simple it all seems to you,' he said to K. as he did so. 'We should settle the matter amicably, you say? No, no, that is just not possible. Which is, however, not to say that you should despair. No, why should you? You have only been arrested, that is all. That is what I had to inform you of. I have done so and also seen how you received the news. That is sufficient for today and we can take our leave, though only temporarily. I presume you'll want to go the bank now?' 'To the bank?' K. asked. 'I thought I'd been arrested.' K. put his question with a certain defiance, for, although his proffered hand had not been accepted, he felt himself more and more independent of all these people, especially since the supervisor had stood up. It was his intention, if they should leave, to run after them to the street door and invite them to arrest him. That was why he repeated, 'How can I go to the bank when I've been arrested?' 'Oh,' said the supervisor, who was already at the door, 'you have misunderstood me. Yes, you have been arrested, but that should not prevent you from going to work. Nor should anything prevent you from going about your daily life as usual.' 'Then being arrested is not too bad,' said K., going up close to the supervisor. 'I never meant it in any other way,' the latter said. 'But in that case telling me I've been arrested does not even seem to have been very necessary,' said K., going even closer. 'It was my duty,' said the supervisor. K. remained adamant. 'A stupid duty,' he said. 'Perhaps,' the supervisor replied, 'but there's no point in wasting time on that. I had assumed you would want to go to the bank. Since you examine every word, I will add: I am not forcing you to go to the bank, I had merely assumed you would want to go. To make that easier for you and to make your arrival at the bank as unobtrusive as possible I have put these three gentlemen here, colleagues of yours, at your disposal.' 'What?' K. exclaimed, looking at the three in amazement. These insignificant, colourless young men, whom he had only registered as a group beside the photographs, were indeed employees from his bank; not colleagues, that would be going too far and indicated a gap in the supervisor's omniscience, but they were subordinate employees from the bank. How could K. not have noticed that? He must have been entirely taken up with the supervisor and the guards not to recognize the three. Rabensteiner, stiff, swinging his arms, Kullich, blond with deep-set eyes, and Kaminer* with the intolerable smile caused by a chronic muscular spasm. 'Good morning,' said K. after a while, holding out his hand to the three, who made formal bows. 'I didn't recognize you. So now we'll go off to work, shall we?' The men nodded, laughing and eager, as if that was what they had been waiting for the whole time; only when K. could not find his hat, which was still in his room, they all three ran, one after the other, to fetch it, which suggested a certain feeling of embarrassment. K. stood there and watched them through the two open doors; the last was naturally the apathetic Rabensteiner, who had simply set off at an elegant trot. Kaminer handed him his hat, and K. had to remind himself, as he frequently had to in the bank, that Kaminer's smile was not intentional, indeed, that he could not smile intentionally at all.

In the vestibule Frau Grubach, who did not look very guilty at all, held the door open for the whole company, and K., as so often, looked down at her apron strings, which cut unnecessarily deep into her massive body. Once out in the street, K., his watch in his hand, decided to take a taxi; he was already half an hour late and did not want to extend that unnecessarily. Kaminer ran to the corner to fetch the cab. The two others were clearly trying to take K.'s mind off what had happened, when Kullich suddenly pointed to the door of the building opposite where the man with the ginger goatee had just appeared. At first, slightly embarrassed at showing himself at his full height, he stepped back to the wall and leant against it. The old couple were presumably still coming down the stairs. K. was annoyed at Kullich for pointing out the man, whom he himself had already seen, had even expected to see. 'Don't look,' he snapped, without noticing how it must strike grown men as odd to adopt such a tone to them. But no explanation was necessary, since the cab was just arriving; they got in and drove off. Then K. realized he had not noticed the supervisor and the guards leaving; the supervisor had blocked his view of the three bank clerks and then the bank clerks his view of the supervisor. It did not show great presence of mind, and K. resolved to keep a better eye on himself in that respect. But he still automatically turned round and leant over the rear of the car to see if he could catch a glimpse of the supervisor and the guards. He immediately turned back again, however, without even having attempted to look for anyone, and leant back comfortably in the corner of the seat. Although that wasn't what it looked like, it was a moment when he would have appreciated some encouragement, but the three men seemed tired, Rabensteiner was looking out of the car to the right, Kullich to the left, leaving only Kaminer with his grin, and unfortunately common humanity forbade making a joke about that.

A Conversation with Frau Grubach
Then Fräulein Bürstner

DURING that spring K. used to spend his evenings whenever possible—he generally stayed in the office until nine o'clock—going for a short walk after work by himself or with friends and then to an inn, where he normally sat with some mostly older men at their regular table until eleven. There were, however, exceptions to this routine, for example when the bank manager, who valued his diligence and trustworthiness very highly, invited K. for a drive in his car or to dinner at his villa. Apart from that, K. went once a week to a girl called Elsa, who worked serving in a wine-bar during the night and well into the morning, and during the daytime only received visitors from her bed.

On that evening, however—the day had passed quickly, with hard work and many people coming to wish him a happy birthday, showing how well liked and respected he was—K. intended to go home straight away. He had been thinking about it during all the little breaks at work; without being able to say precisely what it was he had in mind, he had the feeling that the events of that morning had caused great disorder throughout Frau Grubach's apartment, and that he specifically was needed to restore order. And once order had been restored, all trace of those events would be erased and everything would return to normal. In particular he had nothing to fear from the three clerks, they had once more been swallowed up in the mass of bank employees, there was no change to be observed in them. K. had summoned them to his office several times, both singly and together, for no other reason than to observe them; each time he had been able to dismiss them, satisfied with what he had seen.

When, at half-past nine in the evening, he arrived at the building where he lived, he came across a young lad standing in the entrance, legs apart and smoking a pipe. 'Who are you?' K. immediately asked, putting his face close to the lad, since nothing much could be seen in the dim light of the hallway. 'I'm the janitor's son, sir,' the lad replied, taking the pipe out of his mouth and stepping to one side. 'The janitor's son?' K. asked, tapping the floor impatiently with his stick.

'Is there something you want, sir? Should I fetch my father?' 'No, no,' said K., a note of forgiveness in his voice, as if the lad had done something wrong but he had forgiven him. 'It's all right,' he said, continuing on his way, but he turned round again before he went up the stairs.

He could have gone straight to his room, but since he wanted to speak to Frau Grubach, he knocked at her door first. She was darning a stocking, seated at a table on which was a pile of other old stockings. Flustered, K. apologized for coming at such a late hour, but Frau Grubach was very friendly and waved his apologies away, her door was always open for him, she said, he knew very well that he was her best and dearest lodger. K. looked round the room; it was completely restored to its former state, the breakfast dishes that had been on the little table by the window that morning had been cleared away. A woman's hand can do so much unseen, he thought. He could perhaps have smashed the crockery there on the spot, but definitely not have cleared it away. He regarded Frau Grubach with a certain feeling of gratitude. 'Why are you working so late?' he asked. By now they were both sitting at the table, and from time to time K. buried one hand in the pile of stockings. 'There's a lot of work to do,' she said. 'During the day my time belongs to my lodgers, I only have the evenings if I want to deal with my own things.' 'I must have made extra work for you today.' 'How do you mean?' she asked, becoming slightly more animated, her knitting resting in her lap. 'I mean the men who were here this morning.' 'Oh them,' she said, regaining her former calm, 'that didn't make any extra work.' K. watched in silence as she picked up the stocking again. 'She seems to be surprised I talked about it,' he thought, 'she doesn't seem to think it right I should talk about it. That makes it all the more important I should do so. An old woman's the only person I can talk to about it.' 'I'm sure it did make work for you,' he said, 'but it won't happen again.' 'No, it can't happen again,' she agreed, giving K. an almost melancholy smile. 'Do you mean that seriously?' K. asked. 'Yes,' she said more softly, 'but above all you mustn't take it to heart. Just think of all the things that happen in the world. Since you've taken me into your confidence, I can be honest and tell you that I listened at the door a little, and the two guards told me a few things too. It's your happiness that's at stake and I'm particularly concerned about that, perhaps more than I have a right to be, I'm just your landlady. Well then, I did hear a few things, but I can't say they were particularly bad. No. You have been arrested, true, but not the way a thief's arrested. When someone's arrested like a thief, then it is bad, but this arrest . . . It seems to me like something very learned, excuse me if what I'm saying is stupid, but it seems to me like something very learned that I can't understand, but which one doesn't have to understand.'

'What you just said, Frau Grubach, is by no means stupid.* At least I agree with you to an extent, only I take an even harsher view of the matter, I don't see it as something learned but simply as nothing at all. I was taken by surprise, that was all. If I'd got up as soon as I woke and come straight to you, without allowing myself to be flustered by Anna's non-appearance and not bothering about anyone who might have stood in my way, if for once I'd made an exception, if I'd taken my breakfast in the kitchen and got you to bring my clothes from my room, if, in short, I had behaved sensibly, nothing would have happened, everything that was about to happen would have been nipped in the bud. But one is so ill prepared. In the bank, for example, I am prepared, it's impossible for something like that to happen to me there, I have a man of my own there, the outside telephone and the office telephone are on the desk in front of me, people are always coming in, clients and clerks; moreover, and above all, I'm constantly involved in my work, therefore always on the alert, it would be a real pleasure to be faced with such a situation there. Now it's over and I didn't really want to talk about it again, I just wanted to hear your opinion, the opinion of a sensible woman, and I'm glad we agree. Now you must shake hands with me, agreement like that must be sealed with a handshake.'

Will she shake my hand? The supervisor didn't shake my hand, he thought and looked at the woman differently from before, with a searching look. She stood up because he had stood up, slightly flustered because she hadn't been able to understand everything K. had said. But because she was flustered, she said something she certainly didn't intend and which was certainly out of place. 'Don't take it to heart so, Herr K.,' she said. Her voice was filled with tears and of course she forgot to shake his hand. 'I wouldn't say I was taking it to heart,' said K., suddenly weary and realizing how worthless any assent from this woman was.

At the door he asked, 'Is Fräulein Bürstner in?' 'No,' said Frau Grubach, smiling with belated, sensible sympathy as she made this brief response. 'She's at the theatre. Did you want something? Shall I pass on a message?' 'Oh, I just wanted to have a word with her.' 'Unfortunately I don't know when she'll be back. She's usually late when she's been to the theatre.' 'It doesn't matter,' said K. who, head bowed, was already turning towards the door to leave, 'I just wanted to apologize for having used her room this morning.' 'That won't be necessary, Herr K., you're too considerate, she doesn't know anything about it, she's been out since the early morning and everything's been tidied up, see for yourself.' And she opened the door to Fräulein Bürstner's room. 'That's all right, I believe you,' said K., but then he went to the open door after all. The moon was silently shining in the dark room. As far as could be seen, everything was in its place, even the blouse wasn't hanging from the window-catch any more. The pillows on the bed seemed remarkably high, they were partly in the moonlight. 'Fräulein Bürstner often comes home late,' said K., looking at Frau Grubach as if she were to blame. 'It's the way young people are,' said Frau Grubach in explanation. 'True, true,' said K., 'but it can go too far.' 'It certainly can,' said Frau Grubach, 'how right you are, Herr K. Perhaps even in this particular case. Far be it from me to do Fräulein Bürstner down, she's a nice girl, friendly, tidy, punctual, hardworking, I can appreciate all that, but one thing is true, she should have more self-respect, she should hold back more. This month alone I've twice seen her in out-of-the-way streets, and with a different gentleman each time. I find it painfully embarrassing. As God's my witness, you're the only one I've told, Herr K., but it can't be helped, I'm going to have to have a word about it with the young lady herself. And that's not the only thing I find suspicious about her.' 'You're on the wrong track entirely,' said K., furious and hardly able to conceal it, 'and anyway, you've clearly misunderstood what I said about Fräulein Bürstner, I didn't mean it like that. I warn you, and I mean it, not to say anything to her. You're completely wrong, I know the young lady very well, nothing of what you said is true. However, perhaps I'm going too far, I don't want to stop you, tell her whatever you want. Good night.' 'Herr K.,' said Frau Grubach in pleading tones, hurrying after him to the door, which he had already opened, 'of course I don't mean to talk to Fräulein Bürstner yet, I'm just going to continue to observe her first, you're the only one I've told what I know. After all, it must be in the interest of every lodger to try and keep my guest-house pure,* and that was all I was attempting to do.' 'Purity!' K. exclaimed, through the crack of the door. 'If you want to keep the guest-house pure, you'll have to give me notice first of all.' With that he slammed the door shut, ignoring the soft knocking that followed.

However, since he did not in the least feel like sleeping, he decided to stay up and use the opportunity to see for himself when Fräulein Bürstner came home. Perhaps then it would also be possible, despite the unsuitable hour, to have a few words with her. Looking out of the window, elbows on the windowsill and rubbing his tired eyes, he even wondered for a moment about punishing Frau Grubach by persuading Fräulein Bürstner to join him in giving notice to quit. He immediately felt that was going much too far, and he even suspected himself of being bent on changing his room because of the events of that morning. Nothing would have been more absurd, and above all pointless and contemptible.

Having grown weary of staring out into the empty street, he lay down on the sofa, after first having opened the door into the hall a little so that he could see anyone coming into the apartment. He stayed on the sofa until about eleven o'clock, calmly smoking a cigar. After that, however, he couldn't stand it there any longer and went out into the hall, as if that would make Fräulein Bürstner come home sooner. He felt no particular desire for her, in fact he couldn't even remember exactly what she looked like, but he had decided he wanted to talk to her, and he was irritated that her late return home meant the day ended in more disquiet and disorder. It was also her fault that he had not had any dinner that evening and had not been able to go and see Elsa, as he had intended. He could, of course, remedy both these omissions by going now to the wine-bar where Elsa worked. He decided to do so later, after he'd talked to Fräulein Bürstner.

It was gone half-past eleven when he heard someone coming up the stairs. K. who, lost in thought, had been walking noisily up and down the hall as if it were his own room, fled, hiding behind his door. It was Fräulein Bürstner coming. Shivering, she pulled a silk shawl round her narrow shoulders as she locked the door. The next moment she would go into her room, which K. could certainly not enter around midnight, so he really ought to make his presence known now. Unfortunately he had forgotten to switch on the light in his room, so if he emerged from his darkened room, it might look like an ambush and at the very least would startle her. Not knowing what to do, he whispered through the crack in the door, 'Fräulein Bürstner.' It sounded like a plea rather than a call to attract attention. 'Is someone there?' Fräulein Bürstner asked, looking round, wide-eyed. 'It's me,' said K. and came out. 'Oh, Herr K.,' said Fräulein Bürstner with a smile, 'good evening,' and she held out her hand. 'I just wanted a few words, would you permit me to speak to you now?' 'Now?' Fräulein Bürstner asked. 'Does it have to be now? It's a little odd, isn't it?' 'I've been waiting for you since nine.' 'Well, I was at the theatre. I didn't know anything about you wanting to see me.' 'What prompted me to want to speak to you only happened this morning.' 'Aha. Well, I've no objection in principle, except that I'm dead tired. Come to my room for a few minutes, then. We certainly can't talk here, we'll wake everyone up and I would be more unhappy about that for our own sakes than for the other people's. Wait here until I've put the light on in my room, then switch off the light here.'

K. did so, but waited until Fräulein Bürstner quietly repeated her invitation to come in. 'Sit down,' she said, pointing to the ottoman; she herself stayed standing against the bedpost, despite the tiredness she'd mentioned. She hadn't even taken off her little hat decorated with a profusion of flowers. 'So what do you want? I'm really curious to know.' She crossed her legs slightly. 'Perhaps you will say the matter wasn't so urgent', K. said, 'that it had to be discussed now, but—' 'I always ignore introductory remarks,' said Fräulein Bürstner. 'That makes my task easier,' said K. 'This morning, and through my fault in a way, a certain amount of disorder was caused in your room. It was done by strangers and against my will, though, as I said, through my fault, and I wanted to apologize.' 'My room?' Fräulein Bürstner asked, giving not the room but K. a searching look. 'That's right,' said K., and now for the first time they looked each other in the eye. 'Exactly how it came about is not worth wasting words on.' 'But that's the really interesting part,' said Fräulein Bürstner. 'No,' said K. 'Well,' said Fräulein Bürstner, 'I don't want to pry into your secrets. If you insist it's not interesting, I won't press the point. I'm happy to accept your apology, especially as I can see no trace of disorder.' Her hands pressed flat against her lower hips, she made a circuit of the room. She stopped by the mat with her photographs. 'Look at that!' she exclaimed. 'My photographs have been messed up. That's not very nice. So someone's been in my room who'd no right to be here.' K. nodded, silently cursing Kaminer. The bank clerk could never manage to control his tedious fidgetiness. 'It's strange,' said Fräulein Bürstner, 'that I find myself compelled to forbid you to do something you ought to refrain from of your own accord, that is, to come into my room in my absence.' 'But I explained, Fräulein,' said K., going over to join her by the photographs, 'that I wasn't the one who touched your photographs. Since you don't believe me, however, I have to admit that the commission of inquiry brought along three bank clerks, one of whom—and I will see he's thrown out of the bank at the first opportunity—probably couldn't keep his hands off them. Yes,' K. went on, since she gave him a questioning look, 'it was a commission of inquiry that was here.' 'To see you?' she asked. 'Yes,' K. replied. 'No!' Fräulein Bürstner exclaimed and laughed. 'Yes it was,' said K., 'or do you think I'm guiltless?' 'Well, guiltless . . .' said the young woman, 'I wouldn't want to express a judgement that might have serious consequences, and I don't know you either, but it must be a serious crime if they set a commission of inquiry on someone straight away. Since, however, you are at liberty—at least I deduce from your calm that you haven't just escaped from prison—you can't have committed a crime like that.' 'True,' said K., 'the commission of inquiry might have realized I'm innocent, or at least not as guilty as was assumed.' 'That is possible, certainly,' said Fräulein Bürstner, paying close attention. 'But then,' said K., 'you haven't much experience of matters to do with the courts.' 'No, I haven't,' said Fräulein Bürstner, 'and I've often regretted it. I'd like to know everything and I find matters to do with the courts in particular uncommonly interesting. Courts have an attraction all of their own,* haven't they? But I'm sure I'll improve my knowledge in that area, since next month I'm starting as a secretary in a lawyer's office.' 'That's very good,' said K., 'then you'll be able to help me a little with my trial.' 'Perhaps I could,' said Fräulein Bürstner. 'Why not? I like making use of my knowledge.' 'I do mean it seriously,' said K., 'or at least semi-seriously, as you do. The matter's too trifling to bring in a lawyer, but I could really do with an adviser.' 'Yes, but if I'm to be an adviser I'd need to know what it's about,' said Fräulein Bürstner. 'That's the problem,' said K., 'I don't know myself.' 'Then you've been pulling my leg,' said Fräulein Bürstner, extremely disappointed, 'and this time of night is not the best time to choose for it.' With that she walked away from the photographs, where they'd been standing together for so long. 'Not at all, Fräulein Bürstner,' said K., 'I've not been pulling your leg. How can I get you to believe me? I've told you everything I know. Even more than I know, since it wasn't a commission of inquiry. I called it that because I don't know another name for it. No inquiries were made, I was just arrested, but by a commission.'

Fräulein Bürstner was sitting on the ottoman and laughing again. 'What was it like?' she asked. 'Terrible,' said K., but he wasn't thinking about that at all, he was entirely absorbed in the sight presented by Fräulein Bürstner. She supported her chin on one hand, her elbow resting on the ottoman cushion, whilst with her other hand she slowly stroked her thigh. 'That's too vague,' said Fräulein Bürstner. 'What's too vague?' K. asked. Then he remembered, and asked, 'Shall I show you how it was?' He needed to be moving but didn't want to leave. 'I'm tired,' said Fräulein Bürstner. 'You came back so late,' said K. 'And now I end up getting blamed, though with some justification since I shouldn't have let you in. Nor was it necessary, as it has turned out.' 'It was necessary,' said K., 'as you will now see. May I move the bedside table away from your bed?' 'What are you thinking of?' said Fräulein Bürstner. 'Of course not!' 'Then I can't show you,' said K., getting worked up as if that was doing him immeasurable harm. 'Oh well, if you need it for your demonstration, just move the table,' Fräulein Bürstner said, adding after a while in a weaker voice, 'I'm so tired I'm letting things go farther than is proper.' K. placed the little table in the middle of the room and sat down at it. 'You need to have a true idea of where everyone was, it's very interesting. I'm the supervisor, two guards are sitting on the trunk over there, and three young men are standing by the photographs. There was a white blouse hanging from the window-catch, though that's only by the way. And now we can start. Oh, I'm forgetting myself, the most important person. Well, I'm standing here, on this side of the table. The supervisor is sitting very comfortably, legs crossed, one arm draped over the back of the chair, a real slovenly lout. So now it starts in earnest. The supervisor calls out as if he had to wake me up, he really shouts. Unfortunately I'll have to shout too, if I'm to make everything clear to you, though it's only my name he shouts.' Fräulein Bürstner, laughing as she watched, placed her index finger on her lips to stop K. shouting, but it was too late, K. was too immersed in his role. He slowly called out, 'Josef K.!'* though not as loudly as he'd threatened to, but in such a way that the name, after it had suddenly been uttered, seemed to spread out gradually in the room.

At that there was a knocking on the door to the adjoining room,
sharp, loud, regular knocks. Fräulein Bürstner went pale and put her
hand to her heart. The knocking particularly startled K., because for
a while his mind had been entirely occupied with the events of the
morning and the girl for whom he was acting them out. As soon as
he'd recovered himself, he hurried over to Fräulein Bürstner and
took her hand. 'Don't be afraid,' he whispered, 'I'll sort everything
out. But who can it be? That's the living-room, and there's no one
sleeps there.' 'There is,' whispered Fräulein Bürstner in K.'s ear.
'Since yesterday a nephew of Frau Grubach's, an army captain, has
been sleeping there. No other room happened to be free. I'd forgotten about it. But why did you have to shout like that? It's really upset
me.' 'There's no reason to be upset,' said K. and kissed her on the
forehead as she sank down onto the cushion. 'Go away, go away,' she
said, hurriedly sitting up again, 'please go, please go. What do you
expect, he's listening at the door, he can hear everything. Why must
you torment me so?' 'I'm not going', said K., 'until you've calmed
down a little. Come over into the other corner of the room, he can't
hear us there.' She let him lead her over. 'You're not thinking,' he
said. 'While it's unpleasant for you, it doesn't present a danger. Frau
Grubach is the one who has the decisive voice in this matter, especially since the captain is her nephew, and you know how she really
worships me and believes everything I say. She's dependent on me
as well, since she's borrowed a large sum of money from me. I'm ready
to accept any more or less reasonable explanation you want to give as
to why we're here together, and I guarantee I can get Frau Grubach
not only to support it in public, but to really and truly believe it
herself. You don't have to spare me at all. If you want it spread
abroad that I burst in on you, then that is what Frau Grubach will be
told. And she will believe it without losing her faith in me, such is
her attachment to me.' Fräulein Bürstner stared at the floor, silent,
shoulders drooping somewhat. 'Why should Frau Grubach not
believe I burst in on you?' K. added. He was looking at her hair, reddish with a centre parting, slightly bouffant, and firmly kept in place.
He thought she would turn to look at him, but she did not change her
posture as she said, 'I'm sorry, it was the sudden knocking that startled me rather than any possible consequences because of the presence of the captain. It was so quiet after you shouted and then there
was the knocking, that's what gave me such a shock. I was sitting

quite close to the door as well, the knocking was almost next to me. Thank you for your offer, but I can't accept it. I take responsibility for everything that happens in my room, whoever wants to call me to account. I'm surprised you don't realize how insulting your offer is, despite your good intentions, which I naturally recognize. But go now, leave me, I need to be alone now, even more than before all this. The few minutes you requested have turned into half an hour and more.' K. took her hand and then her wrist. 'But you're not angry with me?' he said. Removing his hand, she replied, 'No, no, I'm never angry with anyone.' He took hold of her wrist again. This time she tolerated it and led him to the door. He had firmly resolved to leave, but just before he reached the door he halted, as if he hadn't expected to see a door there, and Fräulein Bürstner used his moment's hesitation to free herself, open the door, slip out into the hall and whisper to K. from there, 'Will you please come now. Look'—she pointed to the door to the captain's room, with light showing underneath it—'he's put on the light and he's amusing himself at our expense.' 'Right, I'm coming,' said K. He went out, grasped her, kissed her on the lips and then all over her face, like a thirsty animal furiously lapping at the water of the spring it has found at last. Finally he kissed her on the neck, over the throat, and left his lips there for a long time. A noise from the captain's room made him look up. 'I'll go now,' he said. He wanted to call Fräulein Bürstner by her first name, but he didn't know it. She nodded wearily, letting him kiss her hand, though she had already half turned away, as if she were unaware of it, and went into her room, shoulders drooping. A short time later K. was in bed. He quickly fell asleep, but first he thought for a while about the way he had behaved; he was satisfied with it, but was surprised that he wasn't even more satisfied; he was seriously concerned for Fräulein Bürstner because of the captain.

The First Hearing

K. HAD been informed by telephone that a short hearing in his affair would take place the next Sunday. He was advised that these hearings would now proceed regularly, if not every week perhaps, then certainly at fairly frequent intervals. On the one hand, he was told, it was in everyone's interest to bring the trial to a swift conclusion, on the other hand the hearings had to go into every aspect thoroughly but, because of the effort that entailed, should never last too long. The way out of the dilemma had been the choice of a rapid succession of short hearings. Sunday had been set as the day for his hearings so as not to disrupt K.'s work at the bank. They were assuming he was happy with that; should he prefer a different time, they would try to oblige him as far as possible. For example, hearings could take place at night, but in that case K. would presumably not be fresh enough. As long as K. had no objections, therefore, they would leave it at the Sunday. It went without saying, the voice went on, that he had to turn up, presumably that didn't have to be pointed out. He was given the number of the house where he was to present himself, it was in a street in an out-of-the-way, lower-class district where K. had never been before.

Once he had received the message, K. hung up without replying. He immediately resolved to go on Sunday. It was clearly necessary. The trial was getting under way, and he had to take a stand against that; this first hearing must also be the last. He was still standing by the telephone, lost in thought, when he heard the voice of the deputy manager behind him. He wanted to make a call, but K. was in his way. 'Bad news?' the deputy manager asked in an offhand manner, not because he wanted to know, but to get K. away from the telephone. 'No, no,' said K. stepping to one side, but not going away. The deputy manager picked up the receiver and said, while he was waiting to be connected, the receiver still clamped to his ear, 'One thing, Herr K. Would you do me the pleasure of joining us on my yacht on Sunday morning? It will be a large party, including some of your acquaintances. Hasterer, the public prosecutor, for example. Will you come? Do come.' K. tried to concentrate on what the deputy manager was saying. It was not without importance for K., for he had never got on well with the deputy manager, and this invitation was clearly an olive branch and showed how important K. had become in the bank and how valuable his friendship, or at least his neutrality, was for the second-highest employee of the bank. This invitation was a humiliation for the deputy manager, even if he had issued it while waiting to be connected, the receiver clamped to his ear. And K. had to add a second humiliation. He said, 'Thank you. Unfortunately I have no time on Sunday, I have a prior engagement.' 'Pity,' said the deputy manager, turning to his telephone call that had just been put through. It was not a short call, but K. was so preoccupied, he stayed by the telephone all the time. Only when the deputy manager rang off did he come to with a start and said, in order to excuse himself just a little for standing there with no reason, 'A person just rang to ask me to go somewhere, but forgot to tell me what time.' 'Ring back and ask,' said the deputy manager. 'It's not that important,' said K., even though that made his earlier excuse even more threadbare than it was already. As they left, the deputy manager talked of other things and K. forced himself to answer, though what he was mainly thinking was that it would be best to arrive at nine o'clock on Sunday morning, since that was the time all the courts started to work on weekdays.

Sunday was overcast. K. was very tired, because he had stayed up late into the night at the inn for a celebration with the regulars and had almost overslept. He dressed in a hurry, without having time to think and run through the various plans he had worked out during the week, and hastened off to the district indicated in the phone call without having had his breakfast. Oddly enough, even though he didn't have much time for looking around, he saw the three bank clerks, Rabensteiner, Kullich, and Kaminer, who were involved in his affair. The first two were in a tram which crossed K.'s path, but Kaminer was sitting on the terrace of a café and leant over the balustrade in curiosity just as K. passed. Presumably they all watched him go, surprised to see their superior hurrying along. It was a kind of defiance that had stopped K. taking a cab, he abhorred the idea of any, even the most minor assistance in this case of his, he didn't want to call on anyone for help and have to take them into his confidence in any way at all, nor, when all was said and done, did he feel in the least like humbling himself before the commission of inquiry by excessive punctuality. However, he did start to run now, just so as to arrive by nine if possible, even though he had not been given an appointment for a particular time.

He had assumed he would recognize the building from a distance by some sign or other, though he did not have a precise idea of what that would be, or by some particular movement outside the entrance. He stood for a moment at the beginning of Juliusstrasse,* where it was supposed to be, but the street was lined on both sides with almost identical houses, tall, grey tenements where poor people lived. Now, on this Sunday morning there were people at most of the windows, men in their shirt-sleeves smoking or carefully and tenderly holding children on the window-ledges. Other windows had eider-downs piled up in them, above which the tousled head of a woman would appear for a moment. People called to each other across the street, one such call provoking a gale of laughter right above K. At regular intervals in the long street were little shops selling various kinds of groceries; they were below street level, with a few steps lead-ing down to them. Women were going in and out, or standing on the steps, chatting. A fruit-seller, who was hawking his wares to the people at the windows and paying no more attention than K., almost knocked him over with his barrow. At that moment a gramophone, that had seen better days in better districts of the city, started up its excruciating noise.

K. went farther down the street, slowly, as if he were in plenty of time, or as if the examining magistrate could see him from one of the windows and so would know that K. had turned up. It was shortly after nine. It was quite a long way to the house, which was quite unusually extensive. The gateway especially was high and wide, obvi-ously intended for goods being delivered to the various warehouses which, closed at the moment, surrounded the large courtyard and bore the names of firms, several of which were familiar to K. from the bank. He stood at the entrance to the courtyard for a while, taking in, contrary to his usual habit, all these superficial details. Close by him a man with bare feet was sitting on a crate, reading a newspaper. Two boys were in a handcart, rocking to and fro. At a pump a frail young girl in a bedjacket was looking across at K. as the water poured into her jug. In one corner of the yard a line was being fixed between two windows. The washing which was being hung out to dry was already on it, and a man was directing the operation with a few calls from the yard below.

K. turned towards the stairs to go to the room where the hearing would be held, but then he stopped again, for apart from these stairs there were three other flights of stairs in the courtyard; as well as that, a little passageway at the end of the yard seemed to lead to a second courtyard. He was annoyed that he hadn't been told precisely where the room was, the manner in which he was being treated was strangely negligent or offhand, a point he intended to make loudly and clearly. Finally he went up the first staircase after all, with the memory of something the guard Willem had said going through his mind, namely that the court was attracted by guilt, so that logically the hearing should be held in a room on the staircase K. happened to choose.

As he went up, he got in the way of a lot of children who were playing on the stairs and gave him angry looks as he passed through their line. 'If I have to come here again,' he said to himself, 'I'll either have to bring some sweets, to win them over, or my stick to beat them.' Just before the first floor he even had to wait a while for a marble to come to a halt; two small boys with the twisted faces of grown-up miscreants* held on to his trousers until it stopped. If he had tried to shake them off he would have hurt them, and he feared the fuss they would kick up.

The actual search began on the first floor. Since he couldn't really ask for the commission of inquiry, he invented a carpenter called Lanz*—the name occurred to him because that was what the captain, Frau Grubach's nephew, was called—and decided to ask in all the flats if a carpenter called Lanz lived there so that he would get the opportunity to look into the rooms. As it turned out, however, in most cases that was unnecessary, since almost all the doors were open and the children were running in and out. In general they were small rooms with a single window, in which the cooking was also done. Some women had babies in their arm and were working at the stove with their free hand. The busiest at running to and fro were adolescent girls, who appeared to be wearing nothing but pinafores. In all the rooms the beds were still being used, occupied by people who were sick, or sleeping, or lying on them fully clothed. K. knocked at doors that were closed and asked if a carpenter called Lanz lived there. Usually a woman opened the door, listened to his question, and turned to a man just discernible in a bed in the room. 'There's a gentleman asking if there's a carpenter called Lanz lives here.'

'A carpenter called Lanz?' the man asked from the bed. 'Yes,' said K., even though it was obvious the commission wasn't there, so that he had found out what he needed to know. Many of them assumed it was very important for K. to find the carpenter called Lanz and spent a long time racking their brains, before mentioning a carpenter, who, however, was not called Lanz, or a name that bore a fairly remote similarity to Lanz, or they asked the neighbours, or took K. to the door of a flat some distance away where they thought such a man might be a subtenant or where there was someone who would be better informed than they themselves. Eventually K. hardly needed to ask his question any more, since he was dragged from storey to storey in this way. He regretted the plan he had made, which at first had seemed so practical. Before he was taken up to the fifth floor he decided to abandon the search, said goodbye to a friendly young worker who wanted to take him farther, and went back down. Then, however, annoyed at the pointlessness of the whole business, he went back and knocked at the first door on the fifth floor. The first thing he saw in the room was a large clock on the wall showing that it was already ten o'clock. 'Does a carpenter called Lanz live here?' he asked. 'Through there,' said a young woman with lustrous black eyes who was washing nappies in a tub, and gestured with her wet hand at the open door to the neighbouring room.

K. had the impression he was entering a meeting. The medium-sized room with two windows was filled by a jostling throng of all sorts of people, who ignored him when he went in. Just below the ceiling was a gallery running round the room which was also crammed full with people, who had to stand bent over, their heads and backs touching the ceiling. K., finding it too muggy in there, went out again and said to the young woman, 'I was asking about a carpenter, a man called Lanz?' 'Yes,' said the woman, 'please go in.' K. would perhaps not have complied had she not gone up to him and, taking hold of the door-handle, said, 'I have to close the door after you, no one else is allowed in.' 'Very sensible,' said K., 'but it's too full already.' However, he still went back in.

Two men were standing right next to the door talking—one had his hands extended in the gesture of counting out money, while the other looked him sharply in the eye. A hand appeared between them and clutched at K. It was a little, red-cheeked boy. 'Come on, come on,' he said. K. let the boy lead him, and it turned out that there was a narrow way free through the teeming throng, possibly separating two parties. That was also suggested by the fact that in the front rows on either side there was scarcely a face turned towards K.; he could only see the backs of people who were talking and gesturing to those of their own party alone. Most were dressed in black, in old, long Sunday coats* that hung down loosely. K. found their dress puzzling, otherwise he would have assumed it was a district political meeting.

K. was led to the far end of the room, where a little table had been set up across a very low and equally overfilled platform. Sitting at the table, close to the edge of the platform, was a small, fat, wheezing man who, with a great deal of laughter, was chatting with one of those standing behind him—the latter was leaning his elbows on the back of the chair and had his legs crossed. Sometimes he threw an arm up into the air, as if he were caricaturing someone. The boy who was leading K. had difficulty attracting their attention. Standing on tiptoe, he twice tried to get his message across without being noticed by the man. Only when one of those on the platform pointed out the boy did the man turn to him, lean down, and listen to what he had to say in his quiet voice. Then he took out his watch and gave K. a quick glance. 'You should have been here an hour and five minutes ago,' he said. K. was going to reply, but he had no time, since hardly had the man finished speaking than a general muttering arose from the right-hand side of the hall. 'You should have been here an hour and five minutes ago,' the man repeated in a louder voice, and with a quick glance down into the body of the hall. Immediately the muttering grew louder, then gradually died away when the man said nothing more. It was much quieter in the hall now than when K. had first come in. Only the people in the gallery continued to make their remarks. They seemed to be more poorly dressed than those below, as far as one could make anything out in the gloom, smoke, and dust up there. Some had brought cushions, which they placed on their heads so as not to hurt them as they pressed them against the ceiling.

K. had resolved to observe more than to speak, so refrained from defending himself for his late arrival but merely said, 'Perhaps I have arrived late, but now I'm here.' This was followed by a round of applause, again from the right-hand side of the hall. 'They're easily won over,' K. thought; the only thing that bothered him was the silence from the left-hand side, which was immediately behind him and from which only isolated applause had come. He wondered what he could say to win them all over at once or, if that should prove impossible, to get the others on his side at least some of the time.

'Yes,' said the man, 'but I am no longer obliged to question you.' Again the muttering, but ambiguous this time, for the man waved it aside and went on, 'Exceptionally, however, I will do so today. But such a late arrival must not occur again. And now step forward.' Someone jumped down from the platform, making room for K., who climbed up. He was squashed up against the table, the crush behind him was so great he had to brace himself against it to stop himself pushing the examining magistrate's table, and possibly the magistrate himself, off the platform.

The examining magistrate did not bother about that, however, but settled comfortably enough in his chair and, after he had said a final word to the man behind him, picked up a little notebook, the only object on the table. It was like a school exercise book, old and falling to pieces from having been consulted so often. 'Right then,' said the magistrate, leafing through the notebook, and addressing K. as if stating a fact: 'You are a painter and decorator?' 'No,' said K., 'I am senior accountant with a large bank.' This answer was followed by laughter from the right-hand group, that was so hearty K. had to join in. People put their hands on their knees and shook as if they had a violent fit of coughing. Even the odd person in the gallery laughed. Now very angry, the examining magistrate, who was probably powerless against the people below, tried to take it out on the gallery. He jumped up and shook his finger at the gallery, his normally unremarkable eyebrows* gathering in a huge bushy blackness over his eyes.

The left-hand side of the hall was still silent, the people stood in their rows, their faces turned towards the platform, listening to the exchanges there as calmly as they listened to the noise of the other group; they even tolerated individuals from their own group joining in with the others now and then. Presumably the people of the left-hand group, who were less numerous as it happened, were as insignificant as those of the right-hand group, but their calm attitude made them seem more important. When K. now started to speak, he was convinced he was speaking for them.

'Your question, sir, as to whether I am a painter and decorator— though actually it was not so much a question as an outright assertion—is entirely typical of the proceedings which are being taken against me. You may object that they are not proceedings at all and you would be right, for they are only proceedings if I recognize them as such. But for the moment let us say I do recognize them, out of pity, as you might say. Pity is the only possible attitude, if one is to take notice of them at all. Far be it from me to say that the proceedings are a mess, but I am happy to offer you the expression as a means to self-knowledge.'

K. broke off and looked down into the hall. What he had said was harsh, harsher than he had intended, but still true. It deserved a scattering of applause, but all was silence, they were clearly keen to hear what was to come, perhaps in the silence an eruption was brewing which would put an end to the whole business. There was a distracting interruption when the door at the end of the hall opened and the young washerwoman came in, presumably having finished her work, attracting some glances despite all the care she took. The examining magistrate alone was a source of unalloyed pleasure for K., for he seemed immediately struck by what had been said. So far he had listened standing up, for K.'s address had caught him by surprise when he had got up to deal with the gallery. Now, during the pause, he sat down slowly, as if he didn't want anyone to notice. He picked up the notebook again, presumably in order to allow himself time to compose his expression.

'It's no use, sir,' K. went on, 'your little book will only confirm what I say.' Gratified to hear nothing but his own calm words in this gathering of strangers, K. even went so far as to take the notebook away from the examining magistrate, without a by-your-leave, and hold it up by one of the middle pages with his fingertips, as if in disgust, so that the mottled, closely written pages, yellowing at the edges, hung down on either side. 'Behold the examining magistrate's files,' he said, dropping the notebook onto the table. 'Do keep reading, sir, truly I am not afraid of this legal account book,* even though it is a closed book to me since I can only bring myself to touch it with the tips of two fingers.' It could only have been a sign of profound humiliation, or at least that was what it looked like, that the examining magistrate picked up the notebook, after it had been dropped on the table, tried to straighten it out a little, and opened it again in order to read.

The people in the front row were looking at K. with such expectant expressions on their faces that he looked down at them for a while. They were all of them older men, some with white beards. Were they perhaps the ones with the decisive voice who could influence the whole assembly, which even the humiliation of the examining magistrate could not rouse from the immobility into which it had sunk since K.'s speech?

'What has happened to me,' K. went on, in a slightly lower voice than before and looking up and down the front row, which made his speech somewhat disjointed, 'what has happened to me is merely an individual case, and as such not very important, since I do not take it too much to heart, but it is a sign of the way many people are treated and it is for them that I take my stand here, not for myself.'

He had raised his voice automatically. Somewhere someone applauded, hands raised, and shouted, 'Bravo! Why not? Bravo! I say bravo!' One or two of the men in the front row tugged at their beards, but none turned round to see where the shout came from. K. attached no importance to it either, but he did feel encouraged. He no longer thought it was necessary for them all to applaud, it was sufficient if the assembly as a whole started to think about the matter and just the odd one was won over by persuasive argument.

Taking up this idea, K. went on, 'I do not seek to win you over by oratory, that is probably beyond me anyway. The examining magistrate is probably a much better speaker, that is part of his job. What I do want to do is to see that an abuse of public office is brought out into the open. Listen. About ten days ago I was arrested—as to the fact that I have been arrested, it means this to me,' said K. snapping his fingers, 'but that's beside the point. They descended on me early one morning, while I was still in bed. Perhaps—from what the examining magistrate has said it's not impossible—perhaps they'd been ordered to arrest some painter who's as innocent as I am, but they chose me. The neighbouring room was occupied by two hulking guards. They couldn't have taken better precautions if I'd been a dangerous robber. And these guards were corrupt riff-raff, they kept going on at me, they wanted bribes, they tried to get clothes and linen out of me under false pretences, they demanded money in order, so they said, to bring me some breakfast, after they had brazenly eaten my breakfast before my very eyes. And if that was not enough, I was taken before the supervisor in another room. It was the room of a lady I respect highly, and I had to look on as, because of me but through no fault of mine, the room was in a way polluted by the presence of the guards and the supervisor. It was not easy to stay calm, but I managed to do so, and I asked the supervisor perfectly calmly—if he were here he would have to confirm that—why I had been arrested. And what was the reply of this supervisor? I can see him now, sitting in the aforementioned lady's chair, the very picture of dull-witted arrogance. His reply, gentlemen, was basically no reply, perhaps he really did have no idea, he had arrested me and that was enough. He had even gone farther and introduced into this lady's room three petty clerks from my bank, who spent the time touching and messing up photographs belonging to the lady. Naturally there was another purpose behind the presence of these clerks; like my landlady and her servant, they were to spread the news of my arrest, damaging my reputation and, especially, weakening my position at the bank. Without the least success, I have to say. Even my landlady—a simple woman, if I name her here, it is to do her honour: she is called Frau Grubach—even Frau Grubach was sensible enough to realize that such an arrest means no more than an attack boys who are not properly supervised carry out in the street. I repeat: this whole business has caused me nothing more than inconvenience and passing irritation, but could it not have had more serious consequences?'

When K. broke off and looked at the silent examining magistrate, he thought he saw him give a nod to a man in the crowd. K. smiled and said, 'The examining magistrate here beside me has just given one of you a secret sign. That means there are some among you who are directed from up here. I do not know whether the sign is meant to produce booing or applause, but by exposing this before it can take effect, I quite deliberately forgo the opportunity of learning what the sign means. It is a matter of complete indifference to me, and I publicly authorize the examining magistrate to pass on his commands to his paid assistants down there out loud, with words instead of with secret signs, saying, for example, "Boo now" at one point and "Applaud now" at another.'

Whether from embarrassment or impatience, the examining magistrate was shifting to and fro in his chair. The man behind him, whom he'd been talking to before, leant down again, presumably to give him either general encouragement or a specific piece of advice. Down below, the people were talking to each other, quietly but animatedly. The two groups, which earlier seemed to have had such opposing views, intermingled, some individuals among them pointing at K., others at the examining magistrate. The smoky haze in the room was extremely irksome, it even made it impossible to see those standing farther away with any clarity. It must have been particularly annoying for those in the gallery; to find out exactly what was going on, they were forced to ask, quietly and with timid sidelong glances at the examining magistrate, those on the floor of the meeting. And they replied just as quietly, holding their hands over their mouths.

'I have almost finished,' said K., rapping the table with his fist, since there was no bell; the shock caused the heads of the examining magistrate and his adviser to fly apart. 'This whole business is a matter of indifference to me, therefore I can assess it calmly and you can derive great benefit from listening to me, assuming this so-called court is of any interest to you. I beg you to put off your discussions of what I have to say until later, for I have no time and will soon leave.'

Silence immediately fell, such was K.'s control over the meeting. They were no longer all shouting at once, as they had at the beginning, they were not even applauding any more, but they seemed to have been convinced already or were well on the way to it.

'There is no doubt—' said K. very quietly, pleased with the way the whole assembly had pricked up their ears in expectation; in the silence a buzzing arose which was more exciting than the most ecstatic applause. 'There is no doubt that there is a large organization at work behind this court's every operation, in my case the arrest and today's examination. An organization which not only employs venal guards, foolish supervisors, and examining magistrates who are at best unassuming, but which, beyond that, doubtless maintains a bench of judges of high, indeed the highest standing, with their inevitable numerous entourage of ushers, clerks, police officers, and other assistants, perhaps even, I do not hesitate to use the word, executioners. And the point of this large organization, gentlemen? It consists in arresting innocent persons and instituting pointless and mostly, as in my case, fruitless proceedings against them. How would it be possible, given the pointlessness of the whole business, to avoid the worst kind of corruption among its employees? It is not possible. Even the most senior judge could not guarantee it in his own case. That is why the guards try to steal the very clothes off the backs of the people they arrest, that is why supervisors break into apartments that don't belong to them, that is why innocent people are humiliated before packed meetings instead of being interrogated. The guards told me about depots, where the belongings of people under arrest are taken. I would

like to have a look at these depots, where the property which those
arrested have earned by the sweat of their brow is rotting away, that is,
assuming it has not been stolen by thieving employees of the depot.'

K. was interrupted by a screeching from the back of the hall. He
shaded his eyes in order to see, for the dull daylight made the haze
whitish and dazzled him. It was the washerwoman whom K. had
noted as a serious disturbance the moment she had entered. Whether
she was to blame this time or not was impossible to tell. All that K.
could see was that a man had dragged her into a corner by the door
and was pressing her to him. However, it wasn't she who was
screeching, but the man, who had opened his mouth wide and was
staring at the ceiling. A little circle had gathered round the pair, and
those in that part of the gallery seemed delighted to see the serious
note K. had introduced to the meeting interrupted in this manner.
K.'s first impulse was to rush over to them straight away. He assumed
that everyone would want order to be restored and at the very least
the pair ejected from the hall, but the front rows stood firm, no one
moved to let K. through. On the contrary, they stopped him, old
men stuck out their arms, and someone's hand—he didn't have time
to turn round—grasped him by the back of his collar. K. was no
longer really thinking about the man and the woman, he felt as if he
were being restricted in his freedom, as if they were going ahead with
his arrest, and he jumped down off the platform, without consideration for those below. Now he was standing eye to eye with the
throng. Had he misjudged these people? Had he overestimated the
effect of his speech? Had they put on an act, as long as he was speaking, and were they tired of their act now that he was about to draw
his conclusions? And these faces all around him! Small black eyes
darting to and fro, cheeks drooping like a drunkard's, the long beards
stiff and sparse, and if you stuck your fingers in one it was as if you
were making it into claws, not as if you were putting your fingers in
a beard. Beneath the beards, however—and this was the real discovery
K. made—was the gleam of badges of various sizes and colours on
their coat collars. They all had these badges, as far as could be seen.
The groups on the right and the left, that had looked like two parties,
all belonged together, and he saw, as he suddenly swung round, the
same badges on the collar of the examining magistrate who, his hands
in his lap, was calmly looking down. 'So!' K. cried, throwing his arms
in the air—this sudden insight needed space—'You're all officials, as

I see, you're the corrupt gang I was inveighing against, you crammed into this hall as eavesdroppers and snoopers, pretending to be two different parties, and one applauded, just to test me; you wanted to learn how to seduce innocent people. Well, I presume you haven't been wasting your time, either you found it amusing that someone should expect you to defend innocence or—leave me alone or I'll hit you,' K. cried to a trembling old man who had come particularly close to him—'or you really have learnt something. I congratulate you on your occupation.' He quickly picked up his hat, which was on the edge of the table, and elbowed his way to the exit amid general silence, the silence, he was sure, of absolute surprise. But the examining magistrate appeared to have been even faster than K., for he was waiting for K. by the door. 'One moment,' he said. K. halted, not looking at the examining magistrate, however, but at the door, the handle of which he already had in his hand. 'I merely wanted to point out to you,' the examining magistrate said, 'that today—you are probably not aware of this—you have forfeited the benefit a man who has been arrested can always derive from a hearing.' K. directed his laugh at the door. 'You can keep your hearings, you blackguards,' he cried, opened the door and hurried down the stairs. Behind him came the noise of the meeting returning to life. They were probably starting to discuss the events, in the way students do.

In the Empty Conference Hall
The Student · The Offices

DURING the next week K. waited daily for a new appointment. He could not believe they had taken his rejection of hearings literally, and when the expected notification had not arrived by Saturday evening, he assumed there was a tacit summons to be in the same building at the same time. So he returned there on the Sunday, going straight up the stairs and along the corridors. Some people remembered him and greeted him from their doors, but he did not need to ask anyone the way and soon came to the right door. It was opened immediately when he knocked, and he was about to go to the next room, ignoring the woman he'd seen the last time, who stayed by the door, when she said, 'There's no session today.' He refused to believe it. 'Why should there not be a session today?' he asked. But the woman showed him it was true by opening the door to the neighbouring room. It was, indeed, empty, and in its emptiness looked even more squalid than the previous Sunday. On the table, which was still there on the podium, were a few books. 'Can I have a look at the books?' K. asked, not because he was particularly curious, but so that coming here would not have been a complete waste of time. 'No,' said the woman, closing the door, 'that is not allowed. The books belong to the examining magistrate.' 'I see,' said K., nodding. 'The books will be law-books, I suppose, and it's part of this legal system that one is condemned when one is not only innocent, but also ignorant.' 'I expect so,' said the woman, who had not understood exactly what he had said. 'In that case I'll go,' said K. 'Is there any message for the examining magistrate?' the woman asked. 'You know him?' K. asked. 'Of course,' said the woman, 'my husband's a court usher.' Only now did K. notice that the room, where previously there had been just a washtub, was now a fully furnished living-room. The woman saw his surprise and said, 'Yes, we live here rent-free, but we have to clear out the room on days when there's a session. My husband's job does have some disadvantages.' 'It wasn't the room I was surprised at,' said K., giving her an angry look, 'so much as the fact that you're married.' 'Are you perhaps referring to the incident during the last session when I interrupted your speech?' the woman asked. 'Of course,' K. said. 'It's past now and almost forgotten, but at the time I was furious. And now you tell me you're a married woman.' 'It didn't work to your disadvantage that your speech was broken off. Even then, opinion on it afterwards was very unfavourable.' 'That's as may be,' K. said, dismissing the topic, 'but it still does not excuse you.' 'I am excused in the eyes of everyone who knows me,' said the woman. 'That man who embraced me has been pursuing me for a long time. I may not be particularly attractive in general, but for him I am. There's nothing can be done about it, even my husband has accepted it. He has to put up with it if he wants to keep his job, since that man's a student and is likely to become very powerful. He's after me all the time, he left just before you arrived.' 'It doesn't surprise me,' said K., 'it fits in with everything else.' 'I suppose you want to bring in some improvements here,' the woman asked, speaking slowly and weighing every word, as if she was saying something that was dangerous both for her and for K. 'I deduced that from your speech, which I personally liked very much, though I only heard part of it, I missed the beginning and during the end I was lying on the floor with the student.—It's so horrible here,' she said after a pause, clasping K.'s hand. 'Do you think you will manage to make some improvement?' K. smiled, moving his hand about a little in her soft hands. 'Actually,' he said, 'it's not my job to make improvements here, as you put it. If you were to tell that to the examining magistrate, for example, you'd be laughed to scorn or punished. The fact is that I would certainly not have become involved in these things of my own free will, nor would I have lost any sleep over the need for improvement in this court. But having been supposedly arrested—I have been arrested, you see—has compelled me to step in here, if only for my own sake. If, however, in the course of this I can help you in any way, I will of course be very happy to do so. Not simply out of the goodness of my heart, but also because you can help me too.' 'How could I do that?' the woman asked. 'By showing me those books on the table there, for example.' 'But of course,' the woman cried, dragging him along behind her straight away.

They were old books, well thumbed, one cover was almost split across the middle and the pages were only held together by a few threads. 'How dirty everything is here,' said K., shaking his head, and the woman gave the books a swift if superficial wipe with her apron before he could pick them up. K. opened the top book; an obscene picture appeared, a naked man and woman sitting on a sofa. The artist's pornographic intention was clearly recognizable, but his lack of skill was such that it ended up being simply a man and a woman emerging from the picture, their bodies all too evident, sitting there too upright and, because of the false perspective, turning towards each other very awkwardly. K. did not look any further, but just opened the second book at the title-page. It was a novel entitled: *The Torments Grete Had to Suffer from her Husband Hans.* 'So these are the books of law that they study here,' said K. 'And I'm to be judged by people like that?' 'I will help you,' said the woman. 'Will you? Could you really do that without endangering yourself? You said before that your husband was very dependent on his superiors.' 'In spite of that I still want to help you,' the woman said. 'Come, we must discuss it. Forget about the danger to me, I only fear danger when I want to. Come.' She pointed to the platform and asked him to sit down on the steps with her. 'You have beautiful dark eyes,' she said after she had sat down and looked up at K.'s face. 'They tell me I have beautiful eyes too, but yours are much more beautiful. I noticed them the first time you came in, you know. It was because of them that I came into the meeting room here later on. I don't normally do that, in fact in a way I'm even forbidden to do so.' 'So that's what it's all about,' thought K. 'She's offering herself to me, she's depraved like all the others round here, she's fed up with the court officials, which is understandable, and so greets any man who turns up from outside with a compliment about his eyes.'

Not saying anything, K. stood up as if he had spoken his thoughts out loud and thus explained his behaviour to the woman. 'I don't think you could help me,' he said. 'In order to give me real help, you'd have to have connections with senior officials, but I'm sure you only know the minor employees you get in masses round here. I'm sure you know them very well and could get somewhere with them, that I do not doubt, but even the most you could get from them would be of no significance as far as the final outcome of my trial is concerned. And you would have lost some of your friends. I wouldn't want that. Keep up the same relationship with them, it seems to me that's essential for you. It's not without some regret that I say that, for, to return your compliment if I may, I like you too, especially when, as now, you look at me sadly—for which, by the way, there's no reason. You're part of the society I have to fight against, you feel comfortable in it, you even love the student or, if you don't love him, at least you prefer him to your husband. That was clear from what you said.' 'No!' she cried. She stayed sitting on the steps, but grasped K.'s hand, which he didn't manage to withdraw quickly enough. 'You can't go away now, you can't go away with a wrong opinion of me. Could you really bring yourself to leave now? Do I mean so little to you that you won't even do me the favour of staying here a little longer?' 'You misunderstand me,' said K., sitting down, 'if it's really important to you that I stay here, then I'm happy to stay. After all, I have the time, since I came here today expecting there to be a hearing. What I said before was just to ask you not to do anything for me in my trial. You shouldn't feel hurt by that; remember, the result of the trial is of no importance to me, I will just laugh if I'm condemned. That's always assuming there'll be a proper conclusion to the trial, which I very much doubt. In fact I believe that, as a result of laziness or forgetfulness, or perhaps even from fear on the part of the officials, the proceedings have already been broken off, or will be in the near future. Of course, it's always possible they'll make a show of carrying on with the trial in the hope of a large bribe—in vain, as I can tell you now, for I do not give bribes to anyone. There is one favour you could do me, though. You could tell the examining magistrate, or anyone else who likes spreading important news, that none of the many tricks these gentlemen presumably have up their sleeves will ever persuade me to offer a bribe. It would be quite pointless, you can tell them that from me. Perhaps they've already realized that themselves, though even if they haven't, it's not all that important to me that they find out now. It would only save those gentlemen some work—and me a certain amount of inconvenience, but I'm quite happy to accept that if I know that any inconvenience for me is at the same time a blow to them. And it will be, I'll make sure of that. Do you actually know the examining magistrate?' 'Of course,' the woman said, 'that's the first person I thought of when I offered to help you. I didn't know he's only a minor official, but since you say so it will probably be right. Despite that, I think the report he sends to his superiors will still have some influence. And he writes so many reports. You say the officials are lazy, but I'm sure that's not true of them all, especially not of this examining magistrate, he writes a great deal. Last Sunday, for example, the session lasted almost until the evening.

All the people left, but the examining magistrate stayed in the hall. I had to fetch a lamp for him, I only had a little kitchen lamp, but he was happy with that and immediately started to write. By that time my husband had come back—he has every Sunday off—so we brought in the furniture and arranged the room, then some neighbours came and we chatted by candlelight; to cut a long story short, we forgot about the examining magistrate and went to bed. During the night, it must have been quite late on, I suddenly woke up. The examining magistrate was standing beside the bed, shading the lamp with his hand so the light wouldn't fall on my husband. His precaution was unnecessary, the way my husband sleeps the light wouldn't have woken him anyway. I was so startled, I almost cried out, but the examining magistrate was very friendly, told me not to make a noise and whispered that he had been writing all that time, he was returning the lamp, and that seeing me asleep was a sight he would never forget. All that is just to show you that the examining magistrate does write a lot of reports, especially about you, since I'm sure your hearing was one of the main subjects of the Sunday session. Long reports like that can't be entirely without significance. Moreover, that incident shows that the examining magistrate is paying court to me, and that in this early stage—he must only just have noticed me—I will have great influence over him. And I have other tokens of how much I mean to him. Yesterday he sent the student with a pair of silk stockings as a present; the student's his assistant, he trusts him. They were supposed to be a reward for tidying up the conference room, but that's only an excuse, it's part of my job and my husband's paid for it. They're lovely stockings, look'—she stretched out her legs, pulling up her dress to her knees and examining the stockings herself—'they're lovely stockings, though really they're too fine and not suitable for me.'

Suddenly she broke off, placed her hand on K.'s hand, as if to reassure him, and whispered, 'Shh, Bertold's watching us.' K. slowly looked up. A young man was standing in the doorway of the hall. He was short, slightly bow-legged, and was trying to make himself look dignified, with a short, sparse red beard* he kept fingering. K. observed him with curiosity, he was the first student of this unknown legal system he had encountered personally, so to speak, a man who would probably eventually reach a senior position. The student, for his part, appeared to ignore K. entirely, he just took a finger out of his beard for a moment and crooked it to beckon the woman over, then went

to the window. The woman leant over to K. and whispered, 'Don't
be angry with me, I beg you, and don't think ill of me, but I have to
go to him now, to that horrible man, just look at his bandy legs. But
I'll be right back and then I'll go with you, if you'll take me—I'll go
wherever you want, you can do whatever you want with me, I'll be
happy just to get away from here for as long as possible, best of all for
ever.' She stroked K.'s hand, jumped up, and ran over to the window.
K. grasped at her hand involuntarily, but felt only empty air. The
woman really did tempt him and, however much he thought about it,
he could find no plausible reason why he should not yield to the
temptation. He easily dismissed the cursory objection that she would
tie him to the court. In what way could she tie him? Would he not
still remain free enough to crush the court at one blow, at least inso-
far as it affected him? Could he not have confidence in himself to do
that small thing? And her offer of help sounded genuine and was
perhaps not to be discounted. Could there be any better revenge on
the examining magistrate and his entourage, than to deprive them of
this woman and take her to himself? It might then happen that the
examining magistrate, after having worked laboriously on his lying
reports about K., would come late at night to find the woman's bed
empty. And empty because she belonged to K., because that woman
by the window, that warm, supple, voluptuous body in the dark dress
of coarse, heavy material, belonged to K. alone.

After he had thus overcome his misgivings about the woman, he
began to feel the quiet conversation by the window had been going
on too long and rapped the platform with his knuckles, then with his
fist. The student glanced briefly over the woman's shoulder at K.,
but carried on talking to the woman, indeed, he pressed up closer and
put his arms round her. She bent her head low, as if she were listening to him carefully, and he gave her a loud kiss on the neck as she
bent down, with hardly any interruption to the flow of words at all.
K. saw this as confirmation of the tyranny which the woman complained the student exercised over her. He stood up and walked up
and down the room. With sideways glances at the student, he wondered how he could get rid of him, and was not unhappy when the
student, clearly irritated by K.'s walking up and down, which at
times was turning into stamping, remarked, 'If you're impatient, you
can leave. You could have left sooner, no one would have missed you.
In fact, you should have left already, when I came in, and that as

quickly as possible.' This remark might well have been an outburst of anger, but it was certainly an expression of the arrogance of a future official of the court speaking to an unwelcome defendant. K. came to a halt close by him and said, with a smile, 'I am impatient, that is true, but the easiest cure for my impatience would be for you to leave us. If, however, you've come here to study—I have heard that you are a student—I will be perfectly happy to get out of your way and leave with this woman. It will take a lot of study before you can become a judge, you know. It's true that I am not very well acquainted with your legal system, but I assume that rudeness alone, which I admit you already employ to offensive effect, will not get you there by a long chalk.'

'They shouldn't have let him run around free like this,' said the student, as if he felt the need to explain K.'s insults to the woman, 'it was a mistake. I said as much to the examining magistrate. He should at least have been confined to his room between the hearings. Sometimes I don't understand the examining magistrate.' 'Wasted words,' said K. stretching his hand out to the woman. 'Come.' 'So that's it,' said the student, 'no, no, you're not having her,' and, with a strength one would not have expected in him, he picked her up and ran with her to the door, his back bent, and looking up to her with a tender expression on his face. There was undeniably a certain fear of K. in this, but despite that the student still dared to provoke K. by stroking and squeezing the woman's arm with his free hand. K. followed them for a few steps, ready to grab him, to throttle him if need be, when the woman said, 'It's no use, the examining magistrate has sent for me, I can't go with you, this little monster'—as she said that she ran her hand over the student's face—'this little monster won't let me.' 'And you don't want to be freed,' K. shouted, placing his hand on the shoulder of the student, who snapped at it with his teeth. 'No,' cried the woman, pushing K. away with both hands, 'no, no, that's the last thing I want, what are you thinking of! It would be the ruin of me. Let go of him, oh, please let go of him. He's only obeying the examining magistrate's orders and carrying me to him.' 'Then he can go and I don't want to see you ever again,' said K., furious with disappointment, giving the student a push in the back. He stumbled briefly, only to jump up even higher with his burden the next moment, elated at not having fallen. K. followed them slowly. He realized that this was the first undoubted defeat he had suffered at the hands of these people. Naturally there were no grounds for concern because of that, the only reason he had been defeated was because he had taken the fight to them. If he were to stay at home and lead his normal life, he would be a thousand times superior to these people, could clear any of them out of his way with one kick. In his mind's eye he pictured a scene in which this wretched student, this puffed-up child with his bandy legs and his beard, was made to look as ridiculous as possible, on his knees beside Elsa's bed, hands clasped, begging for mercy.* K. was so pleased with this idea that he decided to take the student with him to Elsa, should the opportunity ever arise.

K. hurried to the door out of curiosity. He wanted to see where the woman was carried to—presumably the student would not carry her through the streets in his arms. As it turned out, it was nothing like as far as that. Immediately opposite the door to the apartment was a narrow wooden staircase, presumably leading to the loft; it had a turn so that the top could not be seen. The student was carrying the woman up these stairs, very slowly and groaning, for the previous running had weakened him. The woman waved to K. and tried to indicate, by raising and lowering her shoulders, that she was not to blame for the abduction, though there was not much regret in the gesture. K. regarded her with a blank expression on his face, as if she was some- one he didn't know; he didn't want to reveal that he was disappointed, nor that he could easily overcome his disappointment.

The two of them had already disappeared, but K. was still stand- ing in the doorway. He had no option but to assume that the woman had not only deceived him but, with her claim that she was being taken to the examining magistrate, lied to him as well. Surely the examining magistrate wouldn't be sitting waiting for her in the loft. The wooden stairs told him nothing, however long he stared at them. Then K. noticed a piece of paper on the wall at the bottom, went over, and read, in clumsy, childish handwriting, 'Staircase to the Court Offices'. So the court offices were in the loft of this tenement? That was not calculated to instil much respect in people, and it was reas- suring for a defendant to realize how little money this court had at its disposal if it located its offices in a place where the other tenants, who were themselves among the poorest of the poor, dumped the stuff they had no further use for. Of course, it was not impossible that there was in fact enough money but the staff pounced on it before it could be employed in the service of the court. From K.'s experience so far that even seemed very likely. Having to attend such a dilapidated court was degrading for a defendant, but the fact that the dilapidation was the result of the dishonesty of the staff rather than the impoverishment of the court was, basically, reassuring. Now K. could understand why, for the initial questioning, they were ashamed to summon the defendant to the loft and preferred to molest him in his own home. There was no comparison between the examining magistrate, stuck in his loft, and K., who had a large office in the bank with an anteroom and a view out over the busy city square. Of course, he had no supplementary income from bribes or embezzlement, nor could he get the messenger to carry a woman up to his office. But K., at least in this life, was happy to forgo that privilege.

K. was still standing by the notice when a man came up the stairs, looked through the open door into the living-room, from which one could also see into the conference room, and asked K. if he had seen a woman there a short while ago. 'You're the usher, aren't you?' K. asked. 'Yes,' the man said. 'Oh, you're the defendant called K., I recognize you now, welcome.' And he stretched out his hand, the last thing K. was expecting. 'There's no session down for today,' the usher said, when K. remained silent. 'I know,' said K., looking at the court usher's everyday coat which, along with a few ordinary buttons, had, as its sole official emblem, two gilt buttons which seemed to have been cut off from an old officer's coat. 'I spoke to your wife a short while ago. She's not here any more. The student carried her up to the examining magistrate.' 'There you are,' said the usher, 'they keep on carrying her away. After all, today's Sunday and it's not a working day, but just to get rid of me they send me off with a pointless message. But they don't send me far, so that I can still hope that if I'm very quick I might get back in time. So I run as fast as I can, open the door of the office where I've been sent just a crack, shout my message so breathlessly it can hardly be understood, then run back. But the student's been even quicker than me, he's had a shorter distance to go, of course, he just had to run down the stairs from the loft. If I weren't so dependent on them I'd have long since crushed the student against the wall, here, beside the notice. I keep on dreaming of doing that. He's squashed flat, here, a little above the floor, his arms outstretched, his fingers splayed, his bow legs forming a circle and splashes of blood everywhere. So far it's only been a dream.' 'There's nothing else can be done about it?' K. asked with a smile. 'Not that

I know of,' said the usher. 'And now it's getting even worse. So far he's only carried her off for himself, but now, as I've long expected, he's carrying her to the examining magistrate.' 'Is your wife not partly to blame herself?' K. asked, and as he asked the question he had to keep himself under control, so strong was the jealousy he felt, even now. 'Certainly she is,' said the usher, 'she's even most to blame. She threw herself at him. As for him, he runs after all the women. In this building alone he's already been thrown out of five flats he'd sneaked into. However, my wife's the most beautiful woman in the whole building, and I'm the one person who can't do anything about it.' 'If that's the way things are,' said K., 'then there's certainly nothing can be done about it.' 'Why not?' the usher asked. 'Someone would have to catch the student, who's a coward, just when he's after my wife, and give him such a thrashing he won't dare come near her again. But I can't do that and others won't do me the favour because they're afraid of his power. Only a man like you could do it.' 'Why me?' K. asked in astonishment. 'Well, you're a defendant.' 'Yes,' said K., 'but that means I'd be all the more afraid he'd probably exert his influence on the preliminary examination, if not the result of the trial itself.' 'Yes, of course,' said the usher, as if K.'s views were just as valid as his own. 'But in general we don't proceed with trials we're not certain to win.' 'I don't agree with you there,' said K., 'but that needn't stop me dealing with the student, should the occasion arise.' 'I would be very grateful,' said the usher somewhat formally, he didn't really seem to believe his greatest wish might be fulfilled. 'There may perhaps', K. went on, 'be others of your officials, perhaps even all of them, who deserve the same treatment.' 'Yes, yes,' the usher said, as if that was obvious. Then he gave K. a trusting look, which he had not done before, despite the friendliness of their conversation, and added, 'One always feels a bit rebellious.' But he did seem to feel a little uncomfortable about their discussion after all, for he broke it off, saying, 'I have to report back to the office now. Do you want to come?' 'I've no business there,' said K. 'You could have a look at the offices. No one will bother with you.' 'Are they worth seeing?' K. asked, hesitantly, even though he was very keen to go. 'Well,' said the usher, 'I just thought you'd be interested.' 'Fine,' said K. eventually, 'I'll come along,' and he hurried up the stairs, faster than the usher.

He almost fell over as he went in, for there was a step behind the door. 'They don't show much consideration for the public,' he said.

'They don't show any consideration at all,' said the usher, 'just look
at this waiting room here.' It was a long corridor with crudely made
doors leading to the various cubicles in the loft. Although there was
no direct light from outside, it wasn't completely dark, since, instead
of proper walls, some of the cubicles had wooden slats, which did go
up to the ceiling, but still let in some light, and through which
officials could be seen, writing at desks or standing close up against
the slats watching the people out in the corridor through the gaps.
Probably because it was Sunday, there were only a few people in the
corridor. They all made a very meek impression. They were sitting,
almost equidistant from each other, on the two rows of long wooden
benches that had been set up on either side of the corridor. Their
clothes were neglected, despite the fact that most of them, to go by
their facial expressions, posture, beards, and many almost imperceptible little details, belonged to the middle classes. Since there were no
coat-hooks they had put their hats, one probably following the example of the other, underneath the bench. When those sitting closest
to the door saw K. and the usher, they stood up in greeting; those
farther away saw this and thought they had to greet them as well, so
that they all stood up as the two walked past. They never stood completely upright, their backs were bowed, their knees bent, they stood
there like beggars in the street. K. waited for the usher, who was
walking a little way behind him, and said, 'How they must have been
humiliated.' 'Yes,' said the usher, 'they're defendants, all those you
see here are defendants.' 'Really?' said K. 'Then they're my colleagues.'
And he turned to the nearest, a tall, slim man whose hair was almost
grey already. 'What are you waiting for here?' K. asked politely. But
being addressed unexpectedly only made the man confused, which
was all the more embarrassing because he was obviously a man with
experience of the world who, elsewhere, would surely be able to control himself and would not easily relinquish the superiority he had
achieved over others. Here, however, he was incapable of answering
such a simple question and looked at the others, as if it were their
duty to help him and as if no one could expect an answer from him
if that help were not forthcoming. Then the usher came up and said,
to calm the man down and encourage him, 'The gentleman's only
asking what you're waiting for. Go on, answer him.' The usher's
voice, which was probably familiar to him, was more effective. 'I am
waiting—' he said, then paused. Clearly, he'd started in that way in

order to give a precise answer to the question put, but then he didn't know how to continue. Some of the others who were waiting had come closer and surrounded the group, but the usher said, 'Move away, move away, keep the corridor clear.' They drew back a little, but not to the places where they'd been sitting before. Now the man had composed himself, and even smiled a little as he said, 'A month ago I made several applications for evidence to be produced in my case and I am waiting for the result.' 'You seem to be going to a great deal of trouble,' said K. 'Yes,' said the man, 'after all, it's my case.' 'Not everyone takes that view,' said K. 'I, for example, have also been accused but, as I hope to be saved, I have neither made any application for evidence to be produced, nor have I taken any other similar steps. Do you consider that necessary?' 'I don't really know,' said the man, unsure of himself again. He obviously thought K. was making fun of him, so he would probably most of all have liked to repeat what he had just said word for word, in order to avoid making some further mistake, but when he saw K.'s impatient look, he just said, 'As far as I'm concerned, I've applied for evidence to be produced.' 'I suppose you don't believe I've been accused?' K. asked. 'Oh, to be sure,' said the man, stepping a little to one side, but what came over in his reply was not belief, but fear. 'So you don't believe me?' K. asked, taking him by the arm in an unconscious response to the man's humble manner, as if he wanted to compel him to believe him. Not wanting to hurt him, he had only taken hold of his arm gently, but despite that the man cried out as if K. had touched his arm not with two fingers but with red-hot pincers. This ridiculous screaming was the last straw for K. If the man wouldn't believe he had been accused, all the better; perhaps he even thought he was a judge. In farewell he grasped him really firmly, pushed him back down on the bench, and went on. 'Most of the defendants are very sensitive,' said the usher. Behind them, all those who were waiting gathered round the man, who had stopped screaming, and seemed to be questioning him about precisely what had happened. Coming towards K. now was a guard, mostly recognizable as such from his sabre, the sheath of which seemed, at least from the colour, to be made of aluminium. K. was astonished at that, and even stretched out his hand towards it. The guard, who had come because of the cries, asked what had happened. The usher tried to satisfy him with a few words, but the guard, explaining that he had to go and see for himself, saluted and went on with very hurried but very short steps, probably dictated by arthritis.

K. didn't bother with him and the others gathered there for long, especially when, more or less half-way down the corridor, he saw that it was possible to turn off through an opening without a door on the right. He checked with the usher that it was the right way, the usher nodded, and he took the turn. He found it annoying that he had to walk one or two steps in front of the usher all the time, it could well look, at least in this place, as if he were being taken under escort. K. kept waiting for the usher to catch up, but he immediately dropped back again. Finally, in order to put an end to his discomfort, K. said, 'I've seen what things look like here, so now I'll leave.' 'You haven't seen everything,' said the usher in non-committal tones. 'I don't want to see everything,' said K., who was genuinely feeling tired, 'I want to leave, how do I get to the way out?' 'You haven't got lost already, have you?' the usher asked in astonishment. 'You go to the corner there, then turn right along the corridor and the door's straight ahead.' 'Come with me,' said K., 'and show me the way. There are so many ways here, I'll take the wrong one.' 'It's the only way,' the usher said, his voice now starting to sound reproachful. 'I can't go back with you, I have to deliver my message. I've already lost a lot of time because of you.' 'Come with me,' K. repeated more sharply, as if he'd finally caught the usher lying. 'Don't shout like that,' the usher whispered, 'there are offices everywhere here. If you don't want to go back by yourself, come along with me, or wait here until I've delivered my message, then I'll be happy to go back with you.' 'No, no,' said K., 'I'm not going to wait and you must come with me now.' So far K. hadn't looked round the place where he was, only now, when one of the many wooden doors all around them opened, did he look at it. A young woman, presumably alerted by K.'s loud voice, came in and asked, 'What is it you want, sir?' In the distance behind her a man could also be seen approaching in the gloom. K. looked at the usher. He had said that no one would bother with K. and here were two people coming already; it wouldn't take much and the whole staff would have noticed him and would be demanding an explanation for his presence there. The only understandable and acceptable one would be that he was a defendant and wanted to know the date of his next interrogation, but that was the very explanation he did not want to use, especially as it wasn't true, since he'd only come out of curiosity or—and this was even less acceptable as an explanation—out of a desire to confirm that this court was just as repulsive on the inside as it was on the outside. And since it seemed that this assumption was correct, he didn't want to penetrate any further. He felt constrained enough by what he had seen already and was in no state to face a senior official, who might appear from any of these doors. He wanted to leave, with the usher or, if needs be, without him.

But the way he stood there in silence must have been striking, for the young woman and the usher were looking at him as if he were about to undergo some great metamorphosis* in the very next minute which they didn't want to miss. And in the doorway stood the man K. had seen earlier in the distance; he was holding on to the lintel of the low door and rocking a little on the balls of his feet, like an impatient onlooker. But the young woman was the first to realize that the cause of K.'s behaviour was a slight indisposition. She brought an armchair and asked him, 'Won't you sit down?' K. immediately sat down and rested his elbows on the arms in order to support himself more securely. 'You feel slightly dizzy, don't you?' she asked. Her face was quite close to him now, it had the severe expression some women have when they are young and at their most beautiful. 'There's no need to worry,' she said, 'it's nothing unusual, almost everyone has an attack like that the first time they're here. It is the first time you've been here, isn't it? Well, it isn't unusual, then. The sun burns down on the roof timbers and the hot wood makes it very close and stuffy. That makes it unsuitable as office space, despite all its other advantages. On days when it's open to the public, and that's almost every day, the air is hardly breathable. And when you remember that washing's often hung out to dry here—we can't entirely prohibit the tenants from doing so—you won't be surprised you feel slightly sick. But eventually you get used to the air here. When you come the second or third time you'll scarcely notice how oppressive it is. Do you feel better now?' K. didn't reply, he felt too embarrassed, being at the mercy of these people because of this sudden faintness, and learning the cause of his feeling of nausea didn't make him feel any better, in fact it made it a little worse. The young woman noticed this straight away and, in order to give K. some fresh air, picked up a pole with a hook on the end that was propped up against the wall and pushed open a little skylight just above K.'s head.

But so much soot fell in that she had to close the skylight again immediately and clean the soot off K.'s hands with her handkerchief, since K. was too tired to do it himself. He would have liked to stay sitting there quietly until he was strong enough to leave, but that would have to be sooner rather than later, depending on how long people would look after him. And now, anyway, the young woman was saying, 'You can't stay here, we're in the way,'—K. looked round questioningly to ask what he could be in the way of—'I'll take you to the sickroom, if you like.—Would you help me, please?' she said to the man in the doorway. He immediately approached. But K. didn't want to go to the sickroom, being taken farther was the last thing he wanted, the farther he went, the worse it must be. So he said, 'I can walk,' and stood up, though, having got used to the comfortable chair, he was trembling. But then he couldn't keep on his feet. 'It's no good,' he said with a shake of the head and, sighing, sat down again. He remembered the usher, who, despite everything, could easily have led him out, but he seemed to have gone long ago. K. looked between the young woman and the man, who were standing in front of him, but he couldn't see the usher.

'I think', said the man, who was elegantly dressed—his grey waist-coat ending in two sharp points was particularly striking—'that this gentleman's indisposition is caused by the atmosphere in here. In that case it would be best, and preferable for him, if we took him not to the sickroom but straight out of the offices.' 'You're right,' K. cried, so pleased that he spoke almost before the man had finished, 'I will certainly feel better, I'm not that weak, I just need a little support under the arms, I won't give you much trouble, after all it's not very far, just take me to the door, I'll sit on the stairs for a while and I'll feel better in no time at all, I don't usually get these attacks, it's come as a complete surprise to me. I work in an office myself, so I'm used to office air, but it seems much worse here, you said so yourself. So would you be so kind as to help me along the way a little, I feel dizzy and sick if I stand up by myself.' And he raised his shoulders to make it easier for them to help him up.

But the man did not respond to his request, he kept his hands in his pockets and laughed out loud. 'You see,' he said to the young woman, 'I was right. It's only here the gentleman feels unwell, not in general.' She smiled, but tapped the man lightly on the arm with the tips of her fingers, as if to say he'd gone too far in making fun of K.

'What's all this,' said the man, still laughing, 'I really am going to help the gentleman out.' 'That's all right, then,' said the young woman, putting her dainty head on one side for a moment. 'Don't take his laughter too seriously,' she said to K., who was staring sadly into space once more and didn't seem interested in an explanation, 'this gentleman—I can introduce you, can't I?' The man gave his permission with a wave of the hand. 'You see, this gentleman is the information clerk. He gives defendants who are waiting all the information they need, and since our court is not very well known among the public, there are many enquiries. He knows the answer to all the questions, you can test him out some time if you feel like it. But that's not the only good thing about him, the other is his elegant dress. We, that is the staff here, decided that the information clerk, who is constantly dealing with the public and is their first contact with the court, ought to be given elegant clothes,* in order to make a dignified impression on them. The rest of us, as you can tell from me, are rather poorly dressed and in an old-fashioned style; there's not much point in spending money on clothing, since we are almost perpetually in the offices, we even sleep here. But as I said, we felt fine clothes were necessary for the information clerk. Since, however, they were not obtainable from our administration, which has rather strange ideas in such matters, we had a collection—litigants contributed as well—and bought him this fine suit and others. That would be everything that was needed to make a good impression, but he spoils it by the way he laughs and puts people off.'

'True, true,' said the man in mocking tones, 'but I don't understand why you are telling this gentleman all these intimate details, or, rather, forcing them on him since he's not interested in hearing them. Look at him sitting there, clearly preoccupied with his own affairs.'* K. couldn't even be bothered to contradict him. The young woman was probably motivated by good intentions, perhaps aiming to take his mind off things, or to allow him to compose himself, but it was unsuccessful. 'I had to explain about your laughter,' she said, 'it was insulting.' 'I think he would put up with even worse insults if I showed him the way out.' K. said nothing, didn't even look up; he allowed the two to argue about him as if they were arguing over a case, indeed he preferred it like that. But suddenly he felt the information clerk's hand on one arm and the young woman's on the other. 'Up you get, you weak man,' said the information clerk. 'Thank you both very much,' said K., pleasantly surprised. He stood up slowly and put the others' hands on the places where he most needed support. 'It must look', said the young woman softly in K.'s ear as they made their way towards the corridor, 'as if I'm trying my hardest to show the information clerk in a good light, but believe it or not, I'm telling the truth. He isn't hard-hearted. It's not part of his duties to show sick litigants out of the offices, but he does do it, as you can see. Perhaps none of us is hard-hearted,* perhaps we'd all like to help, but as officials of the court we can often appear to be hard-hearted and not to want to help anyone. I'm really unhappy at having to appear like that.'

'Wouldn't you like to sit down here for a while?' the information clerk asked. They had already reached the corridor and were by the defendant K. had spoken to earlier. K. felt almost ashamed to be seen by him. Previously he had stood up so straight before him, now he needed the support of two people, his hair was dishevelled, hanging down over his sweat-soaked forehead, and the information clerk was balancing his hat on his splayed fingers. But the defendant didn't seem to notice that at all, he stood humbly before the information clerk, who ignored him, and just tried to explain his presence there. 'I know', he said, 'that the decision on my applications cannot be given today, but I've come anyway, I thought I could wait here, it is Sunday, after all, I've plenty of time and I'm not disturbing anyone here.' 'You shouldn't apologize so much,' said the information clerk, 'your efforts are very laudable. True, you're occupying space here unnecessarily, but despite that I will certainly not prevent you from following the progress of your case, as long as it is not a nuisance to me. When one has seen people who shamefully neglect their obligations, one comes to have patience with people like yourself. Sit down.' 'Isn't he good at speaking to defendants,' the young woman whispered. K. nodded, but immediately started as the information clerk asked him again, 'Wouldn't you like to sit down here?' 'No,' said K., 'I don't want to rest.' He said that with absolute firmness, even though in reality it would have done him good to sit down. He felt as if he were seasick, as if he were on a ship in a heavy sea. It was as if the water were crashing against the wooden walls, as if a rushing sound came from the far end of the corridor, like water pouring over, as if the corridor were rocking to and fro and as if the people sitting on either side were going up and down. It made the calm of the young woman and the man who were helping him to the exit all the more incomprehensible. He was completely dependent on them, if they were to let go he would fall down like a plank of wood. Their small eyes shot sharp glances hither and thither; K. could feel their regular steps without taking any himself, for he was more or less being carried from one step to the next. Finally he realized they were talking to him, but he couldn't understand them, all he could hear was the noise filling everything and in it an unchanging high note that seemed to be sounding, as if from a siren. 'Louder,' he whispered, head bowed and ashamed, for he knew they had been speaking loud enough, even if it had been incomprehensible to him.

Finally, as if the wall in front of him had been torn apart, he felt a breath of fresh air and heard a voice beside him say, 'First he wants to leave, but you can tell him a hundred times this is the way out and still he doesn't move.' K. saw that he was standing at the way out and the young woman had opened the door. It was as if all his strength had suddenly returned, and, in order to enjoy a foretaste of freedom, he immediately stepped down one stair, from which he said goodbye to his escorts, who leant down towards him. 'Thank you very much,' he said repeatedly, shaking both their hands repeatedly and only stopping when he thought he saw that they, accustomed to the office air, could not stand the fresh air coming from the stairs. They could hardly answer, and the young woman might have fallen down if K. had not closed the door extremely quickly. K. stood there for a moment, smoothed back his hair with the aid of a pocket mirror, picked up his hat,* which was on the next landing—the information clerk must have thrown it down there—and ran down the stairs so nimbly and so many at a time that the rapid change almost frightened him. His normally sound state of health had never previously given him such a surprise. Could his body be going to rise in revolt and provide a new trial for him, since he bore the old one so effortlessly? He did not entirely reject the idea of going to see a doctor at the earliest opportunity, but he definitely intended—he didn't need any outside advice for this—to make better use of all future Sunday mornings than he had of this one.

The Thrasher

As K. was going along the corridor from his office to the main stairs one evening soon afterwards—on that day he was almost the last to leave, there were just two messengers still working in dispatch in the little circle of light from a lamp—he heard groans coming from behind a door where he had always assumed, without having actually seen it himself, that there was nothing but a lumber-room. He stopped in surprise and listened again to make sure he hadn't been mistaken; for a while there was silence, then the groans came once more. At first he was going to fetch one of the messengers—he might need a witness—but then his curiosity got the better of him and he literally flung open the door. It was, as he had correctly suspected, a lumber-room. Just over the threshold the floor was covered in old, out-of-date printed forms and empty earthenware ink-bottles. In the room itself, however, were three men, bent down because of the low ceiling. The light came from a candle fixed to a shelf. 'What are you doing here?' K. asked. He was so agitated the words came tumbling out, though not too loud. One of the men, who was clearly in charge of the others and immediately drew attention to himself, was dressed in a kind of dark leather outfit which left his arms and much of his chest completely bare.* He didn't reply, but the two others cried, 'Sir! We're going to be given a thrashing because you complained* about us to the examining magistrate.' Only then did K. see that it was the guards, Franz and Willem, and that the other had a cane in his hand with which to thrash them. 'No,' said K., staring at them, 'I didn't complain, I just said what had happened in my apartment. And your behaviour wasn't exactly irreproachable either.' 'Sir,' said Willem, while Franz was obviously trying to keep himself safe from the other man by hiding behind him, 'if you knew how badly we're paid you'd think better of us. I have a family to feed and Franz here would like to get married, we try to make money wherever we can, it's not possible through work alone, not even the hardest work, your fine linen tempted me, naturally we guards are forbidden to behave like that, it wasn't right, but it's a tradition that the linen goes to the guards, it's always been like that, believe me. Anyway, what can such things mean to someone who is so unfortunate as to be arrested?

If, however, someone makes it public, then punishment must follow.' 'I was unaware of that. I didn't ask for you to be punished, it was the principle of the thing that concerned me.' 'Didn't I tell you, Franz?' said Willem, turning to the other guard. 'The gentleman didn't ask for us to be punished. And, as you hear, he didn't even know that we would have to be punished.' 'Don't let what they say move you,' said the other man, 'their punishment is as just as it is inevitable.' 'Don't listen to him,' said Franz, breaking off for a moment to suck his hand, which had been given a stroke of the cane, 'we're being punished because you reported us. Otherwise nothing would have happened, even if they'd found out what we'd done. Can you call that justice? For a long time the two of us, but especially me, had performed our duties as guards satisfactorily—you yourself will have to admit that we guarded you well, from the point of view of the department—we had prospects of being promoted and would certainly soon have been made thrashers, like this man here, who just happened to have the good fortune not to be reported by anyone, for such complaints are really very rare. And now everything's lost, sir, our careers are over, we'll be assigned to much lower-grade work than guarding and, more-over, now we're going to get this terribly painful thrashing.' 'Can the cane hurt so much?' K. asked, examining the cane the thrasher was brandishing before him. 'We'll have to strip naked,' said Willem. 'Oh,' said K., having a closer look at the thrasher. He was bronzed like a sailor and had a fierce, fresh face. 'Is there no possibility of these two being spared the thrashing?' he asked him. 'No,' said the thrasher, shaking his head with a laugh. 'Get undressed,' he ordered the guards. And to K. he said, 'You shouldn't believe everything they say. Their fear of being beaten has made them a little feeble-minded. What this one here, for example,'—he pointed at Willem—'told you about his possible career is quite ridiculous. Look how fat he is, the first strokes will be wasted on fat. Do you know how he got so fat? He has the habit of eating the breakfast of all those he arrests. Didn't he eat your breakfast? There you are. But a man with a belly like that can never become a thrasher, it's out of the question.' 'There are thrashers like that,' insisted Willem, who was just undoing his belt. 'No!' said the thrasher, brushing Willem's neck with the cane in a way that made him flinch. 'You should be getting undressed, not listening.' 'I'd pay you well if you'd let them go,' said K. and, without looking at the thrasher—such deals are best done with eyes lowered on both sides—took out his wallet. 'I suppose you'll go and report me then,' said the thrasher, 'and let me in for a thrashing too. No, no!' 'Be reasonable,' said K., 'if I'd wanted these two to be punished, I wouldn't be trying to buy their freedom now. I could simply close the door behind me, refuse to see or hear anything further, and go home. But I'm not doing that, on the contrary, I'm seriously trying to have them set free; if I'd had any idea that they were to be punished, or even just might have been punished, I would never have named them. I don't consider them guilty, it's the organization that's guilty, the senior officials.' 'That's true,' the two guards cried out, immediately getting a stroke of the cane on their backs, which were already bare. 'If it was one of the senior judges on the receiving-end of your cane,' said K., holding down the cane, which was about to be raised again, 'I would certainly not stop you from striking, on the contrary, I'd give you money to strengthen yourself for the good cause.' 'That all sounds very convincing,' said the thrasher, 'but I refuse to accept bribes. I'm employed as a thrasher, so I'll thrash them.' Franz, who so far had kept very much in the background, perhaps expecting K.'s intervention to be effective, came over to the door, wearing nothing but his trousers, knelt down and grasped K.'s arm, whispering, 'If you can't get both of us spared, then at least try to get him to let me go. Willem's older than me and less sensitive in every respect; he's also already had a mild thrashing, a few years ago, but my reputation is unblemished, I only behaved as I did because of Willem, who has been my guide, in both good and evil. My poor fiancée's waiting outside the bank to see what happens. I'm so terribly ashamed.' He used K.'s coat to dry the tears that were running down his face. 'I'm not going to wait any longer,' said the thrasher, grasped the cane with both hands, and started laying into Franz whilst Willem crouched in a corner, watching furtively, not daring to turn his head. Then Franz let out a scream, one unchanging, uninterrupted scream that didn't sound as if it came from a human being, but from some tortured instrument, the whole corridor echoed with it, the whole building must have heard it. 'Don't scream,' K. cried. He couldn't stop himself, and as he stared intently in the direction from which a messenger must come, he pushed Franz, not hard, but hard enough to knock him to the ground where, distraught, he scrabbled frenziedly over the floor with his hands; but he didn't escape the thrashing, the cane hit him even on the floor, the tip swinging steadily up and down as he rolled this way and that under it.

Already one messenger had appeared in the distance and another a few steps behind him. K. quickly slammed the door shut, went to a window close by that looked out into the courtyard, and opened it. The screaming had stopped completely. To prevent the messengers from coming too close, he called out, 'It's only me.' 'Good evening, Herr K.,' they shouted back, 'is anything wrong?' 'No, no,' K. replied, 'it's just a dog howling* in the courtyard.' When the messengers didn't move, he added, 'You can carry on with your work.' In order to avoid a conversation with the messengers, he leant out of the window. When he looked back along the corridor a while later, they had gone. But K. stayed by the window, he didn't dare go into the lumber room, nor did he want to go home. It was a small, square courtyard he was looking down into, with offices all round. The windows were already dark, just the top ones catching a reflection of the moonlight. K. strained his eyes to try and see into a dark corner of the courtyard, where a few hand-carts were piled up together. He felt anguish at having been unable to prevent the thrashing, but it wasn't his fault. If Franz hadn't screamed—true, it must have hurt a lot, but a man should be able to control himself at decisive moments—if Franz hadn't screamed then K. would, at least very probably, have found some means of winning the thrasher over. If all the lower officials were rogues, then why of all men should the thrasher, who had the most inhuman task, be an exception? K. had seen very well the gleam in his eyes at the sight of the banknote, he'd obviously only continued with the thrashing to increase the bribe a little. And K. would have spared no expense, it really was important to him to free the guards; having already started to combat the rottenness of the court, it was natural that he should take action here as well. But the moment Franz started to scream naturally put an end to all that. K. could not allow the messengers, and goodness knows who else besides, to catch him in his negotiations with the company in the lumber-room. Really, no one could demand such a sacrifice from K. If that had been his intention, then it would have almost been simpler for K. to get undressed and offer himself to the thrasher as a substitute for the guards. However, the thrasher would certainly not have accepted such a replacement, for in so doing he would have been guilty of serious neglect of his duty without gaining any advantage; at the same time he would probably have overstepped his authority, since as long as his case was still in progress K. was presumably untouchable for any employee of the court. Of course, there might be special regulations operating in this case. Be that as it may, K. had had no other choice but to close the door, even though that didn't mean he was entirely out of danger himself. That he had ended up giving Franz a push was regrettable, and only excused by his own agitation.

He could hear the footsteps of the messengers in the distance. So as not to attract their attention, he closed the window and set off towards the main staircase. He stopped for a while and listened at the lumber-room door. All was quiet. The man could have beaten the guards to death, after all, they were completely in his power. K. had already stretched out his hand for the doorknob, but he pulled it back. He couldn't help anyone any more, and the messengers were sure to be there at any moment. However, he vowed to himself that he would bring the matter up and, as far as was in his power, mete out proper punishment to those who were really to blame, namely the senior officials, of whom none had dared to show his face. As he went down the steps outside the bank, he observed all the passers-by carefully, but even in the surrounding area there was no young woman to be seen who was waiting for someone. Franz's claim that his fiancée was waiting for him had turned out to be a lie, though a pardonable lie, the only purpose of which was to arouse greater pity.

During the next day K. could not get the guards out of his mind. He couldn't concentrate on his work, and to get it all done he had to stay a little longer in the office than the previous evening. When he passed the lumber-room on his way out, he opened the door, as if out of habit. He was completely taken aback by what he saw there instead of the expected darkness. Everything was unchanged, was just as it had been when he had opened the door the previous evening: the printed forms and ink-bottles immediately behind the door, the thrasher with his cane, the guards, still fully dressed, the candle on the shelf. The guards began to moan and called out, 'Sir!' Immediately K. slammed the door shut and thumped it with his fists, as if that would make it even more firmly shut. Almost in tears, he ran to the messengers, who were calmly working at the copying machine and looked up from their work in astonishment. 'It's about time you cleared out that lumber-room,' he cried, 'we're drowning in filth.' The messengers said they could do it the following day and K. nodded; that late in the evening he could not compel them to do the task then, as he had actually intended. He sat down for a moment, to keep the messengers close to him for a while, and shuffled some copies around, hoping to give the impression he was checking them, then once he was satisfied that the messengers would not dare leave at the same time as he did, he went home, weary and his mind a blank.

His Uncle · Leni

ONE afternoon—it was just before the post was due to go, and K. was very busy—his Uncle Karl, a small landowner from the country, pushed his way into the room between two messengers who were bringing documents. K. was less horrified to see him than he might have been. His uncle was bound to come, K. had become convinced of that about a month ago, and had at that time been extremely horrified at the very idea of his uncle arriving. He had seen him in his mind's eye, leaning forward slightly, his crushed panama in his left hand, stretching out his right hand towards him while he was still some way away and holding it out to him across the desk in a heedless rush, knocking over everything that was in his way. His uncle was always in a hurry, for he was obsessed by the unfortunate idea that on his visits to the capital, which only lasted one day, he had to do everything he had planned and must not, moreover, neglect any chance opportunity that arose for a conversation, a piece of business, or pleasure. K., who, as his former ward, was under a particular obligation to him, was expected to assist him in every conceivable way and, moreover, had to put him up for the night. He used to call him 'The Ghost from the Country'.

As soon as they had shaken hands—he had no time to sit down in the armchair K. offered him—he asked K. for a word with him in private. 'It's necessary,' he said, swallowing with difficulty, 'it's necessary for my peace of mind.' K. immediately sent the messengers out of the room with instructions to let no one in. 'What's this I hear, Josef?' his uncle cried once they were alone, sitting down on the desk and stuffing various documents under him without looking at them in order to get a more comfortable seat. K. remained silent. He knew what was coming, but, suddenly released as he was from his strenuous work, he abandoned himself to a pleasant weariness and looked out of the window at the opposite side of the street, of which only a small triangular section was visible from his chair, a portion of the wall of a building between two shop-fronts. 'You're looking out of the window,' his uncle cried, arms in the air, 'for heaven's sake, Josef, answer me. Is it true? Can it be true?' 'Uncle,' said K., shaking himself out of his reverie, 'I've no idea what you're on about.' 'Josef,' said his uncle, wagging his finger, 'as far as I know, you've always told the truth. Should I take your words as a bad sign?' 'I suspect I know what you're referring to,' K. said obediently, 'you've probably heard about my trial.' 'That's right,' said his uncle, nodding slowly, 'I've heard about your trial.' 'Who told you?' K. asked. 'Erna wrote to me about it,' his uncle said. 'She doesn't see you at all, unfortunately you don't bother much with her, but she still heard about it. I got the letter today and naturally came into town immediately. For that reason alone, but it seems to me reason enough. I can read out the bit referring to you, if you like.' He took the letter out of his wallet. 'Here it is. She writes:

"I haven't seen Josef for a long time. I did go to the bank last week, but Josef was so busy I wasn't allowed to see him. I waited almost an hour, but then I had to go home because I had a piano lesson. I would have liked to talk to him, perhaps there'll be an opportunity soon. He sent me a big box of chocolates for my name day, which was very kind of him. I forgot to write to you about it at the time, I've just remembered it now that you asked me. I have to tell you that in the school chocolate disappears straight away, hardly have you realized you've been given some chocolate than it's gone. But there was something I wanted to tell you about Josef. As I mentioned, in the bank I wasn't allowed to see him because he was in a meeting with a gentleman. After I had waited quietly for some time, I asked one of the messengers whether the meeting was likely to last much longer. He said that it most likely would, since it was presumably about Herr K.'s trial. I asked what trial that was, was he sure he wasn't mistaken, and he said he wasn't mistaken, it was a trial and a serious one at that, but he didn't know any more about it. He himself, he went on, would gladly help Herr K., for he was a very good and just gentleman, but he didn't know how to go about it and he could only hope some influential gentlemen would take up his cause. And he was sure that was what would happen and that everything would turn out fine in the end, but at the moment, as he could tell from Herr K.'s mood, things were not going very well. Naturally I didn't attach too much importance to what he said. I tried to reassure the simple-minded fellow and also told him not to speak to others about it. I assume it's all idle chatter. Still, I do think it would be a good idea, Father, if you looked into it during your next visit. It will be easy for you to find out the exact truth of the matter and, if it should prove necessary, get your influential acquaintances to intervene. If that's not necessary, which is the most likely outcome, at least it will give your daughter the opportunity to embrace you in the very near future, which she greatly looks forward to."

'A good child,' K.'s uncle said when he had finished reading out the letter, wiping a few tears from his eyes. K. nodded. Because of all the disruption to his life recently, he had completely forgotten Erna, he'd even forgotten her birthday and the story about the chocolate had clearly been invented simply in order to stop him getting into hot water with his uncle and aunt. It was a touching gesture, and the theatre tickets, which he intended to send her regularly from now on, would not be an adequate reward, but he didn't feel in the right mood at the moment for visits to the boarding school and conversations with a little seventeen-year-old schoolgirl. 'So what do you say to that?' his uncle asked. The letter had made him forget all his haste and agitation, and he seemed to be reading it again. 'Yes, Uncle,' said K., 'it's true.' 'True?' his uncle exclaimed. 'What's true? How can it be true? What kind of a trial is it? Surely not a criminal trial?' 'A criminal trial,' K. replied. 'How can you sit here calmly when you've a criminal trial to deal with?' his uncle cried, getting louder and louder. 'The calmer I am, the better it is for the outcome,' said K. wearily. 'Don't worry.' 'That doesn't reassure me at all,' his uncle cried. 'Josef, my dear Josef, think of yourself, think of your relations, of our good name. Until now you were our pride and joy, you mustn't bring down disgrace* upon us. I don't like your attitude,'—he looked at K., his head on one side—'it's not the behaviour of an innocent man who's been accused and who's still in full command of his faculties. Tell me quickly what it's all about. Presumably it's the bank?' 'No,' said K., standing up, 'but you're talking too loud, Uncle, the messenger's probably at the door listening. I'm not happy with that. Let's go somewhere else and then I'll answer all your questions as well as I can. I realize that I owe the family an explanation.' 'Correct,' his uncle shouted, 'quite correct. Now get a move on, Josef, get a move on.' 'I just have to give some instructions,' said K. and telephoned to summon his deputy. He arrived in a few seconds, and K.'s uncle was so worked up that he pointed to K., to indicate that it was he who had called him, which was perfectly clear anyway. The young man listened calmly and attentively as K., standing at his desk, explained in a quiet voice and using various documents what still remained to be done that day in his absence. His uncle was a distraction, first of all simply by standing there, eyes wide and biting his lip nervously, not listening, though the fact that he appeared to be listening was distraction enough. But then he started walking up and down the room, stopping now and then to look out of the window or at a picture, constantly exclaiming such things as, 'I just can't understand it at all' or 'And where's it all going to lead, now tell me that?' The young man behaved as if he hadn't noticed this, calmly listened to K.'s instructions, made a few notes, and left, first bowing to K., then to his uncle, who had his back to him and was looking out of the window, arms outstretched, crumpling up the curtains in his hands.

The door had hardly closed when his uncle cried, 'At last your puppet's gone, now we can go too. At last!' Unfortunately there was nothing K. could do to get his uncle not to ask questions about the trial in the vestibule, where a few clerks and messengers were standing and the deputy manager just happened to be crossing. 'Now Josef,' his uncle said, returning the bows of those around with a wave of the hand, 'tell me honestly what kind of a trial it is.' K. made a few non-committal remarks, laughing a little at the same time. It was only when they were on the steps that he explained to his uncle that he hadn't wanted to talk openly in front of the other people. 'Quite right,' his uncle said, 'but now talk.' He listened, head bowed, taking short, hasty puffs at his cigar. 'First of all, Uncle,' K. said, 'it's not a case that's being tried in the normal court.' 'That's bad,' said his uncle. 'What?' K. said, looking at his uncle. 'I think that's bad,' his uncle repeated. They were standing on the steps outside the bank, and, since the commissionaire appeared to be listening, K. led his uncle down into the street where they were engulfed in the bustling throng. K.'s uncle, who had taken his arm, was no longer questioning him so urgently about the trial, for a time they even walked along in silence. 'But how did it come about?' his uncle finally asked, stopping so abruptly the people behind them were startled and had to take evasive action. 'These things don't happen all at once, they're a long time brewing, there must have been signs, why didn't you write to me? You know I'd do anything for you, in a way I'm still your guardian, and so far that's always been a cause for pride. Naturally I'll help you, even now, only it's very difficult, given that the trial's already under way. It would be best if you took some time off and came to stay with us in the country. You've lost a bit of weight, I've only just noticed. In the country you'd build up your strength, that would be all to the good, I'm sure you have tiring times ahead of you. On top of that, however, you would in a way be out of reach of the court. Here they have all sorts of powers, which they would necessarily, automatically, employ against you; out in the country they would first of all have to dispatch officials or try to work on you by letter, telegram, telephone. That naturally weakens the effect, it doesn't free you, but it gives you breathing-space.' 'Of course, they could forbid me to leave,' K. said, carried along a little by his uncle's train of thought. 'I don't think they'll do that,' his uncle said thoughtfully, 'the loss of power they would suffer through your departure is not that great.' 'I thought', said K., taking his uncle by the arm to prevent him from stopping again, 'that you would think the whole affair even less important than I do, and now you're taking it very seriously indeed.' 'Josef,' his uncle cried, trying to free his arm so that he could stop, but K. didn't let him, 'you're a changed man. You always had such a clear grasp of things, has it deserted you now, of all times? Do you want to lose the trial? Do you know what that means? That means you'll simply be deleted. And all your family will go down with you, or at least be thoroughly humiliated. Pull yourself together, Josef. Your lack of concern is driving me mad. Looking at you, I'm tempted to believe the saying: "To have a trial like that means you've already lost it."' 'My dear Uncle,' said K., 'there's no point in getting all worked up like this; there's no point in your doing so, nor would there be in mine. Getting worked up doesn't win you trials, you must trust my experience, as I always value yours, even though it sometimes surprises me. Since you say the family will also be affected by the trial—which, for my part, I cannot understand at all, but that's just by the way—I am quite happy to follow your advice in everything. It's only going to stay in the country that doesn't seem a good idea to me, even from your point of view, it would imply flight and a sense of guilt. It's true that here I'm more at their mercy, but I can also do more to pursue the case.' 'Correct,' his uncle said, in a tone of voice that suggested they were finally getting closer. 'I only proposed it because I felt that if you stayed here the case would be endangered by your indifference, and thought it would be better if I were to work on it instead of you. If, however, you intend to put all your effort into it, that would be much better, of course.' 'So we're agreed on that,' said K. 'Have you any suggestion as to what I should do first?' 'I'll have to think about that,' his uncle said. 'You must remember that I've been living almost uninterruptedly in the country for twenty years now, and when that happens you lose your feel for these affairs. As a matter of course, various important connections with people who are better acquainted with such matters have become more tenuous. I'm rather isolated out in the country, as you well know. It's really only on occasions like this that one notices it oneself. And to a certain extent your case came as a surprise, although strangely enough, after Erna's letter I suspected something of the kind and was almost sure the moment I saw you today. But that's beside the point, the important thing now is not to lose any time.'

While he was still speaking he stood on tiptoe, waved to a taxi, and pulled K. in with him, at the same time giving the driver an address. 'Now we're going to see Huld,* the lawyer,' he said, 'we were at school together. You'll have heard of him, I'm sure. No? Now that is strange. He has a considerable reputation as defence counsel and as a lawyer for the poor, but it's as a person especially that I have great confidence in him.' 'Whatever you suggest is fine by me,' said K., despite his unease at the hasty and insistent way his uncle was going about it. He wasn't happy with the idea of going as a defendant to see a lawyer for the poor. 'I didn't realize', he said, 'that you could bring in a lawyer on such a case.' 'Of course you can,' said his uncle, 'that goes without saying. Why ever not? And now tell me everything that's happened so far, so that I know all about the case.' At once K. started to tell him, without holding anything back, complete openness was the only way he had of protesting against his uncle's opinion that the trial brought shame on them all. He only mentioned Fräulein Bürstner's name once, and that very briefly, but that did not detract from his openness, since Fräulein Bürstner had no connection with the case.

As he was talking, he looked out of the window and saw that they were approaching the district where the court offices were. He pointed this out to his uncle who, however, saw nothing remarkable in that. The taxi stopped outside a dark house.* His uncle immediately rang the bell by the first door on the ground floor; as they waited, he bared his large teeth in a smile and whispered, 'Eight o'clock, an unusual time for a business call. But Huld won't take it amiss as it's me.' Two large, black eyes appeared in the peephole, examined the two visitors

for a while, and then disappeared; but the door did not open. K. and
his uncle confirmed to each other that they had seen a pair of eyes.
'A new maid who's afraid of strangers,' his uncle said, and knocked
again. Again the eyes appeared, one could almost have said they
looked sad, but perhaps that was just an illusion caused by the open
gas flame that was burning, just over their heads, with a loud hissing
noise but gave little light. 'Open up,' his uncle cried, thumping the
door with his fist, 'we're friends of Herr Huld.' 'Herr Huld's ill,' came
a whisper from behind them. There was a man in a dressing-gown
standing in a doorway at the farther end of the short corridor, who
gave them this news in an extremely quiet voice. K.'s uncle, already
furious at the long delay, swung round and, walking up to him threat-
eningly, as if the man himself were the illness, cried, 'Ill? You say he's
ill?' 'The door's been opened,' said the man, pointing to the lawyer's
door, gathered up his dressing-gown, and disappeared.

The door really had been opened. A young woman in a long, white
apron—K. recognized her dark, slightly protuberant eyes—was
standing in the hall holding a candle in one hand. 'Next time open
up more quickly,' said his uncle in lieu of a greeting, as the girl made
a brief curtsey. 'Come on, Josef,' he said to K., who slowly pushed
his way past the girl. 'Herr Huld is ill,' the girl said, since his uncle
was hurrying towards a door without waiting. K. was still marvelling
at the girl, even while she had turned round to lock the door again;
she had a rounded, doll-like face, not only her pale cheeks and chin
were round but also her temples and the outline of her forehead.
'Josef,' his uncle called again, and asked the girl, 'I presume it's his
heart?' 'I think so,' the girl said. By this time she had managed to go
ahead of them with the candle and open the door to the room. In the
corner of the room, which the light of the candle did not reach, a face
with a long beard rose from a bed. 'Who's that coming, Leni?' the
lawyer asked. Dazzled by the candle, he could not see who his visitors were. 'It's your old friend Albert,'* K.'s uncle said. 'Oh, Albert,'
said the lawyer, falling back into the pillows, as if he didn't need to
pretend for this visitor. 'Are you really that bad?' K.'s uncle asked,
sitting down on the edge of the bed. 'I don't believe it. It's a recur-
rence of your heart trouble* and it'll pass as it did all the other times.'
'Possibly,' said the lawyer in a low voice, 'but it's worse than it's ever
been. I've difficulty breathing, I can't sleep at all, and I'm getting
weaker by the day.' 'Is that so,' said K.'s uncle, his large hand pressing

his Panama hat firmly down on his knee. 'That's bad news. But are you being looked after properly? It's so gloomy here, so dark. It's a long time since I was last here, it seemed pleasanter then. Nor does your little maid seem very cheerful, unless she's putting on a show.' The young woman was still standing by the door with the candle; as far as it was possible to tell from her indeterminate look, her eyes were on K. rather than his uncle, even when the latter was talking about her. K. was leaning on a chair, which he had pushed close to her. 'When you're as ill as I am,' the lawyer said, 'you need peace and quiet. I don't find it gloomy.' After a brief pause he added, 'And Leni looks after me well, she's very good.' However, that was not enough to convince K.'s uncle, he was clearly prejudiced against her. He didn't say anything in reply to his sick friend, but he watched with a stern eye as the nurse went to the bed and placed the candle on the bedside table, whispering to the invalid as she bent over him and arranged his pillows. He almost seemed to forget the consideration due to a sick man, standing up and following the nurse to and fro; K. would not have been surprised if he had grasped her skirts and pulled her away from the bed. K. himself looked on calmly, in fact the lawyer's illness was not entirely unwelcome as far as he was concerned. He hadn't been able to dampen the ardour with which his uncle had thrown himself into the case, but he was happy to see the ardour diverted into other channels without him having to do anything about it. Then his uncle, perhaps just in order to rebuff the nurse, said, 'Would you please leave us alone for a while, Fräulein, I have some personal business to discuss with my friend.' The nurse, who was still leaning far over the sick man and smoothing the sheet by the wall, just turned her head and said, in a very calm voice, in striking contrast to K.'s uncle's outpourings, which kept building up in fury then overflowing, 'You can see that the gentleman is too ill to discuss any business at all.' She had presumably repeated some of his uncle's words for convenience's sake, but even to an outsider they would have sounded mocking; K.'s uncle naturally flew into a rage, like a man who's been stung. 'You damned hussy,' he said. Such was his agitation, it came out as a gurgle and was fairly incomprehensible, but K. was horrified, even though he had expected something of the kind, and he ran over to his uncle with the clear intention of using both hands to shut his mouth. Fortunately, however, the figure of the sick man rose up behind the girl. With a grim look, as if he were swallowing something revolting, K.'s uncle said in calmer tones, 'Naturally we are quite capable of understanding that; if what I am demanding were impossible, I would not demand it. Please go now.' The nurse was standing up straight, facing K.'s uncle; K. thought he noticed her stroking the lawyer's hand. 'You can say everything in front of Leni,' the sick man said in what was undoubtedly the tone of an urgent request. 'It doesn't concern me,' K.'s uncle said, 'it's not my secret.' And he turned away, as if he were refusing to negotiate any more but were allowing them time to think things over. 'Whom does it concern?' the lawyer asked; his voice gave way and he lay back again. 'My nephew,' K.'s uncle said, 'I've brought him along with me.' And he introduced him: 'Josef K., senior accountant at the bank.' 'Oh,' said the invalid in a much livelier voice, holding out his hand to K., 'you must excuse me, I didn't see you.—Leave us, Leni,' he said to the nurse, who didn't resist any longer. He shook her hand, as if they were saying farewell for a long time.

'So you haven't come to call on a sick man,' he eventually said to K.'s uncle, who, appeased, had come closer, 'you've come on business.' He was so reinvigorated it made it look as if the idea of K.'s uncle coming to call because he was sick had drained him of energy. He remained resting on one elbow, which must have been fairly strenuous, and kept tugging at a strand of hair in the middle of his beard. 'You look much better already,' K.'s uncle said, 'now that witch has left.' He stopped, whispered, 'I bet she's listening,' and leapt over to the door. But there was no one at the door. K.'s uncle came back, not disappointed but irritated—the fact that the nurse was *not* listening seemed an even worse piece of devilry to him. 'You misjudge her,' the lawyer said, without saying anything further to defend his nurse; perhaps that was to suggest she didn't need defending. But in a much more sympathetic tone he went on, 'As far as your nephew's business is concerned, I would consider myself very happy should my strength be up to this extremely difficult task. I'm very much afraid it won't be, but at the very least I will try everything possible; if I cannot manage, someone else could always be brought in. To be perfectly honest, I'm too interested in the case to forgo all participation in it. If it should prove to be too much for my heart, then at least that organ will have found a worthy occasion for its complete failure.' K. felt he couldn't understand a single word of all this, and looked to his uncle for an explanation. His uncle, however, simply sat, the candle in his hand, on the bedside table, from which one medicine bottle had already rolled off onto the floor, nodding at everything the lawyer said, agreeing with everything, and glancing up at K. now and then, inviting him to express the same agreement. Had his uncle perhaps told the lawyer about his trial beforehand? But that was impossible. Everything that had happened that afternoon spoke against it. 'I don't understand,' he therefore said. 'Oh, have I perhaps misunderstood you?' the lawyer asked, just as surprised and embarrassed as K. 'Perhaps I jumped to conclusions. What was it you wanted to talk to me about? I thought it was about your trial?' 'Of course,' said K.'s uncle, then asked K., 'What's the matter with you?' 'Yes, but how is it you know about me and my trial?' K. asked. 'Aha,' said the lawyer with a smile. 'I'm a lawyer, I associate with people connected with the courts, we talk about various trials, and one remembers the more striking ones, especially when they concern the nephew of a friend, there's nothing remarkable in that.' 'What's the matter with you?' K.'s uncle asked again. 'Can't you stay calm?' 'You associate with people from this court?' K. asked. 'Yes,' said the lawyer. 'That's the kind of question a child would ask,' K.'s uncle said. 'Who else should I associate with, if not with people in my own field?' the lawyer added. It sounded so irrefutable that K. didn't bother to answer. What he wanted to say was, 'But you work at the court in the Palace of Justice and not at the one in the loft,' but he couldn't bring himself actually to say it. 'You must remember—' the lawyer went on, as if it were a matter of course hardly worth the bother of mentioning, 'You must remember that I derive great and manifold benefits for my clientele from associating with these people, I don't have to keep going on about it. At the moment, of course, I'm a little restricted because of my illness, but despite that good friends from the court do come to visit me and I hear this and that. I perhaps even learn more than some who are in the best of health and spend the whole day at the court. Just at the moment, for example, a dear friend is visiting me.' He pointed to a dark corner of the room. 'Where is he, then?' K. asked, almost rudely because of his surprise. He looked round uncertainly; the light from the little candle didn't come anywhere near to reaching the wall opposite. Yes, something was beginning to move, there in the corner. In the light of the candle, which his uncle now held up high, an oldish man could be seen sitting at a little table. To have remained unnoticed for so long, he couldn't have been breathing at all. He stood up, making heavy weather of it, clearly unhappy that attention had been drawn to him. He flapped his hands like short wings, as if he wanted to wave away any introductions and greetings, as if he didn't want to disturb the others by his presence, and as if he were urgently begging to be returned to the dark and for his presence to be forgotten. It was, however, too late for that. 'You surprised us,' the lawyer explained, waving to the man to encourage him to come closer, which he did, slowly and looking round hesitantly, but still with a certain dignity. 'The head of administration*—oh, sorry, I haven't introduced you, this is my friend, Albert K., and this is his nephew, Josef K., a senior accountant with the bank—the head of administration has been kind enough to pay me a visit. Only someone who is acquainted with the courts and knows how snowed under with work the head of administration is can appreciate the value of such a visit. Well, he came despite that, and we were having a quiet conversation, as far as my weak state allowed. We hadn't forbidden Leni to admit visitors, since none were expected anyway, but we felt we should remain alone. But then came your thumps, Albert, and the head of administration moved to the corner, together with his chair and table. Now, however, it appears we may possibly, if that is what is desired, have a matter of common interest to discuss, in which case we might as well move closer together,' he said, indicating an armchair by the bed with a bow of the head and an obsequious smile to the head of administration. 'Unfortunately I can only stay for a few minutes,' the head of administration said in friendly tones, with a glance at the clock as he settled comfortably in the chair, 'business calls. But I wouldn't want to let slip the opportunity of getting to know a friend of my friend.' He inclined his head slightly in the direction of K.'s uncle, who seemed very satisfied with his new acquaintance but, due to his character, was incapable of expressing humble respects and accompanied the head of administration's words with embarrassed but loud laughter. Not a pleasant sight! K. was able to observe all this undisturbed, since no one bothered with him. As appeared to be his habit, the head of administration, once he had been drawn out, took command of the conversation, and the lawyer, whose initial weakness had perhaps only been a ploy to get rid of his new visitors, listened attentively, his hand behind his ear. K.'s uncle, the candle-bearer— he was balancing the candle on his thigh, the lawyer gave it frequent, worried glances—had soon overcome his embarrassment and was

delighted with both what the head of administration had to say and
the gentle, undulant gestures with which he accompanied it. K., who
was leaning against the bedpost, was completely ignored, perhaps
even deliberately, and served merely as an audience for the old men.
Anyway, he had hardly any idea what they were talking about; soon
his thoughts turned away, now to the nurse and the poor treatment
she had been subjected to by his uncle, now to the head of administration, wondering whether he had not seen him before, perhaps
even among those who had attended his first hearing. Perhaps he was
mistaken, but the head of administration would have fitted in perfectly with the old men with the sparse beards in the front row.

Then a sound like breaking china from the hall gave them all a start.
'I'll go and see what's happened,' said K., leaving the room slowly,
as if giving the others the opportunity to stop him. Scarcely had he
gone out into the hall and was trying to find his bearings in the darkness, when a small hand, much smaller than K.'s, was placed on the
hand with which he was still holding the door and quietly closed it.
It was the nurse, who had been waiting there. 'Nothing's happened,'
she whispered, 'I just threw a plate at the wall to get you to come out.'
Hardly knowing what to say, K. said, 'I was thinking of you too.' 'All
the better,' said the nurse, 'come.' After a few steps they came to a
frosted glass door, which the nurse opened, inviting K. to go in. It
must have been the lawyer's study; as far as could be seen in the
moonlight, by which only a small, square patch of floor below each
of the two large windows was brightly lit, it was full of old, heavy
furniture. 'Over here,' said the nurse, pointing to a dark chest with a
carved wooden backrest. Once he had sat down, K. looked round the
room. It was a large, high room, the lawyer's poverty-stricken clients
must feel lost in it. K. could almost see the small steps his clients took
to approach the massive desk. Then, however, he dismissed the thought
and only had eyes for the nurse, who was sitting close to him, almost
squeezing him up against the armrest. 'I thought you'd come out to
me by yourself,' she said, 'without my having to call you. It was strange.
When you first came in you couldn't take your eyes off me, then you
kept me waiting.—By the way, you can call me Leni,' she added
abruptly, speaking quickly as if not one moment of the conversation
was to be wasted. 'Willingly,' said K. 'As far as the strangeness is
concerned, Leni, that's easily explained. In the first place I had to
listen to the chatter of the two old gentlemen and couldn't leave

without good reason, and in the second place I'm not a brazen type, in fact I'm rather shy, nor did it look as if you could be won over on the spot.' 'That's not it,' said Leni, draping her arm over the backrest and looking at K., 'you didn't find me attractive then and you probably don't find me attractive now.' 'Being attractive isn't everything,' said K., evading the issue. 'Oh!' she said with a smile, gaining the upper hand slightly with K.'s remark and that little exclamation. That silenced K. for a while. Since by now he had become accustomed to the darkness in the room, he could see various details of the furnishings. He was particularly struck by a large picture to the right of the door, and he leant forward to have a better view of it. It represented a man in a judge's gown; he was sitting on a high, throne-like chair with gilding which stood out in many places. The unusual aspect was that the judge was not calm and dignified; he was clasping the back and arm of the chair firmly with his left arm, while his right arm was completely free, only the hand on the armrest, as if at any moment he was about to leap up* with a vehement and perhaps outraged gesture to say something decisive, or even pronounce sentence. Presumably you had to imagine the accused at the foot of the steps; just the top ones could be seen in the picture, covered by a gold carpet. 'Perhaps that's my judge,' said K., pointing a finger at the picture. 'I know him,' said Leni, looking up at the picture, 'he comes here quite often. The picture was painted when he was young, but he can never have looked anything like that, he's quite tiny. Despite that, he had himself stretched out in the picture, for he's ridiculously vain, like all of them here. But I'm vain as well, and very unhappy that you don't find me attractive.' To her last remark K.'s only response was to put his arm round her and draw her towards him; she quietly laid her head on his shoulder. To her comments on the judge, he said, 'What is his position?' 'He's an examining magistrate,' she said, taking the hand of the arm K. had round her and playing with his fingers. 'Only an examining magistrate again,' said K., disappointed, 'the senior officials keep out of sight. But look at the chair he's sitting on, it's like a throne!' 'That's all the artist's imagination,' said Leni, leaning over K.'s hand, 'in reality he sits on a kitchen chair with an old folded-up horse-blanket on it. But do you have to think about your trial all the time?' she added slowly. 'No, not at all,' said K., 'I probably think about it too little.' 'That's not the mistake you're making,' said Leni, 'you're too intransigent, that's what I've heard.' 'Who said that?'

asked K. He could feel her body against his chest, and was looking
down at her thick, dark, firmly plaited hair. 'It would be giving away
too much, if I told you that,' Leni replied. 'Please don't ask me for
names, but stop making this mistake, stop being intransigent, no one
can resist this court, you just have to confess. Confess at the next
opportunity. It's only then there's a possibility of escaping, only then,
though even that's not possible without outside help. But you needn't
worry about that, I'll provide the help myself.' 'You know a lot about
this court and the deceit that is necessary there,' said K., lifting her
up onto his lap, as she was pressing too hard against him. 'That's nice,'
she said, and sat up in his lap, smoothing her skirt and adjusting her
blouse. Then she clasped her hands behind his neck, leant back, and
gave him a long look. 'And if I don't confess, you won't be able to help
me?' K. asked tentatively. I'm enlisting women helpers, he thought
in mild surprise, first of all Fräulein Bürstner, then the usher's wife,
and now this little nurse, who seems to have an incomprehensible
desire for me. The way she sits in my lap, as if it's just the right place
for her! 'No,' Leni replied, shaking her head slowly, 'in that case
I can't help you. But you don't want my help, you don't care about
it, you're obstinate and can't be persuaded.—Have you got a lover?'
she asked after a short while. 'No,' K. said. 'Oh, yes, you have,' she
said. 'Yes, I have,' said K. 'Just imagine, I denied I have one and I've
even got a photo of her with me.' She asked to see it and he handed
her a photo of Elsa. She studied it, curled up in his lap. It was a
snapshot of Elsa after a whirling dance such as she liked to dance in
her wine-bar, the folds of her skirt still twisting round her from the
rotation; her hands were on her hips and she was looking to one side,
her neck stretched out, laughing. It was impossible to tell from the
picture at whom her laugh was directed. 'She's tightly laced,' Leni
said, pointing to the spot where, in her opinion, it could be seen. 'I don't
like her, she's clumsy and coarse. Perhaps towards you, however, she's
kind and gentle, you could deduce that from the picture. Would she
be capable of sacrificing herself for you?' 'No,' said K., 'she's neither
kind and gentle, nor would she sacrifice herself for me. Though I have
to say that so far I haven't asked the one or the other of her. No,
I haven't even looked at her photo before as closely as you have.' 'So
she doesn't mean much to you,' said Leni, 'she's not your lover at all,
then.' 'Yes she is,' said K. 'I don't go back on my word.' 'Maybe she's
your lover now,' said Leni, 'but you wouldn't miss her much if you were

to lose her or to exchange her for someone else, for me for example.'
'Certainly,' said K. with a smile, 'that is conceivable, but she has one
great advantage over you, she knows nothing of my trial, and even if
she did, she wouldn't think about it. She wouldn't try to persuade
me to submit.' 'That's not an advantage,' Leni said. 'If that's her
only advantage I won't lose heart. Has she got a physical defect?' 'A
physical defect?' K. asked. 'Yes,' said Leni, 'I've got a little defect
like that. Look.' She held the middle and ring fingers of her right
hand apart; the skin between them went up almost to the top joint of
her little fingers. 'What a trick of nature,' said K., adding, after he had
examined the whole of her hand, 'What a pretty claw!'* It was with
a kind of pride that Leni watched as K., in wonderment, kept pulling
her two fingers apart and putting them together again, until finally he
gave them a brief kiss and let go. 'Oh!' she immediately cried, 'you
kissed me!' Hastily, mouth open, she clambered up until she was
kneeling on his lap. K. looked up at her in some consternation. Now
she was so close to him he could smell the bitter, provocative odour
she exuded, like pepper. She took hold of his head, leant across him,
and bit and kissed his neck, even bit into his hair, crying from time
to time, 'You've swapped her for me, look, now you've swapped her
for me after all!' Her knee slipped, and with a little cry she almost fell
on the carpet. K. put his arms round her to stop her falling and was
pulled down on top of her. 'Now you belong to me,' she said.

'Here's the front-door key, come whenever you like,' were her last
words, and an aimless kiss landed on his back as he went. As he left
the house, light rain was falling. He was going to step out into the
middle of the street, so that he might perhaps see Leni at the window, when his uncle came rushing out of a taxi that had been waiting
outside the building, but which K. had been too distracted to notice.
His uncle grabbed him by the arms and pushed him back against the
door, as if he wanted to fix him to it. 'Nephew,' he cried, 'how could
you do that! You've done terrible damage to your case, which was
going well. You disappear with a grubby little tart, who, moreover,
is obviously the lawyer's mistress, and stay away for hours. You didn't
even look for a pretext, didn't keep it quiet, no, you just went to her
and stayed with her. And all the time we were sitting there together,
the uncle who is making such efforts for you, the lawyer who was to
be won over to your side, and, above all, the head of administration,
that important gentleman whose influence on your case is decisive at

its present stage. We wanted to discuss how we could help you; I had to treat the lawyer with care, as he did the head of administration, surely that was reason enough for you at least to support me. Instead you stayed absent, and eventually the cause couldn't be concealed. Now they are courteous men of the world, they didn't mention it, they spared me the embarrassment, but eventually even they found it too much for them, and since they couldn't talk about the case, they fell silent. We sat there for minutes on end listening to see if you were going to come back at last. Finally the head of administration, who'd stayed there much longer than he'd originally intended, got up and said goodbye, clearly feeling sorry for me without being able to help me. With an indulgence beyond belief, he waited a while longer in the doorway, then he left. Naturally I was glad he'd left, I could hardly breathe myself and the effect on the sick lawyer was even worse, the poor man couldn't even speak when I took my leave of him. You've probably helped bring about his complete collapse, and will thus have hastened the death of a man you're dependent on. And you left me, your uncle, to wait for hours out here in the rain, just feel, I'm completely sodden.'

The Lawyer · The Factory-Owner · The Painter

ONE winter's morning—outside snow was falling in the murky light—K. was in his office, feeling extremely tired already despite the early hour. In order to prevent himself from at least being disturbed by the clerks, he'd told the messenger not to let any of them in, because he was occupied with an important piece of work. But instead of working, he spun round in his chair, slowly rearranged objects on his desk, and then, without realizing it, left the whole of his arm stretched out across the desktop and sat there, motionless, his head bowed.

He couldn't get the trial out of his mind any more. Several times already he'd wondered whether it might not be a good idea to draw up a written statement and submit it to the court. His intention was to present a brief account of his life, explaining for every event that was in any way important why he'd acted as he had, whether he now looked on his course of action with approval or disapproval, and the reasons he could adduce for either conclusion. The advantages of submitting such a statement in his defence, as against simply being defended by the lawyer, who was open to criticism on other counts anyway, were indubitable. K. had no idea what steps the lawyer was taking; they certainly couldn't have amounted to very much, he hadn't asked him to come and see him for a month, and at none of their earlier meetings did K. have the impression that the man could do much for him. First and foremost, he had hardly questioned him at all. And there were so many questions that could be asked. Asking questions was the most important thing. K. had the feeling he could ask all the necessary questions himself. Instead of asking questions, the lawyer, on the other hand, talked about himself or sat there facing him in silence, leaning forward a little over the table, probably because of his poor hearing, tugging at a strand of his beard and looking down at the carpet, perhaps at the very spot where K. had lain with the nurse. Now and then he gave K. empty exhortations, such as one gives to children, and similarly useless and boring speeches, for which K. resolved not to pay one single penny when the final account came.

After the lawyer thought he had sufficiently humiliated him, he usually started to give him a little more encouragement. He'd already won many similar trials, he would tell him at such points, or at least partly won them, trials which, while in reality perhaps not so difficult as his, had looked as if they were even more hopeless. He had a list of them in the drawer there—at that, he would tap some drawer in his desk—unfortunately he couldn't show him the documents because of professional confidentiality. Still, the vast experience he had acquired through all these trials would of course benefit K. He had, he continued, naturally got down to work immediately, the first submission was almost finished. It was very important, because the first impression the defence made often determined the whole course of the trial. Unfortunately he had to point out to K. that it sometimes happened that first submissions to the court were not read at all. They were simply filed, and the officials declared that hearing and observing the accused was more important than any written material. If the petitioner was insistent they would add that, once all the material had been gathered and before a decision was reached, all the files, including the first submission, would naturally be reviewed as a whole. Unfortunately, he said, that too was mostly incorrect, the first submission was usually mislaid or completely lost, and even if it was kept right to the end it was hardly read, though he, the lawyer, had only heard rumours to that effect. All of this, he went on, was regrettable, but not entirely without justification. K. should not forget that the proceedings were not public; they could be made public, if the court considered that necessary, but it was not required by law. Consequently the court's papers, above all the indictment, were not available to the accused and his defence, so that in general they didn't know, or at least not precisely, what accusation the first submission was trying to refute. Therefore it was only a matter of chance if it should contain something that was important for the case. Truly pertinent and reasoned submissions could only be drawn up later, if, in the course of the examination of the accused, the individual charges and the grounds on which they were based became clearer or could be guessed at. Under those conditions the defence counsel was naturally in a very unfavourable and difficult position. But that, too, was the intention. A defence counsel was not expressly allowed by law, only tolerated, and even the question of whether that particular passage in the law could be interpreted as permitting toleration was a moot point. Therefore, strictly speaking there were no lawyers recognized by the court, all those who appeared before that court as attorneys were, basically, unregistered lawyers. That naturally had the effect of degrading the whole profession, and the next time K. visited the court offices he could have a look at the lawyers' room, just so that he'd seen it. He would probably be horrified at the company he would find gathered there. The narrow, low room they'd been allocated showed the contempt in which the court held those people. The only light came from a small skylight, which was so high up that if anyone wanted to look out—at which the smoke from a chimney just in front of it would fill his nostrils and blacken his face—he had to find a colleague to give him a piggyback. In the floor of this little room—to give just one further example of the conditions—was a hole that had been there for years, not big enough for someone to fall through, but big enough for one foot to get stuck in it. The lawyers' room was in the upper attic, so if one of them did get stuck, his foot would hang down in the lower attic, right in the middle of the corridor where their clients waited. The advocates were not going too far when they described such conditions as disgraceful. Complaints to the administration had not got them anywhere at all, and they were forbidden to change anything in the room at their own cost. But this treatment of the lawyers also had its reason. They wanted to eliminate the defence counsel as far as possible, everything should depend on the accused alone. Not an unreasonable point of view, basically, but nothing could be more wrong than to conclude that lawyers were unnecessary for the accused. On the contrary, there was no court where they were more necessary. In general, the proceedings were kept secret not only from the public but also from the accused. Only as far as possible, of course, but that was to a very great extent. The accused was not allowed to see the court documents either, and it was very difficult to deduce anything from the hearings about the documents on which they were based, especially for the accused, who was prejudiced and had all sorts of worries to distract him. That was where the defence counsel had a part to play. In general, defence counsels were not allowed to be present at the hearings, therefore they had to question the accused about the hearing after it, if possible at the door of the room where it had been held, and extract from these often very hazy reports anything that could be used by the defence. But that was not the most important thing, there was not much that could be learnt in that way, though of course there, as everywhere else, a competent man would learn more than others. It was the advocate's

personal contacts that were the most important, that was the main value
of a defence counsel. Now, he went on, K. had presumably deduced
from his own experiences that the lowest level of the court administration was not exactly perfect, had neglectful and venal employees,
which led to gaps in the strict cordon round the court. That was
where the majority of lawyers found their way in, that was where the
bribery and information-gathering went on, there had even been
cases—at least in earlier times—of files being stolen. It could not be
denied that in this way some surprising, advantageous results for the
accused could temporarily be achieved, and those petty lawyers would
go swaggering round with them, attracting new clients. But they meant
nothing—or nothing good—for the further course of the trial. It was
only honest personal contacts that were of real value, contacts with
senior officials, though of course that meant only the lower grade of
senior officials. That alone could influence the progress of the trial,
only imperceptibly at first, but more and more clearly later on. There
were naturally only a few lawyers who could do that, and here, he
said, K.'s choice was a very good one. There were perhaps only one or
two other lawyers who had such good contacts to show as Dr Huld.
They, of course, did not bother with the crew in the lawyers' room,
they had nothing to do with them. All the closer, however, were their
relationships with the court officials. It was not even always necessary
for Dr Huld to go to the court, to wait around in the antechambers
for the chance appearance of one of the examining magistrates and,
depending on his mood, achieve some usually only ostensible success,
perhaps not even that. No, as K. had seen for himself, the officials,
including quite senior ones, came to him and volunteered quite clear,
or at least easily interpreted, information, discussed the future course
of the trials, even, in individual cases, being persuaded by argument
and happy to accept another man's opinion. Though in that last
respect, he added, one should not put too much trust in them.
However definitely they expressed their new intention, which was
favourable to the defence, they were quite capable of going straight
back to their office and delivering a decision for the next day which
was the exact opposite and perhaps even more unfavourable to the
defendant than their initial intention, which they claimed to have
abandoned completely. Of course, he said, there was nothing one
could do about that, what they said in private had only been said in
private and could not be used in public argument, even if it wasn't in

The Trial

the interests of the defence to keep in favour with these gentlemen anyway. On the other hand, he went on, it was quite correct that they should maintain contact with defence counsel, naturally only with expert defence counsel, and that not merely out of sociability or friendship but because, in certain respects, they were dependent on them. It was here that the disadvantage of a court organization which insisted on secret proceedings from the very beginning made itself felt. The officials lacked any relationship with the people. They were well equipped to deal with the ordinary, average cases; a trial of that kind proceeded along its allotted way almost automatically, just needing a little push now and then. But when faced with the very simple cases, however, as well as with the especially difficult ones, they were often at a complete loss. Because they were stuck in their law day and night, they hadn't a true sense of human relationships, and that was a serious deficiency in such cases. Then they would come running to the lawyer for advice, and behind them would be a court usher carrying the documents which were usually so secret. Many a gentleman whom one would least have expected to see, he declared, could have been seen standing at that window staring out into the street despondently, while the lawyer was at his desk, studying the documents in order to give him some good advice. Moreover, it was such occasions that showed how uncommonly seriously these gentlemen took their work and how they succumbed to profound despair when confronted with obstacles they were, by their very nature, not qualified to deal with. In general their position was not an easy one, it would be an injustice to imagine theirs was an easy position. The hierarchy and upper echelons of the court were endless, stretching beyond the purview even of those who belonged to it. Proceedings in court were in general also kept secret from the lower officials, so that they could hardly ever follow the further progress of any case they were dealing with in its entirety; that meant that the court business turned up on their desk, often without their knowing where it came from, and went on its way without their knowing where it went. So these officials did not benefit from the lessons that could be learnt from the study of the individual stages of the trial, of the final verdict and the reasons behind it. They could only concern themselves with that part of the trial which the law apportioned them, and usually knew less of its further progress, of the results of their own work, than the defence, which as a rule stayed in contact with the accused almost to the end of the trial. So in that respect, too, they could gain valuable information from the defence counsel. Bearing all this in mind, was K. still surprised at how irritable the officials were, at the insulting manner in which they sometimes addressed the defendants? That happened to every one of them at some point or other. All the officials were irritated, even when they appeared to be calm. Naturally, it was the petty lawyers who bore the brunt of it. People recounted the following story, which had all the semblance of truth. An old official, a nice, quiet gentleman, had spent all day and night without interruption—the court officials were indeed harder-working than anyone else—studying a difficult case which had been made particularly complicated by the lawyer's submissions. Towards morning, after twenty-four hours of probably not very productive labour, he went to the entrance, where he lay in wait and threw every lawyer who tried to enter back down the stairs. The lawyers gathered on the landing below and discussed what to do. On the one hand, they hadn't any formal right to be admitted, so that they could hardly take legal steps against the official, and, as already mentioned, they had to be careful not to provoke the officials. On the other hand, any day they did not spend at the court was a day wasted, so it was very important for them to get in. Eventually they agreed that they would try to exhaust the old man. One lawyer after the other was sent out to climb the stairs and allow himself, while offering as much, though only passive, resistance as possible, to be thrown down to the bottom, where he was caught by his colleagues. This lasted for about an hour, after which the old man, already weary from working through the night, did actually become completely exhausted and returned to his office. Initially those below could hardly believe it, and first of all sent out one of their number to see if there really was no one behind the door. Only then did they go in, and probably didn't even dare to grumble about it. The last thing the lawyers—even the least of them had some idea of the situation—would want to do would be to bring about any improvements to the court; on the other hand—and that was typical—almost every defendant, even very simple people, started thinking up suggestions for improvements the moment they became involved in the trial, and often wasted time and energy on it which could have been put to better use. The only correct approach was to accept things as they were. Even if it were possible to improve minor details—which, however, was a foolish superstition—one would at best have achieved something for future cases, but one would have done immeasurable harm to one's own case by attracting the attention of the vindictive officials. The essential thing was not to attract attention, to stay calm, however much it went against the grain, to try to understand that this great legal organism remained eternally in balance, so to speak. If, of your own volition, you changed something at the place you occupied, you would be cutting the ground from under your own feet and might well fall, whilst the great organism could easily find a replacement for the minor disruption at some other part—everything was interconnected—and remained unchanged, assuming it did not, as was in fact likely, become even more self-enclosed, even more vigilant, even more severe, even more malevolent. One should leave the work to the lawyer instead of hindering it. Reproaches never achieved very much, especially when it was impossible to make the full significance of the grounds for them clear, but it had to be said that K. had seriously harmed his case by the way he had behaved towards the head of administration. That influential man could be as good as struck off the list of those who could be approached to do something for K. He deliberately ignored even casual mentions of the trial. In many respects the officials were like children. Often they could be so offended by what were harmless actions—which, however, was not how one would describe K.'s behaviour—that they would even stop speaking to close friends, turn away when they met them, and work against them in all kinds of ways. Then, however, it could happen that a little joke, which one only ventured to make because everything else seemed hopeless, brought a laugh to their lips and they were reconciled. It was, he went on, at the same time difficult and easy to get on with them, there were hardly any principles one could follow. Sometimes it amazed you that a single ordinary life was sufficient to comprehend enough to be able to work there with a certain amount of success. There were, of course, grim times such as everyone had, when you thought you had not achieved anything at all, when it seemed as if only those trials reached a satisfactory con-clusion which had been destined to do so from the very beginning and would have done so without any assistance, while all the others had been lost despite all your attentions, all your efforts, all the little apparent successes with which you were so pleased. Then one felt that nothing was certain, and if you were asked you wouldn't even dare to deny that trials which were going well, because that was the kind of trial they were, had taken a wrong turn through your help. That too showed a kind of self-confidence, but it was the only kind you were left with. Lawyers were particularly prone to such attacks— naturally they were only attacks, nothing more—when a trial, which they had handled for some time, and satisfactorily, was suddenly taken out of their hands. That was probably the worst thing that could happen to a lawyer. Not that the trial was taken away from him by the defendant, that surely never happened, once a defendant had taken a particular lawyer he had to stay with him, come what may. How could he survive alone, once he'd enlisted a lawyer's help? The trial and the defendant and everything were simply taken away from the lawyer, and even the best contacts with the officials were of no use, for they knew nothing about it themselves. It was just that the trial had reached a stage at which no more help was allowed, at which it was processed by inaccessible courts where even the defendant was beyond the reach of the lawyer. You came home one evening and on your table you found all the submissions relating to the case into which you had put such hopes and such hard work; they had been returned because they were not allowed to be transferred to the new stage the trial had reached, they were nothing but scrap paper now. That didn't necessarily mean the trial was lost, not at all, at least there was no compelling reason to assume that, it was just that you didn't know about the trial any more, nor hear any more about it either. Fortunately such cases were exceptions, and even if K.'s trial were such a case, he went on, it was far from having reached that stage at the moment. There was still ample opportunity for a lawyer to do his work, and K. could rest assured that it was an opportunity that would be taken. As he had said, the submission had not yet been handed in, but that wasn't urgent, much more important were the preliminary discussions with influential officials, and those had already taken place. With varying success, as he was ready to admit. It was, he said, much better not to reveal the details for the moment, they might have an unfortunate influence on K., arousing too many hopes or too many fears; all that he would say was that some had expressed themselves very favourably and shown themselves to be very willing, while others had expressed themselves less favourably but had by no means refused their aid. The overall result, then, was very gratifying, only one shouldn't draw any particular conclusions from that, since preliminary negotiations always began similarly, and it was only the further development that revealed the value of those preliminary negotiations. At least nothing had been lost yet and if they should succeed in winning over the head of administration— various steps had been set in motion to that end—then the whole business was a clean wound, as the surgeons said, and they could await further developments with confidence.

The lawyer could go on at interminable length about these and similar matters. It happened at every visit. There was always some progress that had been made, but K. could never be told what kind of progress. The first submission was constantly being worked on but was never completed, which, at his next visit, usually turned out to be of great advantage, since the preceding weeks would have been a very unfavourable time to hand it in, although that could not have been foreseen. If K., wearied by all the talk, happened to remark that things were proceeding at a very slow pace, even considering all the difficulties, he was told that things were not proceeding slowly at all, but that they would certainly have got much farther if K. had consulted the lawyer promptly. That he had unfortunately neglected to do, and his neglect would entail further disadvantages, not only in the matter of time.

The sole agreeable distraction during these visits was Leni, who always managed to arrange matters so that she brought the lawyer his tea while K. was there. Then she would stand behind K. and surreptitiously let him take her hand, while appearing to watch the lawyer as he, bending low over the cup with a kind of craving, poured the tea and drank it. There was complete silence. The lawyer drank, K. squeezed Leni's hand, and sometimes Leni went so far as to stroke K.'s hair gently. 'You're still here?' the lawyer would ask when he'd finished his tea. 'I wanted to remove the tea things,' said Leni, giving K. one last squeeze of the hand as the lawyer wiped his mouth and started to go on at him with renewed vigour.

Was the lawyer's aim reassurance or despair? K. couldn't say, but he soon considered it a fact that his defence was not in good hands. Everything the lawyer said might well be true, even if it was plain to see that he was trying to push himself forward as much as possible; he had probably never before been involved in such an important trial as K. believed his own to be. His constant stressing of his personal contacts with the officials was suspicious. Did that mean they were exploited to K.'s advantage alone? The lawyer never forgot to mention that they were only lower-ranking officials, that is, officials in very subordinate positions for whose advancement certain developments in the trials might be important. Did they perhaps make use of the lawyer to bring about such developments, which would, of course, always be to the defendant's disadvantage? Perhaps they didn't do that in every trial, no, that wasn't likely, there were presumably trials in the course of which they granted the lawyer concessions in return for his services, since it must be important for them to keep his reputation unblemished. If that were indeed the case, in what way would they intervene in K.'s trial, which, as the lawyer explained, was a very difficult and therefore important trial, and had aroused great interest in the court from the very beginning? There could not be much doubt as to what they would do. One could see signs of it in the fact that the first submission had still not been handed in, even though the trial had been going on for months already, and that everything, according to what the lawyer said, was still in the initial stages. All this was naturally calculated to lull the accused into a false sense of security and keep him defenceless, only to catch him unawares with the verdict, or at least with the announcement that the results of the hearing, which had gone against him, were being passed on to the higher courts.

It was absolutely essential for K. to take things into his own hands. He was utterly convinced of this, particularly at times when, as on that winter morning, he was overcome with weariness and had no power to control the thoughts going round and round in his head. The contempt with which he had formerly regarded the trial had gone. If he had been alone in the world it would have been easy to ignore the trial, though it was also certain that in that case the trial would never have come about. But now that his uncle had dragged him off to the lawyer, family considerations were involved; his position at the bank was no longer completely independent of the course of the trial, he himself had incautiously, and with a certain inexplicable self-satisfaction, mentioned the trial to acquaintances, and others had heard about it in ways that were unknown to him; his relationship with Fräulein Bürstner seemed to vary according to the way the trial was going—in brief, he hardly had the choice of accepting or rejecting the trial any more, he was right in the middle of it and had to put up a fight.

For the moment, however, there was no reason for excessive concern. He had managed to work his way up to his present senior position in the bank in a relatively short time, and to maintain himself in that position, respected by all his colleagues. Now it was simply a matter of applying a little of the ability that had enabled him to get so far to the trial, and there was no doubt everything would turn out well. Above all, it was essential, if he was to get anywhere, to discount from the outset any suggestion that he might be guilty. Guilt did not come into it. The trial was nothing more than a piece of business, such as he had often transacted with profit for the bank, a piece of business fraught, as was always the case, with various dangers which had to be averted. To that end he must not even toy with the thought of guilt, but hold as fast as he could to the thought of his own advantage. From that perspective he had no alternative but to dismiss the lawyer as soon as possible, at best that very evening. From what he had told him, it was an unheard-of and probably very insulting action, but K. refused to allow his efforts in the trial to come up against obstacles which might even have been put in his way by his own lawyer. Once his lawyer had been discarded, however, the submission had to be handed in immediately and pressure brought to bear every day, as far as possible, to get them to consider his submission. To achieve that it would, of course, not be sufficient for K. to sit in the corridor like the others, with his hat under the bench. He himself, or the women or other emissaries, would have to importune the officials every day and compel them to sit down at their desks and study K.'s submission, instead of staring through the slats out into the corridor. These efforts had to be unremitting, everything had to be organized and monitored. For once the court was going to find itself confronted by a defendant who knew how to stand up for his rights.

Even though K. was confident of his ability to carry all this out, the difficulty of drawing up the submission was immense. Earlier, until about a week before, it had only been with a feeling of shame that he had been able to contemplate being compelled at some point to write the submission himself, but he had never imagined it could be difficult. He remembered how, one afternoon when he had been snowed under with work, he had suddenly pushed everything to one side and taken out his writing-pad to rough out a possible line of thought for such a submission, which he might then put at the disposal of the sluggish lawyer; at that very moment the door to the managerial suite had opened and the deputy manager had emerged, laughing loudly. It had been very embarrassing for K., even though the deputy manager had not been laughing at his submission, but at a joke he had just heard, a joke which, in order to be explained, needed a drawing, which the deputy manager, bending over K.'s desk and taking K.'s pencil out of his hand, proceeded to draw on the writing-pad K. had intended to use for his submission.

Now K. was beyond shame, the submission had to be prepared. If he couldn't find the time to do it in the office, which was very likely, he would have to do it at home, during the night. If that didn't allow him enough time, he would have to take some leave. No half-measures, it was not only in business that this applied but in everything, all the time. Though preparing the submission was an almost unending task. You didn't have to lack self-confidence to quickly come to feel it was impossible ever to complete the submission. Not out of laziness or deceitfulness, which might be what prevented the lawyer from completing it, but because, ignorant as he was of the charges against him, not to mention any possible extension of them, he would have to pass his whole life in review and describe it right down to the very last detail. And what a sad task that was as well. It was perhaps a suitable occupation for retirement, to help pass the long days once his mind had grown senile and childish. But now, at a time when K. needed to concentrate wholly on his work, when, as he was still climbing the ladder and already represented a threat to the deputy manager, every hour passed with the utmost swiftness, and when, as a young man, he wanted to enjoy the short evenings and nights, now he had to start drawing up this submission. Once more his reflections had ended in lamentation. Almost automatically, simply to put an end to it, his finger felt for the button of the electric bell in the outer office. As he pressed it, he looked up at the clock. It was eleven, he'd dreamt away two hours of valuable time, and was naturally even more weary than before. At least it wasn't wasted time, he'd made decisions which could be useful. Apart from various letters, the messenger brought the visiting-cards of two men who had already been kept waiting for some considerable time to see K. As it happened, they were very important customers of the bank who should on no account have been kept waiting. Why did they have to come at such an inconvenient time and why, the men seemed to be asking themselves behind the closed door, was such a hard-working executive as K. wasting the best hours of the day for business on his private affairs? Tired from what he had already been through, and tired at the thought of what was to come, K. stood up to welcome the first of them.

This was a small, jolly man, a factory-owner whom K. knew well. He apologized for interrupting K. while he was occupied with important work, and K., for his part, apologized for having kept the factory-owner waiting so long. But even his apology was spoken so mechanically, and with almost the wrong emphasis, that the factory-owner would certainly have noticed if he hadn't been so preoccupied with the business that had brought him there. Instead, he started pulling calculations and tables of figures out of his pockets and spread them out before K., explaining various items, correcting a minor error, which he noticed even though he only glanced over the material, and reminding K. of a similar transaction he had concluded with him about a year ago, casually remarking that this time another bank was keen to take on the business at a very advantageous rate; finally he fell silent, awaiting K.'s opinion on the matter. Initially K. had indeed followed the factory-owner's explanations quite clearly, he too had been gripped by the thought of the important piece of business, only not for long, unfortunately, soon he had stopped listening; for a while he had nodded at the factory-owner's louder exclamations, but eventually he stopped doing even that and had confined himself to staring at the bald head bent over the papers, wondering when the factory-owner would finally come to see that all his talk was pointless. When the latter fell silent, K. at first actually thought it was to give him the opportunity of admitting that he was incapable of listening. It was only with regret that he realized from the expectant look of the factory-owner, who was clearly prepared for all possible responses, that he had to continue the business discussion. So he bowed his head, as if responding to an order, picked up his pencil, and began to pass it slowly to and fro over the papers, stopping now and then and staring at a figure. The factory-owner suspected he had objections, perhaps the figures really didn't add up, perhaps they weren't the decisive factor; whatever the case, the factory-owner placed his hand over the papers and, moving quite close to K., started to give a general description of the proposal again.

'It's difficult,' said K., pursing his lips and slumping onto the arm of his chair, since the only thing he could fix on, the papers, were covered over. He only glanced up vaguely even when the door to the managerial suite opened and the deputy manager appeared, not very clearly, as if behind a gauze veil. K. gave it no further thought, but merely observed the immediate effect, which was very welcome to him, since straight away the factory-owner sprang up from his chair and scurried over to the deputy manager. K., however, would have liked him to do it ten times more swiftly, for he was afraid the deputy manager might disappear again. His fear was unfounded, the two men shook hands and came over to K.'s desk together. The factory-owner complained that the senior accountant had shown little enthusiasm for the project, and pointed at K. who, feeling the deputy manager's eyes on him, bent over the papers again. When the two of them leant on the desk and the factory-owner set about trying to win over the deputy manager, K. felt as if two men, whose height he exaggerated in his imagination, were discussing what should be done with him over his head. Cautiously turning his eyes upward, he tried to find out what was happening up there, took, without looking, one of the documents off the desk, placed it on the flat of his hand, and gradually raised it as he stood up himself to join the other two. He had no specific idea in mind as he did this, just the feeling that this was the attitude he would have to adopt once he had completed the great submission which would completely exonerate him. The deputy manager, who was concentrating fully on his discussion, just glanced briefly at the document and, without reading what was in it—what was important to the senior accountant was unimportant to him—took it out of K.'s hand, said, 'Thank you, I know everything already,' and calmly placed it back on the table. K. gave him a resentful sidelong glance, but the deputy manager didn't notice it, or, if he did, was only encouraged by it. He kept laughing out loud, and once clearly embarrassed the factory-owner by a quick-witted response, but immediately allowed him to recover by producing an objection to his own objection, and eventually invited him into his office, where they could conclude the business. 'It's a very important matter,' he said to the factory-owner, 'I fully realize that. And I'm sure our senior accountant'—even when he said this he was really only talking to the factory-owner—'will be glad if we take it off his hands. It requires calm consideration, and he seems rather overloaded with work today. Some people have been waiting for hours in the outer office to see him.' K. still had just about enough control over himself to turn away from the deputy manager and direct his friendly but fixed smile at the factory-owner alone; otherwise he made no attempt to involve himself, merely rested both hands on the desk, leaning forward slightly like a clerk at his high desk, and watched the two men as, still talking, they picked up the documents and went into the managerial suite. The factory-owner turned round in the doorway and said he would, of course, come back to tell the senior accountant the result of their meeting, adding that he also had a small matter to communicate to him.

At last K. was alone. He had no intention of admitting another client, and he was aware, though only vaguely, how pleasant it was that the people outside believed he was still dealing with the factory-owner and therefore no one, not even the messenger, could come in. He went to the window and sat on the windowsill, holding onto the catch with one hand and looking out over the square. The snow was still falling, it hadn't brightened up at all.

He sat there for a long time without really knowing what it was that was worrying him. From time to time he started slightly and looked over his shoulder at the door to the outer office, where he mistakenly thought he'd heard a noise. Since no one came, he calmed down. He went over to the washstand, washed himself in cold water, and returned to his seat by the window with a freezing-cold head. The decision to take over his defence himself now seemed more serious than he had originally assumed. Basically, as long as he had left his defence to the lawyer he had not been much affected by the trial; he had observed it from a distance and it had scarcely touched him directly, he could check how his case stood whenever he liked, but he could also pull back whenever he liked. Now, on the other hand, if he were to conduct his defence himself, he would have to put himself completely at the mercy of the court, at least for the time being. The purpose of this was, of course, to bring about his later absolute and final release, but to achieve that he had for the moment put himself in even greater danger than before. Had he had any doubts about that, today's encounter with the deputy manager and the factory-owner would have convinced him otherwise. The way he had sat there, completely preoccupied with the decision to conduct his defence himself! And how would it be in future? What times were in store for him! Would he find the path that would take him through everything to a happy end? Did not a carefully prepared defence— and anything else was pointless—did not a carefully prepared defence of necessity mean he had to cut himself off as far as possible from everything else? Would he come through it all safe and sound? And how could he manage to achieve all this while still in the bank? It was not only a matter of the submission—a period of leave would probably have been enough for that, even though a request for leave would have been a great risk just at the moment—it was the whole trial, and it was impossible to say how long that would last. What an obstruction had suddenly been placed in the way of K.'s career!

And he was expected to work for the bank at a time like this? He looked across at his desk. He was expected to receive clients and discuss business with them at a time like this? While his trial was inexorably pursuing its course, while the court officials were sitting over the trial documents up there in the loft? Did it not look like a torture, approved by the court, which was connected with his trial and accompanied it? And would the bank, for example, take account of his particular situation in the appraisal of his work? Never! His trial was not entirely unknown, but so far it was not quite clear who knew about it and how much they knew. The rumour couldn't have reached the deputy manager yet, otherwise it would have been obvious that he was using it against K., contrary to the demands of loyalty to one's colleagues and common humanity. And the manager? True, he was well disposed towards K., and once he heard about the trial he would probably want to relieve K. of some of his responsibilities, as far as that lay in his power, but he would certainly not be able to push that through, for at the moment, since the counterweight that K. had up to this point represented was starting to weaken, he was increasingly subject to the influence of the deputy manager, who, moreover, was exploiting the manager's ill health in order to strengthen his own position. So what was there left for K. to look forward to? Perhaps such reflections weakened his power of resistance, but, on the other hand, it was vitally important not to deceive himself and to see everything as clearly as was possible at that moment.

Without any particular reason, just so that he didn't have to go back to his desk for the time being, he opened the window. It was difficult to open, he had to use both hands to turn the catch. Then the fog mixed with smoke* poured in through the whole width and height of the window, filling the room with a faint smell of burning. A few snowflakes were blown in too. 'A horrible autumn,' came the voice of the factory-owner from behind K. He'd come into the room from the deputy manager's office unnoticed. K. nodded, giving his briefcase an uneasy glance. Presumably the factory-owner would now take out the documents to inform K. of the result of his discussions with the deputy manager. However the factory-owner, following the direction of K.'s glance, patted his briefcase and said, without opening it, 'You want to hear the result. Tolerable. The deal's almost in the bag. A delightful man, your deputy manager, but you have to watch him.' He laughed, shook K.'s hand, and tried to get him to laugh too. But now the fact that the factory-owner didn't show him the papers made K. suspicious, and he found nothing to laugh at in his remark. 'Herr K.,' said the factory-owner, 'you must be a bit under the weather. You look so depressed today.' 'Yes,' said K., clasping his forehead, 'a headache, family worries.' 'Quite right,' said the factory-owner, who was always in a hurry and couldn't wait calmly for another person to finish, 'everyone has his cross to bear.' K. had automatically taken a step towards the door, as if to see him out, but the factory-owner said, 'I have something to tell you, Herr K. I'm very much afraid I'm being a nuisance, telling it you today, but I've seen you twice recently and forgotten it both times. If I put it off again it will probably be no use to you at all. That would be a pity, for what I have to tell you is perhaps not without value.' Without giving K. time to reply, the factory-owner came up close to him, gently tapped him on the chest with his knuckle, and said quietly, 'You have a trial, haven't you?' K. stepped back and immediately cried, 'The deputy manager told you that.' 'Not at all,' said the factory-owner, 'how should the deputy manager know?' 'But how do you know?' K. asked, already much calmer. 'I hear things about the court now and then,' the factory-owner said, 'and that is what I wanted to tell you about.' 'So many people have connections with the court!' K. said, his head bowed, taking the factory-owner across to his desk. They sat down in the chairs they had previously sat in, and the factory-owner said, 'There's not a lot I can tell you, I'm afraid, but in such matters one should not ignore the least detail. Moreover I feel I want to help you, however modest my assistance. We've always been good business partners, haven't we? Well—' K. wanted to apologize for his behaviour during the earlier meeting, but the factory-owner refused to be interrupted. He pushed his briefcase tight under his armpit, to show that he was in a hurry, and went on, 'I heard about your trial from a certain Titorelli.* He's a painter, Titorelli's just what he calls himself as an artist, what his real name is I don't know. For years he's been coming to my office now and then bringing little pictures—he's almost a beggar—for which I give him a small sum out of charity. They're pretty pictures, by the way, landscapes, 'Sunset Over the Heath', that kind of thing. These sales became a matter of routine and passed off smoothly. Once, however, they started to get too frequent, I complained, and we got talking. I was interested to know how he could support himself from his painting alone, and was astonished to learn that his main source of income was from portraits. He worked for the court, he told me. For which court, I asked. So then he told me about the court. You yourself will be best placed to imagine how astonished I was at what I heard. Since then I get some news from the court every time he comes to see me, and have thus gradually acquired some understanding of what goes on there. I have to say, though, that Titorelli's very garrulous and I often have to turn him away, not only because I'm sure he sometimes lies, but above all because I'm a businessman and have my own worries, which are almost too much for me, and cannot concern myself overly with other people's affairs. But that's just by the way. Perhaps—this was my idea—Titorelli could be of some assistance to you. He knows lots of judges, and even if it turns out that he doesn't have much influence himself, he can surely give you advice on how to approach various influential people. And even if this advice should not of itself prove decisive, it will, in my opinion, be of great importance for you to possess it. You're almost a lawyer. I always say: "Herr K.'s almost a lawyer." Oh, I'm not worried about your trial. But will you go and see Titorelli? If I recommend you, I'm sure he'll do everything he can. I really think you should go. It doesn't have to be today, of course, some time, any time. I feel I should add that the fact that it is I who am giving you this advice does not in the least commit you actually to visit Titorelli. No, if you think you can do without Titorelli, it will certainly be better to ignore him completely. Perhaps you have a precise plan, and Titorelli might get in the way of it. In that case, naturally you mustn't go. And I'm sure it goes against the grain to accept advice from a fellow like that. It's up to you. Here's the letter of recommendation, and this is the address.'

Disappointed, K. took the letter and put it in his pocket. At best, the advantage he could derive from the recommendation would bear no relation to the damage done by the fact that the factory-owner knew about his trial and that the painter would spread the news

further abroad. He had to force himself to say a few words of thanks
to the factory-owner, who was already on his way to the door. 'I will
go,' he assured him as he said goodbye to the factory-owner at the
door, 'or, since I'm very busy, write and ask him to come and see me
in my office.' 'I knew you'd find the best solution,' said the factory-
owner, 'though I think it would be better if you didn't invite people
like this Titorelli to the bank to discuss your trial with them here. It
isn't always a good idea to put people like that in possession of a letter
from you. But I'm sure you'll have thought everything through, and
know what you should or should not do.' K. nodded, and accompanied the factory-owner through the outer office as well. Despite his
appearance of calm, he was horrified at himself. He had actually only
said he would write to Titorelli as a way of showing the factory-owner
that he appreciated his recommendation and had immediately set about
thinking about possible ways of meeting Titorelli. But if he had
believed Titorelli's support would be valuable, he would not have
hesitated to write to him at once. And it had only been the factory-
owner's comment that had made him aware of the dangers that might
entail. Had he already reached a point where he could put so little
reliance on his own judgement? If it was possible for him to send a
clear letter inviting a dubious individual to come to the bank and,
separated solely by a door from the deputy manager, request advice
about his trial from him, was it not possible, even probable, that he
was failing to see other dangers or even rushing straight into them?
There would not always be someone there to warn him. And it was
now, when he needed all his faculties about him, that these usually
alien doubts about his own alertness had to appear! Were the difficulties he felt doing his work for the bank about to start affecting his
trial? Now he simply could not understand how it had been possible
for him to even think of writing to Titorelli and inviting him to come
to the bank.

He was still shaking his head at this when the messenger came up
to him and pointed out the three men who were sitting on the bench
there in the outer office. They had been waiting a long time to see K.
Now that the messenger was talking to K., they had stood up, each
one trying to take advantage of a favourable opportunity to get hold
of K. before the others. Since the bank was so lacking in consideration as to make them waste their time there in the waiting-room, they
were not going to show consideration either. 'Herr K.,' one of them

was already saying, but K. had told the messenger to bring his coat, and said to all three of them, as he put it on with the help of the messenger, 'You must excuse me, gentlemen, unfortunately I haven't time to see you at the moment. I do apologize, but I have to go out immediately on urgent business. You'll have seen yourselves how long I've been held up. Would you be so good as to come back tomorrow, or at some other time? Or should we perhaps deal with your business by telephone? Or would you like to tell me here briefly what it's about, and I'll reply in full by letter? Though the best thing would be if you came back in the next few days.' The men, whose wait had now turned out to be completely fruitless, were so astonished at K.'s suggestions that all they could do was stare at each other in silence. 'That's agreed then?' K. asked, turning to the messenger who had brought him his hat. Through the open door into K.'s office the snow could be seen falling more heavily, so K. turned up the collar of his coat and buttoned it right up to the neck.

Just then the deputy manager came out of the adjoining room, smiled when he saw K. in his winter coat talking to the men, and asked, 'You're going out now, Herr K.?' 'Yes,' said K., straightening up, 'I have some business to attend to.' But the deputy manager had already turned to the three men who were waiting. 'What about these gentlemen?' he asked. 'I believe you've been waiting a long time.' 'We've already made arrangements,' said K., but now the men refused to hold back any longer. They surrounded K., declaring that they wouldn't have waited for hours if their business hadn't been important and required immediate and detailed discussion in a personal interview. The deputy manager listened to them for a while and observed K. as well, who was holding his hat and cleaning off the dust in places, then he said, 'Gentlemen, there's a simple solution. If you're willing to make do with me, I'd be happy to take over the discussions in place of Herr K. We are just as much businessmen as you and know how valuable a businessman's time is. Would you step this way, please?' And he opened the door leading to his outer office.

How good the deputy manager was at taking over all the things K. was now forced to give up! But was K. not giving up more than was absolutely necessary? While he was going off to see an unknown painter, in whom he put vague and, he had to admit, very slight hopes, his reputation in the bank was suffering irreparable damage. It would probably have been much better to take off his winter coat and win

back at least the two men who would still have to wait in the adjoining room. K. would perhaps have tried that, if he hadn't caught sight
of the deputy manager in his office looking for something on the
bookshelves as if they were his own. As K., agitated, approached the
door, he said, 'Ah, you haven't left yet.' The many lines in the face
that turned towards him seemed to betoken strength rather than age.
Immediately the deputy manager returned to his search. 'I'm looking
for the copy of a contract,' he said, 'which the representative of the
firm says you have. Won't you help me look?' K. took a step forward,
but the deputy manager said, 'Thanks, I've found it,' and went back
into his office carrying a large package of documents which must
have contained much more than just the contract.

'I'm not a match for him just at the moment,' K. said to himself,
'but once my personal difficulties are out of the way, he'll be the first
to feel the effects, and pretty sharply too.' Calmed a little by these
reflections, he told the messenger, who had been holding the door to
the corridor open for him for a long time, to inform the manager,
when the opportunity arose, that he was out on business, and left the
bank, almost happy at being able to devote himself more completely
to his case for a while.

He took a cab at once to the painter, who lived in a district on the
opposite side of town from that where the court offices were. It was
an even poorer area, the houses even darker, the streets full of rub-
bish slowly floating round on the melted snow. In the building where
the painter lived only one of the big double doors was open; at the
bottom of the other, beside the wall, a hole had been broken from
which, as K. approached, a revolting yellow, smoking liquid shot out,
sending a rat scurrying for the nearby drain. At the bottom of the
steps a child was lying on its belly, crying, but it could hardly be
heard because of the noise from the plumber's workshop on the other
side of the doors which drowned out everything. The door to the
workshop was open. Three apprentices were standing in a semicircle
round some piece of work and hitting it with hammers. A large sheet
of tinplate hanging on the wall threw a pale light between two of the
apprentices, lighting up their faces and aprons. K. merely glanced at
it all, he wanted to get this over with as quickly as possible, just ask
the painter a few penetrating questions and go back to the bank
straight away. He was determined that the merest hint of success
here would have a positive influence on his work at the bank that

same day. On the third floor he had to slow down, he was out of breath, the storeys were excessively high, the stairs steep, and he had been told the painter lived in an attic right at the top. The air was very oppressive as well, there was no stairwell, the narrow stairs were enclosed on both sides by walls, with only the occasional tiny window almost right at the top.

While K. was standing still for a moment, a few girls came running out of one of the flats and hurried, laughing, up the stairs. K. followed them slowly. He caught up with one of the girls, who had stumbled and fallen behind the others, and asked her, as they continued up the stairs beside each other, 'Does a painter called Titorelli live here?' At that the girl, hardly thirteen and slightly hunchbacked, jabbed him with her elbow and gave him a sidelong look. Neither her young years nor her physical defect had prevented her from becoming quite depraved already. She didn't even smile, but regarded K. seriously, with a sharp, provocative look. K. pretended not to notice and asked, 'Do you know Titorelli, the painter?' She nodded and put a question herself: 'What do you want from him?' It seemed to K. a good opportunity to quickly find out a bit about Titorelli. 'I want him to paint me,' he said. 'Paint you?' she asked, opening her mouth as wide as she could and flapping her hand at K., as if he'd said something exceptionally surprising or inept, lifted up her skirt, which was very short anyway, with both hands, and ran as fast as she could after the other girls, whose cries were already fading to indistinctness far above. At the next turn of the stairs, however, K. encountered all the girls again. The hunchback had obviously told them what K. intended to do, and they were waiting for him. They stood on either side of the staircase, pressing back against the wall to let K. pass comfortably, and smoothing their pinafores. Their expressions, as well as the way they lined the stairs, showed a mixture of childishness and depravity. The hunchbacked girl now assumed the leadership of the group and led them as they set off behind K., laughing. It was due to her that K. found the right way at once. He was going to keep on straight ahead up the stairs, but she indicated that he should take a branch off them to get to Titorelli. The stairs up to his flat were particularly narrow and very long, with no turns; the whole flight could be seen, ending at Titorelli's door. This door, relatively brightly lit* compared with the rest of the staircase by a small, crooked skylight, was made of unpainted planks, on which the name Titorelli was written

in red with broad brushstrokes. K. and his retinue were scarcely half-
way up the stairs when, clearly because of the sound of all the steps,
the door at the top was opened a little and a man, seemingly only wearing his nightshirt, appeared in the gap. 'Oh!' he exclaimed, when he
saw the throng coming, and disappeared. The hunchback clapped
her hands in delight, and the other girls crowded together and jostled
K. to make him go more quickly.

They hadn't even reached the top when the painter opened the
door wide and, with a low bow, invited K. to enter. The girls, on the
other hand, were waved away, he refused to let any of them in, however much they begged and however much they tried to get in, if not
with his permission, then against his will. Only the hunchback managed to slip through underneath his outstretched arm, but the
painter raced after her, grabbed her by her dress, whirled her round
once, then deposited her outside the door with the other girls, who
had not ventured to cross the threshold after the painter abandoned
his post. K. didn't know what to make of all this, it looked as if
everything was being done in an amicable spirit. One after the other,
the girls by the door stretched their necks, calling out various things,
meant as a joke, to the painter; he laughed too, and the girl he was
holding almost flew through the air. Then he shut the door, bowed
once more to K., held out his hand, and introduced himself, saying,
'Titorelli, artist.' K. pointed at the door, behind which the girls
could be heard whispering, and said, 'You seem to be very popular
here.' 'Oh, the little rascals!' said the painter, trying in vain to button
up his nightshirt at the neck. Otherwise he was barefoot and wore
just a pair of wide, yellowish linen trousers, fastened by a belt with a
long end dangling to and fro. 'Those rascals are a real pest,' he went
on, giving up trying to fasten his nightshirt, the top button of which
had just come off. He fetched a chair and insisted K. sit down. 'I once
painted one of them—she isn't with them today—and since then
they're all of them after me. When I'm here, they only come in when
I let them, but once I'm out there's always at least one here. They've
had a key to my door made and they lend it out to each other. You
can hardly imagine what a nuisance it is. For example, I come back
with a lady I'm to paint, open the door, and find, say, the hunchback
at the table there, painting her lips red with my brush, while the little
brothers and sisters she has to look after are rampaging round the
room, leaving their mess in every corner. Or, as happened to me only

yesterday, I come home late in the evening—please excuse my own state and the mess the room's in, but that's the reason—so I come back late in the evening and I'm climbing into bed when something nips my leg. I look under the bed and pull out another of these brats. I don't know why they feel this urge to come and see me, I don't try to lure them, as you must have seen. Naturally it distracts me from my work. If this studio hadn't been put at my disposal free of charge, I would have moved out long since.' At that moment a voice, soft and timorous, was heard outside the door: 'Can we come in, Titorelli?' 'No,' the painter replied. 'Not even me, all by myself?' 'Not even you,' said the painter, went to the door and locked it.

In the meantime K. had looked round the room. It would never have occurred to him to call this miserable little room a studio. You couldn't take much more than two long steps either up and down or across it. Everything, floor, walls, and ceiling, was of wood, with narrow gaps visible between the planks. Against the wall opposite K. was the bed, with sheets and blankets of varying colours piled up on it. On an easel in the middle of the room was a picture covered with a shirt, the arms of which were hanging down to the floor. Behind K. was the window, through which nothing but the snow-covered roof of the neighbouring building could be seen because of the fog.

The turn of the key in the lock reminded K. that he had wanted to get away quickly, so he took the factory-owner's letter out of his pocket and said, handing it to the painter, 'This gentleman, an acquaintance of yours, told me about you, and it's on his advice that I've come here.' The painter quickly glanced through the letter and tossed it onto his bed. If the factory-owner had not spoken of Titorelli in the most certain terms as an acquaintance, as a poor man who was dependent on his charity, K. really could have believed that Titorelli didn't know him, or at least couldn't recall him. On top of that, the painter now asked him, 'Have you come to buy paintings or to have yourself painted?' K. gave the painter an astonished look. Naturally, he had assumed that the factory-owner would have told the painter in his letter that all K. wanted was to enquire about his trial. He had rushed here too hurriedly, without thinking. But now he had to find some answer for the painter, so he said, glancing at the easel, 'You're working on a painting at the moment?' 'Yes,' said the painter, throwing the shirt that hung over the easel to join the letter on his bed. 'It's a portrait. A good piece of work, but not quite finished yet.'

Chance had smiled on K., the opportunity to talk about the court was literally staring him in the face, for it was obviously the portrait of a judge. It was, moreover, strikingly similar to the picture in the lawyer's study. True, the subject was a quite different judge, a fat man with a black bushy beard reaching far up his cheeks; also the lawyer's picture was in oils whilst this was lightly sketched out in pastels. But everything else was similar, for in this picture as well the judge was gripping the arms of a thronelike chair, from which he was about to rise menacingly. 'But that's a judge,' K. was going to say, but he held back for the moment and went up to the picture, as if he wanted to study the details. There was a large figure above the middle of the chair which he couldn't explain, so he asked the painter about it. 'It still needs a little more work doing,' the painter replied, picking up a pastel crayon from a small table and going over the edges of the figure a little, without making it any clearer for K. 'It's Justice,' the painter said eventually. 'Ah, now I can see,' said K., 'there's the blindfold over her eyes and there's the scales. But aren't those wings on her heels, and isn't she running?' 'Yes,' said the painter, 'it was in the commission that I had to paint her like that, it's actually Justice and the Goddess of Victory* at the same time.' 'That's not a good combination,' said K. with a smile, 'Justice has to be in repose, otherwise the scales will wobble and a just verdict will not be possible.' 'I'm following my client's wishes,' the painter said. 'Yes, of course,' said K., who had not intended to offend anyone with his remark. 'You'll have painted the figure as it is on the chair.' 'No,' said the painter, 'I've never seen either the figure or the chair, but I was told what I was to paint.' 'What?' said K., deliberately pretending he didn't quite understand the painter. 'But it is a judge sitting on the chair, isn't it?' 'Yes,' said the painter, 'but he's not a very senior judge and he's never sat in a chair like that.' 'And yet he has himself painted in such a ceremonial posture? He's sitting there like a senior high-court judge.' 'Yes, they're vain, those gentlemen,' said the painter. 'But they have permission from on high to have themselves painted like that. Each one has precise instructions about the way he's allowed to have himself painted. Unfortunately, in this particular picture you can't judge the details of the costume and the seat, pastel isn't suited for such depictions.' 'Yes,' said K., 'it's strange that it's done in pastel.' 'That's what the judge wanted,' said the painter, 'it's for a lady.' Seeing the picture seemed to have stimulated his appetite for work. He rolled up his sleeves, took several crayons, and K. looked on as, round the head of the judge, the quivering points of the crayons created a reddish shadow like a sunburst, which faded away towards the edge of the picture. Gradually the shadow encircled the head, like an adornment or a sign of distinction. Around the figure of Justice, however, it remained bright, apart from some imperceptible shading, and in the brightness the figure seemed to advance more than ever, it hardly recalled the Goddess of Justice any more, nor the Goddess of Victory either, rather, it looked completely like the Goddess of the Hunt.

K. found himself more attracted by the painter's work than he wanted, and eventually he reproached himself for spending so much time there without doing anything for his case. 'What's that judge called?' he suddenly asked. 'I'm not allowed to say,' the painter replied. He was bent low over the picture, pointedly neglecting the visitor whom he had at first received with such attention. K. thought it was a mere whim, and was annoyed at it because he was wasting his time. 'I presume you're a confidential agent of the court?' At once the painter put down the crayons, straightened up, rubbed his hands, and looked at K. with a smile. 'At last we get to the truth,' he said. 'You want to learn about the court, as it said in the factory-owner's letter, but first of all you talked about my pictures to win me over. But I don't hold it against you, you couldn't know that doesn't work with me. Please!' he said sharply, dismissing K.'s attempted protest. Then he went on, 'As it happens, you're quite right, I am a confidential agent of the court.' He paused, as if to give K. time to come to terms with this. Now the girls could be heard on the other side of the door again. They were probably crowding round the keyhole, perhaps it was possible to see in through the gaps in the door. K. refrained from apologizing because he didn't want to distract the painter. But he didn't want the painter to feel too superior, either, and thus put himself beyond his reach in a way, so he asked, 'Is that a publicly recognized position?' 'No,' the painter replied curtly, as if K.'s question had left him almost speechless. But K. didn't want him to clam up either, so he said, 'Well, unrecognized positions like that are often more influential than publicly recognized ones.' 'That's just how it is with mine,' the painter said and nodded, knitting his brow. 'I was talking to the factory-owner about your case yesterday. He asked whether I might be able to help you and I said, "The man can come and see me some time." I'm glad to see you've come so soon. You seem to have taken the matter very much to heart, which doesn't surprise me at all. Would you perhaps like to take your coat off?'

Despite the fact that K. only intended to stay for a very short while, he welcomed the painter's suggestion. He had started to find the air in the room oppressive, several times he'd glanced at a small iron stove in the corner which was clearly not lit; the muggy atmosphere in the room was inexplicable. As he took off his winter coat and also unbuttoned his jacket, the painter said apologetically, 'I need warmth. It's very cosy in here, isn't it. From that point of view the room's very well situated.' K. did not respond, but it wasn't actually the heat that was making him uncomfortable, it was more the musty air that made breathing difficult; the room couldn't have been aired for ages. The unpleasantness was increased when the painter invited him to sit on the bed, while he himself sat down by the easel on the only chair in the room. Moreover, the painter seemed to misunderstand why K. stayed on the edge of the bed. He told him to make himself comfortable, and when K. hesitated, he went over himself and pushed him deep into the blankets and pillows. Then he went back to his chair and asked his first pertinent question, which made K. forget everything else. 'Are you innocent?' he asked. 'Yes,' said K. Answering that question gave him real pleasure, especially as it was to a private individual, and therefore placed him under no obligation. Until now no one had asked him so openly. To enjoy this pleasure to the full, he added, 'I am completely innocent.' 'Well, then,' the painter said, bowing his head and appearing to think this over. Suddenly he looked up and said, 'If you're innocent, then the matter's very simple.' The sparkle left K.'s eyes. This man, who was supposed to be in the confidence of the court, was talking like an ignorant child. 'My innocence doesn't simplify the matter at all,' said K. Despite everything, he couldn't repress a smile and slowly shook his head. 'It depends on the many subtleties the court gets caught up in. In the end, however, they manage to produce a great burden of guilt from somewhere or other, where originally there was nothing at all.' 'Yes, yes, to be sure,' said the painter, as if K. were needlessly distracting him from his train of thought. 'But you are innocent?' 'Well, yes,' said K. 'That's the main thing,' said the painter. He was impervious to counter-arguments, only, despite his unequivocal tone, it wasn't clear whether he said this out of conviction or indifference. K. wanted to establish that first and foremost, so he said, 'I'm sure you know the court much better than I do. I don't know much more than what I've heard about it, though from very different people. But they all agreed on one thing: charges are not brought lightly, and when the court does bring charges it is firmly convinced of the guilt of the accused and can only be persuaded to change its mind with difficulty.' 'With difficulty?' the painter asked, throwing up one hand. 'The court can never be persuaded to change its mind. If I were to paint all the judges on a canvas here and you defended yourself before the canvas, you'd have more chance of success than before the real court.' 'Yes,' K. said to himself, forgetting that his purpose had been to sound out the painter.

One of the girls at the door started up again: 'Isn't he going to go soon, Titorelli?' 'Shut up,' the painter shouted in the direction of the door, 'can't you see I'm in a discussion with the gentleman?' But that wasn't enough to stop the girl, who asked, 'You're going to paint him?' And when the painter didn't reply, she went on, 'Please don't paint him, such an ugly man.' A hubbub of cries ensued, incomprehensible but expressing agreement. The painter leapt over to the door, opened it a little—the girls' hands clasped in supplication could be seen—and said, 'If you're not quiet I'll throw you all down the stairs. Sit down on the stairs here and be still.' They probably didn't obey immediately, so that he had to order them: 'On the stairs!' Only then was it quiet.

'Sorry about that,' said the painter when he had joined K. again. K. had hardly turned towards the door at all, he had left it entirely up to the painter whether and in what way he would stand up for him. And he still hardly moved when the painter bent down to him and whispered in his ear, so as not to be heard outside, 'The girls belong to the court too.' 'What?' asked K., moving his head away to one side and looking at the painter. But the painter went back to his chair and said, half as a joke, half in explanation, 'But everything belongs to the court.' 'I didn't realize that before,' said K. The painter's general remark had nullified the disturbing nature of what he had said about the girls. Despite that, K. stared for a while at the door, on the other side of which the girls were now sitting quietly on the stairs. Only, one of them had pushed a straw through a gap between the planks and was slowly moving it up and down.

'You don't seem to have an overall view of the court yet,' said the painter. He had spread his legs wide and was tapping his toes on the floor. 'However, since you're innocent, you won't need one. I'll get you out on my own.' 'How are you going to do that?' asked K. 'Just now you said yourself that the court is completely impervious to argument.' The painter raised his forefinger, as if there was a subtle distinction K. had not noticed. 'Only impervious to arguments which are brought forward in court,' he said. 'But it's quite a different matter with things of that kind that are tried behind the back of the public court, so to speak, that is, in the interview rooms, in the corridors, or, for example, here in the studio.' What the painter was now saying no longer seemed so implausible to K., indeed, it largely agreed with what he had heard from other people. Yes, it even sounded very hopeful. If the judges could really be as easily led by personal connections as the lawyer had suggested, then the painter's connections with the vain judges were particularly important and certainly not to be underestimated. In that case the painter was a very good addition to the circle of helpers K. was gradually assembling round himself. His talent for organization had once been praised in the bank, and here, where he was completely on his own, was a good opportunity to put it to the ultimate test. The painter observed the effect his explanation had on K., and then said, with a certain anxiety in his voice, 'Haven't you noticed that I speak almost like a lawyer? It's the influence of my constant dealings with the men from the court. Naturally I profit considerably from that, but at the cost of most of my artistic creativity.' 'How did you first come into contact with the judges?' asked K. He wanted to gain the painter's trust before taking him, one might almost say, into his service. 'That was very simple,' the painter said, 'I inherited the connection. My father was a court painter before me. It's a position that is always handed down. New people are no use. There are so many different and, above all, secret rules for painting the officials of the various ranks that they are unknown outside certain families. In that drawer there, for example, I have my father's notes, which I don't show to anyone. But only someone who knows them is capable of painting the judges. Even if I were to lose them, however, there are still so many rules which I alone have inside my head that no one could try to take my position away from me. Every judge wants to be painted the way the great judges of the past were painted, and only I can do that.' 'You are to be envied,' said K., thinking of his own position at the bank. 'So your position is unassailable?' 'Yes, unassailable,' said the painter with a proud shrug of the shoulders. 'That's the reason why I can take the risk now and then of helping a poor man who has a trial.' 'And how do you do that?' asked K., as if it wasn't him the painter had just referred to as a poor man. The painter, however, was not to be put off. He said, 'In your case, for example, since you're completely innocent I would do the following.' K. was beginning to find the repeated mention of his innocence irritating. Sometimes he felt that with these remarks the painter was making a favourable outcome of the trial a prerequis-ite for his help, which naturally completely nullified its usefulness. K., however, put these doubts on one side and didn't interrupt the painter. He wasn't going to refuse the painter's help, on that he was resolved, it certainly didn't seem to be any more dubious than the lawyer's assistance. In fact K. far preferred it to that, because it was offered in a more artless and open fashion.

The painter had dragged his chair closer to the bed and continued, keeping his voice low, 'I forgot to ask you earlier what kind of release you want. There are three possibilities: genuine acquittal, apparent acquittal, and protraction of the proceedings. Genuine acquittal is, of course, the best, only I haven't the least influence on that kind of solution. There is, in my opinion, no person at all who can influence genuine acquittal. In those cases it is presumably solely the defend-ant's innocence that is the deciding factor. Since you're innocent, it would actually be possible to rely on your innocence alone. Then you won't need my help, nor anyone else's.'

At first K. was somewhat taken aback by this well-ordered presen-tation, but then he said to the painter, speaking just as softly, 'I think you have contradicted yourself.' 'In what way?' the painter asked, leaning back with an indulgent smile. This smile gave K. the feeling that now he was getting down to discovering contradictions not in what the painter had said, but in the court proceedings themselves. Despite that, he still went on and said, 'Earlier on you remarked that the court is completely impervious to argument; later you restricted that to the open court, and now you're even saying that an innocent person does not need any help in court. That in itself is a contradic-tion. Moreover, you said before that the judges are open to personal influence, but now you deny that a genuine acquittal, as you call it, can ever be obtained by personal influence. That is the second con-tradiction.' 'These contradictions are easily explained,' said the painter. 'We're talking about two different things here: what is written in the law and what I have experienced personally, and you mustn't confuse the two. Of course the law says—though I haven't read it myself—that an innocent man is to be acquitted; on the other hand, it doesn't say that judges can be influenced. My experience, however, is the exact opposite. I have never heard of any genuine acquittal, but I have heard of many cases of influence being exerted. It is, of course, possible that none of the cases known to me involved an innocent person. But is that not unlikely? Not a single innocent person in all those cases? Even when I was a child, I used to listen carefully when my father talked about trials at home; the judges who came to his studio used to talk about the court too, people in our circles talk about nothing else. Whenever I had the opportunity to go to the court myself, I always availed myself of it, I've listened to countless trials at important stages and followed them as long as they were held in open court, and, I have to admit, I have never come across a single genuine acquittal.' 'Not one single acquittal, then,' said K., as if he were talking to himself and to his hopes. 'That only serves to confirm the opinion I already have of the court. So there's no hope from that side either. The whole court could be replaced by a single executioner.' 'You shouldn't generalize,' said the painter, displeased, 'I was only speaking of my own experiences.' 'But that's sufficient,' said K., 'or have you heard of acquittals from earlier times?' 'People do say', the painter replied, 'that there have been such acquittals, only that's very difficult to ascertain. The court's final decisions are not published, they're not even available to the judges. The result is that all we have of old court cases is legends, and the majority of them are certainly about genuine acquittals. You can believe them, but they can't be proved. Despite that, they shouldn't be entirely ignored, I'm sure they contain a certain element of truth, and they're very beautiful, I myself have painted a few pictures on the subject of these legends.' 'Mere legends won't change my opinion,' said K. He'd decided to accept all the painter's opinions for the time being, even if he considered them unlikely and they contradicted other reports. At the moment he hadn't time to check the truth of everything the painter said, let alone refute it, the most he hoped to achieve was to persuade the painter to help him in some way or other, even if it wasn't decisive. So he said, 'Let's forget about genuine acquittals. You mentioned two other possibilities.' 'Apparent acquittal and protraction of the proceedings. Those are the only ones,' said the painter. 'But before

we talk about them, won't you take your jacket off? You must be hot.'
'Yes,' said K. So far he'd been concentrating on the painter's explanations, but now the heat had been mentioned he started dripping
with sweat from his forehead. 'It's almost unbearable.' The painter
nodded as if he could well understand K.'s discomfort. 'Can't the
window be opened?' asked K. 'No,' said the painter, 'the pane's fixed,
it can't be opened.'*

Now K. realized that the whole time he'd been hoping the painter
or he himself would suddenly go to the window and fling it open.
He'd been prepared to suck in even the fog with open mouth. The
feeling of being completely cut off from the air made him dizzy. He
patted the eiderdown beside him and said in a faint voice, 'That's
uncomfortable and unhealthy.' 'Oh no,' said the painter, defending
his window, 'despite just being a single pane, the fact that it can't be
opened means the heat is kept in better than with a double window.
If I need ventilation, which is not very necessary, since the air comes
in everywhere through the gaps, I can open one of my doors, or even
both.' K., slightly reassured by this explanation, looked round for
the second door. The painter noticed that and said, 'It's behind you.
I had to block it with the bed.' Only now did K. see the little door in
the wall. 'It's much too small in here for a studio,' the painter said,
as if to forestall criticism from K., 'I have to make the best of it. In
front of the door is a very bad place for the bed, of course. For example, the judge I'm painting just now always comes in through the
door by the bed, I've even given him a key to that door so that he can
wait for me in the studio when I'm out. He usually comes early in the
morning, however, when I'm still asleep. Naturally I'm rudely woken
from my deep sleep when the door beside my bed opens. You'd lose
all respect for the judges if you could hear the curses I hurl at him as
he climbs over my bed in the morning. Of course, I could take the
key back from him, but that would only make matters worse. It
doesn't take much at all to break down any of the doors here.'

All the time the painter was speaking K. was wondering whether
to take his jacket off, eventually coming to the conclusion that if he
didn't, he would be unable to stay there any longer. So he took his
jacket off, but laid it across his knees so that he could put it on again
immediately once the discussion had ended. Hardly had he taken his
jacket off than one of the girls cried out, 'He's got his jacket off
already,' and they could all be heard crowding round the gaps to see

the spectacle for themselves. 'You see, the girls all think I'm going to paint you,' the painter said, 'and that you're getting undressed for it.' 'Do they now,' said K., only mildly amused, for he didn't feel any better despite the fact that he was in his shirtsleeves. It was almost in a grumpy voice that he asked, 'What did you call the two other possibilities?'—he'd already forgotten the terms. 'Apparent acquittal and protraction of the proceedings,' said the painter. 'It's up to you which you choose. With my help either is attainable, though not without difficulty, of course. The difference in that respect is that apparent acquittal demands a concentrated effort over a limited period, protraction a much more modest but interminable effort. First of all apparent acquittal, then. If that is what you should want, I'll write a statement confirming your innocence on a sheet of paper. The wording of such a statement has been handed down to me by my father, and cannot be faulted. I would then do the rounds of the judges I know with the statement, starting, for example, with the judge I'm painting at the moment. When he comes to sit for me this evening, I'll submit the statement to him. I'll submit the statement to him, explain that you're innocent, and give a personal guarantee of your innocence. And that is not a merely ostensible, but a real, binding pledge.' The look in the painter's eyes seemed to reproach K. for his intention of placing such a burden on him. 'That would be very kind,' said K. 'And the judge would believe you and still not grant me a genuine acquittal?' 'As I have already said,' the painter replied. 'Anyway, it's not at all certain that every judge would believe me. Some, for example, would insist I take you to them. So then you'd have to come with me one of the times. Though I have to say that in such a case we'd be halfway there already, especially as beforehand I would naturally give you precise instructions as to how you were to behave before the judge in question. It's worse with the judges—this does happen too—who refuse to see me. I would, of course, make several attempts, but we would have to proceed without these, but we can do that, these matters are not decided by individual judges. When I have a sufficient number of judges' signatures appended to the statement, I take it to the judge who is conducting your trial at the moment. I might even have his signature, in which case everything will proceed a little more quickly. When that point is reached there are, in general, not many obstacles in the way any more, for the accused it's the time of greatest optimism. It's strange but true that at this point people feel more optimistic than after their acquittal. From now on it doesn't take any great effort. In the statement the judge has the guarantee of a number of judges, so he can acquit you without worrying, which he will doubtless do, though only after completing various formalities, as a favour to me and other acquaintances. But you are released from the court and are free.'

'So then I'll be free,' said K. hesitantly. 'Yes,' said the painter, 'but only ostensibly. You see, the lowest-ranking judges, to whom my acquaintances belong, do not have the right to grant a final acquittal, that right is reserved to the highest court, which is quite out of the reach of you, of me, of us all. We don't know what things are like there and, I have to add, don't want to know. That is, our judges do not possess the supreme right: to release the accused from the charge. So if you are acquitted in this way, it means you are freed from the charge for the moment, but it continues to hover over your head and can come into effect at once the moment the order comes from on high. Since I have such good connections with the court, I can tell you the purely outward signs of the difference between real and apparent acquittal as they appear in the regulations for the court offices. In a case of genuine acquittal, the trial documents are to be completely discarded, they disappear for good from the proceedings, not only the charge, the trial and even the acquittal are destroyed as well, everything's destroyed. It's different with an apparent acquittal. Then the only change to the file is that the statement confirming innocence, the acquittal, and the grounds for acquittal are added to them. Otherwise, however, it remains active and is, in line with the uninterrupted communication between the court offices, forwarded to the higher courts then returned to the lower ones, and continues swinging up and down, with longer or shorter oscillations, with longer or shorter pauses. Their ways are unpredictable. From outside it can sometimes seem as if everything has long since been forgotten, the file is lost, the acquittal absolute. Anyone who knows how the courts work will not believe that. No file is ever lost, the court never forgets. One day, when no one's expecting it, some judge will take a closer look at the file, will realize that the accused is still living, and order his immediate arrest. Here I'm assuming a long time has passed between the apparent acquittal and the second arrest; that is possible, I have heard of such cases, but it's also possible for the person acquitted to arrive home from the court and find people waiting who have been sent to arrest him again. Of course, that means the end of his life of freedom.' 'And the trial starts again?' K. asked, almost in disbelief. 'Of course,' said the painter. 'The trial starts again but, just as before, there is the possibility of obtaining an apparent acquittal. You have to summon up all your strength again and refuse to submit.'

The painter's last comment was perhaps a response to the impression K., who had slumped a little, made on him. 'But is it not more difficult', K. said, as if to anticipate any revelations the painter might make, 'to obtain a second acquittal than the first?' 'It's not possible to say anything definite about that,' the painter replied. 'I presume you mean that the second arrest will influence the judges against the accused? That is not the case. The judges will have foreseen this arrest even when they granted the acquittal, so that it hardly has any effect. But, of course, the judges' mood as well as their legal view of the case may have changed for countless other reasons, so that your efforts to obtain a second acquittal have to be adjusted to take account of these changed circumstances, and must generally be as energetic as those before your first acquittal.' 'But this second acquittal won't be final either,' said K., turning his head away coldly. 'Of course not,' said the painter, 'the second acquittal is followed by the third arrest, the third acquittal by the fourth arrest, and so on. That's all part of the concept of apparent acquittal.' K. remained silent. 'You clearly don't see much advantage in apparent acquittal,' said the painter, 'perhaps protraction will suit you better. Should I explain the nature of protraction?' K. nodded.

The painter was leaning back comfortably in his chair. His nightshirt was wide open, and he'd put a hand inside it with which he was stroking his chest and sides. 'Protraction,' said the painter, staring into space for a moment, as if he were looking for a completely accurate explanation, 'protraction is when the trial is kept permanently at the lowest stage. To achieve that, it is necessary for the accused and his helper, especially his helper, to remain in uninterrupted personal contact with the court. I repeat: this does not demand the expenditure of energy such as is necessary to obtain an apparent acquittal, but it does require much closer attention. It is essential not to lose sight of the trial, you have to go and see the judge in question at regular intervals and on special occasions as well, and try in every way to keep him well disposed towards you. If you're not personally acquainted with the judge, you must get judges you do know to influence him, but without giving up the direct approach. If you leave nothing undone, you can assume with reasonable certainty that the trial will never progress beyond the first stage. The trial doesn't come to an end, but the accused is almost as sure of not being condemned as if he were free. The advantage of protraction, compared with apparent acquittal, is that the defendant's future is less uncertain, he's spared the terror of the sudden arrests, and he needn't fear he will be faced with the exertions and anxieties associated with obtaining an apparent acquittal just at a time when it least suits his general situation. Naturally, protraction also has certain disadvantages for the defendant which must not be underestimated. It's not the fact that the accused is never free that I have in mind here, he's not truly free with an apparent acquittal either. It's another disadvantage. The trial can never rest, unless there are at least what appear to be good reasons for it; to outward appearances it must look as if something's happening in the trial. From time to time, therefore, various proceedings have to be arranged, the accused has to be questioned, investigations have to be carried out, etc. The trial has to be kept going round and round in the little circle to which it is restricted. The consequence of that is a certain inconvenience for the accused, though it isn't as bad as you might imagine. It's all just for show, the hearings, for example, are very short, and if at some point you have no time or inclination to go, you can send your apologies, with certain judges you can even arrange things together with them well in advance. All it means, basically, is that as a defendant you have to report to your judge from time to time.'

Even as the painter was speaking these last words, K. had put his jacket over his arm and stood up. 'He's already standing up,' came the immediate cry from outside the door. 'You're leaving already?' the painter asked, also getting to his feet. 'I'm sure it's the air in here that's driving you away. I find it very embarrassing, there's lots more I could tell you. I had to be very brief, but I hope I was comprehensible.' 'Oh yes,' said K. his head aching from the effort he'd had to make to listen. Despite K.'s affirmation, the painter summarized everything once more, as if to comfort him on his way home: 'What is common to both methods is that they prevent the accused being sentenced.' 'But they also prevent him being really acquitted,' said K. softly, as if he were ashamed to have seen that. 'You've grasped

the crux of the matter,' the painter said quickly. K. placed his hand
on his winter coat, but couldn't even make up his mind to put his
jacket on. What he really wanted to do was to grab everything and
run out into the fresh air. Even the girls couldn't persuade him to put
on his jacket and coat, despite the fact that they were calling out to
each other prematurely that he was getting dressed. The painter felt
it was important to interpret K.'s mood somehow or other, so he said,
'I presume you haven't come to a decision as regards my proposals.
I think that's right. You have to weigh everything up precisely. But
you mustn't lose too much time.' 'I will come back soon,' said K.,
putting on his jacket in a sudden fit of resolution, throwing his coat
over his shoulder, and hurrying to the door. Now the girls on the
other side started screaming. K. felt as if he could see the screaming
girls through the door. 'But you must keep your word,' said the
painter, who had not followed him, 'or I'll come to the bank to get
your answer myself.' 'Do open the door,' said K., pulling at the handle which the girls outside, as he could tell from the resistance, were
holding tight. 'Do you want to be pestered by the girls? Use this way
out instead,' the painter said, pointing to the door behind the bed.
K. was happy with that, and rushed back to the bed. However, instead
of opening the door, the painter crawled under the bed and asked
from underneath, 'Just one moment. Wouldn't you like to see another
picture, one that I could sell you?' K. didn't want to seem discourteous, the painter had really made an effort for him and had promised
to continue to help him; also, because of K.'s forgetfulness they had
not discussed the question of payment for his assistance. For all these
reasons K. felt he couldn't refuse, and let him show him the picture,
even though he was quivering with impatience to get out of the studio.
From under the bed the painter pulled out a pile of unframed pictures, which were so covered in dust that, when the painter blew it
off the top one, it swirled round before K.'s eyes and left him gasping
for breath. 'Sunset Over the Heath,'* the painter said, handing it to
K. It showed two spindly trees, standing far apart in the dark grass.
In the background was a multicoloured sunset. 'Good,' said K., 'I'll
buy it.' K. had spoken curtly without thinking, so he was glad when
the painter, instead of taking it amiss, picked up another painting off
the floor, saying, 'Here's a companion piece to that picture.' It was,
perhaps, intended as a companion piece, but not the slightest difference could be seen: there were the trees, there the grass, and over there

the sunset. But that didn't bother K. 'They're beautiful landscapes,' he said, 'I'll buy both and hang them in my office.' 'You seem to like that subject,' the painter said, picking up a third painting, 'fortunately I happen to have another similar picture here.' It wasn't similar, however, but rather another completely identical sunset over the heath. The painter was really seizing the opportunity to sell off old paintings. 'I'll take that one as well,' said K. 'How much do the three pictures cost?' 'We'll talk about that the next time,' said the painter. 'You're in a hurry, but we'll stay in contact. And I'm delighted you like the pictures, you can take all the pictures I have under here. They're all of the heath, I've already done lots of pictures of the heath. Some people reject pictures like that because they're too gloomy, while others, and you're one of them, are particularly fond of gloominess.' But K. had no time for the painter's professional experiences. 'Pack up all the paintings,' he said, interrupting the painter, 'I'll send my messenger to fetch them tomorrow.' 'That won't be necessary,' the painter said, 'I hope I can get a porter who can go along with you now.'

At last he leant over the bed and unlocked the door. 'Climb over the bed,' he said. 'Don't worry, everyone who comes in here does it.' K. would have gone ahead even without this invitation, indeed, he had already placed his foot in the middle of the eiderdown, but when he looked out of the door, he withdrew it. 'What is that?' he asked the painter. 'Why are you surprised?' the painter asked, surprised himself. 'It's the court offices. Didn't you know that there are court offices here? There are court offices in almost every attic, so why not here? My studio's actually part of the court offices, but the court's put it at my disposal.' It was not so much finding court offices here that had shocked K., it was mainly his own ignorance of matters concerning the court. It seemed to him that a basic rule of behaviour for a defendant was always to be prepared, never to allow oneself to be caught by surprise, not to look, all unsuspecting, to the right when the judge was standing beside one on the left—and it was precisely this rule that he ignored again and again. A long corridor stretched out in front of him, sending out air compared with which the air in the studio was refreshing. Benches ran along either side of the corridor, just as they did in the waiting-room of the office dealing with K.'s case. There seemed to be precise regulations for the way the offices were furnished. At the moment there were not many defendants there. One man was half sitting, half lying down, with his face buried in his arms on the bench; he seemed to be asleep. Another was standing in the semi-darkness at the end of the corridor. Now K. did climb over the bed, the painter following him with the pictures. They soon came across an usher—by now K. could recognize the ushers by the gold button they wore among the ordinary buttons of their everyday clothes—and the painter ordered him to accompany K. with the pictures. K. was staggering more than walking, his hand-kerchief pressed over his mouth. They had almost reached the exit when the girls came rushing towards them, so that K. was not spared them either. They had obviously seen that the second door of the studio had been opened, and had gone round to come in from this side. 'I can't come any farther with you,' the painter cried, laughing at the girls crowding round him. 'Goodbye! And don't spend too long thinking it over.' K. didn't even turn round. In the street he took the first cab that came along. He was very keen to get rid of the usher, whose gold button kept catching his eye, even though no one else probably noticed it. The usher was so eager to be of assistance that he tried to get up on the box seat, but K. forced him down. It was long past midday when K. arrived back at the bank. He would have liked to leave the paintings in the cab, but he was afraid some occasion might arise when he had to show the painter that he had them. So he got a messenger to take them up to his office and locked them in the bottom drawer of his desk, where they would at least be safe from the eyes of the deputy manager for the immediate future.

K. HAD finally decided to take his case out of the lawyer's hands. He couldn't entirely rid himself of doubts as to whether this was the correct course of action, but they were outweighed by his conviction that it was necessary. On the day he intended to visit the lawyer his decision had severely reduced his capacity for work, he had to stay very late in the office, and it was already after ten when he finally reached the lawyer's door. But before he rang, he wondered whether it might not be better to dismiss the lawyer by telephone or by letter; the personal interview was bound to be very awkward. Despite that, K. decided he had to go ahead with it. Dismissal by any other method would be accepted in silence, or with a few formal expressions, and, unless Leni could discover something, K. would never find out how the lawyer had taken his dismissal and what consequences, in the lawyer's not-unimportant opinion, it might have for K. If the lawyer was facing K. and was taken by surprise by the dismissal, K. would easily be able to deduce from his expression and behaviour everything he wanted to know, even if he didn't get much out of him in the way of words. It was even possible that he might be persuaded that it would be better to leave the handling of his case to the lawyer and withdraw the dismissal.

As usual, the first ring at the lawyer's door produced no result. 'Leni could be quicker,' K. thought. But at least it was a good thing that another tenant didn't intervene, as they usually did, whether it was the man in the dressing-gown or anyone else who started to pester him. As K. pressed the bell for the second time he looked back at the other door, but this time it remained closed. Finally a pair of eyes appeared in the peephole of the lawyer's door, but they were not Leni's eyes. Someone unlocked the door, but kept his weight against it while he shouted back into the apartment, 'It's him.' Only then did he open the door wide. K. had been pushing at the door, for he could hear the key being hastily turned in the door of the other apartment behind him. Thus, when the door finally opened he really shot into the hall, and caught a glimpse of Leni, to whom the warning from the man who opened the door had been addressed, running off in her shift down the corridor between the rooms. He watched her for a

moment, then turned to the man who had opened the door. He was
a small, scrawny man with a beard, holding a candle in his hand. 'Do
you work here?' K. asked. 'No,' the man replied, 'I don't belong here,
it's just that the lawyer is representing me. I'm here on legal business.' 'Without your jacket?' K. asked, indicating the man's *déshabille*
with a sweep of the arm. 'Oh, forgive me,' the man said, regarding
himself in the light of the candle as if he only now realized his state
of dress. 'Leni's your mistress?' K. asked curtly. He was standing,
legs slightly apart, clasping his hat behind his back. The mere possession of a heavy overcoat gave him a feeling of great superiority
over the skinny little man. 'Oh, God,' he said, raising one hand in
front of his face in horror, 'no, no, what makes you think that?' 'You
look like a man who can be believed,' K. said with a smile, 'but still—
come with me.' K. waved him on with his hat and made him walk in
front of him. 'So what's your name?' K. asked as they went. 'Block,
I'm a corn merchant,' the little man said, turning round to face K. as
he introduced himself. But K. didn't let him stop. 'Is that your real
name?' K. asked. 'Certainly,' was the reply, 'why do you doubt it?'
'I thought you might have some reason to keep your name secret,'
said K. He felt a freedom one usually only feels when talking to lowly
people away from home. One keeps everything concerning oneself to
oneself and talks calmly of the others' concerns alone, raising them
in their own estimation, but also dropping them when it suits one.

When they reached the door to the lawyer's study, K. stopped,
opened it, and called out to the corn merchant, who had obediently
carried on, 'Not so fast! Give me some light here.' K. thought Leni
might be hiding there, so he made the corn merchant look in every
nook and cranny, but the room was empty. In front of the picture of
the judge K. pulled the corn merchant back by his braces. 'Do you
know him?' he asked, pointing with his forefinger. The corn merchant
held the candle high and said, screwing up his eyes as he looked at it,
'It's a judge.' 'A senior judge?' K. asked, standing beside the corn
merchant to observe the impression the picture made on him. The
corn merchant looked up, an expression of awe on his face. 'It's a
senior judge,' he said. 'You don't know much about these things,'
said K. 'He's the lowest of the examining magistrates, and that's the
lowest rank.' 'Now I remember,' the corn merchant said, lowering
the candle, 'I have heard that.' 'But of course,' K. cried, 'I was forgetting. Of course you must have heard that.' 'But why must I, why

must I?' the corn merchant asked as K. pushed him towards the door.

Out in the corridor K. said, 'You know where Leni's hiding, of course?' 'Hiding?' said the corn merchant. 'No, but she's probably in the kitchen making soup for the lawyer.' 'Why didn't you say that right away?' K. asked. 'I was going to take you there, but you called me back,' the corn merchant replied, as if confused by the contradictory commands. 'I presume you think you're being very clever,' said K. 'Right then, take me there.' K. had never been in the kitchen before, it was surprisingly large and well equipped. The range alone was three times the size of ordinary ones; no details of the rest could be seen, since the only light came from a lamp hanging over the door. Leni was at the stove, in a white apron as always, pouring eggs into a pan on a spirit stove. 'Good evening, Josef,' she said with a sidelong glance. 'Good evening,' said K., pointing to a chair to one side where the corn merchant was to sit down, which he did. K. went up close behind Leni, leant over her shoulder, and asked, 'Who is the man?' Leni, clasping K. with one hand, and beating the soup with the other, drew him closer and said, 'He's a sad case, a poor corn merchant, Block's his name. Just look at him.' They both looked round. The corn merchant was sitting on the chair where K. had told him to sit. He'd blown out the candle, as it was no longer needed, and was squeezing the wick with his fingers to stop it smoking. 'You were in your shift,' said K., using his hand to turn her head back to the stove. She said nothing. 'He's your lover?' asked K. She tried to pick up the soup pot, but K. took both her hands and said, 'Come on, answer me.' She said, 'Come to the study and I'll explain everything.' 'No,' said K., 'I want you to explain it here.' She clung on to him and tried to kiss him, but K. wouldn't let her and said, 'I don't want you to kiss me just now.' 'Josef,' said Leni, looking K. in the eye with a pleading but open look, 'don't say you're jealous of Herr Block.—Rudi,' she then said, turning to the corn merchant, 'come and help me, can't you see I'm under suspicion. Leave that candle alone.' It looked as if he wasn't paying attention, but he knew precisely what was going on. 'I've no idea why you should be jealous,' was his rather lame reply. 'I've no idea either,' said K., looking at the corn merchant with a smile. Leni laughed out loud and, using K.'s distraction to take his arm, whispered, 'Leave him alone, you can see what kind of person he is. I've been looking after him a bit because he's an important client of the lawyer, and that's the only reason. What about you? Do you want to speak to the lawyer now? He's very ill today, but I'll announce you if that's what you want. You'll stay the night with me, of course. It's so long since you were here, even the lawyer's been asking after you. Don't neglect your trial. I've got various things I've heard to pass on to you as well. But take your overcoat off for a start.' She helped him take it off, took his hat from him, and went to hang them up in the hall, then came back and checked the soup. 'Shall I announce you first or take him his soup first?' 'Announce me first,' said K. He was annoyed. He'd originally intended to discuss his business, especially the possible dismissal of the lawyer, in detail with Leni, but the presence of the corn merchant had taken away all desire to do so. Now, however, he decided his case was too important for this little corn merchant to have a, perhaps decisive, influence on it. Leni was already in the corridor, so he called her back. 'Take him his soup first after all,' he said. 'Let him build up his strength for his discussion with me, he's going to need it.' 'You're a client of the lawyer as well,' the corn merchant said quietly in his corner, as if in confirmation. It wasn't well received. 'What's that to do with you?' said K. 'Do be quiet,' said Leni, adding, 'So I'll take him his soup first,' as she poured the soup into a bowl. 'The only problem is, he might fall asleep, he goes to sleep quickly after he's eaten.' 'What I have to tell him will keep him awake,' said K., hinting all the time that there was something important he intended to discuss with the lawyer. He wanted Leni to ask him what it was and only then to ask her advice. As she passed him with the bowl, she deliberately bumped into him gently and whispered, 'I'll announce you as soon as he's finished his soup, so that I get you back as quickly as possible.' 'Off you go,' said K., 'off you go.' 'You could be nicer to me,' she said, turning right round again in the doorway with the tray.

K. watched her go. Now it had been finally decided that the lawyer would be dismissed. It was probably better that he hadn't been able to talk to Leni about it beforehand, she really didn't have a proper overall picture of the matter. He was sure she'd have advised against it, she might possibly even have persuaded K. not to go ahead with the dismissal for the moment, leaving him still in doubt and uncertainty; but after a while he would eventually have carried out his decision, the arguments for it were overwhelming. But the sooner he did so, the more damage would be prevented. Perhaps the corn merchant could tell him something about that.

K. turned round. Scarcely had the corn merchant seen that, than he immediately started to get up. 'Don't get up,' said K., pulling a chair along beside him. 'Are you an old client of the lawyer?' asked K. 'Yes,' said the corn merchant, 'a very old client.' 'How long has he been handling your affairs?' asked K. 'I don't know what you have in mind,' the corn merchant said. 'The lawyer has been handling legal matters connected with my business ever since I took it over, that is, for twenty years. He's also been representing me in my trial, which is probably what you're getting at, since it began, that's more than five years.—Yes, well over five years,' he added, taking out an old wallet. 'I've everything written down here, if you want I can show you the exact dates. It's hard to remember everything. My trial has probably been going on much longer, it started shortly after my wife died, and that was over five-and-a-half years ago.' K. moved his chair closer to him. 'So the lawyer handles ordinary legal business as well?' he asked. This connection between the different courts and legal systems seemed immensely reassuring to K. 'Of course,' the corn merchant said and then whispered to K., 'People even say he's better at that business than at the other.' Then, however, he seemed to regret having said that, placed his hand on K.'s shoulder, and said, 'I beg you, please don't give me away.' K. patted him reassuringly on the thigh and said, 'No, I don't go telling tales.' 'He's very vindictive, you know,' said the corn merchant. 'I'm sure he won't do anything to harm such a loyal client,' said K. 'Oh, but he would,' said the corn merchant. 'When he gets angry it doesn't matter who you are; anyway, I've not actually been loyal to him.' 'In what way?' K. asked. 'Can I confide in you?' the corn merchant asked sceptically. 'I think you can,' K. said. 'Well then,' the corn merchant said, 'I'll tell you part of it, but you have to tell me a secret as well, so that we're in the same position vis-à-vis the lawyer.' 'You're very cautious,' said K., 'but I'll tell you a secret which will completely reassure you. So what does your disloyalty to the lawyer consist of?' 'I have—' said the corn merchant hesitantly, and in a tone that suggested he was admitting something dishonourable, 'I have other lawyers apart from him.' 'But there's nothing wrong in that,' said K., a little disappointed. 'There is here,' said the corn merchant, still breathing heavily after his confession, though somewhat reassured by K.'s remark.

'It's not allowed. Least of all is it allowed to employ unregistered lawyers as well as a so-called proper lawyer. And that's exactly what I've done. Besides him, I have five unregistered lawyers.' 'Five!' K. exclaimed. It was the number that amazed him. 'Five lawyers apart from this one?' The corn merchant nodded. 'I'm just negotiating with a sixth.' 'But why do you need so many lawyers?' asked K. 'I need them all,' said the corn merchant. 'Could you explain why?' asked K. 'Willingly,' said the corn merchant. 'Above all, I don't want to lose my trial, that goes without saying. Consequently, I can't afford to ignore anything that might help me. Even if my expectation of help in any particular case is slight, I cannot reject it. That's why I've spent everything I possess on this trial. For example, I've taken all the money out of my business. Before, my offices took up almost a whole storey, today a box-room at the back of the yard is enough for me and an apprentice. It's not only the withdrawal of money that has caused the decline in my business, but also the withdrawal of my own labour. If you're trying to do something for your trial, you have little time for anything else.' 'So you've been working at the court yourself?' K. asked. 'That's something I'd particularly like to hear about.' 'There's not much I can tell you about that,' said the corn merchant. 'I did try it at the beginning, but I soon desisted. It's too exhausting and doesn't produce much in the way of results. Even just working and dealing with people there proved completely impossible, at least for me. The sitting and waiting alone is very strenuous. You'll have come across the heavy air in the offices yourself.' 'How do you know I've been there?' K. asked. 'I was in the waiting-room when you went through.' 'What a coincidence!' K. exclaimed, all attention now. He'd quite forgotten how ridiculous he had originally found the corn merchant. 'So you saw me! You were in the waiting-room when I passed through!' 'It's not such a great coincidence,' the corn merchant said, 'I go there almost every day.' 'I'll probably have to go there quite often myself now,' K. said, 'though I'm unlikely to be given such a deferential reception again. Everyone stood up. Presumably they thought I was a judge.' 'No,' said the corn merchant, 'that was for the usher. We knew you were a defendant, that kind of news gets round very quickly.' 'So you knew already,' said K. 'Then perhaps my behaviour seemed arrogant to you? Didn't you discuss it among yourselves?' 'No,' said the corn merchant, 'on the contrary. But that's all nonsense.' 'What's all nonsense?' K. asked.

'Why do you ask?' said the corn merchant, irritated. 'You don't seem to know the people there yet, and you might misunderstand. You must remember that in these proceedings lots of things keep cropping up which are beyond our understanding, we're simply too tired and distracted for many things, so to make up for it we turn to superstition. I'm talking about the others, but I'm no better myself. One of these superstitions, for example, is that many claim they can see the outcome of the trial in the defendant's face, especially in the marking of the lips.* Going from your lips, those people maintained that you would definitely, and soon, be condemned. I repeat: it's just a ridiculous superstition, and in most cases it's completely disproved by events, but when you live among those people it's hard to avoid such opinions. You can imagine what a great effect this superstition can have. You spoke to someone there, didn't you? He could hardly stammer a reply. There are, of course, many reasons why people there are confused, but one was the sight of your lips. Afterwards, he told us he saw on your lips the sign telling him he himself was going to be condemned.' 'On my lips?' K. asked, taking out a pocket mirror and looking at himself. 'I can't see anything special about my lips. Can you?' 'I can't either,' said the corn merchant, 'not at all.' 'How superstitious these people are!' K. exclaimed. 'Didn't I tell you,' the corn merchant replied. 'Do they see each other and discuss things that often?' K. asked. 'Up to now I've kept away.' 'In general they don't see each other,' said the corn merchant. 'There are so many of them it would hardly be possible, and they have very little in the way of common interests. If, from time to time, the belief in a common interest does arise in some group, it soon turns out to be a mistake. Acting in common gets you nowhere against the court, every case is examined on its own merits, it is a most meticulous court. So acting in common gets them nowhere, only an individual can sometimes achieve something in secret, but it's only after it's been achieved that the others get to hear about it, and no one knows how it happened. So there is no common ground. They do meet now and then in the waiting-rooms, but there's not much discussion there. The superstitions have existed from time immemorial. They keep multiplying, they're positively self-generating.' 'I saw the men in the waiting-room there,' said K., 'the waiting seemed so pointless.' 'Waiting is not pointless,' said the corn merchant, 'the only thing that is pointless is acting on your own initiative. As I told you, beside this one

I have five other lawyers. You would think—as I thought at first—that now I could leave my case entirely to them. That would be quite wrong, however. I can leave it to them even less than when I only had one. I suspect you don't understand that?' 'No, I don't,' said K., placing his hand on the corn merchant's hand in a calming gesture to stop him talking too quickly. 'But I would ask you to speak a little more slowly. All these things are very important for me and I can't quite keep up with you.' 'A good thing you reminded me of that,' said the corn merchant, 'you're new to this, of course. Your trial's only six months old, isn't it? Yes, I've heard about it. Such a young trial! I, on the other hand, have thought these things over countless times, for me nothing could be more natural.' 'I presume you're happy your trial has made such progress?' K. asked. He didn't want to ask the corn merchant straight out how things stood in his affairs. Nor did he get a clear answer. 'Yes, I've kept my trial going for five years,' said the corn merchant, bowing his head, 'it's no mean achievement.'

Then he fell silent for a while. K. listened to see if Leni was perhaps coming. On the one hand he didn't want her to come, there were many questions he still had to ask, and he didn't want Leni to find him in this confidential discussion with the corn merchant; on the other hand he was annoyed that, despite the fact that he was there, she was spending so long with the lawyer, much longer than was necessary to give him his soup.

The corn merchant resumed, and immediately K. was all ears. 'I well remember the time when my trial was as old as your trial. At that time I just had this lawyer, and I wasn't very happy with him.' 'Now I'm going to find out everything,' K. thought, nodding vigorously, as if that would encourage the corn merchant to tell him everything he needed to know. 'My trial', the corn merchant went on, 'wasn't getting anywhere. There were hearings, I attended every one, collected material, did all my business accounts at court—which, as I later heard, wasn't even necessary—kept going to see the lawyer, and he sent in various submissions—' 'Various submissions?' K. asked. 'Yes, of course,' said the corn merchant. 'I find that very important,' said K., 'in my case he's still working on the first submission. He hasn't produced anything yet. Now I see that he's neglecting me scandalously.' 'There could be various legitimate reasons why the submission isn't finished yet,' said the corn merchant. 'Moreover, it turned out later that my submissions were quite worthless. One of the court officials was even obliging enough to let me read one. It was very learned, but basically it said nothing. First of all lots of Latin, which I can't understand, then pages of general appeals to the court, then flattery of particular individual officials who, although not named, must have been obvious to those in the know, then the lawyer praised himself, humbling himself before the court in the most sycophantic manner, before finally examining cases from former times which, he claimed, were similar to mine. I must say, however, that the examinations of the cases were, as far as I could tell, very meticulously done. All this is not to make a judgement on the lawyer's work, the submission I saw was only one of several. However—and this is what I want to talk about—at that time I couldn't see any progress in my trial.' 'What kind of progress did you want to see?' asked K. 'That's a very sensible question,' said the corn merchant with a smile. 'In these proceedings it is only rarely that you can see progress. But at the time I didn't know that. I'm a businessman—at the time even more so than now—and I wanted to see tangible results, the whole thing moving towards an end, or at least showing a regular upturn. Instead there were just interrogations, mostly on the same subject, I had the answers ready just like a litany; several times a week messengers from the court came to my business premises, to my apartment, or wherever else they could find me. Naturally it was a nuisance (in that respect it's much better today, a telephone call is less of a disruption), and as well as that rumours about my trial started to spread among my business associates and especially among my relations, with the result that I suffered all kinds of damage without the slightest indication that even the first hearing would take place in the near future. So I went to the lawyer and complained. He gave me long explanations, but firmly refused to do anything I suggested. No one, he said, could influence the setting of times for the hearings; to present a submission insisting that a time be set—as I was demanding—was simply unheard-of, and would be the ruin of both me and himself. I thought: there's sure to be someone else willing and able to do what this lawyer can't or won't do. So I looked around for other lawyers. And before you ask: not one has got them to set a date for the main hearing or even demanded they do so, that is—with one proviso I'll talk about later—impossible, so in that respect this lawyer did not deceive me; otherwise, however, I have no regrets at having taken other lawyers. I imagine you'll have heard quite a few things from Dr Huld about the unregistered lawyers; he probably described them as very contemptible, and they really are. Though I have to say that when he talks about them, and compares them with his colleagues, he does make a small mistake which I will just point out briefly. He always distinguishes the lawyers of his circle from the others by calling his colleagues the "great lawyers". That is wrong. Naturally, anyone can call himself "great" if he likes, but in this case it is the court usage that is decisive. According to that, there are, apart from the unregistered lawyers, also the petty lawyers and the great lawyers. This lawyer and his colleagues, however, are only the petty lawyers. The great lawyers, of whom I've only heard—I've never seen one—are incomparably higher in rank above the petty lawyers than the latter are above the despised unregistered lawyers.' 'The great lawyers?' asked K. 'Who are they? How do you approach them?' 'So you've never heard of them?' said the corn merchant. 'There's hardly a defendant who, once he's heard of them, doesn't dream of them for a while. But don't be tempted. I don't know who the great lawyers are, and I presume you can't get to them. I know of no case where it can be said for certain that they took part. They defend some people, but you can't get them to do that through your own efforts, they only defend the ones they want to defend. But I assume a case they take on must have progressed beyond the lower court. It's better not to think of them at all, otherwise you'll find the consultations with the other lawyers, their advice and their assist- ance, extremely disgusting and useless. I've been through that myself, you feel like throwing everything up, taking to your bed, and ignor- ing everything. Of course, that would be the stupidest thing to do, and anyway, you wouldn't be left in peace in your bed for long.' 'So back then you didn't think of the great lawyers?' asked K. 'Not for long,' the corn merchant said, smiling once more. 'Unfortunately you can't entirely forget about them, the night-time in particular seems to encourage such thoughts. But back then I wanted immediate results, that's why I went to the unregistered lawyers.'

'Just look at the two of you, sitting there together!' Leni exclaimed. She had come back with the tray and was standing in the doorway. They really were sitting close together, the slightest turn and their heads would clash. The corn merchant, who, apart from being small, was sitting with his back bowed, had forced K. to bend down low if he wanted to hear everything. 'Just a little while longer,' said K., to

keep Leni away, impatiently flapping his hand, which was still on
that of the corn merchant. 'He wanted me to tell him about my trial,'
the corn merchant said to Leni. 'Go on then, tell him,' she said. She
spoke to the corn merchant in an affectionate but also condescending
tone, which displeased K. As he now realized, the man did after all
have something about him, at least he had experience, which he was
good at putting across. Leni's judgement of him was probably wrong.
He looked on in irritation as Leni now took the candle, which the
corn merchant had been holding all the time, away from him, wiped
his hand with her apron, and then knelt down beside him to scratch
off some wax that had dripped on to his trousers. 'You were going to
tell me about the unregistered lawyers,' said K., pushing Leni's hand
away without comment. 'What are you doing?' Leni asked, aiming a
gentle slap at K. then continuing with her task. 'Oh yes, the unregistered lawyers,' said the corn merchant, wiping his brow as if he were
thinking. K., trying to jog his memory, said, 'You wanted immediate
results, and so you went to the unregistered lawyers.' 'That's right,'
said the corn merchant, but did not continue. 'Perhaps he doesn't
want to talk about it while Leni's here,' K. thought, controlling his
impatience to hear what he had to say, and not pressing him.

'Have you told him I'm here?' he asked Leni. 'Of course,' she
said,' he's waiting for you. Leave Block now, you can talk to Block
later, he's staying here.' K. was still hesitating. 'You're staying here?'
he asked the corn merchant. He wanted him to answer, he didn't
want Leni to talk about him as if he wasn't there. Today he was seeth-
ing inside with irritation at Leni, but again it was she who answered:
'He quite often sleeps here.' 'Sleeps here?' K. cried. He had assumed
the corn merchant would just wait for him while he dealt with his
interview with the lawyer as quickly as possible, so that they could
leave together and discuss everything thoroughly and in peace and
quiet. 'Yes,' said Leni, 'not everyone is allowed to see the lawyer at
any time he wants. You don't seem to be at all surprised that the
lawyer will see you at eleven o'clock at night, despite his illness. You
take everything your friends do for you too much for granted. Well,
your friends do it willingly, or at least I do. I neither want nor need
any other reward than for you to be fond of me.' 'Be fond of you?'
was K.'s immediate reaction. Only then did the thought occur to him:
'Well, yes, I am fond of her.' Despite that he said, ignoring everything else, 'He sees me because I'm his client. If other people's help

was necessary for that as well, you'd be saying please and thank you at every step.' 'Isn't he terrible this evening?' Leni asked the corn merchant. 'Now I'm the one who's not here,' K. thought, and was even almost angry with the corn merchant when he said, adopting Leni's impoliteness, 'The lawyer sees him for other reasons too. His case is more interesting than mine. Moreover, his trial is just at the start, so it probably hasn't reached such an impasse yet, the lawyer will still enjoy dealing with him. It'll be different later on.' 'Yes, yes,' said Leni, laughing as she looked at the corn merchant. 'The way he chatters!' she said, turning to K. 'You know, you can't believe a thing he says. He may be nice, but he's a terrible chatterbox. Perhaps that's why the lawyer can't stand him. At least, he only sees him when he's in the mood. I've done everything I can to change that, but it's impossible. Just imagine, sometimes I tell him Block's here and he only sees him three days later. And if Block isn't there when he's called, then it's all over and he has to start from the beginning again. That's why I allow Block to sleep here. It has happened that the lawyer has rung for him during the night, and that means Block is ready during the night as well. On the other hand, it does now sometimes happen that when it turns out that Block is here, the lawyer cancels his order to show him in.' K. gave the corn merchant a questioning look. He nodded and said, speaking as frankly as he had previously to K.—perhaps his embarrassment had made him unguarded—'Yes, eventually you get very dependent on your lawyer.' 'His complaining's just pretence,' said Leni. 'He likes sleeping here, he's often told me as much.' She went to a little door and pushed it open. 'Do you want to see his bedroom?' K. went over and stood in the doorway, looking into the low, windowless room which was completely taken up with a narrow bed. To get into bed you had to climb over the bottom of the bedstead. At the head of the bed there was a cavity in the wall in which, meticulously arranged, were a candle, an inkwell and pen, as well as a bundle of papers, probably documents to do with the trial. 'You sleep in the maid's bedroom?' K. asked, turning back to face the corn merchant. 'Leni's let me have it,' the corn merchant replied, 'it's very convenient.' K. gave him a long look; his first impression of the corn merchant was perhaps the right one after all. He had experience, because his trial had been going on for a long time, but he had paid dearly for it. Suddenly K. couldn't stand the sight of the corn merchant any longer. 'Put him to bed,' he cried to Leni, who didn't seem to understand at all. He had resolved to go to the lawyer and, by dismissing him, free himself not only from the lawyer, but also from Leni and the corn merchant. But before he had reached the door, the corn merchant spoke to him in a low voice: 'Sir,' he said. K. turned round, an angry look on his face. 'You've forgotten your promise,' said the corn merchant, reaching out towards K. pleadingly from his chair. 'You were going to tell me a secret.' 'Indeed I was,' said K., glancing at Leni, who was watching him intently. 'Well, listen, though it's not going to be a secret much longer: I'm going to see the lawyer now to dismiss him.' 'He's dismissing him!' the corn merchant exclaimed, leapt up from his chair, and ran round the kitchen, arms in the air. He kept on crying, 'He's dismissing the lawyer.' Leni tried to attack K., but the corn merchant got in her way, for which she gave him a punch. She then ran after K., fists clenched, but he was too far ahead. He was already in the lawyer's room when she caught up with him. He'd almost closed the door behind him, but Leni, who had stuck her foot in the door, grasped his arm and tried to pull him out. But he squeezed her wrist so hard she was forced to let go, with a groan. She didn't dare come into the room immediately, and K. locked the door with the key.

'I've been waiting a very long time for you,' said the lawyer, who was in bed. He placed a document he'd been reading by the light of a candle on the bedside table, put on his spectacles, and scrutinized K. Instead of apologizing, K. said, 'I'll be going soon.' Since it was not an apology, the lawyer ignored K.'s remark and said, 'In future I won't see you at such a late hour.' 'That fits in well with the matter I have to discuss today,' said K. The lawyer gave him a questioning look. 'Sit down,' he said. 'As you wish,' said K., drawing a chair up to the bedside table and sitting down. 'It seems to me you've locked the door,' said the lawyer. 'Yes,' said K. 'It's because of Leni.' He did not intend to spare anyone. 'Has she been making advances again?' 'Making advances?' asked K. 'Yes,' said the lawyer. He laughed as he spoke, had a fit of coughing, and then, when he'd got over it, laughed again. 'I'm sure you'll have noticed how she makes advances?' he asked, patting K.'s hand which he had absent-mindedly placed on the table and now quickly withdrew. 'You don't attach much importance to it,' the lawyer said, when K. remained silent, 'all the better. Otherwise I might have had to apologize to you. It's one of Leni's peculiarities, which I've long since forgiven her, and which I wouldn't have mentioned if you hadn't locked the door. This peculiarity—you're the last person I need to explain it to, but you're giving me such a horrified look, so I will—this peculiarity is that Leni finds almost all the defendants attractive. She becomes attached to them all, and does appear to be loved by them all; sometimes, in order to amuse me, she tells me about it, if I allow her. I'm not as surprised by all this as you seem to be. If you have an eye for it, you really can often find the defendants attractive. It's a strange phenomenon, a scientific one, in a way. Of course, that doesn't mean that being accused produces a clear change in appearance that can be precisely determined. After all, it's not like cases connected with other courts; if they have a good lawyer to look after them, most of the defendants continue in their normal way of life and are not particularly hampered by the trial. Nevertheless, people with experience are able to pick out every last man of those who've been accused, no matter how big the crowd. "How?" you'll ask. My answer won't satisfy you. Those who've been accused are the most attractive. It can't be guilt that makes them attractive, for—as I at least, as a lawyer, have to say—they're not all guilty; nor can it be the punishment that is to come that makes them attractive now, for not all are punished; it can only be the proceedings instituted against them that somehow become part of them. There are, however, particularly attractive ones among these attractive men. But they're all attractive, even that miserable worm Block.'

By the time the lawyer had finished, K. had himself completely under control. He had even given several distinct nods at his final words, in confirmation of his old opinion that the lawyer was trying, as always, to distract him with irrelevant generalizations and thus divert him from the main point, namely, what work he had actually done on K.'s case. The lawyer must have noticed that this time K. was resisting more strongly than usual, for he fell silent to give K. the opportunity of speaking himself, then, when K. didn't speak, said, 'Have you come with something specific in mind today?' 'Yes,' said K., shielding his eyes from the candle a little in order to see the lawyer better, 'I wanted to tell you that, as from today, you no longer represent me in my trial.' 'Do I understand you correctly?' said the lawyer, half sitting up in bed and supporting himself with one hand on the pillows. 'I assume so,' said K., sitting bolt upright, as if on the alert. 'Well, we can discuss this plan,' said the lawyer after a short while.

'It isn't a plan any more,' said K. 'That's as may be,' said the lawyer, 'but we still don't want to rush into anything.' He used the word 'we' as if he had no intention of releasing K., and was determined, if he could not continue to represent him, to remain his adviser. 'Nothing has been rushed,' said K., slowly standing up and going behind his chair, 'it has been carefully thought over, perhaps even for too long. My decision is final.' 'In that case, allow me just a few words,' said the lawyer, removing the eiderdown and sitting on the edge of the bed. His bare, white-haired legs were trembling with cold. He asked K. to give him the blanket off the sofa. K. brought him the blanket and said, 'You're quite unnecessarily running the risk of catching cold.' 'This is important enough,' said the lawyer, wrapping the eiderdown round his top half then putting the blanket over his legs. 'Your uncle is my friend, and over the last few months I've become fond of you as well. I admit that quite openly, it's nothing to be ashamed of.'

These mawkish remarks were unwelcome to K., since they forced him into a more detailed explanation, which he would have preferred to avoid. Moreover, as he openly admitted to himself, they confused him, even if they would never make him reverse his decision. 'Thank you for your kind sentiments,' said K. 'For my part I recognize that you have done everything for my case that it was in your power to do and that you felt was of benefit to me. However, I have recently come to the conclusion that that is not enough. I would, of course, never attempt to bring you, a much older and more experienced man, round to my opinion; if I have sometimes tried, without thinking, to do so, then I ask you to forgive me, but the matter is, as you yourself put it, important enough, and it is my considered opinion that the time has come to take more vigorous steps as far as my trial is concerned.' 'I can understand how you feel,' said the lawyer, 'you're impatient.' 'I'm not impatient,' said K., slightly irritated, and no longer taking such care as to how he expressed himself. 'You will probably have realized at my very first visit, when I came with my uncle, that the trial wasn't that important to me; I completely forgot about it, if I wasn't forcibly reminded of it, so to speak. But my uncle insisted I appoint you to represent me, and I did so to please him. And one would have expected that, from then on, the trial would have been less of a burden to me, after all, one appoints a lawyer to represent one in order to shift some of the load on to him. The opposite happened, however. I never had so much worry about the trial as I've had since you've been representing me. When I was alone, I did nothing for my case, but I scarcely felt it; once I had a lawyer representing me, on the other hand, I was constantly on tenterhooks waiting for you to do something, but nothing ever happened. I did get various pieces of information about the court from you, which I might perhaps not have got from anyone else. But that's not enough for me now that the trial is getting too close for comfort, and as good as in secret too.'

K. had pushed the chair away and was standing up, his hands in his jacket pockets. 'There comes a time in a legal practice,' said the lawyer quietly and calmly, 'after which nothing really new happens. How many clients, at a similar stage in their trials, have stood before me as you are standing and spoken in a similar way!' 'Then,' said K., 'all those similar clients were just as right as I am. That doesn't prove me wrong.' 'I wasn't trying to prove you wrong,' said the lawyer, 'but I was just going to add that I would have expected better judgement from you than from the others, especially since I've given you a better insight into the way the court works and what I do than I usually give clients. And now I find that, after all, you haven't sufficient trust in me. You're not making things easy for me.'

How the lawyer was humbling himself before K.! With no thought for the honour of his profession, which would surely be most sensitive on precisely that point. Why was he doing it? After all, he was to all appearances greatly in demand as a lawyer, and a rich man into the bargain, the loss of income and of a client couldn't mean much to him. Moreover, he was in poor health and should have been keen to have his workload reduced. And despite that he was clinging on to K. Why? Was it personal sympathy for his uncle, or did he really regard K.'s trial as so exceptional and hoped to distinguish himself through it, either in K.'s eyes or—this possibility couldn't be disregarded—in those of his friends at the court? His expression gave nothing away, however openly K. scrutinized him. You could almost have assumed he was waiting, with a deliberately blank look on his face, to see what effect his words would have. But he was obviously putting too favourable an interpretation on K.'s silence when he went on, 'You will have noticed that I have a large office but employ no assistants. It used to be different. There was a time when several young lawyers worked for me, nowadays I work by myself. This is partly connected with a change in the work I do, concentrating more and more on cases of the type of your trial, partly with the increasingly profound understanding I have developed of this type of case. I realized I could not leave this work to anyone else, if I didn't want to break faith with my clients and with the task I had taken on. The natural consequence of my decision to do all the work myself was that I had to refuse almost all requests for legal representation, and could only accept those which particularly interested me. Of course, there are plenty of wretches, even quite nearby, who are only too glad to snap up any scraps I throw away. Moreover, I became ill from overwork. But despite all this I did not regret my decision, although it is possible that I should have refused more requests than I have done. I have devoted myself fully to the trials I have taken on, and that has proved to be absolutely essential and has been rewarded with success. In a book I found a very nice description of the difference between representing a client in normal cases and in these cases. It said: One lawyer leads his client by a thread to the verdict, but the other lifts his client up on to his shoulders straight away and carries him to the verdict, and even beyond, without putting him down. That's how it is. But it wasn't entirely correct when I said that I never regret this great task. When it is so completely misunderstood, as in your case, then I do almost regret it.'

All this talk made K. impatient, rather than convincing him. He felt he could somehow tell from the lawyer's tone of voice what would await him if he were to give way: he would once more be fobbed off with allusions to progress made with the submission, to the improved mood of the court officials but also to the great difficulties facing the task—in brief, everything he had already heard ad nauseam would be brought out again to delude him with vague hopes and torment him with vague threats. An end had to be put to that, once and for all, so he said, 'What do you propose to do in my case, should you continue to represent me?' The lawyer accepted even this insulting question and replied, 'To continue with what I have already done for you.' 'I knew it,' said K., 'now further discussion is futile.' 'I will make one more attempt,' said the lawyer, as if the things over which K. was getting agitated were not happening to K., but to him. 'You see, I suspect that your false assessment of my legal advice, as well as your behaviour in general, are due to the fact that, even though you are a defendant, you have been treated too well, or, to be more precise, treated carelessly, as it would seem. This, too, has its reason; it is often better to be in chains than free. But I would like to show you how other defendants are treated, perhaps you will manage to learn from it. I'm going to call Block now, unlock the door and sit here by the bedside table.' 'With pleasure,' said K., doing as the lawyer asked; he was always ready to learn. However, in order to secure himself against any eventuality, he asked, 'But you have taken note that you are no longer my legal representative?' 'Yes,' said the lawyer, 'but you can still rescind your decision today.' He got back into bed, pulled the eiderdown up to his chin, and turned to the wall. Then he rang.

Leni appeared almost simultaneously with the ring, and looked quickly round the room to try and find out what had been happening. She seemed reassured to see K. sitting calmly beside the lawyer's bed. Smiling, she nodded at K., who gave her a fixed stare. 'Fetch Block,' said the lawyer. However, instead of fetching him, Leni simply went out, shouted, 'Block! The lawyer wants you,' then, probably because the lawyer was still turned to the wall and not bothering with anything, slipped behind K.,'s chair. From that point on she distracted him by leaning over him or running her fingers through his hair and stroking his cheeks, though very cautiously and gently. Eventually K. tried to stop her by grasping one of her hands, which, after a short struggle, she let him keep.

Block came as soon as he was called, but stood outside the door, as if wondering whether he should come in. He raised his eyebrows and inclined his head, seemingly listening for the lawyer's command to be repeated. K. could have encouraged him to come in, but he had resolved to make a complete break not only with the lawyer, but with everything there in the apartment, so he remained motionless. Leni didn't speak either. Block saw that at least no one was sending him away, so he came in on tiptoe, a tense expression on his face, hands clutched tightly behind his back. He left the door open as a possible escape route. He didn't look at K. at all, but kept his eyes fixed on the piled-up eiderdown under which the lawyer could not even be seen, since he'd pushed himself quite close up to the wall. But then his voice was heard. 'Block's here?' he asked. Block had advanced quite far into the room, and the question positively hit him in the chest and then in the back, he stumbled, came to a halt, and said, bent low, 'At your service.' 'What d'you want?' asked the lawyer.

'You come at an inconvenient time.' 'Wasn't I called?' asked Block, speaking more to himself than to the lawyer. He put his hands out to protect himself, and was ready to run away. 'You were called,' said the lawyer, 'but you still come at an inconvenient time.' And after a pause he added, 'You always come at an inconvenient time.' Once the lawyer had started speaking, Block didn't look at the bed any-more but stared at some corner or other instead and just listened, as if the sight of the speaker were too dazzling for him to bear. But even listening was difficult, since the lawyer was turned towards the wall and speaking both softly and very fast. 'Do you want me to leave?' asked Block. 'You're here now,' said the lawyer. 'Stay!' You would have thought that, instead of fulfilling Block's wish, the lawyer had threatened to have him thrashed, for now Block really did start to tremble. 'Yesterday,' said the lawyer, 'I visited my friend, the third judge, and gradually brought the conversation round to you. Do you want to know what he said?' 'Oh, please,' said Block. Since the law-yer didn't continue immediately, Block repeated his request and stooped low, as if he were about to kneel. At that K. berated him. 'What d'you think you're doing?' he shouted. Since Leni had made an attempt to stop him crying out, he grasped her other hand. It wasn't love that made him hold it tight, and she kept groaning and trying to pull her hands free. But it was Block who was punished because of K.'s cry, for the lawyer asked him, 'Who is your lawyer?' 'You are, sir,' said Block. 'And apart from me?' the lawyer asked. 'No one apart from you, sir,' said Block. 'Then don't listen to anyone else,' said the lawyer. Block accepted that entirely, giving K. an angry look and shaking his head at him. If his gestures had been translated into words they would have been gross insults. And K. had imagined he could have a friendly conversation about his own case with a man like that! 'I won't interrupt you again,' said K., leaning back in his chair. 'Do as you like, you can kneel down or crawl on all fours for all I care.' But Block still had his self-respect, at least as far as K. was concerned, for he went over to him, waving his fists, and shouted at him, as loud as he dared in the lawyer's presence, 'You can't talk to me like that, it's not permitted. Why are you insulting me? And here, before the lawyer, where both of us, you as well as me, are only allowed on sufferance, out of compassion? You're no better a person than I am, for you have been accused and have a trial as well. If, despite that, you remain a gentleman, I am just as much a gentleman too, perhaps a greater one even, why not? And I insist on being addressed as such, by you of all people. If you think you are privileged because you can sit there calmly and calmly listen, whilst I, as you put it, crawl on all fours, then I will remind you of the old axiom: "For a suspect, movement is better than staying still, for someone who is still can always, without realizing it, be in the scales and be weighed with his sins."'

K. said nothing, he merely stared in astonishment, unable to take his eyes off this confused man. What changes he had gone through in the last hour alone! Was it the trial which threw him this way and that, so he could no longer tell who was his friend, who his enemy? Could he not see that the lawyer was deliberately humiliating him, his only intention this time being to show off his power to K. and perhaps, by so doing, make K. subject to him as well? If Block was incapable of understanding that, or if he was so afraid of the lawyer that no understanding was of any help to him, how was it that he was cunning or bold enough to deceive the lawyer and keep it from him that he had other lawyers working for him. And how was it that he was bold enough to attack K., since he could betray his secret. But he was even bolder. He went to the lawyer's bed and started to complain to him about K. 'Sir,' he said, 'did you hear the way this man spoke to me? His trial can still be measured in hours, and he's telling me, a man whose trial has been going on for five years, how to behave. He even insulted me. He knows nothing and he insults me, a man who has studied, as far as his weak powers would allow, the demands of propriety, duty, and court etiquette.' 'Don't concern yourself with anyone else,' said the lawyer, 'just do what you feel is right.' 'Certainly,' said Block, as if to give himself courage, then, with a brief sideways glance, knelt* right beside the bed. 'I'm kneeling, my Lawyer,' he said. The lawyer, however, remained silent. Cautiously, Block stroked the eiderdown with one hand.

In the ensuing silence Leni freed herself from the grip of K.'s hands, saying, 'You're hurting me. Let go. I'm going to Block.' She went over and sat down on the edge of the bed. Block was delighted at that, and immediately begged her, mutely but with vigorous signs, to intercede with the lawyer for him. He clearly needed the lawyer's information urgently, though perhaps only for his other lawyers to make use of. Leni probably knew exactly how to get round the lawyer, she pointed to the lawyer's hand and pursed her lips, as if in a kiss. Immediately Block kissed his hand, and repeated it twice more at Leni's insistence. But the lawyer stayed silent. Then Leni leant over the lawyer, revealing the beautiful lines of her body as she stretched, and stroked his long white hair as she bent low over his face. That did elicit an answer. 'I hesitate to tell him,' said the lawyer, and one could see him shaking his head slightly, perhaps the better to feel the pressure of Leni's hand. Block listened, his head bowed, as if by listening he were breaking a commandment. 'Why do you hesitate?' Leni asked. K. had the feeling he was listening to a well-rehearsed dialogue that had been repeated many times before, that would be repeated many times again, and retained its freshness for Block alone. Instead of replying, the lawyer asked, 'How has he been behaving today?' Before replying, Leni looked down at Block and watched him for a while as he raised his hands to her and rubbed them together pleadingly. At last she nodded earnestly, turned to the lawyer, and said, 'He's been quiet and hard-working.' An old businessman with a long beard was begging a young woman for a favourable report! Even if he had some ulterior motive, nothing could justify his behaviour in the eyes of a fellow human being; the observer almost felt degraded by it. K. couldn't understand how the lawyer could have imagined this performance might win him over. If he hadn't already got rid of him, this scene would have made him do so. So that was the way the lawyer's method worked: eventually the client forgot everything else and plodded along this one route, which was actually the wrong track, hoping it would lead to the end of his trial. Fortunately, K. had not been exposed to it long enough for that. Such a person was no longer a client, he was the lawyer's dog. If the lawyer had ordered him to crawl under the bed, as if going into a kennel, and bark, he would have done so with pleasure. K. sat back and listened intently, as if he had been charged with noting precisely everything that was said here and reporting it to a higher authority.

'What has he been doing all day?' the lawyer asked. 'So that he wouldn't distract me while I was working,' said Leni, 'I locked him in the maid's bedroom, where he usually stays. I could check up on him from time to time through the hatch to see what he was doing. Every time he was kneeling on the bed, reading the books you'd lent him which he had open on the window-ledge. It made a good impression on me; you see, the window just looks out on to a ventilation shaft and gives almost no light at all. That Block was reading despite that shows how obedient he is.' 'I'm delighted to hear that,' said the lawyer, 'but was he reading the books with understanding?' During this conversation Block was constantly moving his lips; clearly he was formulating the replies he hoped Leni would give. 'Of course, I can't answer that with any certainty,' said Leni, 'but I could see that he was reading everything thoroughly. He spent the whole day reading the same page, moving his finger along the lines as he read. Every time I looked, he was sighing, as if he found the reading very laborious. The books you lent him are probably difficult to understand.' 'Yes,' said the lawyer, 'they are that. I don't imagine he can understand them at all. They're just to give him an inkling of how difficult the fight is that I have to undertake in his defence. And for whom am I undertaking such a difficult fight? For—it's almost absurd to say it out loud—for Block. And he is about to learn what that means. Has he been studying uninterruptedly?' 'Almost uninterruptedly,' Leni replied, 'just once he asked me for a drink of water, so I handed him a glass through the hatch. And at eight o'clock I let him out and gave him something to eat.'

Block glanced at K. out of the corner of his eye, as if all this redounded to his credit and ought to impress K. Now he seemed to be filled with hope, moving more freely and shifting to and fro on his knees, so that the way he froze at the lawyer's next words came out all the more clearly. 'You praise him,' said the lawyer, 'but that makes it all the more difficult for me to speak. What the judge had to say about him was not good, neither for Block himself, nor for his trial.' 'Not good?' Leni asked. 'How is that possible?' Block was looking at her intently, as if he thought she was capable of turning the judge's words, which had been spoken long since, into something favourable for him. 'Not good,' said the lawyer. 'He even reacted with displeasure when I started talking about Block. "Don't talk about Block," he said. "He's my client," I said. "You're being exploited," he said. "I don't think his case is lost," I said. "You're being exploited," he repeated. "I don't think so," I said, "Block works hard at his trial, he's always engaged on his case. He stays in my house almost all the time so as to keep up to date with it. True, as a person he's unpleasant, has no manners and is grubby, but as far as his trial's concerned, he's impeccable." I said impeccable, I was deliberately exaggerating. To that the judge replied, "Block's just cunning. He's gathered a lot of experience and knows how to draw out the trial. But his ignorance is greater than his cunning. What do you think he'd say if he were to learn that his trial hasn't even begun, if he were to be told that the bell for the start of his trial hasn't even been rung yet?" Stay still, Block!' said the lawyer, for Block had started to get up, his knees wobbling, clearly about to ask for an explanation.

Now the lawyer spoke for the first time at greater length directly to Block. With tired eyes, his gaze now drifted aimlessly round the room, now settled on Block, making him slowly sink back down on his knees. 'These remarks by the judge are of no significance whatever for you,' said the lawyer. 'Stop taking fright at every word. If it happens once more, I won't reveal anything at all to you ever again. One can't even start a sentence without you looking at me as if the final verdict were about to come. You should be ashamed of yourself in front of my client. And you're destroying the trust he has in me. What do you want? You're still alive, you're still under my protection. Your fear is pointless. You've read somewhere that in some cases the final verdict can come unexpectedly, at any time at all, from anyone's lips. That, with many reservations, happens to be true, but it is equally true that your fear fills me with disgust, and that I see in it a lack of the necessary trust. What did I say? I repeated the remark of a judge. You know that the various opinions pile up round the proceedings to the point of impenetrability. This judge, for example, sees the proceedings beginning at a different point than I do. A difference of opinion, nothing more. According to an old custom, a bell is sounded at a particular stage of a trial. The judge's view is that that is when the trial begins. I can't tell you everything that speaks against that just now, you wouldn't understand anyway, suffice it to say that there is much that speaks against it.' In embarrassment Block plucked at the sheepskin bedside rug with his fingers. The fear the judge's remarks had caused him made him at times forget the submissiveness he normally showed the lawyer, As he examined the words of the judge from all sides, his only thought was for himself. 'Block,' said Leni in warning tones and pulling him up a little by his jacket collar, 'leave the sheepskin alone and listen to the lawyer.'

In the Cathedral

K. WAS given the task of showing a very important Italian business associate of the bank, who was visiting the city for the first time, some of its artistic treasures. It was a task which at any other time he would have regarded as an honour. Now, however, at a time when it was taking all his effort to maintain his reputation in the bank, he accepted it reluctantly. Every hour he spent away from the office caused him concern. Although he could no longer make anything like as good use of his time in the office as formerly, sometimes spending hours making only a thin pretence of doing proper work, he was even more worried when he was not in the office. He imagined he could see the deputy manager, who had always been on the lookout for any chance to take advantage, going into his office from time to time, sitting down at his desk, looking through his papers, seeing clients with whom K. had been almost friends for years and turning them against him, perhaps even uncovering errors, by which K. now saw himself menaced from all sides during his work and which he could no longer avoid. Consequently, whenever he was sent out on business or, even worse, on a short trip—and such tasks happened to have piled up recently—there was always the natural suspicion, however much of an honour it was to be chosen, that they wanted to get him out of the office for a while to check his work, or at least that they thought they could easily do without him in the office. There would have been no difficulty refusing most of these requests, but he didn't dare. If there was the slightest justification for his concern, refusing a request would have been an admission of his fear. For that reason, he accepted these tasks with apparent equanimity; indeed once, when he was to undertake a strenuous two-day business trip, he even kept quiet about a heavy cold merely so as to avoid the danger that they might stop him going on the trip because of the rainy autumn weather at that time.

It was when he came back from this trip, with a blinding headache, that he heard he had been deputed to accompany the Italian business associate the next day. The temptation to refuse, at least just this once, was very great, especially since the task was not something that was directly connected with the bank's business. It was a social obligation, which was doubtless important enough, only not for K., who knew very well that he could only survive through success in his work; if he didn't manage that, it would make no difference whatsoever even if, contrary to expectation, he were to charm this Italian. He didn't want to be kept out of the domain of work, even for one day, for his fear that he would not be let back in again was too great. He quite clearly recognized that this fear was exaggerated, but it still gripped him. In this particular case, though, it was almost impossible to find an acceptable reason for refusing; K.'s knowledge of Italian was limited but still sufficient, but the decisive factor was that K. had earlier acquired some knowledge of art history. This had become known—and exaggerated—in the bank, because for a while K. had been a member, though only for business reasons, of the Association for the Preservation of the City Monuments.* Now, it was rumoured that the Italian was interested in art, so that the choice of K. to show him round was a matter of course.

It was a very rainy, blustery morning when K., annoyed at the day ahead, arrived in the office at seven o'clock, early enough to get at least some work done before the visitor took him away from it all. He was very tired, having spent half the night studying an Italian grammar in order to prepare himself a little, and he was more attracted by the window, where he had spent too much time sitting recently, than by his desk. However, he resisted the temptation and set to work. Unfortunately, at that moment a messenger came, saying the manager had sent him to see if Herr K. was already in; if he was, would he be so good as to come through to the reception room, the gentleman from Italy was already there. 'I'm coming,' said K. Sticking a small dictionary in his pocket, and clasping under his arm an album of the sights of the city he'd prepared for the Italian, he went through the deputy manager's office to the manager's suite. He was glad he'd come to the office so early and was immediately available, which presumably no one had seriously expected. The deputy manager's office was still empty, of course, as if it were the middle of the night; the messenger had probably been told to summon him to the reception room as well, but in vain.

Two men got up from the low armchairs when K. entered the reception room. The manager gave him a friendly smile, clearly delighted to see K. there, and immediately performed the introductions. The Italian shook K.'s hand vigorously and laughed as he called someone an early riser. K. didn't quite know who he was referring to; it was,

moreover, an odd word, the meaning of which it took K. a little while
to work out. He responded with a few bland sentences, which the
Italian once more accepted with a laugh, his restless hand several
times stroking his dark, bushy moustache speckled with grey. His
moustache was clearly perfumed, it almost made you want to go up
and smell it. When they had all sat down and a brief introductory
conversation began, K. was greatly disturbed to realize that he only
understood fragments of what the Italian was saying. When he spoke
calmly, K. could understand nearly everything, but that was a rare
exception, mostly the words positively poured out of his mouth, and
he shook his head as if he were enjoying it. But when he talked like
that, he regularly slipped into some dialect or other which didn't
sound Italian at all to K., which the manager, however, not only
understood, but also spoke. K. could have foreseen that, since the
Italian came from southern Italy, where the manager had also spent
several years, but it meant that K. had little possibility of communi-
cating with him, since his French was difficult to understand as well.
Furthermore, his moustache concealed his lip movements, which
might have helped K. understand. K. began to suspect there were
many irritating problems to come. For the moment he gave up trying
to understand the Italian—it would have been wasted effort anyway,
when the manager was there and could understand him so easily—
and concentrated on observing him morosely, the way he sat in the
armchair, low down but at ease, the way he kept plucking at his fash-
ionably tailored jacket, the way he once, with his arms raised and
waving his hands loosely, tried to demonstrate something K. couldn't
understand, even though he leant forward and kept his eyes on the
man's hands. Eventually K., with nothing to occupy him, was just
mechanically following the to and fro of the conversation, and his
earlier tiredness reasserted itself. He was so bemused that he caught
himself—to his horror but, fortunately just in time—about to stand
up, turn away, and leave.

At last the Italian looked at his watch and jumped up. After he had
said goodbye to the manager, he came over to K., pressing up so
close to him that K. had to push his chair back to be able to move.
The manager, who must have been able to tell from the look in K.'s
eyes that he was having problems with this Italian dialect, joined in
the conversation. He did it so cleverly and tactfully that it sounded
as if he were just giving little pieces of advice, while in fact, with his

brief remarks, he was making sure that K. understood everything the Italian, who insisted on interrupting him all the time, said. K. learnt that the Italian had business to attend to first, that unfortunately he did not have much time anyway, that he certainly had no intention of rushing round all the sights, that instead he had decided—only if K. was in agreement, of course, he was the one to make the decision—to have a look round the cathedral alone, but to do that properly. He was delighted, he said, to be able to do this in the company of such a learned and charming man—by this he was referring to K., who was concentrating on ignoring the Italian and quickly picking up what the manager said—and, if it was convenient, he suggested they meet in two hours' time, at around ten o'clock, in the cathedral. K. made some appropriate reply, the Italian shook first the manager by the hand, then K., then the manager again, and headed for the door, followed by the pair of them, only half-turned towards them, but still not stopping speaking.

Afterwards K. stayed for a while with the manager, who looked particularly ill that day. He felt that he had in some way to apologize to K., and said—they were standing close together in friendly conversation—that at first he had intended to show the Italian round himself, but then—he gave no specific reason—he'd decided to send K. instead. If he couldn't understand the Italian at first, he went on, he shouldn't let himself be put off, understanding would come very quickly, and even if he couldn't understand very much it wouldn't be a disaster, since for the Italian it wasn't that important to be understood. Anyway, K.'s Italian was surprisingly good, he was sure he would handle the matter perfectly.

With that, K. was dismissed. He spent the time still at his disposal copying unusual words he would need for the guided tour out of the dictionary. It was exceedingly tedious: messengers brought the mail; clerks came with various enquiries and, when they saw K. was busy, remained standing in the doorway and didn't move until K. had listened to them; the deputy manager availed himself of the opportunity to disturb K., coming in several times, taking the dictionary out of his hand and leafing through it, obviously with no specific purpose; even clients appeared in the semi-darkness of the anteroom whenever the door opened, bowing hesitantly, trying to bring themselves to his notice, but uncertain whether they'd been seen. All this revolved round K. as if he were its centre, while K. himself compiled a list of the words he needed, then looked them up in the dictionary, then wrote them down, then practised their pronunciation, and finally tried to learn them off by heart. His former good memory seemed to have completely abandoned him, however, and sometimes he got so furious with the Italian, who was the cause of all this drudgery, that he buried the dictionary beneath a pile of papers with the firm intention of not doing any more preparation. But then he realized he could not stand looking mutely at the works of art in the cathedral with the Italian and, even more furious, pulled the dictionary out again.

At half past nine, just as he was about to leave, there was a telephone call. Leni wished him good morning and asked how he was. K. thanked her hurriedly, saying it wasn't possible for him to talk to her just then as he had to go to the cathedral. 'To the cathedral?' Leni asked. 'Er, yes, to the cathedral.' 'Why ever to the cathedral?' Leni asked. K. tried to explain briefly, but hardly had he started than Leni suddenly said, 'They're hunting you down.' K. had no time for pity that he had neither invited nor expected, and simply said goodbye, nothing more, but as he replaced the receiver he said, half to himself, half to the far-off young woman he could no longer hear, 'Yes, they're hunting me down.'

Now, however, it was getting late, there was almost a danger he would not reach the cathedral in time. He drove there in a taxi. At the last minute he remembered the album, which he had not had the opportunity to hand over earlier, so he took it with him. He had it on his knees, and drummed his fingers on it restlessly all the time during the journey. The rain was lighter, but it was damp, cold, and dark, they wouldn't see much in the cathedral, but all the standing around on the chilly stone flags was sure to make K.'s cold worse.

The cathedral square was completely deserted. K. remembered that even as a small child it had struck him that the curtains of the houses in the narrow square were nearly all always drawn. True, with the weather as it was, that was more understandable than normally. The cathedral* seemed to be empty as well. Naturally, no one thought of going there at this time. K. walked up and down both of the side aisles. The only person he met was an old woman wrapped in a warm shawl, who was kneeling before a picture of the Virgin and looking at it. Then in the distance he saw a lame sexton limp out through a door in the wall. K. had arrived on time, the clock was just striking eleven* as he came in, but the Italian wasn't there yet. K. went back to the main entrance, stood there for a while, unsure what to do, then walked round outside the cathedral in the rain to see if the Italian was perhaps waiting at one of the side entrances. He was nowhere to be seen. Could the manager have misunderstood the time he had suggested? How could anyone understand the man correctly? However that might be, K. would certainly have to wait at least another half-hour. Since he was tired and wanted to sit down, he went back into the cathedral, found a scrap of some kind of carpet material on a step, dragged it with the tip of his toe to the floor in front of a nearby pew, wrapped his coat more tightly round him, and sat down. To pass the time, he opened the album and leafed through it for a while, but he soon had to stop, for it had grown so dark that when he looked up he could hardly see any of the details in the nearby aisle.

Far away on the main altar was the glitter of a large triangle of candles. K. couldn't have said for certain whether he had seen them earlier. Perhaps they'd only just been lit. Sextons are professional creepers, you never notice them. When K. happened to turn round he saw, not far behind him, a tall, thick candle fixed to a pillar. It was also lit but, beautiful as it was, it was insufficient to illuminate the altarpieces, which were mostly hanging in the darkness of the side altars. In fact it only served to increase the darkness. In not coming, the Italian had been sensible if discourteous, there would have been nothing for him to see, the most they could have done would have been to scan a few pictures inch by inch by the light of K.'s electric torch. In order to try that out, K. went to one of the side chapels close by, climbed a couple of steps up to a low marble balustrade, and, leaning over, shone his torch on the altarpiece. The sanctuary lamp hanging in front of it got in the way. The first thing K. partly saw, partly guessed at, was a tall knight in armour at the very edge of the picture. He was leaning on his sword, which he had stuck into the bare earth—there were only a few blades of grass here and there—in front of him. He appeared to be closely observing something that was going on before him. It was astonishing that he stayed there and didn't go closer. Perhaps it was his job to stand guard. K., who had not seen any pictures for ages, spent quite a long time looking at the knight, even though he had to keep on blinking because he couldn't stand the green light of his torch. When he then shone the light on the rest of the picture he found a standard treatment of the Entombment

of Christ;* it was, incidentally, a recent picture. He put the torch in
his pocket and went back to his seat on the pew.

By now it probably wasn't necessary to wait for the Italian any
longer. It was sure to be pouring with rain outside, and since it wasn't
as cold as K. had expected in the cathedral, he decided to wait there
for the time being. Near him was the great pulpit. Two bare golden
crosses, the extreme ends of which overlapped, were fixed, sloping at
an angle, to its little round canopy. The outer wall of the pulpit, including the part that tapered to the column supporting it, was covered in
green foliage at which cherubs, some lively, some in repose, were
clutching. He went up to the pulpit and examined it from all sides.
The workmanship on the stone was meticulous, the deep darkness
among the foliage and beneath it seemed to have been captured and
confined. K. put his hand into one such gap and then ran it carefully
over the stone; he had not known of the existence of this pulpit
before. Then he happened to notice, in the next row of benches, a
sexton standing there in a loosely hanging, creased black coat, holding a snuffbox in his left hand and watching him. 'What does the man
want?' K. wondered. 'Do I look suspicious here? Does he want a tip?'
When the sexton saw that K. had noticed him, he raised his right
hand, in which he had a pinch of snuff between two fingers, and
pointed in some vague direction. His action was almost incomprehensible. K. waited a little while, but the sexton continued to point
at something with his hand, emphasizing his gesture by nodding his
head. 'What do you want?' K. asked quietly, not daring to call out in
the church. But then he took out his purse and pushed his way along
the next pew to get to the man who, however, immediately waved
him away, shrugged his shoulders, and limped off.* His hurried limp
was similar to the way K. had tried to imitate riding a horse as a child.
'Second childhood,' thought K., 'his mind's not up to more than
being a sexton. Look at the way he stops when I stop, waiting to see
if I'm going to continue.' With a smile on his face, K. followed the
old man all the way along the side aisle until he was almost level with
the main altar. The old man kept pointing at something all the time,
but K. deliberately didn't look round, the only aim of the pointing
was to stop him following the old man. Eventually, however, he did
let him go, he didn't want to frighten him too much, nor did he want
to drive the apparition away entirely in case the Italian should come
after all.

When he went into the main aisle in order to find the seat where he had left the album, he noticed a little secondary pulpit against a pillar almost right next to the chancel. It was quite plain, made of pale, bare stone, and so small that from a distance it looked like an empty niche ready to take a statue. A preacher would definitely not be able to take a full step backwards in it. Moreover, the stone vaulting over the pulpit started at an unusually low point; it was undecorated, but swept up at such an angle that a man of medium height would not be able to stand upright, but would have to lean forward over the ledge of the pulpit all the time. It looked as if it was all designed as a torture for the preacher, and it was not obvious why this pulpit was needed, since there was the other, elaborately decorated one available.

K. would certainly not have noticed this little pulpit had it not been for the lamp fixed above it, which was lit, as is usual before a sermon. Was a sermon to be given now? In the empty church? K.'s eyes followed the line of the steps which, clinging to the pillar, led up to the pulpit. They were so narrow they looked as if they weren't meant for a person to use, but rather as a decoration of the pillar. At the bottom however—the surprise brought a smile to K.'s lips—there really was a priest with his hand on the banister, ready to climb up, and looking at K. Then he gave a slight nod, at which K. crossed himself and bowed, as he should have done sooner. With a little pull on the banister, the priest went up to the pulpit, taking short, swift steps. Was there really going to be a sermon? Perhaps the sexton wasn't so simple-minded after all, and had been trying to steer K. towards the preacher, which, given the empty church, was highly necessary. Of course, there was also an old woman kneeling somewhere at a picture of the Virgin, she should have come as well. And if there was to be a sermon, why wasn't it being introduced by the organ? But the instrument remained silent, just glinting faintly from the darkness of its great height.

K. wondered whether he shouldn't get away as quickly as possible. If he didn't now, there would be no chance of him being able to do so during the sermon, he'd have to stay as long as it lasted, losing all that time he could be in the office, since he wasn't obliged to wait for the Italian any longer. He looked at his watch; it was eleven. But was a sermon really going to be given? Could K. alone be the congregation? What if he'd been a stranger who just wanted to look round the church? Basically that was all he was. It was stupid to imagine a sermon could be given now, at eleven o'clock on a weekday morning, during the most awful weather. Obviously the priest—it definitely was a priest, a young man with a smooth, dark complexion—must be going to the pulpit just to put out the lamp, which had been lit by mistake.

But that was not the case. In fact, the priest checked the flame and turned it up a little higher, then turned slowly to the front, grasping the square moulding of the ledge with both hands. He stood like that for a while, looking round without moving his head. K. had retreated some way, and was leaning with his elbows on the front pew. With uncertain eyes he saw, somewhere, he couldn't say exactly where, the sexton squatting down contentedly, his back bowed, as if after a task well done. How silent it was in the cathedral now! But K. was going to have to break the silence, he had no intention of staying there. If it was the priest's duty to preach at a particular time, regardless of the circumstances, then let him do so, he could manage that without K.'s support, just as K.'s presence would do nothing to improve its effect. So K. slowly started to walk, inching his way on tiptoe along the pew, reached the wide main aisle, and continued down it unhindered, except that the stone floor rang out at the softest step and echoed along the vaulted ceiling, faintly but uninterruptedly, in multiple regular progression. K. felt a little forsaken as he walked by himself, perhaps observed by the priest, between the empty pews; also, the vastness of the cathedral seemed to be at the very limit of what was still bearable for human beings. When he came to the place where he had been sitting, he positively grabbed at the album he'd left there, without stopping at all, and tucked it under his arm. He had almost come to the end of the area with the pews, and was approaching the open space between them and the exit, when he heard the priest's voice for the first time. A powerful, practised voice. How it filled the cathedral waiting to receive it! But it was not the congregation the priest was addressing, it was quite unambiguous and there was no escape. He called out, 'Josef K.!'

K. paused, looking at the floor in front of him. For the moment he was still free, he could still walk on and make off through one of the three dark little wooden doors which were not far ahead. It would just mean that he hadn't understood, or that he had understood but didn't intend to do anything about it. But if he did turn round he was

caught, for then he would be admitting that he had clearly understood, that he really was the person addressed, and that he was ready
to obey. If the priest had called out again, K. would certainly have
left, but since all remained silent as long as K. was still waiting, he
turned his head a little, for he wanted to see what the priest was
doing. He was standing calmly in the pulpit as before, but it was clear
that he had noticed K.'s turn of the head. If K. didn't turn round
fully, it would make it into a childish game of peekaboo. He did turn
round, and the priest beckoned him closer with his finger. Since
everything was now out in the open, he went—out of curiosity and
to get the business over with quickly—with long, hurrying steps
towards the pulpit. He stopped beside the front pews, but the distance still seemed too great for the priest. He stretched out his arm
and indicated, his forefinger pointing sharply downwards, a place
just in front of the pulpit. K. obeyed him in this as well, from that
spot he had to bend his head right back to see the priest. 'You are
Josef K.,' said the priest, raising one hand from the pulpit in a vague
gesture. 'Yes,' said K., thinking how freely he used to say his name
in the past. For some time now it had become a burden to him, and
now people he had not met before knew his name; how good it was
to introduce oneself first and only then to be known. 'You have been
accused,' said the priest, speaking particularly quietly. 'Yes,' said K.,
'so I have been informed.' 'Then you are the man I am looking for,'
said the priest, 'I am the prison chaplain.' 'Oh,' said K. 'I have had
you summoned here,' said the priest, 'so that I can talk to you.'
'I didn't know that,' said K. 'I came here to show an Italian round the
cathedral.' 'Forget such matters, they are irrelevant,' said the priest.
'What is that you have in your hand? Is it a prayer-book?' 'No,'
replied K., 'it's an album of the sights of the city.' 'Put it down,' said
the priest. K. threw it away so violently that it opened up and skidded
across the floor, crumpling some pages. 'Do you know that things are
going badly in your trial?' asked the priest. 'That seems to be the
case,' said K., 'I've done everything I can, but so far without success,
though I haven't completed my submission yet.' 'How do you imagine it will end?' asked the priest. 'I used to think that it would turn
out all right,' said K., 'now I sometimes even doubt that myself. I don't
know how it will end. Do you know?' 'No,' said the priest, 'but I fear
it will end badly. They think you are guilty. Your trial will perhaps
not get any farther than one of the lower courts. At least for the

moment they think your guilt is proven.' 'But I'm not guilty,' said K., 'it's a mistake. How can a person be guilty anyway? We're all human, every single one of us.' 'That is correct,' said the priest, 'but that's the way guilty people talk.' 'Are you prejudiced against me as well?' asked K. 'I'm not prejudiced against you,' said the priest. 'Thank you,' said K. 'But all the others who are involved in the proceedings are prejudiced against me. And they even pass their prejudice on to those who are not involved. My position is getting more and more difficult.' 'You misunderstand the situation,' said the priest, 'the verdict does not come all of a sudden, the proceedings gradually turn into the verdict.' 'So that's how it is,' said K., bowing his head. 'What is the next thing you intend to do for your case?' the priest asked. 'I intend to seek more help,' K. said, raising his head to see how the priest reacted to that. 'There are still certain possibilities I've not yet exploited.' 'You seek too much help from others,' said the priest disapprovingly, 'especially from women. Do you not see that that is not true help?' 'Sometimes, often even, I could agree with you,' said K., 'but not always. Women have great power. If I could persuade some women I know to work together for me, I would be bound to get through. Especially with this court, that consists almost entirely of skirt-chasers. Show the examining magistrate a woman in the distance and he'll knock over the court desk and the accused in his hurry to get to her in time.' The priest lowered his head to the ledge, only now did the canopy over the pulpit seem to be pressing down on him. What terrible weather could that be outside? No, that wasn't a dull day any longer, it was already the dead of night. None of the large stained-glass windows managed to cast even a shimmer of light on the darkness of the walls. And now, of all times, the sexton was starting to put out the candles on the main altar, one after the other. 'Are you angry with me?' K. asked the priest. 'Perhaps you don't know what kind of court you're serving.' There was no reply. 'Of course, that's only my experience,' said K. It was still silent above him. 'I didn't mean to insult you,' said K. Then the priest shouted down at K., 'Can't you see even two steps in front of you?' It was shouted angrily, but at the same time as if by a person who can see someone falling and shouts out automatically, throwing caution to the winds because he is horrified himself.

Now both remained silent for a long time. In the darkness below him the priest couldn't have been able to see K. very well, whilst K.

could see the priest clearly in the light of the little lamp. Why didn't
the priest come down? He had not given a sermon but had just made
some comments to K. which, if he were to follow them closely,
would probably do more harm than good. On the other hand, K. was
convinced of the priest's good intentions, it was not impossible, if he
were to come down, that he would agree with him, it was not impossible that he would get from him a decisive and acceptable piece of
advice, which would show him not how the trial could be influenced,
but how he could break out of the trial, how he could circumvent it,
how he could live outside the trial. That possibility must exist, K.
had thought about it quite often recently. But if the priest was aware
of such a possibility, he might reveal it if he were asked, despite the
fact that he belonged to the court, and despite the fact that when K.
had attacked the court he had suppressed his natural gentleness and
had even shouted at K.

'Won't you come down?' said K. 'You don't have to give a sermon,
come down and join me.' 'Now I can come,' said the priest; perhaps
he regretted having shouted. As he lifted the lamp from its hook, he
said, 'I had to speak to you from a distance at first, otherwise I let
myself be too easily influenced and forget my official duty.'

K. waited at the bottom of the steps. The priest stretched out his
hand to him while he was still coming down. 'Have you a little time
for me?' asked K. 'As much time as you need,' said the priest, handing K. the lamp to carry. Even from close to there was still a certain
solemnity about him. 'You're very kind to me,' said K. They were
walking together up and down the dark side aisle. 'You're an exception to all those belonging to the court. However many I've already
met, I trust you more than any of them. I can speak openly to you.'
'Do not deceive yourself,' said the priest. 'In what way would I be
deceiving myself?' asked K. 'You are deceiving yourself about the
court,' said the priest. 'In the introduction to the Law it has this to
say about being deceived:

'Outside the Law* there stands a doorkeeper. A man from the
country* comes to this doorkeeper and asks to be allowed into the
Law, but the doorkeeper says he cannot let the man into the Law just
now. The man thinks this over and then asks whether that means he
might be allowed to enter the Law later. "That is possible," the doorkeeper says, "but not now." Since the door to the Law is open as
always and the doorkeeper steps to one side, the man bends down to

see inside. When the doorkeeper notices that, he laughs and says, "If you are so tempted, why don't you try to go in, even though I have forbidden it? But remember, I am powerful. And I am only the lowest doorkeeper. Outside each room you will pass through there is a doorkeeper, each one more powerful than the last. The sight of just the third is too much even for me." The man from the country did not expect such difficulties; the Law is supposed to be available to everyone and at all times, he thinks, but when he takes a closer look at the doorkeeper in his fur coat, with his large pointed nose, his long, thin, black Tartar moustache, he decides he had better wait until he is given permission to enter. The doorkeeper gives him a stool and lets him sit down at the side of the door. He sits there for days and years. He makes many attempts to be let in, and wearies the doorkeeper with his requests. Quite often the doorkeeper gives him a brief interrogation, asking him questions about the place he comes from and many other things, but they are dispassionate questions, such as important people ask, and at the end he always says he cannot let him in yet. The man, who has equipped himself well for his journey, uses everything, no matter how valuable, to bribe the doorkeeper, who accepts everything, but says, as he does so, "I am only accepting this so you will not think there is something you have omitted to do." Over the many years the man observes the doorkeeper almost uninterruptedly. He forgets the other doorkeepers and comes to see the first one as the only obstacle to his entry into the Law. He curses his misfortune, out loud in the first years, later, as he grows old, he just mutters to himself. He grows childish, and since, as a result of his years of studying the doorkeeper, he has come to recognize even the fleas in his fur collar, he asks the fleas to help him and persuade the doorkeeper to change his mind. Finally his vision grows weak, and he does not know whether it really is becoming dark around him or whether his eyes are deceiving him. But now, in the dark, he can distinguish a radiance which streams, inextinguishable, from the entrance to the Law. Now he does not have much longer to live. Before he dies, all the things he has experienced during the whole time merge in his mind into a question he has not yet put to the doorkeeper. He beckons him over, since he can no longer raise his stiffening body. The doorkeeper has to bend down low, for the difference in height has changed considerably, to the man's disadvantage. "What is it you want to know now?" the doorkeeper asks. "You are insatiable."

"Everyone seeks the Law," the man says, "so how is it that in all these years no one apart from me has asked to be let in?" The door-keeper realizes that the man is nearing his end, and so, in order to be audible to his fading hearing, he bellows at him, "No one else could be granted entry here, because this entrance was intended for you alone. I shall now go and shut it."'

'So the doorkeeper deceived the man,' K., who was very taken with the story, said straight away. 'Don't be over-hasty,' said the priest, 'don't accept someone else's opinion unchecked. I told you the story exactly as it is written. It says nothing about being deceived.' 'But it's obvious,' said K., 'and your initial interpretation* was quite right. The doorkeeper only gave the man the information that would have released him once it was too late for him.' 'It was only then that he was asked,' said the priest, 'and you must remember that he was only a doorkeeper, and as such he did his duty.' 'Why do you think he did his duty?' asked K. 'He didn't do it. His duty was perhaps to turn away all other people, but he should have let the man in, the entrance was intended for him.' 'You don't respect what is written, you change the story,' said the priest. 'The story contains two import-ant statements from the doorkeeper regarding admission to the Law, one at the beginning, one at the end. One is that "he cannot let the man into the Law just now", and the other that "this entrance was intended for you alone". If there were a contradiction between these two statements, then you would be right and the doorkeeper would have deceived the man. But there is no contradiction. On the con-trary, the first statement even points to the second. One might even say that the doorkeeper exceeded his duty by suggesting the man might be let in at some time in the future. At that point his only duty would seem to be to turn the man away. Indeed, many explicators of these writings are surprised that the doorkeeper gave that hint at all, for he seems to like precision and is strict in carrying out his office: for many years he doesn't leave his post, and only closes the door right at the end; he is very aware of the importance of his position, for he says, "I am powerful"; he respects his superiors, for he says, "I am only the lowest doorkeeper"; when it is a matter of doing his duty he can be moved neither to pity nor to anger, for it says of the man that he "wearies the doorkeeper with his requests"; he is not garrulous, during all the years he only asks "dispassionate questions", as the text puts it; he is not corruptible, for he says of a gift, "I am only accepting this so you will not think there is something you have omitted to do"; finally, his outward appearance, his large pointed nose and his long, thin, black Tartar moustache, suggests a pedantic character. Can a doorkeeper show greater devotion to duty? But as well as these, the doorkeeper has other characteristics which are very much to the advantage of the man wanting to be let in, and which at least make it understandable how he could exceed his duty somewhat in hinting at the future possibility. It cannot be denied that he is a little simple-minded, and, connected with that, a little conceited. Even if his comments about his power, and about the power of the other doorkeepers and about the sight of them, which is too much even for him—I say that even if all these comments are basically correct, yet the way he makes these comments shows that his opinion is clouded by simple-mindedness and arrogance. Regarding this, the explicators comment: correct understanding of something and mis-understanding of the same thing are not entirely mutually exclusive. At least one has to assume that his simple-mindedness and arro-gance, however slight the effect may perhaps be, will still weaken the guarding of the entrance, they are deficiencies in the doorkeeper's character. In addition, the doorkeeper seems to be of a friendly nature, he is by no means always standing on his official dignity. In the very first moments he jokingly invites the man to enter, despite repeating that it was forbidden, then he does not send him away, instead he gives him a stool, as it says, and lets him sit at the side of the door. The patience with which he puts up with the man's requests through all the years, his little interrogations, his acceptance of the presents, the delicacy of feeling he shows in allowing the man beside him to curse out loud the misfortune that has put the doorkeeper there—all this suggests feelings of pity. Not every doorkeeper would have behaved like that. And finally, when he is beckoned over he bends down low to the man to give him the opportunity of asking one final question. The words "You are insatiable" express only mild impatience—the door-keeper knows that everything is over. Some people take this kind of explication even farther, assuming that the words "You are insatiable" express a kind of friendly admiration, which, it is true, is not entirely free of condescension. At least in this interpretation the figure of the doorkeeper turns out differently from the way you see him.'

'You know the story better than I do,' said K., 'and you've known it for longer.' They were silent for a while. Then K. said, 'So you don't think the man was deceived?' 'Do not misunderstand me,' said the priest, 'I am merely showing you the opinions there are on that subject. You shouldn't pay too much attention to opinions. What is written is unchanging, and opinions are often just an expression of despair at that. In this case there is even an opinion according to which it is the doorkeeper who is deceived.' 'That is an extreme opinion,' said K., 'what is it based on?' 'It is based on the doorkeeper's simple-mindedness,' the priest replied. 'It is claimed that he does not know the inside of the Law, only the path outside the entrance which he has to keep walking up and down. The ideas he has of the inside are considered childish, and it is assumed that he himself fears the things he wants to make the man afraid of. Indeed, he is more afraid of them than the man is, whose sole desire is to be let into the Law, even when he is told about the terrible doorkeepers inside, while the doorkeeper does not want to enter, at least we are told nothing about that. There are others who say that he must already have been inside, since at some point he will have entered the service of the Law and that can only have taken place inside. The response to that is that he could well have been engaged as doorkeeper by a call from inside, but that if he has been inside at all it cannot have been very far, since the sight of the third doorkeeper is too much for him. Moreover, there is no mention of him saying anything about the inside during all those years, apart from his remark about the doorkeepers. He could have been forbidden to do so, but he says nothing about that either. The deduction from all this is that he knows nothing about the appearance or the significance of the inside, and is deceiving himself about it. But, according to this interpretation, he is also deceiving himself about the man from the country, for he is subordinate to the man and is unaware of it. That he treats the man as a subordinate can be seen in many details which I am sure you will remember. That it is he, however, who is actually subordinate to the man is, according to that opinion, supposed to come out just as clearly. Above all, a free man stands above a bound man. Now, the man is certainly free, he can go wherever he wants, only the entrance to the Law is forbidden him, and that only by one single person, the doorkeeper. If he sits down on the stool at the side of the entrance and stays there for the rest of his life, he does so of his own free will, there is no compulsion mentioned in the story. The doorkeeper, on the other hand, is bound as an official to his post, he cannot leave it and go elsewhere, nor, to all appearances, can he go inside, even if he wanted to. Moreover, he is in the service of the Law, but only for this one entrance, that is, only for this one man for whom alone this entrance is intended. For that reason he is subordinate to him. The assumption is that for many years, as many as it takes for a man to grow to maturity, his task was purely symbolic, for it says that a man comes, that is, a person who has reached manhood, so consequently the doorkeeper had to wait a long time before his purpose was fulfilled, the length of time depending on the man, who came of his own free will; and also, the end of his official duties is determined by the end of the man's life, therefore he remains subordinate to the man until the end. And it is repeatedly emphasized that the doorkeeper seems to be unaware of all this. This is not seen as at all remarkable, for according to this opinion the doorkeeper is deceived in a much more profound way. This concerns his official duties. At the end he says of the entrance, "I'm going to go and shut it now," but at the beginning it says that the door to the Law was open as always. But if it is always open, "always" meaning independently of the lifespan of the man for whom it is intended, then even the doorkeeper will not be able to shut it. Opinions vary as to whether, with his announcement that he is going to shut the door, the doorkeeper simply wants to give an answer, or to emphasize his duty, or to make the man feel remorse and sorrow in his final moment. But many agree that he will not be able to shut the door. They even believe that, at least at the end, he is subordinate to the man in his knowledge as well, for the man can see the radiance that streams from the entrance to the Law, whilst the doorkeeper is presumably standing, as his task demands, with his back to the door, nor does he say anything to show that he has noticed a change.'

'That is well reasoned,' said K., who had repeated some parts of the priest's explanation to himself in a low voice. 'It's well reasoned, and now I too believe that the doorkeeper has been deceived. But that doesn't change my former opinion, in fact they partially coincide. The decisive fact is not whether the doorkeeper sees clearly or is deceived. I said that the man has been deceived. If the doorkeeper sees clearly, then one might doubt that, but if the doorkeeper is deceived, then he must of necessity pass that on to the man. The doorkeeper is not a deceiver, but he is so simple-minded he ought to be sacked immediately. You must remember that the fact that the doorkeeper is deceived does no harm to him, but infinite harm to the man.' 'Here you run into a contrary opinion,' said the priest. 'Some people say that the story does not give anyone the right to judge the doorkeeper. However he appears to us, he is, after all, a servant of the Law, he belongs to the Law and is, therefore, beyond human judgement. Nor can one think that he is subordinate to the man. To be bound as a servant of the Law, even if only at its entrance, is incomparably more than to live in freedom out in the world. The man has only just come to the Law, the doorkeeper is already there. He is appointed by the Law, to doubt whether he is worthy would be to doubt the Law.' 'I don't agree with that opinion,' K. said, shaking his head. 'If one accepts it, one has to take everything the doorkeeper says as the truth. But that isn't possible, as you yourself have demonstrated at great length.' 'No,' said the priest, 'one doesn't have to take everything as the truth, one just has to accept it as necessary.' 'A depressing opinion,' said K. 'It means that the world is founded on untruth.'

K. said this as a final comment, but it was not his final verdict. He was too tired to be able to take into account all the deductions that could be made from the story; it also led him into unusual trains of thought, unreal things, more suited to a discussion among court officials than for him. The simple story had become misshapen, he wanted to shake it off, and the priest, now showing great tact, allowed this and received K.'s comment in silence, even though it certainly did not correspond to his own opinion.

They continued to walk up and down in silence for a while. K. stuck close to the priest, not knowing where he was in the dark. The lamp he was holding had long since gone out. Once the silver statue of a saint glinted in front of him, but it was only the gleam of the silver and immediately faded back into darkness. In order not to be completely dependent on the priest, K. asked him, 'Aren't we close to the main entrance now?' 'No,' said the priest, 'we're a long way away from it. Do you want to go already?' Although that hadn't been in his mind when he asked his question, K. immediately said, 'Definitely, I have to go. I am senior accountant at a bank, people are waiting for me, I only came here to show an Italian business associate round the cathedral.' 'In that case,' said the priest, holding out his hand, 'off you go.' 'But I can't find my way in the dark,' said K. 'Go to the wall on your left,' said the priest, 'then keep following it until you come to an exit.' The priest had only taken a few steps away from him, but still K. called out very loudly, 'Please wait a moment.' 'I am waiting,' said the priest. 'Is there anything else you want from me?' asked K. 'No,' said the priest. 'At first you were very friendly,' said K., 'and explained everything, but now you're dismissing me as if I meant nothing to you.' 'But you have to go,' said the priest. 'Well, yes,' said K., 'but you must understand.' 'First of all you must understand who I am,' said the priest. 'You are the prison chaplain,' said K., going closer to the priest—his immediate return to the bank was not as necessary as he had made out, he could well afford to stay there longer. 'That means I belong to the court,' said the priest, 'so why should I want anything from you? The court does not want anything from you. It receives you when you come and dismisses you when you go.'

The End

On the day before his thirty-first birthday—it was towards nine o'clock in the evening, the time when the streets are quiet—two men came to K.'s apartment, pale and fat, wearing frock coats and top hats that looked as if they were stuck on. Brief formalities at the apartment door* were followed by more extensive formalities at the door to K.'s room. Although he had not been told in advance the men were coming, K., similarly dressed in black,* was sitting in a chair close to the door, pulling on a new pair of gloves that stretched tight over his fingers, in the posture of someone who was expecting visitors. He stood up at once, looking at the men with an expression of curiosity. 'So you're the ones who've come for me?' he asked. The men nodded, each pointing to the other with his top hat. K. admitted to himself that he had expected different visitors. He went over to the window and looked out into the dark street once more. Almost all the windows on the other side were dark as well, many had the curtains drawn. In one lighted window two small children could be seen in a playpen; not yet able to walk or crawl, they were feeling for each other with their hands. 'They send old, second-rate actors for me,' K. said to himself, looking round to confirm that. 'They're trying to get rid of me on the cheap.' K. suddenly turned to them, asking, 'At which theatre* are you engaged?' 'Theatre?' one of the men, the corners of his mouth twitching, asked the other. The other grimaced, like a mute desperately trying to produce a sound from a recalcitrant vocal organ. 'They're not prepared for questions,' K. said to himself, and went to fetch his hat.

As soon as they were on the stairs the men tried to take his arms, but K. said, 'Not until we're in the street, I'm not ill.' But the moment they reached the street door they linked arms with him in a way K. had never walked with anyone before. They put their shoulders close behind his and didn't bend their arms, but used them to entwine the whole length of his arm, grasping K.'s hands at the bottom in an irresistible, practised, textbook grip. K. walked between them, stiffly upright, the three of them forming such a single unit that knocking one down would have meant knocking all of them down. It was a kind of unit only inanimate objects can usually form.

In the light of the street-lamps K. tried several times, despite the difficulty when they were so tightly squeezed together, to see his escorts more clearly than had been possible in the dimness of his room. 'Perhaps they're tenors,' he thought, at the sight of their large double chins. He found the cleanliness of their faces nauseating. One could positively see the cleansing fingers that had poked in the corners of their eyes, rubbed their upper lips, and scraped out the folds under their chins.

When K. noticed this, he halted, with the result that the others halted too. They were at the side of an open, deserted square with flowerbeds. 'Why did they send you, of all people!' he cried out rather than said. The men appeared to have no answer to that, they waited with their free arms hanging down, like hospital orderlies when the patient wants to rest. 'I'm not going any farther,' K. said by way of experiment. The two men didn't need to reply, they simply kept their grip tight and tried to move K. on by lifting him, but K. resisted. 'I won't need much strength any more,' he thought, 'I'll use it all now.' The image of flies tearing their legs to get away from the flypaper occurred to him. 'It's going to be hard work for these gentlemen.'

Then Fräulein Bürstner appeared in the square, coming up a small set of steps from a lower street. It wasn't quite certain that it was her, though the similarity was great. But K. wasn't bothered whether it was definitely Fräulein Bürstner or not, it was just that he immediately became aware of the futility of his resistance. There was nothing heroic about his resistance, about making things difficult for the two men, about trying to enjoy the last semblance of life as he defended himself. He started to walk, and something of the joy that gave the two men transferred itself to him. Now they were happy to allow him to determine the direction, and he took the direction the woman in front of them was taking, not because he wanted to catch up with her, not because he wanted to see her for as long as possible, but solely so as not to forget the admonition she represented for him. 'The only thing I can do now—' he said to himself, and the regularity of his steps and the steps of the three others confirmed what he was thinking: 'The only thing I can do now is to retain a calm clarity of mind right to the end. I was always trying* to interfere in the world with ten pairs of hands—and for an unacceptable goal at that. That wasn't right, and am I now going to show that I have not learnt anything from a trial that has lasted a year? Am I going to depart as a slow-witted person? Are people going to be able to say that at the beginning of the trial I wanted to end it, and now, at the end, 'I want to start it all over again? I don't want people to say that. I'm grateful that I've been given these two half-mute, uncomprehending men to accompany me on my way and it's been left to me to tell myself everything that is needful.'

Meanwhile the young woman had turned into a side-street, but by this time K. could manage without her and let his escort lead the way. They proceeded across a bridge in the moonlight, all three now fully in accord, the two men readily giving way to every slight move-ment K. made; when he turned a little towards the railings, they swung right round in that direction. The water, glittering and quiv-ering in the moonlight, parted round a little island on which masses of leaves from trees and bushes were piled up as if squashed together. Now invisible beneath them were gravel paths with comfortable benches on which K. had stretched out and relaxed on many a sum-mer's day. 'I didn't want to stop,' he said to his escort, shamed by their ready compliance. One of them seemed to address a mild reproach to the other behind K.'s back for the misunderstanding about stopping; then they continued.

They went uphill through some streets where policemen were standing or walking, some very close, some far away. One, with a bushy moustache, his hand on the hilt of his sabre, came, as if intentionally, up to the somewhat suspicious-looking group. The two men paused, and the policeman seemed about to open his mouth when K. pulled them forwards with all his might. Several times he looked round carefully to see if the policeman was following, but when they had put a corner between themselves and the policeman, K. started to run and the men had to run with him, despite being very short of breath.

They quickly left the city behind; on that side it bordered directly on the fields. There was a little quarry, deserted and desolate, close to a house which was still urban in character. There the men stopped, either because that was were they had been heading all the time, or because they were too exhausted to go any farther. Now they let go of K., who waited in silence, took off their top hats, and wiped the sweat from their foreheads with their handkerchiefs as they looked round the quarry. Everything was bathed in moonlight, with the naturalness and calm no other light possesses.

After a series of polite exchanges about who was to perform the next tasks—they didn't seem to have been allocated to them separately—one of them came up to K. and took off his jacket, his waistcoat, and finally, his shirt. K. couldn't stop himself shivering, at which the man gave him a reassuring pat on the back. Then he folded up the clothes carefully, like things that are going to be used again, if not in the immediate future. The night air was cool, and so as not to leave K. exposed to it unmoving, he took him by the arm and walked up and down with him a little, while the other man inspected the quarry for some suitable spot. When he had found one, he waved, and the other man escorted K. to it. It was close to the quarry face, there was a stone there that had broken off. The men laid K. on the ground, leant him against the stone, and gently placed his head on top of it. Despite all the efforts they made, and despite all the cooperation K. showed, his posture remained very strained and unconvincing. Therefore one of the men asked the other to leave the laying-out of K. to him for a while, but that didn't make it any better. Finally they left K. in a position which wasn't even the best of those they had already tried. Then one of the men unbuttoned his frock coat and took out, from a sheath hanging from a belt round his waistcoat, a long, thin, double-edged butcher's knife, held it up, and checked the edges in the light. Now the odious polite exchanges began again, as one handed the knife across K. to the other and he handed it back. K. knew very well that it would have been his duty to grasp the knife himself as, going from hand to hand, it hung in the air above him, and plunge it into his own body. But he didn't do that, instead he turned his neck, that was still free, and looked around. That final test was beyond him, he could not do all the authorities' work for them, the responsibility for this last failing lay with the one who had refused him the necessary strength to do that. His eye fell on the top storey of the house beside the quarry. Like a flash of light, the two casements of a window parted and a human figure, faint and thin from the distance and height, leant far out in one swift movement then stretched its arms out even farther. Who was it? A friend? A kind person? Someone who felt for him? Someone who wanted to help? Was it just one? Or all of them? Was help still possible? Were there still objections he'd forgotten? Of course there were. Logic may be unshakeable, but it cannot hold out against a human being who wants to live. Where was the judge he had never seen? Where was the high court he had never reached? He raised his hands and splayed his fingers.

But the hands of one of the men were placed on K.'s throat,* whilst the other plunged the knife into his heart and turned it round twice. As his sight faded, K. saw the two men leaning cheek to cheek close to his face as they observed the final verdict. 'Like a dog!' he said. It seemed as if his shame would live on after him.

FRAGMENTS

B.'s Friend

In the days that followed K. found it impossible to speak to Fräulein
Bürstner at all, even to exchange a few words with her. He tried all
sorts of different ways of approaching her, but she always managed
to avoid contact with him. He would come straight home from work
and stay in his room with the light off, sitting on the sofa doing nothing but keep the hall under observation. If the maid happened to go
past and close the door of the apparently empty room, after a while
he would get up and open it again. He got up an hour earlier than
usual in the morning, hoping perhaps to see Fräulein Bürstner alone
when she went to the office. But none of these attempts succeeded.
Then he wrote a letter, which he sent to her both at her office and her
apartment, and in which he tried once more to justify his behaviour.
He offered to make amends in any way she liked, and promised he
would never again overstep the bounds she set him; all he wanted
was the chance to talk to her just once, especially as he could do nothing with regard to Frau Grubach until he had discussed the matter
with her beforehand. Finally he informed her that he would be in his
room all day the next Saturday, waiting for an indication that she was
ready to accede to his request, or at least an explanation of why she
could not do so, despite the fact that he had promised to fall in with
her wishes in everything. The letters were not returned, but no answer
came. On the other hand, Sunday brought an indication which left
nothing to be desired as to its clarity. Very early in the morning K.
noticed, through the keyhole, particular activity in the hall. It was
soon explained. A French teacher, a pale young woman, frail and
with a slight limp—she was German, as it happened, and was called
Montag—who until then had had a room of her own, was moving in
with Fräulein Bürstner. For hours she could be seen shuffling across
the hall; there was always an item of underwear or a mat or a book
that had been forgotten and had to be fetched separately and taken to
her new room.

When Frau Grubach brought K. his breakfast—since the evening
when she had made K. angry, she had not left anything that needed

to be done for him to the housemaid—K. could not refrain from addressing her for the first time in five days. 'Why is there such a noise in the hall?' he asked as he poured his coffee. 'Can't it be stopped? Does the tidying-up have to be done on Sundays, of all days?' Although K. did not look up at Frau Grubach, he noticed that she gave a sigh of relief. She took even K.'s harsh questions as forgiveness, or as the beginnings of forgiveness. 'It's not the tidying-up, Herr K.,' she said, 'it's just Fräulein Montag who's moving in with Fräulein Bürstner, she's bringing her things over.' She stopped there, to see how K. would take it and whether he would permit her to continue. But K. put her to the test, reflectively stirring his coffee while remaining silent. Then he did look up, and said, 'Have you abandoned your former suspicions about Fräulein Bürstner?' 'Herr K.,' cried Frau Grubach, who had been waiting for just that question, and held out her clasped hands towards him, 'just recently you took a casual remark very seriously. I hadn't the least intention of offending you or anyone else. You've known me long enough, Herr K., to realize that. You've no idea what I've been through these last few days. That I should speak ill of my tenants! And you thought so, Herr K.! And said I should give you notice to quit! You of all people!' Her last exclamation was already choked with tears, as she buried her face in her apron and gave a loud sob.

'Please don't cry, Frau Grubach,' said K., looking out of the window. He was thinking solely of Fräulein Bürstner, and that she had taken a stranger into her room. 'Please don't cry,' he repeated, when he turned back to the room and saw that Frau Grubach was still crying. 'I didn't mean you to take it so seriously either. It was just a mutual misunderstanding. It can happen, even between old friends.' Frau Grubach pulled her apron down below her eyes, to see whether K. really had forgiven her. 'Yes, that's the way things are,' said K., and, since Frau Grubach's behaviour suggested the captain had not revealed anything to her, now ventured to add, 'Do you really think I would fall out with you over some girl I don't know?' 'That's just it, Herr K.,' said Frau Grubach, whose misfortune it was immediately to make some ill-advised comment as soon as she felt less constrained, 'I kept asking myself: why is Herr K. taking Fräulein Bürstner's side like that? Why is he quarrelling with me over her, when he knows the slightest harsh word from him keeps me awake at night? All I said about the young lady was what I've seen with my own eyes.' K. said nothing to this, he would have had to throw her out of the room with the first words he uttered, and he didn't want to do that. He contented himself with drinking his coffee and letting Frau Grubach feel she was superfluous. Outside, the limping footsteps of Fräulein Montag could be heard going down the whole length of the hall again. 'Do you hear that?' K. asked, gesturing towards the door. 'Yes,' said Frau Grubach, with a sigh. 'I wanted to help her and to get the maid to help her, but she's obstinate, she insists on transferring everything herself. I'm surprised at Fräulein Bürstner. I often find it tiresome having Fräulein Montag as a tenant, and now Fräulein Bürstner's even sharing her room with her.' 'You don't need to let that bother you,' said K., crushing the last bits of sugar in his cup. 'Are you any worse off?' 'No,' said Frau Grubach, 'in fact it suits me very well, it means I have a room free for my nephew, the captain. I've been worried that he might have disturbed you during the last few days, when I had to put him up in the living-room next door. He doesn't show much consideration for others.' 'What an idea!' said K., standing up. 'There's no question of that. You seem to think I'm highly sensitive, because I can't stand Fräulein Montag traipsing to and fro—there she is, going back again.' Frau Grubach felt it was all beyond her.* 'Should I tell her to put off the rest of the move to another time, Herr K.? I'll do that right away, if you like.' 'But she's moving in with Fräulein Bürstner!' said K. 'Yes,' said Frau Grubach, who didn't quite understand what K. meant. 'Well,' he said, 'then she has to transfer her things.' Frau Grubach simply nodded. This mute helplessness, which outwardly looked no different from defiance, irritated K. even more. He started walking up and down the room, from the window to the door, thus depriving Frau Grubach of the opportunity to leave, which she would otherwise probably have done.

K. had just reached the door again when there was a knock. It was the maid, to say that Fräulein Montag would like a few words with K. and that she was waiting for him in the dining-room. K. listened thoughtfully to what the maid had to say, then turned to the startled Frau Grubach with an almost scornful expression on his face. His expression seemed to say that K. had long since anticipated this invitation from Fräulein Montag, and that it fitted in very well with the torments he had had to suffer from Frau Grubach's tenants that Sunday morning. He sent the maid back with the message that he would come at once, then went to the wardrobe to change his jacket. His only answer to Frau Grubach's low mutterings about this tedious woman was a request to clear away the breakfast things. 'But you've hardly touched anything,' said Frau Grubach. 'Oh, take it away all the same,' cried K. He felt as if everything was tainted with Fräulein Montag, making it unpalatable.

As he went across the hall, he looked at the closed door of Fräulein Bürstner's room. However, he hadn't been invited to go there, but to the dining-room, the door of which he flung open without knocking.

It was a very long but narrow room, with one window. There was just enough space for two cupboards to be placed across the corners of the wall beside the door, while the rest of the room was completely taken up by the long dining table, which started close to the door and almost reached the large window, making it virtually inaccessible. The table was already set, and for a large number of people, since on Sundays nearly all the tenants took lunch there.

As K. entered, Fräulein Montag came from the window along one side of the table to meet him. They greeted each other in silence. Then Fräulein Montag, her head, as always, tilted at an unusual angle, said, 'I don't know if you know me.' K. peered at her, his eyes screwed up. 'Of course,' he said, 'you've been living at Frau Grubach's for some time now.' 'But I think you don't bother much with the boarding-house,' said Fräulein Montag. 'No,' said K. 'Won't you sit down,' said Fräulein Montag. In silence, they each pulled a chair out from the top end of the table and sat down facing one another. But Fräulein Montag immediately got up again, for she had left her handbag on the window-ledge and went to fetch it. She limped down the whole length of the room. When she came back, gently swinging her handbag, she said, 'I would like a few words with you, on my friend's behalf. She intended to come herself, but she is feeling a little under the weather today. She asks you to excuse her and to give me a hearing instead. She would not have said anything other than what I have to say to you. On the contrary, I think I can even say more, since I am relatively uninvolved. Don't you agree?' 'So what is there to say?' replied K., who was tired of seeing Fräulein Montag's eyes permanently fixed on his lips, arrogating to herself a kind of control over what he was going to say. 'Clearly Fräulein Bürstner is unwilling to grant me the personal discussion I requested.' 'That is the case,' said Fräulein Montag, 'or, rather, that is not the case at all, you put it in strangely blunt terms. In general, discussions are neither granted nor does the opposite happen. But it can happen that people consider discussions unnecessary, and that is the case here. After what you have just said, I can now speak openly. You asked my friend, either by letter or by word of mouth, if you could see her to discuss something. Now my friend knows—at least that is my natural assumption—what it is you want to discuss, and is convinced, for reasons of which I am unaware, that no one would benefit from this discussion actually taking place. It was, by the way, only yesterday that she told me about this. It was only a brief mention, and she said she was sure the discussion could not be of great importance to you, since the idea had only occurred to you by chance and you would now, or at least very soon, come to realize yourself, without the need for any specific explanation, how pointless the whole thing was. I replied that, while that might well be true, I thought it would be of advantage, in order to resolve the situation completely, if you were given an explicit response. I offered to take this task upon myself, and my friend, after some hesitation, agreed. And I hope the action I have taken is in your interest as well, for even the slightest uncertainty in the most trivial matter is always a torment, and if, as in this case, it can easily be cleared up, then it were best done immediately.' 'Thank you,' K. said at once, stood up slowly, looked at Fräulein Montag, then across the table, then out of the window—the sun was shining on the house opposite—and went to the door. Fräulein Montag followed him for a few steps, as if she didn't quite trust him. But when they reached the door they both had to step back, for it opened and Captain Lanz came in. It was the first time K. had seen him from close to. He was a tall man, about forty years old, with a fleshy, sunburnt* face. He made a slight bow, which included K., then went up to Fräulein Montag and respectfully kissed her hand. He was very graceful in his movements. His courtesy towards Fräulein Montag was in striking contrast to the way she had been treated by K. Despite that, Fräulein Montag did not seem to bear him any ill-will, for she was even, K. sensed, about to introduce him to the captain. But K. did not want to be introduced, he would have been incapable of being at all friendly, either to the captain or to Fräulein Montag; for him, the captain's kiss on her hand had united them as a group who, under the appearance of innocuous altruism, wanted to keep him away from Fräulein Bürstner. K., however, felt that was not the only thing he had seen; he had also seen that the argument Fräulein Montag had chosen, though good, could cut both ways. She exaggerated the significance of the relationship between Fräulein Bürstner and K., above all she exaggerated the significance of the meeting he had requested, at the same time trying to twist things so that it looked as if it was K. who was exaggerating everything. She couldn't be more wrong. K. was not exaggerating at all, he knew that Fräulein Bürstner was just a little typist, who would not keep up her resistance to him for long. And that was deliberately not taking into account what he had learnt about Fräulein Bürstner from Frau Grubach. All this was going through his mind as he left the room with little more than a nod to the others. He was about to go straight to his room, but a little laugh from Fräulein Montag coming from the dining-room behind him gave him the idea of perhaps giving the two of them, Fräulein Montag and the captain, a surprise. He looked around and listened to check whether he might be interrupted from any of the surrounding rooms, but everywhere was quiet, all that could be heard was the conversation in the dining-room and Frau Grubach's voice coming from the corridor leading to the kitchen. It seemed a good opportunity, so K. went to the door of Fräulein Bürstner's room and knocked quietly. Since there was no response he knocked again, but still no answer came. Was she asleep? Or was she really not well? Or was she pretending not to be in, because she suspected it could only be K. knocking so quietly? K. assumed she was pretending not to be in and knocked louder, finally, since his knocking produced no result, opening the door, cautiously and not without the sense that he was doing something wrong, not to say pointless. There was no one in the room. Moreover, it hardly looked like the room as K. remembered it at all. Now there were two beds end to end along the wall, clothes and underwear were heaped up on three chairs close to the door, one wardrobe was open. Fräulein Bürstner had probably gone out while Fräulein Montag had been going on at K. in the dining-room. K. was not particularly dismayed by this, he had hardly expected to get to see Fräulein Bürstner so easily, almost the only reason for this attempt was to spite Fräulein Montag. It was, therefore, all the more embarrassing to see, as he closed the door, Fräulein Montag and the captain talking in the doorway of the dining-room. Perhaps they had been standing there ever since K. had opened the door; they avoided giving the appearance that they were observing K., talking quietly and following K.'s movements in the way you glance around absent-mindedly during a conversation. But these glances weighed heavily on K., and he made his way hastily along the wall to get back into his room.

The Lawyer from the State Prosecution Service

DESPITE the knowledge of human nature and experience of the world that K. had acquired during all the years he had worked for the bank, the company he was part of at their regular table* in the inn had always seemed to him to consist of estimable men, and he was forever telling himself that it was a great honour for him to belong to such a group. It consisted almost entirely of judges, lawyers from the prosecution service, and barristers; a few quite young officials and articled clerks were also admitted, but they sat right at the bottom of the table, and were only allowed to participate in debate when specific questions were addressed to them. Mostly, however, such questions were only asked in order to amuse the assembled company; Hasterer in particular, who belonged to the state prosecution service and generally sat next to K., loved to embarrass these young gentlemen in that way. When he splayed out his large, hairy hand on the middle of the table and turned to the lower end, everyone pricked up their ears. And when one of those from down there responded to the question, but either couldn't even work out what it meant, or stared at his beer ruminatively, or simply opened and closed his mouth without speaking, or even—and that was the worst—expressed an incorrect or non-recognized opinion in an interminable flood of words, then the older men would settle down in their chairs, only then did they seem to feel comfortable. The really serious, specialized discussions were reserved to them.

K. had been introduced to this group by a lawyer who represented the bank. There had been a time when K. had had to have long discussions with this lawyer, lasting late into the evening, so it was quite natural that he should dine together with the lawyer at the table reserved for the regulars, and he enjoyed their company. He was surrounded by learned, respected, and in a certain way, powerful men whose relaxation consisted of striving to solve difficult questions which were only distantly connected with ordinary life. Even though there was, of course, little he could contribute himself, he had the opportunity to learn much that would be of advantage to him sooner or later in the bank, and moreover, it allowed him to establish personal contacts with the courts, which were always useful. And the company seemed to like having him around. He was quickly acknowledged as an expert in business, and his opinion on such matters was accepted—though not without a certain irony—as absolute. It sometimes happened that, when two of the company had a different view on some legal question, they would ask K. his opinion of the matter. Then K.'s name would keep cropping up in all the arguments and counter-arguments, even in the most abstract deliberations which had long since left K. behind. Much did gradually become clearer to him though, especially since he had a good adviser at his side in Hasterer, with whom he was soon also on friendly terms. K. even frequently walked home with him at night. It did, however, take him a long time to get used to going arm in arm with this huge man, who could quite easily have hidden him under his cloak without anyone noticing.

In the course of time, however, they became such close friends that all the differences in education, profession, and age faded away. When they were together, it was as if they had always belonged together, and if in their relationship one sometimes appeared to have the advantage in worldly matters, then it was not Hasterer but K., for it was mostly his practical experience which proved correct, since it had been acquired at first hand in a way that was impossible in the courtroom.

Of course, this friendship was soon generally known among the group; whilst it was more or less forgotten who had actually introduced K., it was Hasterer who vouched for him. If anyone should cast doubt on K.'s right to sit at their table, he could confidently refer them to Hasterer. As a result of this, K. enjoyed a privileged position, for Hasterer was both respected and feared. The power and acuity of his legal mind were admirable, but in that respect many of the others were at least his equal; none, however, could match the fierceness with which he defended his opinions. K. had the feeling that even if he could not convince an opponent, Hasterer at least put the fear of God into him; many drew back merely at the sight of his outstretched forefinger. It was as if his opponent had forgotten that he was in the company of good friends and colleagues, that they were only theoretical questions they were dealing with, that in reality nothing could happen to him—he would fall silent, merely to shake his head demanded courage. When his opponent was sitting a good way away, it was almost embarrassing to see Hasterer, realizing that at that distance no agreement could be reached, push away his plate and stand up slowly to go and confront the man himself. Those close by would lean back in order to observe his face. However, such incidents were relatively rare, since it was almost exclusively legal questions about which he got worked up, and principally ones concerning trials in which he had been, or was still, involved. As long as such questions were not under discussion he was calm and friendly, with a pleasant laugh and a passion for food and drink. Sometimes he would even ignore the general conversation, turn to K., put his arm over the back of K.'s chair, and question him in a low voice about his work at the bank, then talk about his own work or about his lady friends, who caused him almost as many problems as the court. He was never seen to talk like that to anyone else in the group, and people often came first of all to K. if they wanted something from Hasterer— usually to arrange a reconciliation with a colleague—and asked him to mediate, which he always did, willingly and with ease. But he did not exploit this aspect of his relationship with Hasterer, he was always polite and modest to everyone as a matter of course, and what was more important than politeness and modesty, he had the ability to distinguish between the various differences in rank and treat each one according to his status. Though it has to be said that this was something on which Hasterer repeatedly gave him advice, these being the sole rules Hasterer himself did not break, even in the most heated debate. That was also why he always addressed the young men at the bottom of the table, who had almost no rank at all, in general terms alone, as if they were not individuals but just an undifferentiated mass. But it was precisely these men who showed him the greatest respect, and when, towards eleven, he stood up to go home, there was always one of them there to help him on with his heavy cloak, and another who opened the door for him with a low bow and, naturally, held it open when K. followed Hasterer out of the room.

Initially K. would accompany Hasterer—or Hasterer K.—part of the way home, but later such evenings generally ended with Hasterer inviting him up to his apartment for a while, where they would spend an hour or so sitting together over schnapps and cigars. Hasterer liked these evenings so much that he was even unwilling to forgo them during the few weeks when he had a woman called Helene living with him. She was fat and middle-aged, with a yellowish complexion and a black, wavy fringe. At first K. only saw her in bed, where she lay without shame, reading the latest instalment of a novel and ignoring the men's conversation. Only when it started to get late would she stretch out, yawn, and, if there was no other way of attracting attention, throw an issue of her novel at Hasterer. He would then get up with a smile, and K. would take his leave. Later, however, when Hasterer was beginning to tire of Helene, she disturbed their evenings together appreciably. She would await the two of them fully clothed, and usually in a dress which she probably considered very luxurious and becoming, but which in reality was an old, over-elaborate ball-gown, rendered particularly unpleasant-looking by a few rows of fringes with which it was adorned. K. couldn't say exactly what the dress was like, he refused to look at her, and sat there for hours, his gaze slightly lowered, while she walked up and down the room, swaying her hips, or sat down close to him; later, when her position became more and more precarious, she was so desperate she even tried to make Hasterer jealous by showing a preference for K. It was simply desperation, not malice, when she leant across the table with her plump, bare back, bringing her face close to K., trying to force him to look up. All she achieved by that was that K. refused to go to Hasterer's apartment any more, and when, after some time, he did so, Helene had been sent away for good. K. accepted that as a matter of course. That evening they stayed together for a particularly long time, and, at Hasterer's suggestion, agreed to move to the familiar *du*.* On the way home K. was almost a little dazed from all the smoking and drinking.

The very next morning, in the course of a business discussion in the bank, the manager remarked that he thought he had seen K. the previous evening. If he wasn't mistaken, he said, K. had been walking arm in arm with Hasterer from the state prosecution service. The manager seemed to find this so remarkable that—though this did correspond to his usual precision—he named the church by the long side of which, close to the fountain, the meeting had taken place. Had he been describing a mirage, he could not have put it in any other way. K. explained that Hasterer was a friend of his, and that they really had gone past that church the previous evening. The manager gave an astonished smile, and invited K. to sit down. It was one of those moments for which K. loved the manager so much, moments when this frail, sick old man with the hacking cough, and overburdened with responsibility, revealed a certain concern for K.'s well-being and future, a concern which one could, as did other employees who had encountered the same response from the manager, call cold, mere outward show, nothing more than a means of tying valuable employees to him for years by the sacrifice of two minutes—however that might be, they were moments when K. fell under the manager's spell. Perhaps the manager talked a little differently to K. than he did to the others, he didn't forget his superior position and come down to K.'s level—that was something he did regularly during their normal business dealings—instead, it seemed that it was K.'s position he forgot, and he talked to him as to a child or an inexperienced young man, who was just applying for a post and for some inexplicable reason had found favour with the manager. K. would certainly not have tolerated being spoken to like that by another person, not even by the manager himself, if the manager's concern had not seemed genuine, or at least if he had not been completely captivated by the possibility of the concern that he perceived at such moments. He was aware of his weakness, perhaps it was based on the fact that there truly was still something of the child about him, since he had never experienced the concern of his own father, who had died very young. K. had left home early, and had always rejected rather than sought to arouse the tenderness of his mother, who still lived, half-blind, in the unchanging small town, and whom he had last visited about two years ago.

'I was completely unaware of this friendship,' said the manager, the sternness of his comment tempered only by a faint, friendly smile.

Going To See Elsa

ONE evening, shortly before going home, K. received a telephone call summoning him to the court offices. He was warned, the voice said, not to disobey.* His outrageous remarks that the hearings were pointless, that they produced no result and never would, that he would no longer attend, that he would ignore all calls to attend, whether issued by telephone or in writing, and would throw messengers out—all these remarks, he was told, had been noted down and had already seriously damaged his case. Why did he refuse to comply? Had they not made every effort, sparing neither time nor money, to sort out his complicated case? Was he determined to disrupt it and compel them to resort to more drastic measures, which until now he had been spared? The present summons, the voice went on, was one final attempt. He could do as he saw fit, but he should remember that the court would not be mocked.*

K. had told Elsa he would go and see her that evening, and so could not go to the court for that reason, if for no other. He was glad to have this to justify his non-appearance at the court, though, of course, he would never make use of that justification and, moreover, would very probably not have gone to the court anyway, even if he had not had any engagements at all that evening. Still, he asked, as he felt he had every right to do, what would happen if he did not turn up. 'We know where to find you,' was the answer. 'And will I be punished because I didn't come of my own free will?' asked K., smiling in expectation of what he would hear. 'No,' was the reply. 'Excellent,' said K. 'What reason should I have, then, to comply with this summons?' 'People do not usually deliberately lay themselves open to the court's power,' said the voice, growing weaker and finally fading away.* 'It's very careless not to do that,' K. thought as he left, 'after all, one should try to acquaint oneself with the extent of the court's powers.'

Without further ado, he set off to see Elsa. Leaning back comfortably in the cab, his hands in his coat pockets—it was already beginning to get chilly—he looked out over the bustle in the streets. He thought, not without a certain satisfaction, that if the court really was in session he would be causing it no little inconvenience. He had not made it clear whether he would go or not, so the examining magistrate would be waiting, perhaps even the whole assembly, only K. would not appear, to the especial disappointment of the gallery. Undeterred by the court, he was going where he wanted. For a moment he wasn't sure whether he hadn't absent-mindedly given the cabbie the address of the court, so he shouted out Elsa's address to him. The cabbie nodded, he had been given no other address. From then on K. gradually forgot the court, and, as in earlier times, thoughts of the bank began to occupy his mind entirely.

The Fight with the Deputy Manager

ONE morning K. felt much fresher and more robust than usual. He scarcely thought of the court at all, but when he did so, it seemed to him that there was some place where, even though he would have to feel for it in the dark, he could easily get a grip on this huge, quite impenetrable organization, drag it out, and smash it to pieces. This exceptional state even induced K. to invite the deputy manager to his office to discuss a business matter which had needed dealing with jointly for some time. On such occasions the deputy manager always behaved as if his relationship with K. had not changed in the slightest over the last few months. He came in calmly, as in the former times of constant competition with K., listened calmly to what K. had to say, made brief, friendly, even supportive comments showing that he was taking it in, and only confused K., although that wasn't necessarily his intention, by refusing to let anything divert him from the piece of business under discussion, by demonstrating his readiness to involve himself positively body and soul in the matter, while this model of devotion to duty sent K.'s thoughts swarming out in all directions, forcing him to hand the matter over, almost without resistance, to the deputy manager. There came a point where it was so bad that finally K. merely registered the fact that the deputy manager had suddenly stood up and gone back to his office. K. didn't know what had happened, it was possible that the discussion had come to a proper conclusion, however, it was equally possible that the deputy manager had broken it off because K. had unwittingly offended him, or because he had talked nonsense, or because it had become clear to the deputy manager that K. wasn't listening and was occupied with other things. It was even possible, however, that K. had made some ridiculous decision or that the deputy manager had enticed him to do so, and that he was now hurrying off to put it into effect, to K.'s detriment. Whatever the case, the matter was never mentioned again, K. didn't want to bring it up and the deputy manager kept his own counsel; for the moment, however, there were no noticeable consequences. And at least K. had not let himself be deterred by the incident; whenever a suitable opportunity presented itself and he felt reasonably up to it, he was at the deputy manager's door to go and see him or to invite him to come to his office. It was no longer a time to hide from him, as he had done in the past. He no

longer hoped for a swift, decisive victory which would free him at a
stroke from all his cares and automatically restore his old relationship
with the deputy manager. K. realized that he must not let up, if he
were to draw back, as the situation perhaps demanded, there was a
danger he might never get ahead again. The deputy manager must
not be left believing K. was finished, he must not be allowed to sit
calmly in his office believing this, he had to be unsettled, he had to
be made aware as often as possible that K. was alive and that, however harmless he might appear at the moment, he could, like everything that was alive, suddenly turn up one day with new abilities.
Sometimes K. told himself that with this method he was fighting for
nothing but honour, for in his weak state he could gain no real advantage from constantly opposing the deputy manager, strengthening
his sense of power and giving him the opportunity to make observa-
tions and adapt his measures to the current conditions. But K. could
not have changed his behaviour in the slightest, he was subject to
delusions, sometimes he was convinced that now of all times he could
confidently vie with the deputy manager, he learnt nothing from the
most disastrous experiences, and even though everything uniformly
went against him all the time, he would imagine he could achieve at
the eleventh attempt something which he had failed to do ten times
over. When such a meeting left him exhausted, sweat-soaked, his
mind a blank, he couldn't say whether it was hope or desperation that
had driven him to confront the deputy manager; another time, however, it was absolutely clear that it was hope with which he hurried
over to the deputy manager's door.

That's how it was that day too. The deputy manager came in
straight away, but then stopped by the door, cleaned his pince-nez in
accordance with a newly acquired habit, scrutinized K., and then, so
as not to make his curiosity about K. too obvious, the whole room. It
was as if he were taking the opportunity to check his eyesight. K.
resisted his gaze, even smiled a little, and invited the deputy manager
to sit down. He flung himself into his own armchair, pulled it up as
close to the deputy manager as possible, picked up the papers he
needed from his desk, and began his report. At first the deputy manager hardly seemed to be listening. K.'s desk had a low carved rail
running round it. The desk as a whole was an excellent piece of
workmanship, and the rail was firmly set in the wood. But the deputy
manager behaved as if he had just noticed that it was coming loose,

and tried to remedy the defect by thumping away on the rail with his index finger. At that K. broke off his report, but the deputy manager insisted he continue since, he explained, he was listening closely and following everything. While K. found it impossible to wring a comment on the matter in hand out of him, the rail seemed to demand special treatment, for now the deputy manager took out his penknife and, using K.'s ruler as a counter-lever, tried to lift the rail up, probably to enable him to push it back in more easily. K. had included a very innovative proposal in his report, and had high hopes of its effect on the deputy manager. Now, when he came to this proposal in his report, he was so taken with his own work, or rather, so delighted by the feeling, which was becoming rarer and rarer, that he still had something to say in the bank and that his ideas had the power to justify him, that he simply couldn't stop. Perhaps this method of defence was the best, not only in the bank but in his trial as well, much better, perhaps, than all the other methods he had already tried or was planning. In his rush to get on with his report he had no time to tell the deputy manager to stop his work on the rail in so many words, but while he was reading he stroked the rail reassuringly with his free hand a couple of times in order, although he was not really aware of it, to show the deputy manager that there was no defect in the rail, and that even if there should turn out to be one, at the moment listening was much more important and also more courteous than any repairs. But, as is often the case with lively people whose work makes solely intellectual demands on them, the deputy manager had become carried away with this manual task, a piece of the rail had already been lifted out and now the posts had to be replaced in the appropriate holes. This was more difficult than everything that had gone before. The deputy manager had to stand up and try to push the rail back in with both hands, but despite all the effort he put into it, it refused to go. Whilst reading out his report—to which he added many unscripted comments—K. had only vaguely noticed that the deputy manager had stood up. Although he had hardly ever entirely lost sight of the deputy manager's supplementary task, he had assumed the movement was somehow connected with his report, so he also stood up and held out a sheet of paper to the deputy manager, his finger placed on it under a figure. By this time, however, the deputy manager had realized that the pressure of his hands alone was not sufficient, and without pausing for thought put his whole weight on the balustrade. It worked—with a screech of protest the little posts slipped into the holes, but in his haste he snapped one of them, and in one place the delicate upper rail broke. 'Poor-quality wood,' the deputy manager said irritatedly, gave up tinkering with the desk and sat

The Building

ON various occasions K. had tried, without at first being motivated by any specific intention, to discover the location of the office which had issued the initial indictment in his case. There was no difficulty in finding this out, as soon as he asked, both Titorelli and Wolfhart* told him the precise number of the building. Later Titorelli, with a smile he always had ready for secret plans that had not been submitted to him for approval, had supplemented his information with the assertion that this office was of no significance whatsoever, it merely said what it had been told to say, and was only the external mouthpiece of the great organization whose business it was to seek out guilt, which was, of course, inaccessible to defendants and their lawyers. So if, he went on, one wanted something from the authority—naturally there were always many things one wanted, but it was not always wise to express them—one had to turn to the aforementioned subordinate office, though that would neither gain one access to the actual authority, nor would one's request ever reach it.

K. was already familiar with the painter's manner, so he didn't object or ask any further questions, but simply nodded and noted what had been said. Once more he felt, as he had several times recently, that Titorelli amply replaced the lawyer as far as torture was concerned. The only difference was that K. was not as dependent on Titorelli, and could have got rid of him without further ado had he so desired; also that Titorelli was very communicative, even garrulous, albeit more so earlier on than now; and finally, that K. for his part was equally able to torture Titorelli.

And that is what he did in connection with this matter, mentioning the building now and then in a tone of voice which suggested that he was concealing something from Titorelli, that he had established relations with the office but that they had not yet reached the stage where they could be revealed without danger. If, however, Titorelli then tried to press him for details, K. would suddenly change the subject and let some time elapse before he mentioned the office again. He derived pleasure from these little victories, they made him feel he understood these people with connections to the court much better, he could play with them, almost became one of them himself; at least for a few moments he enjoyed the clearer perception of the structure of the court which the first step, on which they stood, allowed them. What difference would it make if he should finally lose his position here below? There was another opportunity for salvation there as well, he just had to slip into the ranks of these people; even if, because of their lowly status or for some other reason, they had not been able to help him in his trial, at least they could take him in and hide him, indeed, if he thought everything through sufficiently and carried it out in secret, they couldn't avoid serving him in this way, especially Titorelli, now that K. had become a close acquaintance and patron.

These and similar hopes were not something K. cherished every day. In general, he could make clear distinctions and took care not to overlook or miss out any difficulty, but sometimes—mostly when in a state of complete exhaustion in the evening after work—he found comfort in the least and, moreover, most ambiguous events of the day. At such times he was usually lying on the sofa in his office—he could no longer leave his office without spending an hour recovering on the sofa—and stringing one observation after another together in his mind. In this he did not limit himself strictly to people connected with the court—as he dozed, they all merged and he forgot the extensive work of the court, he felt as if he were the only defendant and all the others intermingled, like officials and lawyers in the corridors of the court building, and even the dullest had his chin on his chest, his lips pursed, and the fixed stare of conscientious thought. On such occasions Frau Grubach's tenants always appeared as a single group, they stood together, a row of heads with mouths open, like an accusing chorus. There were many among them whom K. did not know, for a long time now he had not paid the least attention to the affairs of the boarding-house. Because of the many unknown people, he felt uneasy about closer contact with the group, which, however, was necessary when he was looking for Fräulein Bürstner among them. For example, he would scan the group and suddenly two completely unknown eyes would blaze out at him and hold him. Then he would not find Fräulein Bürstner, but when, to avoid the possibility of a mistake, he searched again, he would find her right in the middle of the group, her arms round two men who were standing on either side of her. The impression it made on him was infinitely small, especially since the sight was nothing new, it was merely the indelible memory of a photo of the beach he had seen once in Fräulein Bürstner's room. But the sight did drive K. away from the group, and even though he returned several times, when he did he was rushing to and fro round the court building with long strides. He always knew his way round all the rooms, remote corridors which he could never have seen looked familiar to him, as if he had always lived there, details kept impressing themselves on his brain with painful clarity, a foreigner, for example, was taking a walk in one of the anterooms, his dress was similar to a bullfighter's, the waist cut in sharply, as if with knives, his very short jacket, wrapped stiffly round him, consisted entirely of yellowish lace made of coarse threads, and this man exposed himself the whole time to K.'s astonished gaze without for a moment interrupting his walk. K. crept round him, bent low, and gaped at him, straining to keep his eyes wide open. He knew all the patterning of the lace, all the missing fringes, all the undulations of the little jacket, and still could not take his eyes off it. Or, rather, he could have taken his eyes off it long ago, or, to be more precise, he had never wanted to look at it, but it kept a hold on him. 'What fancy outfits they have abroad!' he thought, opening his eyes even wider. And he continued in this man's wake until he turned over on the sofa and pressed his face into the leather.

Going To See His Mother

DURING lunch it suddenly occurred to him that he ought to go and see his mother. Spring was almost over, and with it the third year since he had last seen her. On that occasion she had asked him to come and visit her on his birthday, and he had complied with her request, despite a number of obstacles, and had even promised to spend every birthday with her, a promise which, however, he had already twice failed to keep. But now he had decided not even to wait for his birthday, even though it was only a fortnight away, but to set off immediately. He told himself there was no special reason to go at that particular time, on the contrary, the news he was sent every two months from a cousin who had a shop in the little town and looked after the money K. sent for his mother was more reassuring than it had ever been. True, his mother's sight was fading, but K., going by what the doctors had said, had been expecting that for years, and otherwise her general health had improved, various afflictions of old age had got better instead of worse, at least she complained about them less. In his cousin's opinion, all this was perhaps connected with the fact that over the last few years—when he went to see her K. had noticed signs of this almost with a sense of revulsion—she had become exceedingly devout. In a letter, his cousin had given a very vivid description of the way the old woman, who had previously dragged herself along laboriously, now stepped out really well when he took her on his arm to church on a Sunday. And K. could believe his cousin, for usually he was cautious and in his reports tended to exaggerate the bad rather than the good news.

But however that might be, K. had decided to go. Recently he had noticed a tendency to feel sorry for himself, an almost unbridled determination to yield to his every wish—well, at least in this case this weakness was serving a good purpose.

He went over to the window to gather his thoughts a little, then had the lunch things cleared away and sent one of the messengers to Frau Grubach to tell her he was leaving and to ask her to pack a small suit-case with anything she thought necessary, which the messenger was to bring back. Then he gave Herr Kühne* some instructions regarding business matters for his period of absence, hardly irritated this time by what had become a bad habit with Herr Kühne, namely, turning his face to the side when he was given instructions, as if he knew perfectly well what he had to do and only tolerated the issuing of instructions as a ceremony; finally he went to see the manager. When he asked him for two days' leave of absence, since he had to go and see his mother, the manager naturally asked if she was ill. 'No,' said K., without any further explanation. He was standing in the middle of the room, his hands clasped behind his back. He was thinking, his brow knitted. Had he perhaps been too hasty in preparing to go away? Would it not be better to stay here? Why was he doing it? Could he be going there out of sentimentality? And out of sentimentality possibly leaving himself liable to miss something important here, an opportunity to intervene which now might well crop up at any moment of any day after his trial appeared to have been in abeyance for weeks, with scarcely any news of it coming to him at all? And would he, moreover, perhaps give the old woman a fright, which was naturally not his intention but which could easily happen against his will, since at the moment many things were happening against his will. And his mother had not even asked for him. His cousin's letters used regularly to repeat his mother's pressing invitations, but not for a long time now. He wasn't going for his mother's sake, that much was clear. But if he was going with some hopes for his own sake, then he was a complete fool and would reap the reward of his foolishness in the despair that would eventually engulf him there. But as if all these doubts were not his own, as if it were others who were trying to persuade him of them, he stuck, as he literally woke with a start, by his decision to go. In the meantime the manager had, either by chance or, more likely, out of particular consideration for K., bent over a newspaper; now he looked up too, held out his hand to K. as he stood up, and, without asking any further questions, wished him a safe journey.

K. then had to wait, pacing up and down his office, for the messenger. With hardly a word he waved away the deputy manager, who came in several times to ask why K. was leaving, and when he finally had the suitcase he immediately hurried down to the cab that had been ordered. He was already on the steps when, at the last moment, Kullych appeared at the top, an unfinished letter in his hand about which he clearly wanted a decision. K. waved him away but, dull-witted as this blond man with the large head was, he misunderstood the sign and raced after K. with death-defying leaps, waving the sheet of paper. This so angered K. that, when Kullych caught up with him on the steps, he grabbed the letter from him and tore it up. When K. looked back from the cab, Kullych, who had probably not yet realized what he had done wrong, was standing on the same spot, watching the cab depart, while the commissionaire beside him had doffed his cap. So K. was still one of the top employees of the bank, if he were to deny it, the commissionaire would contradict him. And, despite all denials, his mother even thought he was the manager and had thought so for years. He would not sink in her estimation, even though his reputation had suffered elsewhere. Perhaps it was a good sign that it was just before his departure that he had proved to himself that he was still able to take a letter away from a clerk, and one who had connections with the court at that, and tear it up without a by-your-leave. However, he had not been able to do what he would most like to have done, that is, give Kullych two loud slaps on his pale, plump cheeks.

EXPLANATORY NOTES

5 *arrested*: Kafka originally wrote 'caught', but stroked it out. Later Kafka repeated the word 'caught' where this translation has 'you are our prisoner' (p. 6).

an outfit for travelling: hence equipped with many pockets. However, as the purpose of all these features is not quite clear, this garment presents K. with a puzzle, heralding the enigmatic character which the court will retain.

7 *Which department did they belong to?*: 'department' translates *Behörde*, which has powerful and not fully translatable connotations of officialdom and authority.

10 *apple*: the obvious association is with the biblical Fall (Genesis 3: 6), but there is no sustained pattern of allusion.

11 *Fräulein Bürstner*: the name suggests the vulgarism *bürsten* ('to have sex with', literally 'to brush'); Osman Durrani points out that an approximate English translation would be 'Miss Scrubber' (*The Cambridge Companion to Kafka*, ed. Julian Preece (Cambridge, 2002), 226).

a man with an open-necked shirt: the first of a series of aggressively masculine figures including Captain Lanz, the thrasher, and the student whom K. encounters in the court offices.

13 *Hasterer*: we learn more about this character in one of the fragmentary chapters below.

14 *a shake of the hands*: this gesture of solidarity is very important to K., but for him it is also a means of manipulation, as in his conversation with Frau Grubach (p. 19).

15 *Rabensteiner . . . Kullich . . . Kaminer*: the three names suggest the national and religious groups in Prague, Rabensteiner being recognizable as a German name, Kullich (later Kullych) as Czech, and Kaminer as characteristically Jewish. *Rabenstein* means a place of execution, 'Kullich' (Czech *kulich*) an owl; *Rabe* by itself means 'raven', and since Kafka means 'jackdaw', references to ravens, crows, and jackdaws in Kafka's texts are often taken as private allusions to himself.

19 *by no means stupid*: this paragraph is a fine illustration of the self-serving illogicality by which Kafka's characters can wrest a statement into its opposite.

20 *pure*: the word *rein*, meaning both 'clean' and 'pure', seems excessive for its context, and the reaction it produces in K. may be correspondingly revealing.

23 *Courts have an attraction all of their own*: in view of K.'s increasing obsession with the court, this is a piece of dramatic irony.

24 *'Josef K.!'*: anticipates the chaplain's summons in the cathedral (p. 150).

29 *Juliusstrasse*: a name presumably chosen for its ordinariness. Hartmut Binder suggests an allusion to Kafka's birthday on 3 July (*Kafka— Kommentar zu den Romanen, Rezensionen, Aphorismen und zum Brief an den Vater* (Munich: Winkler, 1976), 209).

30 *miscreants*: not an objective description, but K.'s perception of them.

Lanz: suggests *Lanze* ('lance'), and thus has sexual, phallic connotations.

32 *long Sunday coats*: possibly suggesting the black gaberdines of Eastern European Jews. The 'long beards' (p. 38) also suggest Eastern Jews, while 'students' (p. 39) may imply Talmud students.

33 *eyebrows*: bushy eyebrows are a recurrent symbol of the court's authority.

34 *legal account book*: the original, *Schuldbuch*, normally means a register of debts, but since *Schuld* means both 'debt' and 'guilt', the latter sense is strongly suggested here.

44 *red beard*: a link with the 'ginger goatee' (p. 11) of the man living opposite K.

47 *begging for mercy*: K. may be fantasizing about beating the student in Elsa's presence. If so, the later beating of the guards corresponds to K.'s unacknowledged fantasies.

53 *some great metamorphosis*: Marson suggests that this change might consist in K.'s abandoning his posture of arrogant superiority towards the court, 'an admission that he cannot understand the court and is ignorant of its motives and intentions. And this could be the necessary precondition for a beginning awareness of guilt' (Eric L. Marson, *Kafka's Trial: The Case Against Josef K.* (St Lucia, Queensland: University of Queensland Press), 154).

55 *elegant clothes*: again, clothes seem significant, but it is not clear what they signify. Contrast the 'neglected' clothes of the defendants (p. 50).

clearly preoccupied with his own affairs: ironically, at a time when K. has the chance to learn something about the court.

56 *none of us is hard-hearted*: here and elsewhere the novel distinguishes sharply between people's private characters and the characters they must assume as employees of an organization. Thus the prison chaplain, to whose personal kindness K. mistakenly appeals (p. 153), emphasizes that he belongs to the court (p. 160).

57 *his hat*: regaining his self-mastery, K. combs his hair and picks up his hat, which by synecdoche suggests his reasoning faculties. Cf. the commentary by Marson, *Kafka's Trial*, 160–2.

58 *completely bare*: this figure's appearance and attire suggest the homoerotic fantasies which can occasionally be found elsewhere in Kafka's fiction and diaries: see Mark M. Anderson, 'Kafka, Homosexuality and the Aesthetics of "Male Culture"', *Austrian Studies*, 7 (1996), 79–99.

complained: see p. 35.

61 *a dog howling*: the first of three references to dogs, all implying the degrad-
ation of a human being: see pp. 139, 165. The original verb, *schreit* (screams),
is unusual for a dog and reminds us that K. is talking about a person.

66 *disgrace*: disgrace and shame are prominent motifs: cf. K.'s 'shame' at
composing a submission (p. 90) and the last sentence of the novel (p. 165).

69 *Huld*: 'grace' or 'homage', in a courtly rather than a religious sense.

a dark house: within the novel's imagery of light and darkness, this augurs
badly.

70 *Albert*: Kafka must have forgotten that he earlier called the uncle 'Karl'.

heart trouble: figures of authority in Kafka's fiction are often bedridden or
feeble. The frail fathers in *The Judgement* and *The Metamorphosis*, however, regain their strength, as Huld does later, albeit less dramatically,
when dealing with professional business.

74 *head of administration*: making this person suddenly emerge from the
darkness is Kafka's way of introducing a new character whom he did not
have in mind when beginning the chapter.

76 *about to leap up*: it has been suggested that Kafka knew Freud's essay on
Michelangelo's *Moses*, a figure sculpted in a similar threatening posture:
see Malcolm Pasley, 'Two Literary Sources of Kafka's *Der Prozeß*',
Forum for Modern Language Studies, 3 (1967), 142–7.

78 *'What a pretty claw!'*: Leni's webbed fingers suggest an evolutionary
throwback, and make her seem like a primitive, semi-animal creature.

95 *fog mixed with smoke*: symbolizing the obscurity of K.'s situation.

96 *Titorelli*: a pseudonym presumably intended to suggest such painters as
Titian and Signorelli.

101 *relatively brightly lit*: in contrast to the dark approach to the lawyer's
house.

104 *Justice and the Goddess of Victory*: Kafka resorts to allegory to provide
some indication of the nature of the court.

111 *can't be opened*: the jammed window and the stifling atmosphere underline
K.'s entrapment in his case.

116 *'Sunset Over the Heath'*: K.'s purchase of three identical paintings may
suggest that for him all three possible outcomes are equivalent.

125 *marking of the lips*: a further suggestion that a guilty person is distinguished from others by his appearance: see the account of Hanns Gross's
criminology in the Introduction, p. xxi.

138 *knelt*: Block's submission to the lawyer may allude disparagingly to
Catholic ritual (see Marson, *Kakfa's Trial*, 254), and thus to the error of
relying on mediators instead of confronting one's situation directly.

143 *Association for the Preservation of the City Monuments*: as an interest in
anything outside business is uncharacteristic of K., Kafka hastens to tell
us that he joined it only for business reasons. It is a necessary plot device
to get him to the cathedral.

146 *cathedral*: besides St Vitus' Cathedral in Prague, the atmosphere may
have been suggested by Milan Cathedral, which Kafka visited in September
1911. The candlelight, including the 'sanctuary lamp' (p. 147), contrasts
with the electric light of K.'s modern pocket-torch.

striking eleven: Kafka must have forgotten that K. was supposed to meet
the Italian at ten (p. 145).

148 *Entombment of Christ*: by referring to Christ's burial, with no hint of res-
urrection, Kafka intensifies the atmosphere of foreboding.

limped off: cf. the hunchbacked girl who leads K. to Titorelli. A limp
further suggests the Devil. The servant is an ambivalent figure who, with
his sinister limp, leads K. to the chaplain and to possible salvation. Cf. how
in *The Castle* a summons from the limping Erlanger accidentally leads K.
to the one official, Bürgel, who can do something for him.

153 *Outside the Law*: suggests the Jewish Law, while the 'doorkeeper' appears
in Jewish legends as guardian of the various forecourts leading to heaven.
Kafka himself described this story as a 'legend' (diary, 13 December
1914). On its affinities with Jewish legends, see Iris Bruce, *Kafka and
Cultural Zionism* (Madison, Wisc.: University of Wisconsin Press, 2007),
99–103.

man from the country: an *'am ha'aretz*, literally 'countryman', also implies
someone ignorant of the Jewish law; the Yiddish equivalent, *amorets*,
means 'ignoramus'. Kafka's diaries confirm that he knew this expression
(see diary, 26 November 1911).

155 *interpretation*: the debate about the meaning of the parable suggests the
subtle technique of interpreting passages from the Talmud (the commentary on the Jewish Law).

161 *Brief formalities at the apartment door*: here Kafka departs from K.'s point
of view, since he cannot see what is happening outside his door.

dressed in black: cf. the requirement that K. should don a black suit to
meet the supervisor (p. 11).

theatre: this image is hard to interpret, but may be linked with 'hoax'
(p. 7), where Kafka's original word, *Komödie*, implies play-acting in the
widest sense.

162 *I was always trying*: this sentence might be taken as K.'s final insight into
his faults; but it does not quite match the way K.'s character has developed during the novel.

165 *throat*: anticipated by the reference to K.'s placing his lips on Fräulein
Bürstner's throat (p. 26); the original word, *Gurgel* (windpipe), is even
more precise.

FRAGMENTS

169 *Frau Grubach felt it was all beyond her*: another change of narrative
perspective.

171 *sunburnt*: cf. the thrasher, 'bronzed like a sailor', p. 59.

173 *regular table*: in German-speaking countries it is common for a table (*Stammtisch*) in a pub to be reserved for a specific group of regulars.

176 *the familiar du*: in German, the second-person singular pronoun is a familiar form of address, in contrast to the formal *Sie*.

177 *not to disobey*: the court is here bullying and menacing, unlike its co-operative manner in early chapters.

178 *would not be mocked*: cf. 'God is not mocked' (Galatians 6: 7).

fading away: perhaps implying that K. has on this occasion successfully defied the court?

182 *Wolfhart*: this character is mentioned nowhere else.

185 *Herr Kühne*: a bank employee, not mentioned elsewhere.

The Oxford World's Classics Website

www.worldsclassics.co.uk

- Browse the full range of Oxford World's Classics online

- Sign up for our monthly e-alert to receive information on new titles

- Read extracts from the Introductions

- Listen to our editors and translators talk about the world's greatest literature with our Oxford World's Classics audio guides

- Join the conversation, follow us on Twitter at OWC_Oxford

- Teachers and lecturers can order inspection copies quickly and simply via our website

www.worldsclassics.co.uk

American Literature

British and Irish Literature

Children's Literature

Classics and Ancient Literature

Colonial Literature

Eastern Literature

European Literature

Gothic Literature

History

Medieval Literature

Oxford English Drama

Poetry

Philosophy

Politics

Religion

The Oxford Shakespeare

A complete list of Oxford World's Classics, including Authors in Context, Oxford English Drama, and the Oxford Shakespeare, is available in the UK from the Marketing Services Department, Oxford University Press, Great Clarendon Street, Oxford OX2 6DP, or visit the website at www.oup.com/uk/worldsclassics.

In the USA, visit www.oup.com/us/owc for a complete title list.

Oxford World's Classics are available from all good bookshops. In case of difficulty, customers in the UK should contact Oxford University Press Bookshop, 116 High Street, Oxford OX1 4BR.

	Six French Poets of the Nineteenth Century
HONORÉ DE BALZAC	Cousin Bette
	Eugénie Grandet
	Père Goriot
CHARLES BAUDELAIRE	The Flowers of Evil
	The Prose Poems and Fanfarlo
BENJAMIN CONSTANT	Adolphe
DENIS DIDEROT	Jacques the Fatalist
	The Nun
ALEXANDRE DUMAS (PÈRE)	The Black Tulip
	The Count of Monte Cristo
	Louise de la Vallière
	The Man in the Iron Mask
	La Reine Margot
	The Three Musketeers
	Twenty Years After
	The Vicomte de Bragelonne
ALEXANDRE DUMAS (FILS)	La Dame aux Camélias
GUSTAVE FLAUBERT	Madame Bovary
	A Sentimental Education
	Three Tales
VICTOR HUGO	The Essential Victor Hugo
	Notre-Dame de Paris
J.-K. HUYSMANS	Against Nature
PIERRE CHODERLOS DE LACLOS	Les Liaisons dangereuses
MME DE LAFAYETTE	The Princesse de Clèves
GUILLAUME DU LORRIS and JEAN DE MEUN	The Romance of the Rose

	Late Victorian Gothic Tales
JANE AUSTEN	Emma
	Mansfield Park
	Persuasion
	Pride and Prejudice
	Selected Letters
	Sense and Sensibility
MRS BEETON	Book of Household Management
MARY ELIZABETH BRADDON	Lady Audley's Secret
ANNE BRONTË	The Tenant of Wildfell Hall
CHARLOTTE BRONTË	Jane Eyre
	Shirley
	Villette
EMILY BRONTË	Wuthering Heights
ROBERT BROWNING	The Major Works
JOHN CLARE	The Major Works
SAMUEL TAYLOR COLERIDGE	The Major Works
WILKIE COLLINS	The Moonstone
	No Name
	The Woman in White
CHARLES DARWIN	The Origin of Species
THOMAS DE QUINCEY	The Confessions of an English Opium-Eater
	On Murder
CHARLES DICKENS	The Adventures of Oliver Twist
	Barnaby Rudge
	Bleak House
	David Copperfield
	Great Expectations
	Nicholas Nickleby
	The Old Curiosity Shop
	Our Mutual Friend
	The Pickwick Papers

CHARLES DICKENS	A Tale of Two Cities
GEORGE DU MAURIER	Trilby
MARIA EDGEWORTH	Castle Rackrent
GEORGE ELIOT	Daniel Deronda
	The Lifted Veil and Brother Jacob
	Middlemarch
	The Mill on the Floss
	Silas Marner
SUSAN FERRIER	Marriage
ELIZABETH GASKELL	Cranford
	The Life of Charlotte Brontë
	Mary Barton
	North and South
	Wives and Daughters
GEORGE GISSING	New Grub Street
	The Odd Women
EDMUND GOSSE	Father and Son
THOMAS HARDY	Far from the Madding Crowd
	Jude the Obscure
	The Mayor of Casterbridge
	The Return of the Native
	Tess of the d'Urbervilles
	The Woodlanders
WILLIAM HAZLITT	Selected Writings
JAMES HOGG	The Private Memoirs and Confessions of a Justified Sinner
JOHN KEATS	The Major Works
	Selected Letters
CHARLES MATURIN	Melmoth the Wanderer
JOHN RUSKIN	Selected Writings
WALTER SCOTT	The Antiquary
	Ivanhoe